WHISPERS IN THE DARK

COURTNEY KONSTANTIN

FOREWORD

We all know that Courtney Konstantin writes about zombies. Maybe, like me, she enjoys the utter relentlessness of the undead, their ability to throw a wrench into any moment of our characters' lives, and how something so slow can be so dang terrifying.

However, this CK book has nary a zombie. As part of the *Ravaged Skies Universe*—a shared universe created by fifteen apocalyptic authors—this world ends with a solar flare. But does it really matter how the world ends?

I think what we apocalypse authors find most intriguing is our characters' responses to the end, whether that comes about due to solar flares, aliens, robots, climate change, or whatever else our twisted minds can imagine.

It's the perseverance of the people that we love. We knock them down and pick them up again. We explore the humanity of some and the cruelty of others. We test them and pressure them and wound them in a hundred ways.

Man, we authors are brutal. Clearly, there's something very wrong with us.

Perhaps we should check into that? Nah.

Because we also give them hope. Moments of grace. Connection with each other. Humor. The ability to heal. People to trust.

We know that when it comes down to it, the human spirit is stronger and more relentless than anything—even zombies.

I hope you enjoy Courtney's newest story of survival against the odds. I'm sure I will!

Sarah Lyons Fleming
February 2025

CONTENTS

CHAPTER
ONE
MARLOWE

"He's not guilty!"

I fought the urge to pound my forehead onto the table. Serving on a Washington County jury seemed exciting to me in the beginning. I didn't even mind the thirty-minute drive each day from my house in Beaverton. But after sitting through the case for two days, I felt the conviction was clear. Instead, there was one guy that just refused to agree with the rest.

Don—the lone holdout—leaned back in his chair, crossing his arms over his chest like an overgrown toddler. He didn't even try to hide his smirk. Standing from my seat, I went to the large window. They didn't have a view, just the sky and the concrete building next to them. I watched people moving behind the windows. None of them looked as frustrated as I felt.

Missing two days of work as the shift manager at my neighborhood Target wasn't so bad. I had always been obsessed with true crime, making the robbery trial interesting. I loved listening to podcasts during my bus rides to and from work. Anytime I had free, I had earbuds in and was listening to something gruesome. What I hadn't realized was how one person could throw a wrench into everything.

Thinking about my job, I checked my backpack again. I'd

crammed my uniform into the small bag. The uniform would be wrinkled, like the crumpled paper balls I'd been playing basketball with. I cringed, knowing I never cared about being wrinkled. The director of my store had mentioned I should be a better example for my employees. I wasn't planning on staying in Target forever, so my impact on those employees mattered little to me.

"Come on, Don. We've gone over this. His fingerprints were on the gun, he had motive, and the security footage—" The foreperson was a saint. Clearly frustrated like everyone else, the older woman calmly addressed the man, who was keeping them in the room longer than expected.

"Yeah, yeah." Don waved a dismissive hand. "That video is grainy as hell. Could be anyone. You all just want to convict someone so you can get home faster."

"No, we want to convict the guy who actually did it," I snapped before I could stop myself.

Don's eyes flicked to me, his expression shifting ever so slightly. For a second, something passed over his face—something cold, assessing. Then his smirk returned.

"You seem real eager to put a man away, sweetheart."

The word sweetheart made my teeth grind.

I pressed my fingers against the bridge of my nose, trying to control my irritation. "It's not about what I want, Don. It's about evidence."

His smirk widened, like he enjoyed getting under my skin. "I'm just saying, maybe you shouldn't be so quick to believe what the system tells you. You ever think about that, Miss Perfect Juror?"

A few people shifted uncomfortably in their chairs.

"His fingerprints were on the gun, even though it was only a paintball gun," another juror said from the other end of the table.

"He could have handled the gun prior to the robbery. There's no way to know."

Exclamations of disbelief popped up around the room.

"You have to be kidding —"

"What did he just say?"

"I just want to go home."

Bursting from his chair, another man paced. His anger was a heat wave coming off his body. "Don, man, none of us want to continue to be stuck in this room. Trying to claim the guy had somehow touched a gun, that his defense says he never owned, is really reaching."

I had to agree. Since the beginning of the two-day trial, Don had been disagreeable. Though he answered all the questions correctly when they all were being chosen for the jury, his attitude toward the entire process appeared after they had been led into the jury room the first time. His disdain for the court, the prosecution, and the trial, was clear. He had hidden it from the judge, so the entire jury was stuck with him.

"Michael is right. You have to have more solid evidence to discount the clear forensics being presented, Don." The foreperson spoke up again, working to bring down the tension in the room.

Don's face screwed up into a snarl. "He's being railroaded, and I say he's not guilty."

A collective groan rose around the room, and I opened my mouth in a silent scream, throwing my head back. When I looked across the room, my eyes met a woman sitting there and we shared a knowing look.

"Ok." The foreperson sighed loudly; even her even temper had been pushed by Don's inability to get on board. "I guess we start from the beginning."

Plopping back into my chair, I didn't think twice before resting my head on the table, tuning out the chaos as arguments and curses erupted around me. My shoulder length dark hair curtained my face, and I fought the urge to close my eyes and sleep. I had taken jury duty very seriously, so my hair was controlled, the waves sleek and professional. The sheath dress I was wearing was cheap from Target and definitely not very comfortable. And Don was delaying me from changing out of it.

I hated people like Don—people who just wanted to be difficult for the sake of it. And worse, I could feel his eyes on me.

I lifted my head sharply, and sure enough, Don was still staring, his smirk fading into something unreadable. He didn't look away. Something about the way he studied me, like I was a puzzle he was trying to solve, sent a cold prickle down my spine.

It was just after lunch, and we hadn't gotten past the first vote, all thanks to Don's stubborn "not guilty." Every other juror seemed unwavering in their stance, convinced they knew the truth, yet here we were, grid locked.

Lifting my head, I stared down the table at Don. "I'm guessing you either don't have a job to get to, or you're avoiding the one you do have. But some of us don't have that luxury. So maybe, I don't know, stop making things harder than they need to be?"

The mumbling that had been going on around the room screeched to a halt, as everyone looked over at me and then at Don to see his reaction. His mouth was hanging open. His lack of immediate argument surprised me.

"Close your mouth dear, you're going to catch flies like that," the foreperson said in a sweet voice.

Chuckles sounded around the room and Don's face went beet red. I had to contain my urge to cringe away as his angry eyes locked on me specifically.

The door opened and a bailiff appeared. The woman had been assigned to the jury since the beginning and she looked around, taking in the scene. A small frown appeared between her brows before her gaze landed on me.

"Marlowe Reed?"

My voice squeaked as I replied in surprise. "Yes?"

"There's a phone call for you."

I didn't move at first, remembering that the jury wasn't supposed to have access to their cellphones while in deliberation. That thought was fleeting, as I realized the only person that could be trying to reach me was my mother.

"Hey! I thought we couldn't have phone calls!" Don, the

dissenter, dropped his fist on the table, causing the foreperson to jump.

"There are exceptions, and that's not your concern." Every day, the bailiff had been forced to cater to his absurdly specific lunch requests, as if this were some five-star hotel instead of a courthouse. The jury's patience had worn thin—everyone was completely over him.

I moved to follow the bailiff out of the room. The woman was much taller than me, making me feel like a child behind her. When we got to a separate office, she smiled warmly at me. "Your mother is the only one I would bring you out for. The judge made sure to note that she's sick. I'm sorry to hear that."

I looked at my feet, studying the cheap shiny dress shoes I wore. "Thanks."

Cancer. There wasn't a word in existence that scared me more. It loomed over everything, made even worse by the fact that I hadn't been able to talk to her much while stuck serving jury duty. Every time I called, it seemed she was with the doctors or trying to rest, and I couldn't bring myself to interrupt her. The weight of it all twisted my stomach into knots as I took the phone the bailiff handed me. She gave me a kind smile before quietly leaving the room, shutting the door behind her.

The handset felt heavier than it should have, like it carried the weight of everything I couldn't say. I pressed it to my ear, my voice coming out shaky.

"Mom? Are you okay?"

Her voice on the other end was soft, weaker than I remembered, but still hers. "Hi, sweetheart. I didn't mean to bother you at the courthouse, but I—I just needed to hear your voice."

Guilt hit me like a freight train. "You're not bothering me. God, Mom, I've been trying to call you. I didn't want to interrupt if you were with the doctors or resting—"

"Marlowe," she interrupted gently, her tone a mix of exhaustion and warmth. "I know. I didn't call to make you feel guilty."

"Well, mission failed," I muttered, earning a light chuckle from her, thin but genuine.

There was a pause, long enough for my stomach to twist into tighter knots. "How are you feeling?" I asked, bracing myself.

"About the same," she admitted. "Tired. The treatments are…" she trailed off for a moment. "They're hard this time, Marlowe. Harder than I expected."

I swallowed the lump in my throat, forcing my voice to stay steady. "But they're working, right? They're still working?"

A beat of silence. "The doctors are hopeful," she said carefully, her tone dancing around the truth. "And that's what I'm holding on to."

I closed my eyes, leaning back in the chair as the tension in my chest pressed down harder. "I hate that I'm not there. I hate that I'm stuck here, doing something that doesn't even matter in the grand scheme of things."

"Don't say that," she said firmly, her energy spiking just enough to make her words sharp. "What you're doing is important. You're doing your part, something I know you don't want to do, but you're doing it, anyway. That's the Marlowe I raised. The strong one."

"Strong," I scoffed quietly. "I feel like I'm falling apart every time I think about you."

Her voice softened again. "Sweetheart, you're allowed to fall apart sometimes. Just don't stay there. Okay?"

I nodded, even though she couldn't see me, biting back the tears that threatened to spill. "Okay."

"I'll let you get back to…whatever it is they've got you doing," she said, her voice lighter, but I could hear the fatigue bleeding through. "I just needed to remind myself I have the best daughter in the world."

"Mom…" My voice cracked.

"Love you, Marlowe."

"Love you too, Mom. I'll call as soon as I'm done here, I promise."

"Don't stress yourself over it," she said gently. "Just…stay strong. For both of us."

The line clicked, and I sat there, gripping the phone like it was the only thing keeping me tethered to the world. The bailiff peeked in a few moments later; her face was kind but cautious.

"Ready?" she asked softly.

No. Not even close. But I nodded, stood up, and walked back into the room where none of these people had any idea how much weight I was carrying. It was the second round of cancer for my mother. She'd beat it the first time, when I was a teenager. When I turned eighteen, I got a wild idea to travel from our home in Red Bluff, California, along the entire West Coast. It had been a celebration of my adulthood, but also, the adventure I had never had because my mother had been sick for so long.

She told me to go. As I plotted my route, she helped me mark the best places to stop for food, lodging and any important sights along the way. I saved up what I could, thinking I would settle somewhere and get a job to pay the rest of the way. It was a wild idea, but one many eighteen-year-old kids had.

I travelled south first, getting to the Mexican border before turning around. I passed places like Disneyland and Universal Studios, without the cash to actually go into any of the parks. Standing outside, I imagined what it would have been like to be one of those kids with memories of theme parks, princesses and talking mice.

Instead, my mom raised me as a single mom, working two jobs most of my life. I didn't blame her for anything. She gave me everything she could. Vacations for us were overnight trips that took us to the coast. We collected seashells we took home and glued to furniture to remember our trips. My mom would make wind chimes and carve the date into a small piece of driftwood. She taught me how to enjoy the simple things.

When I travelled back north, I found myself stopping in Portland, Oregon, to find a job. That was six years ago. Many times I thought about moving back to be with my mom, or at least closer to her. However, she always told me to stay in Oregon. I was on my way to becoming a store manager at Target and the opportunities in Red Bluff were limited.

Earlier in the year, when they found that her cancer had returned, I renewed my efforts to come back. She insisted I didn't uproot the life I had built for myself. I visited as often as my days off allowed. With each visit, I could see her getting skinnier and weaker, giving me the impression that the treatment wasn't working.

Now, in July, it had been five months since they found the cells again. Her voice on the phone sounded even weaker than before, a fragile thread holding together what little strength she had left. Every word she spoke felt like a reminder of how little time we might have, and it made the distance between us feel unbearable. The guilt gnawed at me constantly. Guilt for not being there, for not knowing how to help, and for the selfish part of me that dreaded what might come next. I wanted to believe in the doctors, in the treatments, but every strained syllable in her voice chipped away at that hope, leaving only a raw, aching fear.

The bailiff let me back into the jury room and she looked down at me with a regretful face. I knew what she was thinking. I should have bolted the moment she let me use the telephone. When I returned to the room, it was clear that the judge had instructed everyone to stop talking. We weren't supposed to have side conversations or discuss things without everyone present.

As I entered, Don let out a vast sigh, throwing up his hands. "It's about time. You're just holding us all up."

Before I could even muster up a decent response, the foreperson stood, looking at the bailiff that was still standing in the room. Her hand rested on her gun belt, and I had to wonder if she didn't think about shooting Don. I had never touched a gun, but I was thinking about shooting Don.

"Bailiff, I think we have a problem. We have one juror that is refusing to follow the letter of the law and follow the evidence as presented. He is disagreeing without explanation, causing us to sit as a hung jury."

The bailiff nodded, her eyes on Don. Even with the foreperson not using his name, the officer was under no misunderstanding who the troublemaker was.

"I'll let the judge know. You'll need to wait here until we hear from his office."

With that, we were left alone. We had no devices, no TV. Some had books they fished from their bags, settling in for the long haul. At that moment, I was mad at myself for loading all my books onto my e-reader and not having a physical one in my hand. Thinking the e-reader counted as a device, I hadn't bothered to bring it in.

Resting my head on my hand, I closed my eyes for a moment, trying to block out the quiet noises around me. My body hummed with tension, every muscle coiled from anxiety I couldn't shake. The case was important. I knew that. It was my duty, my responsibility. But none of it mattered compared to my mother. The thought of her suffering alone while I was stuck here felt like a knife twisting in my chest, cutting deeper with every passing hour.

CHAPTER
TWO
CRISTIAN

The suit itched. Of course, it wasn't the suit's fault—I was the one who hadn't worn it in over a year, stuffed in the back of my closet next to a pile of things I'd been meaning to throw out since the divorce. I tugged at the collar and resisted the urge to adjust the tie for the hundredth time. The courthouse air was stale, the kind of stale that clings to old wood and bureaucratic bullshit.

My knee wouldn't stop bouncing, a nervous tic I hadn't shaken since rookie days. My shoulder ached, the dull throb radiating into my chest, but I ignored it. I had bigger things to worry about.

Delays in a courthouse were to be expected. This case was no different. They scheduled my testimony for early morning. The prosecution wanted to add additional charges, and the defense team didn't love the last-minute changes. Which left everyone, including me, waiting in a holding pattern. If I didn't live almost an hour from the courthouse, I would have gone home.

I leaned back on the unforgiving bench and let my eyes drift to the crowd milling around the hallway—jurors, attorneys, anxious families. I'd seen them all before, on the job. But being on this side of things felt foreign. Like I'd been invited to someone else's disaster but wasn't allowed to leave.

My gaze landed on my shoes, polished but scuffed around the edges. Sarah always hated when my shoes were scuffed. "It's the first thing people notice," she'd say, shaking her head as if I'd committed some cardinal sin.

A woman walked by in the hallway, laughing softly into her phone. The sound of it—the warmth in her voice—hit me harder than it should have. I knew that tone. I used to hear it in my own home, before Sarah stopped laughing at anything I said.

I hadn't wanted the divorce. Not really. But Sarah had decided long before the papers were served. She wanted out of the marriage, and honestly, I couldn't blame her. It was often said I was married to the job, and maybe she was right. I'd lost count of the times I'd missed dinner, an anniversary, or some family gathering because I was chasing down leads or stuck on patrol.

But what else could I have done? People don't sign up to be cops because they want a simple life. They sign up because they want to protect people, to make a difference, and sometimes that means sacrifices. What Sarah never understood, or maybe just didn't care to, is that protecting people isn't something you can clock out of.

Still, the way it had ended wasn't because of a few missed dates. I knew that. It was only the start. Eventually, Sarah's eye wandered, and she found someone else that would be at the table every night. He probably cooked occasionally, too. I didn't. While there was anger and hurt in my heart, I knew it was the best thing for her. And like with every aspect of my life, other's needs came before my own.

Scrubbing a hand over my face, I tried to push all the emotions back into the box I kept them in. It was all just more things I didn't face. Sarah had been the only woman I wanted in my life for any length of time. Letting her go was the only decision to make, but that didn't mean it was easy. The aftermath wasn't simple either.

"Officer Cristian Reyes?"

I glanced up to see a bailiff leaning against the doorframe, his voice cutting through the murmur of the hallway. "They need to see you."

I groaned. The bailiff lifted his shoulders with an understanding smile. Anytime you had to go over your testimony with lawyers again before a trial meant things were just going to take longer. My patience level was incredibly low, especially after sitting and thinking about Sarah for hours.

Standing, I stretched my stiff back. I had to rotate my shoulder, which always gave me trouble after a high school football injury. The bailiff walked down the hall without checking to see if I followed. I rubbed my shoulder with the opposite hand. The pain made me wonder if it was from waiting, or the tension I couldn't seem to shake.

The prosecutor's office was as nondescript as they come—standard government beige walls, cheap carpeting, and a filing cabinet that looked like it had survived a couple of administrations too many. The fluorescent lights buzzed faintly overhead, adding to the room's dull ambiance.

"Officer Reyes," the prosecutor said as I stepped through the door, motioning toward the chair across from his desk. "Thanks for coming in. I know waiting around isn't fun."

The man looked like he hadn't slept in a week, his suit slightly rumpled and dark circles under his eyes. I'd met his type before: overworked and under-rested, driven by some innate need to win every case no matter how much it cost him. It wasn't much different from how I approached my own job. The work came before everything, including sleep.

"I wanted to go over your testimony before we bring you in," he said, sifting through a stack of papers on his desk until he pulled out a familiar case file. He flipped it open and scanned it briefly, tapping a pen against the desk. "Your statement is pretty straightforward, but I want to make sure we're clear on a few key pieces. We are adding some additional charges and want to make sure all the pieces fit."

I leaned back in the chair, trying to look as relaxed as possible despite the tightness in my shoulder that radiated into my chest. Momentarily, I wondered if it was possible that I was having a heart attack. "I heard. Go ahead."

Pushing his glasses up his nose, he glanced up at me. "On the night in question, you responded to a 911 call reporting suspicious activity at the victim's residence. You were the first officer on the scene?"

"Right," I said. "It was approximately 10:30 p.m. I arrived, noticed the front door was ajar, and called for backup before entering."

"And inside, you found the defendant standing over the victim, correct?"

I nodded. "Yes. The victim was on the floor, unresponsive. The defendant had blood on his hands and was holding a knife."

The scene seared itself into my brain. In the years I had been a police officer, I had seen things that convinced me evil was real in the world. I'd heard people on drugs spew at me in languages, that when sober, swore they didn't know. There were attacks, attempted murders, domestic violence, and so much more. The worst ones, they never truly went away. They were just filed in my brain, like everything else.

The prosecutor scribbled a note on the margins of the file. "Good. When you ordered him to drop the weapon, what was his response?"

I hesitated for a second, replaying the moment in my head. "He didn't say anything. Just dropped the knife and raised his hands. He looked... confused. Like he wasn't sure what had just happened."

The prosecutor looked up sharply. "Confused?"

"Yeah," I said, shifting in my chair. "Not like someone caught in the act. More like... someone in shock."

He frowned and leaned back, tapping the pen against his chin. "That's not ideal."

"Doesn't change the fact that he was holding the knife," I said firmly. "And there's plenty of forensic evidence to back that up. The blood on his clothing was clear spray from the wounds of the victim."

"True," he conceded, though his frown didn't disappear. "But the defense is going to latch onto anything that paints him as less than fully culpable. They're already pushing this narrative that he was framed or acting under duress. Your testimony about his demeanor might give them ammunition. It could even lend to a plea of insanity."

I folded my arms, pulling against my sore shoulder, my jaw tightening. "You want me to lie about what I saw?"

It wouldn't be the first time a legal type asked me to brush past the facts or push something under the proverbial rug. My ethical code ran deeper than some legal types. Their goal was to win, to add to their record, to maybe get elected to some position they were gunning for. My job was to protect the public and get people off the streets that threatened others. In instances where there was doubt about guilt, I wouldn't lie to get that verdict.

"No," he said quickly, holding up a hand. "Absolutely not. I just want you to be precise. Stick to the facts. No embellishments, no speculations."

"That's all I ever do," I shot back, my voice sharper than I intended.

The prosecutor held my gaze for a moment before nodding. "Good. Just make sure to keep it that way on the stand. The defense is going to try and trip you up, make it seem like you're uncertain about what you saw. Don't let them."

"I won't," I said evenly, though the tension in the room made my spine straighten.

"Great." He closed the file and set it aside, leaning forward with his hands clasped. "One last thing, how are you feeling about this? Testifying can be... tricky, even for officers."

"I've testified before," I said curtly. "I know my job."

He studied me for a beat, his expression unreadable, before nodding again. "All right, then. We'll call you in as soon as possible. Thanks for your time, Officer Reyes."

I stood and left the office, my thoughts spinning. The prosecutor had his job to do, but he didn't know the half of it. How moments like this stuck with you, long after the testimony and verdict were in the books.

Back in the hallway, I adjusted my tie and leaned against the wall, taking a deep breath. The case might have been clear-cut to the prosecutor, but to me, it felt like another reminder of everything I couldn't fix, on the job, and in my life.

Closing my eyes, I tried to picture how I'd gotten to the place I was in. The bitterness was long before Sarah and the divorce. Thinking about the moments that brought me to where I was standing made me feel hollowed out. It was the reason I stayed as busy as I could, to avoid that feeling, the bone jarring sadness and the desperation to feel anything else.

I was a walking contradiction. I'd dedicated my life to what was just and right, but the optimism I'd had to make a change in the world had died long ago. After years of seeing humanity at its worst, I still tried to be the exception. But the more I carried, the more I started to wonder, how much longer before it crushed me completely?

CHAPTER
THREE
MARLOWE

The jury room was getting warmer. I opened my eyes and lifted my head to glance around. Being stuck in the room with the group that was no longer speaking to each other felt oppressive. The air felt thick in my throat. I stood and made my way to the window, hoping the view of the outside would make me feel less nauseous.

Honking from down the street caught my attention. I leaned closer to the window, trying to see what the confusion was. I couldn't see the vehicles, however. There was a small group of people moving slowly toward the street that was in front of the courthouse. It was enough of a distraction to get my mind off the warmth in the small jury room.

"What the hell," one woman muttered under her breath, as she tapped at her e-reader.

The lights in the room flickered before going dark completely. I looked around the room, expecting to see someone at the light switch, but everyone remained seated. The room was quiet, while those with electronics fidgeted with their devices. Something nagged my mind about what was happening, but I couldn't put my finger on it.

As I turned back toward the window, movement caught my attention out of the corner of my eye.

"Oh, my god!" I exclaimed.

As I watched, a gray shape from the sky grew in size as it moved closer. The low mechanical groan of an engine sputtering, until it cut off completely. The passenger plane's descent was too steep, its nose pointed toward the Earth. The fuselage reflected the sun, blinding me for a moment, before it disappeared behind the large neighboring building.

An earth-shaking boom I felt in my chest followed a second later. The ground beneath my feet shuddered and a violent ripple tore through the air. I dropped just as the window shattered, shooting shards of glass all over the juror room. The sound of the destruction filled the space, and I could feel the power in my body. I braced myself against the wall beneath the window opening.

Jurors scrambled for cover, unsure if there was something more coming toward the window. I could see Don hiding under the table, his hands over his ears. Absently, I wondered why nothing seemed loud to me. Their voices, raised in shouts or screams, seemed muffled and distant.

The door burst open, and the bailiff rushed in. In seconds, she assessed the situation in the room and started guiding jurors out of the room. I pushed myself up on shaking legs. A huge billow of smoke rose just beyond the building. Broken windows lined the courthouse-facing side of the building. I could see people moving around in a panic, as everyone tried to react to the plane falling from the sky.

I stared at the street below. The blackened husk of the plane was barely visible through the rising smoke, but the pieces were there. Jagged metal twisted around burning parts of the building, bodies sprawled like broken dolls in the wreckage. A woman stumbled away from the fire, her arms wrapped around herself like she was trying to hold her skin together.

"Marlowe?" The bailiff's voice was quiet, and it was her hand on my arm that turned me from the chaos outside.

Her eyes scanned my face. Spinning, she grabbed a tissue from a box on the table and pressed it against my right cheek. I hadn't even felt the sting of the wound until she pressed against it. Looking at my bare arms, I saw other scratches, but none seemed to bleed badly. The bailiff motioned for me to follow her, and I stumbled toward the open door. My legs were jelly and my adrenaline was spiking.

My whole body trembled, but I wasn't sure if it was from fear or the explosion's aftershock. My breath came in short bursts, chest tight, and I realized my hands were shaking violently. I wasn't hurt, not really. But my knees felt like they might give out any second.

It felt miraculous that I had been spared. The plane had crashed less than two hundred yards from me. But even as I thought that, a realization struck me, turning my stomach. Someone, likely dozens of someones, hadn't been spared the same fate.

The hallway outside of the juror room was bustling with people moving erratically. I felt dazed and confused. Pressing the tissue to my face, I could still feel the sting of the cut and I absently wondered if I needed stitches. My insurance was for emergencies at best, costing any meager savings I had if I ever needed to use it. My brain was already calculating costs, wondering if I could afford that and also afford to get to my mom.

"What's happening?" I spoke to the bailiff's back, as she had stopped in the middle of the hallway.

"Power is out. Everything just stopped. And the plane…," she trailed off.

"It fell out of the sky." I glanced back toward the juror room, as if I could see the crashed plane clearly. "Those people."

The bailiff turned to look at me, and her gaze followed.

"There's nothing we can do for them right now. Emergency services should get there any minute."

My hearing still felt muffled, and the only sounds that came to me were people panicking. No sirens, no loud vehicles. The bailiff pulled a cellphone from her pocket, and I realized all of my stuff was back in the jury room. Turning away from the bailiff, I stumbled back down the corridor. I needed my backpack. The bailiff caught up with me, stopping me before I got into the jury room.

"Where did you take our cellphones?" I asked.

The woman shook her head. "None of them are working."

"What do you mean, not working? I need my phone. My mom could try to call. Hell, if she sees this on the news, she'll panic. I need to call her."

"You aren't hearing me. Nothing's working. None of the phones I've tried. Everyone is talking about their cellphones not turning on. I don't think yours is going to be any different," she replied.

I stared at her. It was the first time I noticed she had a name tag on. Becker. Why hadn't I noticed that before? My hands shook and I couldn't keep the tissue pressed to my cheek. Pulling it away, I looked at the dark red stain on the Kleenex. Confusion was setting in.

"No phones? Nothing is working?" I asked, hearing how ridiculous the question sounded even to my ears.

"No, Marlowe. Nothing is working."

Another officer interrupted our conversation. They shared a few quick words and Becker nodded. She turned to me again. "Will you be ok? I have to go."

I nodded, knowing my voice would give away the lie. My gut was twisting, and I didn't understand what was happening. But I wouldn't tell Becker I needed someone to hold my hand. No, I had figured out how to be strong in the world. On my own.

Becker didn't look like she believed me, but her responsibility won out and she walked away. As she disappeared around the corner, fear set in. I moved toward another door that had been left ajar. When I glanced in, I found an office. Someone had left in a hurry, leaving papers strewn across the floor. But it was the phone on the desktop that I was interested in.

Sitting on the chair, I picked up the handset and pressed it to my ear. I shouldn't have been surprised when it was silent. In front of me, a laptop sat half open. I hesitated, thinking about privacy and if I was breaking the law by even being at the desk. But when I remembered the plane crashing not far away, I didn't think anyone was going to be looking for me.

I pushed the laptop lid until it was fully open. Nothing came on. When I ran my finger over the touchpad, still nothing. Frustrated and not ready to accept what felt impossible, I held my finger down on the power button. Nothing. After verifying the laptop was actually plugged into power, I gave up.

The strange stillness of the building struck me. The sudden, absolute silence of the air-conditioning and fluorescent bulbs dying together left a void that even the collective panic in the building couldn't fill.

Outside the office, I could still hear the fear-stricken throng of people moving around the courthouse. Louder voices rose above, bailiffs and other law enforcement trying to control the situation. Going to the door, I tried to figure out what they were advising people. It sounded like they were trying to keep people inside while the plane crash was handled.

"It's not safe! We need everyone to stay inside until law enforcement and fire officials release us."

The officer faced a barrage of shouted questions he couldn't keep up with. He held up his hands, trying to slow everyone down, but it didn't work. Another man, in a suit, stood next to him with a scowl on his face. He leaned toward the bailiff and motioned wildly with his hands. The bailiff barely spared him a glance and shook his head. I watched from the doorway, worried about moving out into the crowd and being stuck. Everything was giving me the feeling that this was about to get worse before it got better.

"This is just a power outage," he assured us, though his voice betrayed the slightest quiver. "The building has protocols for this. We're safe."

But I didn't feel safe. Not even close.

Then came the shots. Three of them, in rapid succession.

Crack! Crack! Crack!

My body reacted before my mind caught up, instinctively ducking low next to the wall. The bailiff was already gone, rushing toward the commotion. My fellow courthouse refugees looked as pale and shell-shocked as I felt, their faces frozen in wide-eyed terror.

"What's happening?" one of them whispered, but no one had an answer.

Another round of shots rang out, closer this time, followed by a guttural yell that sent ice through my veins. I heard the unmistakable sounds of a struggle—shouts, a scuffle, and then something heavy crashing against the wall.

"We need to get out of here," I said, my voice shaky but firm.

"But they said to stay!" someone protested, clinging to the bailiff's earlier assurance.

"Did those gunshots sound like we're safe to you?" I snapped, already moving toward the door.

Cautiously, I peered into the hallway. It was chaos. People were running in every direction. The dim light that could reach from windows cast long, disjointed shadows. Papers were scattered everywhere, fluttering like panicked birds in the rush of feet. Across the hall, I could see directly into the courtroom I had spent the last few days in.

That's when I saw him. The defendant from my trial, the armed robber. He had a reputation for violence, and it showed now in the way his face twisted with fury, blood dripping down his knuckles. A bailiff lay crumpled at his feet, unmoving, his sidearm now clutched in the defendant's trembling hands.

He had been kept in custody after he broke his bail agreement. I could see a handcuff still secured to one of his wrists. I tried to focus on the bailiff on the ground, but there wasn't enough light for me to see if his chest was rising and falling.

Ducking low, I moved into the hallway, running into some of my fellow jurors, including Don.

"He's got a gun," I whispered, panic lacing every word.

Don grabbed my arm, his grip too tight. "What do we do?" he hissed, eyes darting wildly. "We have to get out of here!"

I yanked my arm back, glaring at him. "No shit, Don."

The question hung in the air like the charged silence before a storm.

"Run," I said, my voice firmer than I felt. "We run."

The hallway was chaos—people screaming, running, tripping over one another as they tried to escape. I crouched low, moving as quickly as I could while staying under the line of sight. The defendant's wild, erratic shouting echoed behind me, along with the deafening bark of gunfire.

Someone bumped into me hard, nearly knocking me over. I scrambled to stay upright, the instinct to survive overriding everything else. My cheap heels weren't meant for running or trying to move fast across linoleum floors. My hands brushed against the cool, gritty surface of the wall as I used it to guide myself forward.

"Move!" a man barked, shoving past me and nearly toppling a woman in front of him. The crowd was a living, breathing thing now. Frantic and unpredictable, surging toward the exits.

The problem was, everyone was moving toward the exits, including the man with the gun. More shots sounded and screams echoed in the lobby. Without a destination in mind, I turned back and started down another dark hallway.

"Where are you going?" Don hissed over my shoulder. He was entirely too close to me. I walked faster, using my hand along the wall to guide me in the dark.

"There has to be an emergency exit. Something in the back. Away from the maniac with the gun," I explained.

As we walked down a familiar hallway, I found our way back to the side of the building where we could see the fire from the plane. I glanced into one room, where I could see through the window and I stopped short. For the moment, my escape was forgotten. Moving toward the window, I covered my mouth with shaking fingers.

"Oh, my lord." The foreperson had caught up with our group, and she was standing next to me at the window.

Outside, the world was on fire.

A massive plume of smoke filled the sky. The blaze from the plane had spread, and we could see flames licking up the side of the neighboring building. Inside, there were still people panicking and trying to escape. I leaned forward, trying to see the end of the courthouse or the road. There were no flashing lights, no water being sprayed. Nothing.

"Why aren't they putting the fire out?" I mumbled.

The courthouse building was old, with the lobby being down a short set of stairs. The courtrooms and juror room I had been in were technically on the second floor. When I looked down from the window, I realized we were too high to jump without serious injury. The fire also put the building we were in at risk.

Shouts and gunshots, seemingly closer now, pulled my attention from the window. "We need to go."

I turned and sprinted out of the room and down the hall, my heart slamming against my ribs. The walls felt like they were closing in, the dim light from outside sunlight, casting long, distorted shadows that seemed to claw at my peripheral vision. I could hear the jurors keeping pace behind me, giving me courage to keep going.

At the end of the hall, we found a door marked 'Stairs' and had no choice but to try it for an exit. People packed the steps, jostling from the floors above and shoving as they fought to descend. The air was thick with the scent of sweat and fear. I shoved my way through, gripping the railing tightly as I took the steps two at a time.

"Keep moving!" someone shouted above the din.

A loud crack rang out—a gunshot—and the crowd surged forward, people screaming as they pushed harder to escape. The crush caught me, pressing my body between strangers as we stumbled down the stairs. I felt a hard shove between my shoulder blades, and I felt myself going over. There was no doubt that if I fell, the panicked crowd would trample me.

Suddenly, someone gripped my arm and yanked me back onto my feet, pressing my back against a hard chest.

"Hold on. I'll get you out of here." The voice was gruff and unknown, but he held onto me tightly as we descended the stairs together.

By the time we reached the bottom, my legs were shaking, adrenaline making every movement feel surreal. We stumbled through the emergency exit door. The chaos spilled out onto the streets, where the fiery aftermath of the crash loomed in the distance.

The man holding my arm didn't let go, and I didn't have the strength to pull away. Angling my head, I glimpsed a severe frown and a low brow. I realized it was the same suited man that had been trying to work with the bailiff. Who was likely dead on the courtroom floor now.

Any thought of speaking to the man vanished as my attention shifted to the chaos outside the courthouse. The fire from the plane crash was far more devastating than it had first appeared. Flames roared, consuming not only the building next to the court-house but also the towering trees and the park nearby. Thick smoke billowed into the sky, and the fire's relentless advance had already devoured a nearby strip of businesses, turning the area into an inferno that showed no signs of slowing.

The heat was stifling, and I held up my free hand to shield my face. A pull on my arm got my attention, and I looked over at the man again.

"We need to get away from here," he said.

"Where do we go?" The voice from behind me made me realize we weren't alone.

Turning, I found Don, the foreperson, and two others from my jury. They had all stopped outside the exit door. Everyone looked lost as to what they should do. The man holding my arm finally released me, glancing down at me as if he just noticed me. Looking around, he pointed down the street, toward the opposite side of the courthouse.

"As far away from the fire as we can."

He started a slow jog away from the courthouse. Don easily followed with two jury members. The foreperson huffed out a deep breath, before picking up her pace to try and keep up. I stumbled in my low heels, but my desperate desire to get away from the crashed plane and growing flames encouraged me to continue moving forward. I berated myself for dressing up for jury duty, as if it made any difference to the process of the case.

Around the corner, we approached a road, and it was immediately clear there was more wrong than just a plane crash. There was a car, smashed into a storefront, with a bloodied driver hanging half out of the open door.

When I slowed to look, I saw a leg beneath the car. "We need to help them!"

The man leading us hesitated long enough to see what I was looking at before replying, "Which one do you want to help? What can we do? There's too many."

I stared at him for a moment, shocked at his words. Though I heard what he said, it was as if he was chewing on glass as he spoke. His attention bounced around, from the fire in the distance, to the multiple accidents on the road. I followed his gaze and I realized he was right. Destruction surrounded us.

Without another word, he turned away and went toward a four-way intersection. Mangled cars blocked the middle. None of the traffic lights were on. No solid colors and nothing blinked. Passengers and drivers from the cars stumbled around in confusion, talking to each other. A shoving match broke out as two men accused each other of running the light, while a woman tried to break it up, telling them the lights weren't on.

I filed away my observations and continued to follow the group. Something about the man in the suit felt like he knew what he was doing. He moved as if he had a specific goal in mind and we were all along for the ride. None of us spoke. At the next intersection, we found a commuter train stalled and blocking the street. A pickup truck had crashed into one of the train cars, but the doors of the train were being pried open, and people were climbing out.

"I don't understand. I thought it was just a plane crash?" I said to no one in particular.

No one answered at first. But when we entered a parking garage, the man leading us stopped in a shaded corner. "I think this might be well beyond the plane and further than Hillsboro."

"How do you know that? You seem awful comfortable with all of this," Don said, crossing his arms in front of him.

I groaned audibly and the disagreeable man turned his heated gaze to me. "Have something to say?"

"I think it's pretty clear you know very little, Don. So maybe you try not attacking the guy that's trying to help us."

"Do you even know him? How do you even know he's trying to help us?"

I didn't have an answer for that, and I turned to look at the man we had been following. His brow was still pulled low, as if he was deep in thought. Handsome, even with the slash of a scowl across his face. As we all waited for an answer, he turned narrowed eyes on Don.

"Well, I saved her from falling down the stairs when you shoved her." The stranger motioned toward me and Don's face went bright red.

"I didn't—"

The man cut him off. "Don't bother. I watched you shove her right in the back. You were content in trampling her to save yourself. You're lucky I didn't do more than save her."

As Don sputtered, trying to find a defense, the man stepped toward him. Don stumbled back, fear highlighting his features.

"Either get on board so we can get everyone home. Or you can go on your own." The man spoke low, his voice a sugar laced knife edge.

Don just nodded his head, unable to speak. With his agreement, the man stepped back and took in the group again.

"Maybe introductions are in order. I'm Cristian. I do know something about what's happening. And I'm a Washington County Sheriff's Deputy. We are all trained on mass disasters like this. It's clear there's more going on here than just that plane crash."

Everyone nodded. The jury foreperson raised her hand tentatively. "I'm Colleen. I live in Forest Grove with my husband. And I really need to get home to him."

The other two jurors looked at each other and back at us. The women had been nice during the days we had spent together, but I could see the panic on both of their faces.

"We both live here in Hillsboro. We're going to go. Good luck."

Cristian lifted his hand, as if to reach out to them and keep them from running off. But they turned and sprinted into the parking garage.

"They're not going to get far going that way," he mumbled.

"Why?" I asked.

"I don't think their cars, or most current model vehicles, are going to work."

When I just stared at him, waiting for more, his frown deepened.

"Who are you?" Cristian finally asked. Without warning, his hand snapped out, and he grabbed my chin, tilting my face so he could study the cut on my cheek.

"Marlowe. I live in Beaverton. But if this isn't just happening here, I need to get to Northern California. My mom is there. And she's sick. Why aren't cars going to work?" I talked carefully, making sure I didn't yank my face out of his hands.

"Do you ever watch the news?"

"Sometimes." I shrugged. He released me with a nod, and I assumed my face didn't look horrible.

"I guess sometimes wasn't any of the times that they were talking about some sort of massive solar storm coming. I think I heard about it yesterday."

"How does that have anything to do with what's happening?" Don asked.

Cristian rolled his eyes and curled his hands into fists. I found myself hoping he would punch Don in his argumentative face.

"I'm not a damn scientist. They were just talking about how something this large could mess with communications and electronics."

"This is a lot worse than that. A plane fell out of the sky," I said.

Cristian nodded, and his head turned toward the fire that was still raging. The orange of the flames was visible in the smoke-filled sky. It seemed so much larger than just twenty minutes before. I wanted to keep going.

"I live in Tualatin. I have a house. You're all welcome there," Cristian said.

I debated. My apartment wasn't any closer than Cristian's house. And I would be completely alone if I went there. I didn't know my neighbors. Most of my friends lived in downtown Portland, and I had no way to reach any of them. The three people in front of me were the only connections I had at the moment. Glancing at Don, I didn't consider him a trustworthy connection. But Cristian and Colleen were better than nothing.

"I'll go with you. I don't have anyone else to meet up with," I said.

"It would be the opposite direction for me. I really need to get home," Colleen said.

"I could try to find you a way home before we split up. Maybe people that are going that direction. I don't think traveling alone would be safe," Cristian replied.

Don huffed. "What about me? What am I supposed to do?"

Cristian regarded him, dark eyes shrewd. I stared at his face, trying to see the color of his eyes clearly, but the shade made them look almost black.

"You do whatever you need to do, Don. These ladies need assistance, and I'm not going to just leave them on their own."

"Or you could always leave us on our own, Don. We wouldn't want you to accidentally shove someone else down a flight of stairs," I interjected.

I didn't miss the slight smirk on Cristian's face before he pasted on a neutral look. Clearly, it didn't take long for him to also understand what type of man Don was.

"I'll help," Don muttered under his breath.

"That seemed painful," I replied.

Cristian didn't wait for more of a fight before heading into the parking garage. I looked at Colleen and we nodded to each other before following the man that claimed to be a sheriff deputy, hoping he would know what the next steps were.

CHAPTER
FOUR
CRISTIAN

What was I even doing? I could hear the woman named Marlowe's heels clicking behind me. The sound echoed in the quiet parking garage. I immediately noted the lack of engine noises. Still, I wanted to check my SUV. It was likely a waste of time. However, it gave me the time I needed to think up a plan.

I had tried to follow some sort of disaster planning with the court law enforcement, but they immediately denied my request to have access to my weapon. It was not normal to butt heads with bailiffs during trial. We were typically friendly during the usual waiting and procedures. But as soon as the power went out, and the plane crashed, absolute chaos ensued. There was no telling them anything at that point.

A plane had fallen from the sky. Those were the words Marlowe used. I did not see the plane crash, but everyone in the courthouse felt the impact. I had only heard what had happened from other witnesses as we were trying to control the panic within the building. Until I saw the raging fire with a passenger plane in the center, I hadn't truly believed what I was hearing.

What I had said about the news was true, but I didn't know if that had caused everything to stop working. I could feel the useless weight of my cellphone in my suit pants pocket. As soon as the power had gone out, I'd checked it. It seemed to flicker a few times before dying completely. Now, I had it in my pocket on the long chance that this was an isolated event, and it might start working again.

We arrived at my gray SUV, and I pulled my keys from my pocket. Pressing the fob buttons, nothing happened. Fidgeting with the fob, I pulled the hidden physical key from the housing. At the driver's side door, I used the key to pop open the door and climbed in.

Glancing in the rearview mirror, I caught sight of Marlowe, her short dark hair curtaining her face as she seemed to look at her feet. She did that a lot. Seeing Don shove her from behind infuriated me. I had joined the evacuating group, thinking I could help once we got outside. Instead, I watched as Don put his hand on Marlowe's back and shoved her out of his way. I was certain that if I hadn't grabbed her, she would have been badly injured, or worse.

Now, when she looked at me, it felt like I couldn't leave her behind. I shouldn't have cared. I barely knew her. But leaving her behind felt wrong. Felt like failure. My gut twisted at the thought. Sarah would have called it my savior complex. Maybe she was right. Maybe I hadn't learned a damn thing. There had been people I couldn't save in my life, and I was determined to not have that happen again. Even if the people were strangers.

Pushing the key into the ignition, I wasn't surprised when the engine didn't even try to turn over. Don stood near my open door. He watched with a hopeful look, quickly snuffed as I pulled out the key.

"I didn't really think it would work. But until I tried, I couldn't be sure," I said aloud, once I climbed from the vehicle.

Marlowe and Colleen came around from the back of the SUV and looked at me with expectation on their faces. I ran my hand through my hair, trying to think of another plan. My house was over twenty miles away. A two-day walk, even with the right gear, which neither Marlowe nor Colleen had. I really didn't want to walk twenty miles in my dress shoes, either.

Colleen's house was in the opposite direction and was likely no closer. I couldn't get to both on foot. That left us with few options. In my mind, I listed needs in the order of necessity. Water, food, clothing and possibly overnight shelter. I could tell the events of the day had already taken a lot out of the three people in front of me.

"I think we need to find food and water first. No matter which way we go, we have a long walk ahead of us if we can't find any sort of vehicle that works."

Marlowe's warm brown eyes locked on me, and I had to look away from the intense feeling of responsibility that hit me. The sound of shattering glass caused everyone to jump, and I whirled toward the noise. I reached to my belt and cursed when I remembered the bailiff refusing to give my weapon back before all hell broke loose inside the courthouse. Weaponless, I felt exposed and unprepared.

"We should move," I whispered.

Another crash and loud yelling from one group to another punctuated my words. It wasn't easy to make out the words with the echoing, but it was clear they were looking for something. And we didn't want to be in the way when they got to us.

I started walking toward the exit of the parking garage, motioning for the three to follow me. Don looked back with a frown, but he got in line behind Marlowe and Colleen. As we walked into the late afternoon sun, the smashing glass was closer and I moved behind the concrete wall. Reaching out, I grabbed Marlowe's wrist and tugged her to follow.

Marlowe, Colleen, and Don huddled where I indicated, and I leaned around the wall to see what was happening to the vehicles. Two small groups of people crept between cars, peering into windows. When something caught their attention, one of them whistled a sharp, deliberate signal. Another man approached, dragging a crowbar against the concrete, the metal scraping loud in the quiet. A second later, the window shattered. Together, they would yank things from the vehicles and move onto the next.

Shaking my head, I moved back to my group and pointed down the street, away from the threat. Marlowe tripped, and I steadied her with a hand on her elbow. She glanced up with a grateful smile and I looked away.

"Stupid shoes. Worst day to try to dress the part," she muttered just loud enough for me to hear.

"What part were you trying to play?"

"I was on a jury. It was a day of deliberation. The defendant was the man who shot the bailiff." She raised her eyes from her feet and glared at the back of Don's head. "Guess he was probably guilty, wasn't he, Don?"

Don's shoulders came up around his ears and I saw him tense, but he didn't respond to her curt comment. I wasn't sure what it meant, but they clearly didn't agree on something regarding the trial. No matter what the situation, I saw the man break away from the bailiff that was trying to take him to a holding cell. The next thing I knew, he had a gun and had shot another officer. I could confirm he was at least guilty on that charge.

On the next street, general chaos ensued. People wandered around cars that were crashed or abandoned along the road. Some, still on their pedal bikes, wound through traffic, their general need to get to their destination clear by the swiftness in which they pumped their legs. Bicycles were famous in Portland, Oregon, and the surrounding areas. I filed that away as an idea for later.

A piercing scream cut through the chaos, sharper and louder than anything else. I whipped my head around, searching for the source. Not far away, a smoking car sat still, its front end crumpled against a tree that had halted its deadly momentum. A woman leaned into the open driver's side window, her desperate cries ringing out as she called a name over and over, her voice raw with anguish.

Before I could say anything, Marlowe pulled from my grip and ran as best as she could toward the woman. I sighed, but followed, feeling like I didn't have much of a choice. The woman at the car spun as soon as we approached.

"Please, help him. He's my husband. I…can't get him out."

Marlowe's eyes were soft and kind as she laid her hand on the woman's shoulder, carefully guiding her away from the vehicle. She glanced at me, and I could see the instructions she had for me. Check on the man. Help him and his wife. I gave her a curt nod, before leaning into the car window myself.

Blood covered the man's face, and I guessed the woman recognized her husband by his car. The airbag didn't seem to have deployed, and the connection of his face with the steering wheel rearranged his nose. There was a huge gash across his forehead that had caused the blood to gush down the rest of his face.

I pressed two fingers against his throat, waiting for something. Anything. But there was nothing. Just the eerie stillness of death. The blood flowing down his face started to slow, streaking darkly along his skin. I exhaled through my nose, steeling myself. This wasn't the first time I'd had to tell someone their loved one was gone. But it never got easier.

When I turned, the woman read the grim look on my face. She began to wail, and Marlowe immediately folded her into an embrace. I stood awkwardly on the side, not sure what to do. Colleen joined Marlowe in consoling the wife, while Don came to the car next to me.

"You're a cop, right?" Don asked.

"Deputy, yeah."

He waved his arms around wildly, indicating the insanity near us and the billowing smoke that was still rising into the sky from the direction of the courthouse. His voice was high, frantic. "Where are the cops, man? What the hell is this? Shouldn't someone be in charge?" He spun in place, eyes darting wildly, like he was waiting for someone in uniform to come rescue him.

It was the same question I had been asking myself. A lot of men and women in positions similar to mine had been through the disaster preparedness classes. We had to hear the plans. I sat through several lectures and procedure explanations. It was clear to me now that those plans broke down. Maybe it was the lack of access to real-time communications. Or maybe humans did what they did. Panicked and did what they needed to protect themselves and their families.

"I don't know," I replied.

The wife of the deceased man pulled away from Marlowe and Colleen, coming back to the car to continue to cry over her husband. I grabbed a gawking Don and pulled him out of the way. Marlowe stood, watching the woman, tears in her eyes. I had to look away when one escaped and slid down her freckled cheek. Distancing from grief was a survival technique for doing the work I did.

Eventually, Marlowe and Colleen convinced the woman to go home. Her apartment was nearby and her sister was visiting. She walked away in a dazed state, with Marlowe and Colleen watching after her. The time it took for us to help the woman cost us daylight hours. Despite the destruction, I could feel my strength waning and knew I needed to eat. If I felt that way, I was positive the others did, too.

"We need to find supplies. It's going to be dark soon. And I'm not sure we want to be out in the open when that happens."

Marlowe swiped a hand through her shoulder-length brown hair. It was tangled. What was likely styled to perfection for jury duty was now limp and messy. Strands of it stuck to her skin, where sweat had popped up. Exhaustion was showing on her face, though she nodded in agreement with my plan. When I started making my way down the street, looking for somewhere to stay for the evening, she marched on without hesitation.

We found a cafe with its glass front window completely

smashed. I slowed and looked inside, hoping to see if there were any items left. The inside was dim, with little sunlight able to shine in.

"Wait here. I'll check and see if there's anything to salvage," I said.

Carefully, I stepped across the threshold of the shattered glass door. My dress shoes crunched on the glass littering the ground. Someone had destroyed the inside of the cafe. Tables flipped over. Chairs broken into pieces. Thieves completely emptied the cooler facing the lobby. People knew what they needed to get.

I made my way around the counter and into the darkness of the kitchen. Pulling my keys from my pocket, I tried the small penlight attached to the ring. It flickered and for a moment I didn't think it would stay on. When it did, the beam was dim, just enough to help me find my way around the counter.

Despite the mess in front, the kitchen appeared untouched. That gave me a bit of hope as I found the cooler. The power had been out less than four hours and if the door hadn't been opened, I was sure the temperature would have kept for a little while. With bated breath, I opened the door, and cool air rushed over me.

Inside, I found pre-made sandwiches and small salad kits. There was a section with drinks and condiments as well. I didn't bother to look inside the containers with premade materials that would need to be cooked. For now, there was enough we could eat cold and fill our stomachs.

I propped the door open to ensure I didn't get locked inside. Taking off my jacket, I made a sling, filling it with enough food for the four of us for at least 24 hours. I added waters and juices that didn't need to be kept cold until they were opened. Just as I was turning to leave the cooler, I heard footsteps.

"Cristian?"

Marlowe's voice reached me in the kitchen.

"I'm here," I called back.

I met her at the entrance of the kitchen and found her looking around worriedly.

"I told you to stay outside. There's too much glass."

"You were taking a long time. I got nervous and thought maybe you needed help."

I scoffed. "I don't need your help, Marlowe."

The moment I said the words, I could see the flash of hurt go across her face. But then her eyes narrowed, and she nodded curtly before turning on her heel and stalking back toward the door. I didn't know why the woman got under my skin. As I watched her walk across the glass in the cheap heels, I found myself on edge. It took a second of reflection to realize it was because I was worried she would get hurt.

Outside, I caught up with Marlowe as she stalked down the sidewalk to follow Colleen and Don. They peered through the windows of a neighboring business that remained undamaged. When I walked up, Colleen was shading her eyes with her hands as she pressed against the window, trying to see.

"It's a book and tea store. I don't think anyone sees it as a place to break in. I can see chairs and a couch. Might be a place to wait out the night," the older woman said.

Don tried the door, but found it locked. He looked at me, an eyebrow raised. "I'm not breaking and entering with a deputy hanging with us."

I shoved the food into Don's arms and crouched to look at the lock. What a lot of places didn't have were decent locks, relying instead on surveillance and alarms. None of those things would help anyone now. I rattled the door slightly, confirming I knew what type of lock I was dealing with. Then, pulling a small kit from my pocket, I played with the lock until it clicked open.

"Deputies know how to pick locks?" Don asked.

"This one does."

I had no desire to explain to Don that it wasn't being a deputy that taught me that skill, though the talent had come in handy more than once on the job. I routinely kept a few pieces of a kit in my pocket, on the off chance an emergency came up. Turned out, that was today. With the door open, I lead the group into the bookstore.

It smelled the way bookstores in the Pacific Northwest often did. Musty paper, floral scents and a bit of patchouli. Don dumped the food on the check-out counter and Marlowe walked directly to a lounge chair and collapsed into it. Slipping off her shoes, she rubbed her feet and I felt a bit of guilt for making her move so quickly. I shook off that feeling. I was only doing what was best for her.

I locked the front door again, to protect against anyone doing exactly what we were doing. There were shades on each window and I pulled them, even if it blocked out the last of the light from the sun. The fewer prying eyes, the safer we would be. Light flared from behind me, and I turned to find Colleen with a lit candle on the counter. Now, I could see there were many candles around the shop. Some were open and partially burned. And there was an entire section of book themed candles for sale. Perfect.

"Let's not light too many, and maybe we put them behind the counter," I suggested. "Just don't want anyone being curious."

Colleen nodded and disappeared behind the counter with the flame. It almost completely hid it from the front of the store, which was my goal. I followed and found a spot against the wall where I could see the door and also be in the light. Marlowe, barefoot now, stepped over my legs so she could sit next to the older woman.

They each took a bottle of water and it was clear how thirsty everyone was, even though they hadn't said it. With the thirst slaked, everyone picked a packaged meal and the only noise was plastic wrap and chewing. The sandwich I chose was something with ham and turkey on wheat bread. It hit the spot, even for prepackaged food.

I kept my eyes on the front of the store, often noticing the forms of people walking or running by the windows. There were distant noises of chaos. Gunshots, breaking glass, screams. Even though the power was gone, the world wasn't quiet. If anything, it felt louder. And completely unstable.

Despite being next to the courthouse and almost smashed by a plane, there was no law enforcement presence. While I was under no pretenses in believing everyone would just follow the disaster lessons, I thought there would be someone. Yet, there was no control. No guidance or safety for those that were out in the open. I let my head fall against the wall, closing my eyes for a moment. The weight of the destruction and lawlessness pushed down on me.

"How long will everything be like this?" Marlowe's quiet voice broke into my self-despair.

I shrugged. I had no idea how any of this worked or why it had happened. "Nothing on the news predicted this."

A loud fight sounded right outside the shop, and I jumped to my feet. I motioned for the other three to stay down and out of sight. Slowly, I approached the front window and adjusted the shade. Two men were throwing fists, with a new flat screen tv on the ground next to them. I watched as they yelled over who had the tv first and I shook my head.

Colors out of the corner of my eyes caught my attention, and I turned my gaze away from the looters. My mouth went dry. The sky shouldn't have looked like that. Swirls of purple, pink, and green stretched across the darkness, shimmering like something alive. The colors bled into one another, too bright, too unnatural. It was beautiful, but in the way a funeral song was beautiful. The Pacific Northwest had seen the Northern Lights before, but I had seen nothing as bright as this.

The looters completely forgotten, I made a hissing noise toward the back of the store. Looking back, I saw Marlowe pop her head around the corner of the counter. I motioned for her to come and all three did so. One by one, we took turns looking at the sky.

"It's beautiful," Marlowe breathed.

"I think it's from the solar flare." I replied. "That's the only thing that makes sense. It was strong enough to cause an EMP-like effect, at least here. And this is the aftermath of that."

Marlowe looked up at me, her face highlighted by the slight moonlight coming in. The cut on her face marred an otherwise perfect complexion. I frowned, trying to get a better look at her face. Her eyebrows pulled together under my scrutiny.

"They should have a first aid kit here. We should clean that," I said, motioning to her cheek.

Her hand came up to touch it, but I caught her fingers before she could make contact. "Don't. Your hands aren't sterile. No need to get more germs on it."

"Oh, right," she said, letting her hand fall to her side again once I released her.

"Are those guys really fighting over a TV?" Colleen stepped back from the window, letting the shade fall back into place.

I nodded. "I guess they figure they'll have it when the power comes back on."

"If it comes back on," Marlowe whispered.

Before moving to the back of the store, she lifted the shade to peek out again. Her eyes were round with wonder and a slight smile appeared on her face. Then, as if remembering everything that had happened in the day, her face fell and her gaze dropped to the ground again.

"What is it?" I knew the answer and witnessing her sadness pulled at something inside me.

"So many people died today. Just here, in the area around the courthouse. What does the rest of the Portland metro area look like?"

I'd been thinking the same thing. If this power outage was caused by the solar flare like I surmised, there was no way it was only happening in Hillsboro, or Washington County. I strongly suspected the event extended beyond Oregon, though there was currently no proof.

"We need to worry about surviving until tomorrow. Then we

worry about the next day. And right now, we find a first aid kit for your face."

Turning, I moved away from her. Her innocent eyes looking up at me were more than I could deal with. I didn't want to say anything that would upset her. The truth was, nothing I said would make things ok. Everything just stopped. We were trapped by it.

Behind the desk, I lit another candle and sorted through drawers. When I didn't find what I was looking for, I went further into the back of the store, finding a single stall bathroom with a fancy shelving unit. I glanced at the toilet. We had all relieved ourselves outside before finding the bookstore. I wasn't sure what impact the power would have on water flow.

The shelving unit proved to be a valuable find. It held the first aid kit, which I tucked under my arm. There were also many rolls of toilet paper. If we were going to be on foot, without facilities, the paper would be important. It could also be a fire starter if we were stuck outside without cover for the night. Mentally, I made notes about what we needed to take with us when we left.

Rejoining the group, I found Don lying on his side, pressed against the back wall. His eyes were closed, but I doubted he slept. I knew I wouldn't be able to. I blew out my candle. If we didn't need something burning, I wanted to save the supply. I added the matches, lighter and a handful of brand new candles to my mental list of things we would take when we left.

I chose a seat next to Marlowe. She turned her face toward me without question. Colleen held the candle, so I had all the light I needed. For a moment, I sorted through the first aid kit. It was brand new and overflowing with products. Pulling out an alcohol prep pad, a gauze pad and tape, I set them nearby. I also had a bottle of water to flush the wound.

"How did this happen?" I asked.

"I was too close to the window when the plane went down."

My hand froze, and she looked over at me questioningly. "Too close? You saw it happen?"

Marlowe nodded. "I was thinking about wanting to be outside to get air. I could see people in the building next to us. And I saw something falling out of the sky. The plane. It shattered the window, and I didn't duck fast enough."

"Damn. I'm sorry. That must have been traumatic." I meant it. I saw the aftermath of the crash, but I didn't see it happen.

"I'm not sure I realize how traumatizing it was. Not yet, at least."

Her sad smile pulled a consoling one from me. It felt foreign on my face, but I saw the moment it did the job.

CHAPTER
FIVE
MARLOWE

Cristian's fingers were soft on my cheek. He carefully poured the water along the cut. I hissed quietly. The pain hadn't bothered me, but we had been constantly moving. Now it felt like my entire body was crashing down.

"Sorry. Good news, I see nothing stuck in it. But it started bleeding a bit again." Cristian's voice was too much honey, too much kindness, when things were such a wreck.

"It's ok," I mumbled without moving my cheek.

"I'm going to clean around it with the alcohol. I'll try to not touch the cut."

I started to nod, then stilled, remembering he was trying to clean up my cheek.

"Did you learn first aid through your job?" Colleen asked.

I'd almost forgot she was sitting there, holding the candle for light. Pulling on my internal strings, I yanked myself back into place and stopped looking at Cristian in a way other than a fellow survivor. And the man that was patching up my face.

"Yeah. Everyone is required to learn basic first aid. I've had reason to use it more than once. I was also a Boy Scout."

"Was that a joke, Deputy?" Colleen said with a snort.

"Sort of, but it's also true."

He carefully folded and taped the gauze to keep my eyesight clear. Leaning back, he nodded to himself.

"That should do it. You probably could have used stitches, but it clotted on its own earlier. It should do that again." He turned my chin with his fingers again, looking over my face. He grimaced when he met my eye. "It's going to scar."

"As soon as possible, I'll find a plastic surgeon." I smirked as best I could with the tape stuck to my cheek.

"I'm sure we'll run into one any moment." Though he didn't smile, his eyes crinkled, and I was sure if I had more light, there would be humor dancing there.

"You're full of laughs."

He cleared his throat and moved away to pack the first aid kit. Colleen smiled and handled me a bottle of apple juice. I carefully sipped.

"I'm not sure how much blood you lost, but should make sure to hydrate and keep your blood sugar up, just in case," she said.

Looking down, I was glad I wore a black dress. There were no visible stains from the blood. I also inspected the other scratches along my arms. Nothing was deep, but they stung, reminding me of a cat scratch. I laid my head back against the check stand I leaned against.

Exhaustion was washing over me. But fear also sat deep inside my gut. A part of me was worried about falling asleep, thinking I would wake up and find myself alone in the bookstore. There was no reason for any of the three people I was with to stay with me. I was no better than a drifter. I had only settled in Oregon a couple of years prior and barely knew anyone.

Thinking about my travels made me think about the people I met along the way. What was happening to any of them? During my stay in Los Angeles, I worked for a meal delivery service for the elderly. There were a few regulars, some of them with conditions that made it impossible for them to cook for themselves.

I pictured sweet Mrs. Hendricks, who had dementia. She used to talk about her children when I brought her meals. Were any of them close to her when all this happened? I wrapped my arms around myself. The idea of people like Mrs. Hendricks trying to survive this on their own terrified me. A shiver shook me for a moment, and I picked up my head and opened my eyes.

Colleen was working to make herself a small bed off to one side. Cristian had moved to the front of the store and was sitting in one armchair. He faced the door and sat like a statue. The loveseat near a reading nook caught my attention, and I climbed to my feet.

Cristian's head turned when my movement caught his attention. I lay on the soft cushions and curled my legs tight so I would fit. I wasn't that tall, but even my 5'4" frame was too long. Turning, I hung a leg over the arm of the couch. When that wasn't comfortable either, I turned back onto my side and just dealt with my legs being jammed up with me.

I was startled by Cristian standing and walking over to me. He motioned for me to get up. Jumping up, I watched as he pulled the cushions off of the piece of furniture. With the two seat cushions and one back cushion, he created a bed on the floor for me. He didn't speak as he motioned for me to lie down. With as little movement as possible, I lay on the cushions.

"Thank you."

All I got in response was a grunt, and he walked away. Returning a moment later, he had his suit jacket in his hands. He put the garment over my bare shoulders and sat back in the armchair. Despite it being summer, Oregon tended to get cool in the evenings. The sleeveless sheath dress did little to keep me warm.

Since he didn't speak, I just smiled in the dim light. I pulled the coat close around me, feeling my body warm with it already. I propped my head up on an arm, lying on my left side to avoid my injured cheek. The position meant I faced Cristian's seat. He didn't look down at me. His sole focus appeared to be on our safety.

Closing my eyes, I didn't think it was possible to sleep. But the stress and panic of the day caught up. I felt the ache in my cheek. The stings of all the scratches on my arms. The aching in my feet from the cheap heels I'd been running in. There wasn't much that didn't hurt in one way or another. And as I tried to relax, every pain made itself known.

Somehow, I fell asleep for a short time. A nightmare of a plane crash greeted me. Instead of watching the plane fall to the ground, I was a passenger on the plane. And somehow, as it crashed, I could look out of my window and see myself in the courthouse. The impact of the plane in my dream shocked me awake and my eyes flew open to take in the surrounding bookstore.

There was a dim light sneaking in around the window shades. Not the full sun of the morning. But it wasn't far off. When I looked at the armchair, Cristian still sat in the same position. I wondered if he had moved at all during the night. There had been nothing to disturb me. It seemed looters didn't find the bookstore interesting, at least not yet.

Slowly, I uncurled. The movement caught Cristian's attention, and his gaze moved to me. I couldn't hide the grimace as all of my tight muscles tried to relax. My cheek throbbed, but the gauze was still in place. Pushing myself into a sitting position, I held my arms out in front of me. The scratches had all either never bled or had scabbed over easily.

I limped to the back of the store and found Colleen with the candle lit again. She handed me a water bottle and a package of cheese, crackers, and salami.

"There's a toilet in the bathroom," she said. "But it probably won't fill if we flush it. So, I think we should all use it, then flush it only once everyone is done."

"So disgusting," Don muttered.

I hadn't realized he was sitting in the corner, away from the candlelight. The man was disagreeable, and he seemed to get worse as the minutes passed.

"I guess it's better than having to do it outside," I said, keeping my voice upbeat to drown out Don's negativity.

Don just grunted, but Colleen shot me a small smile.

My eyes were so used to the dark, with just the dim light of the candle by the counter, I found the bathroom. I left the door open, knowing no one was going to walk in on me. Quickly, I finished my business and limped back to sit with Colleen and eat my morning snack.

Cristian came back then and sat within the circle of light. I didn't miss the circles under his brown eyes. They answered the question of his night. He stayed up to keep us safe.

"We could have taken shifts watching the door," I said.

His serious gaze locked on me, and the furrow that seemed permanent between his eyebrows deepened.

"Sure. What would you have done if someone broke in, Marlowe?"

Instead of answering, I slid a cracker and piece of cheese into my mouth. I shrugged and looked away. With just a few words, he flayed me, making me feel completely useless. A small pity party started up in my mind, reminding me I had no actual skills that could help in a powerless world. But I wouldn't let Cristian see how he had hurt my feelings.

Colleen didn't seem to have the same intentions of keeping quiet. She turned an accusing look on him and spoke in a low tone. "And how many nights can you just not sleep before it becomes dangerous for you? For all of us?"

"Hopefully, this was the only night of this," Don said.

Cristian nodded his head in agreement. "I've been thinking. Forest Grove and my place in Tualatin are opposite directions. I don't want to leave anyone alone. But I think we need to find you a mode of transportation, Colleen. Then you could get back to your husband."

"Are you sure about going to your house?" I asked.

I didn't know what I should do. Not being alone felt like the first right decision to make. But then I thought about my mom. Likely sitting alone in a powerless hospital, hoping to keep getting her treatments. The pain of that picture cut so deeply, I felt short of breath for a moment.

"If we can get there, I have supplies for camping. I even have some dried food that's meant for survival. While I was worried about the big earthquake everyone always talks about, turns out it was a solar flare that was the real threat. And I have weapons in a safe. I'm not sure I want to fight to find something to protect us. You are all welcome."

What he said made sense, but that didn't work for me long term. "If this doesn't get better, I have to get to California. My mom…" My throat tightened, and I swallowed hard. "She's alone."

Cristian was silent. I knew he was waiting for me to finish, but I wasn't sure I could without falling apart.

"She called me at the courthouse," I finally whispered. "I think she was saying goodbye."

"One step at a time, Marlowe. Let's get to my place. Then I'll figure out how to get you transportation to your mom," Cristian replied.

I looked at him for a few heartbeats. "You'd help me with that?"

"Of course. I'm not just going to leave you to fend for yourself," he replied with a huff.

I crossed my arms and glared at him. "Right. Because I'm useless."

"I never said that," Cristian replied.

Colleen's eyes bounced back and forth between us. Don sat in the dark corner, his fingers tapping an uneven rhythm against his knee. He wasn't looking at any of us. But every so often, I'd catch his eyes flicking toward me—watching, calculating. Like he was waiting for something.

I hated conflict and really wished one of them would interject. Neither of them did. Cristian stared at me, and uncomfortable, I avoided his gaze, drawing out the silence.

"Ok, well, about transportation," Colleen finally said.

Cristian looked at her and nodded, his face completely changed from frustration to thoughtful. "How do you feel about a bicycle?"

"I haven't ridden one in quite a while, but I see where you're going with this."

"My guess is, older model vehicles might work. But we'd have to find one with keys that someone else hadn't taken. We're in Portland. And what do Portlanders love? Their nonelectric modes of transport. I don't think we'd have to search long to find one that would work for you. If we did, maybe you could get home today," Cristian explained.

"What about us?" Don demanded from the darkness.

Cristian didn't spare him a glance when he replied. "Once we get Colleen on the road, we can make our way to my house. It would be great if we all found bikes, but getting Colleen one first is the first priority."

"Why does she get to go first? Because she's old? I can probably ride a bike much better than she can," Don said. Venom packed his words.

Now Cristian's eyes did move toward the dark corner. I didn't miss his hands tightening into fists as his eyes narrowed. "If you have a problem with it, Don, you are free to go wherever you please."

"Thank you, Cristian," Colleen said in her calming way. That's why they'd chosen her as foreperson. She commanded respect but also had a kindness that came through in everything she said and did.

Cristian watched Don for another long, tense minute. Then he stood and grabbed a few of the reusable canvas shopping bags hanging on a rack by the check-out counter. He disappeared without a word and came back with one canvas full of toilet paper and the first aid kit. The other he packed full of the remaining water, juices, and sandwiches we had. He also added candles from the display. Finally, he tossed in the small box of matches we'd found, as well as the lighter next to a pack of cigarettes in a drawer.

He folded his jacket over one of the bags and put it over his shoulder. I held out my hand for the other, but he shook his head. Instead of arguing, I made my way over to where I had left my shoes. The pain of squeezing my feet into them was bearable, but I was pretty sure I was going to be miserable by mid-morning.

We gathered at the door while Cristian checked through the window at our surroundings. Once he signaled, we unlocked the bookstore door and made our way back out onto the street. Off in the distance, the smoke from the plane crash and raging fires still smudged the sky, though less than yesterday. I guess it had run out of fuel, since there'd been no way for the fire department to respond.

Cristian turned away from the bookstore and headed down the sidewalk. The street was a mess. Besides the abandoned vehicles we had passed the day before, there was trash everywhere. Vandals had smashed car windows and those of most of the businesses along the street.

A broken suitcase lay open on the sidewalk, clothing strewn across the asphalt. I wondered what happened to the person who owned the case. Even though it had broken, they could have taken their belongings. I realized there were a few unpleasant reasons for them not to take their things. And I decided I didn't want to continue to debate that with myself.

Suddenly, Cristian changed his direction and he started to jog down another road. Colleen and I exchanged a look, following his lead. I saw what had caught his attention on the street. A police car was parked partially on the sidewalk, as if the driver had swerved to ensure they didn't hit someone in front of them. At the trunk, a man in uniform was sorting through his belongings.

When Cristian approached, the cop's gaze snapped up, and he took a defensive posture. To show that he was unarmed, Cristian held up his hands.

"I'm Officer Reyes. I have my badge in my pocket, if you let me get it out."

The cop nodded, but he studied Cristian and us as we slowly approached. Pulling out his wallet, Cristian showed a badge to the officer and the cop relaxed just slight.

With a nod, the cop moved forward, putting out his hand for Cristian. They shook.

"I'm Stephen," the man said.

"What's happening Stephen?" Cristian asked.

"I wish I knew," Stephen replied. "Everything just stopped. As if one massive switch was thrown. I haven't been able to reach anyone from any precinct. I ran into a few firefighters, that were off duty when this started. They said the death toll is way higher than either of them could imagine. Car accidents, plane crashes, trail derailments. It all happened at once."

My stomach turned, realizing the plane crash I had almost been in the middle of wasn't the only horrible thing happening. Colleen's hand found mine, and we gripped each other tightly.

"Who's in charge?" Cristian asked.

"Your guess is as good as mine, man," Stephen replied.

Cristian turned and looked back at us. I was frozen in my spot, desperate for any information the cop could give us. But it was becoming clear that his knowledge was as limited as ours. I could see Cristian's turmoil, causing his eyes to harden before he turned back to Stephen.

"So, who is helping? Where are people going if they're injured or can't get home?" Cristian asked.

Stephen went back to sorting through his trunk, replying over his shoulder. "Lincoln Street Elementary and the Methodist church across the street are the nearest ones to here. But," Stephen turned and pointed to a cloud of smoke in the distance, "the school is going up in smoke as we speak."

"What happened to it?" Cristian asked.

Stephen finally stopped what he was doing and faced Cristian.

He wore an exasperated expression. "You have a lot of questions. We all do. But there are no answers. I'm heading home to be with my wife and baby. I suggest you all do the same. For now, you're on your own."

We all stood in silence for a beat before Cristian put out his hand again. "It was nice to meet you. Good luck, man. Do you have an extra weapon? My weapon was lost in the courthouse—long story.

Stephen rubbed the back of his neck and shook his head. "I wish I did. But I have to admit, thieves looted my car while I was checking the school and church. When I got back over here, every-thing was gone."

I had been so interested in what he was saying, I hadn't real-ized the windows of the car were all smashed. The two men spoke quietly for a few more minutes. With a quiet goodbye, Cristian guided us away from the police car and back in the original direc-tion we had been heading.

At the end of the next street lay a small park which included a bike rack. Though Cristian seemed to know what he was looking for, the rack was empty. That didn't stop him. He changed direc-tion without a word and started down another street.

"Jesus, how far are we going?" Don exclaimed.

"As far as we have to. Unless you want to wait here. I'm sure there will be someone by anytime to pick you up," Cristian replied without looking back.

Don's face screwed up as if he had sucked on a lemon. It was clear that the man was used to being catered to. The darkness in his eyes had only increased in the last 24 hours. I hadn't trusted him before, just from spending time with him during the case. Now, I'd be sure not to turn my back on him.

We searched the area for about an hour before we found ourselves in front of REI. Cristian had us wait on the outskirts of the parking lot to watch the store. Randomly, people would come out, bundles of products under their arms or large bags on their backs. We didn't see any altercations.

"Wait here," Cristian said. "I'll go in, find a bike for Colleen. Then maybe figure out a way for the rest of us to get to my house."

He set the bags at my feet and then looked up at me. "What size shoe do you wear?"

"Seven and a half." I raised an eyebrow at him, wondering what he was thinking.

He didn't answer my unspoken question. Instead, he nodded and headed toward the store. I shifted on my sore feet, watching as he disappeared into the darkness of the building. No one entered after him, but that didn't mean there weren't people inside, lying in wait.

When too much time seemed to have passed, I worried. Every minute felt like an hour. My foot tapped against the pavement, an unconscious, restless beat. I hated this. Waiting. Wondering.

"How long should we wait before going after him?" My voice was steadier than I felt.

Colleen patted my arm. "I think he knows what he's doing."

"I know. But anything could happen in there and we wouldn't know."

Just as I was debating following him in, he appeared at the store entrance. He was conversing with another man who walked out with him. They shook hands before parting ways. Cristian was pushing a mountain bike their way and a large hiking pack was on his back. It looked like it was bulging with items.

"There were no other bikes except this. I know it's a little big for you, Colleen, but I think it's your best bet to get home to your husband," he said.

Colleen took the handlebars with a grateful smile. "Thank you, Cristian."

He then swung his pack from his shoulders. Opening it, he pulled out a smaller bag. Digging through the bags we brought from the bookshop, he added food, water and toilet paper to the smaller pack. He also added a smaller first aid kit that he brought from REI. After packing it, he helped Colleen put it on her back.

"I'm sorry it's not more. But hopefully enough to get you home," Cristian said.

Colleen nodded and lifted her arms to embrace him. He patted her back before pulling away. She moved to me and put her hands on my shoulders. "You've got this, Marlowe. Keep your chin up and stay strong."

She hugged me, and I had to push back tears. I couldn't remember the last time someone had hugged me. I squeezed her tightly. The embrace ended long before I wanted it to, but the emotions stayed in my heart. She turned and looked at Don, but didn't move toward him. She just nodded politely before swinging her leg over the seat of the bike.

With one final look back, she waved and slowly pedaled away. Quickly gaining her balance, she sped off down the street. I didn't stop watching until she turned a corner.

Silence closed in around us. Colleen was just another person I would worry about, as the entire world fell apart.

"I guessed your size for the clothes." Cristian's voice pulled my attention to where he was holding out a stack of clothing on top of a box of shoes.

I took the pile and looked at him blankly. Glancing down, I realized he was now wearing hiking boots and not his dress shoes from the courthouse.

"Unless you wanted to keep walking in heels and a dress?"

"No, of course not. Thanks. I'll just, uh…," I spun, looking around for somewhere hidden that I could change.

"Don't go too far," Cristian said, realizing what I was trying to do.

I moved toward a parked truck, thinking I would just change behind it. With the way Don's eyes followed me, I wasn't willing to change in front of them. Once I was behind the truck, I put the clothes on the ground and looked around. I could see Don waiting with Cristian, his head still turned in my direction. It made me queasy to notice the way he paid attention to me.

There was no one else in sight. I slipped the hiking pants on under my dress. They fit almost perfectly. Mentally I high-fived Cristian. The material was soft and so much more comfortable than my sheath dress. Unzipping it in the back, I yanked it over my head and tossed it into the planter next to the truck. I yanked the t-shirt over my head and breathed a deep sigh of relief. I was a jeans and t-shirt kind of girl.

I sat down and pulled on the wool socks Cristian had gotten for me. They were thick for the summer, but I was thankful since I was pulling on brand new hiking boots. I walked back and forth for a moment, testing the shoes. Other than the initial soreness, the shoes felt fantastic. And were likely more expensive than I could ever afford myself.

Walking back to the guys, Cristian looked over at me with an assessing gaze. "Everything fit?"

"Probably even better than if I had picked it myself." I ran a hand over the fabric of the shirt, realizing just how much thought he'd put into this. He hadn't just grabbed the first thing he saw. He'd actually tried to make sure it fit.

I looked up at him. "Thank you."

Cristian just nodded, his face unreadable. But for the first time, I had the strange feeling that I wasn't just another problem for him to solve.

"Are we done with the fashion show? There were really no other bikes in there? How are we supposed to travel?" Don demanded.

I could clearly see Cristian's jaw tense and I wondered why Don couldn't take the same signals.

"We need to head southwest from here. I'm sure we could cut through farmland and make the trip faster. But we'll need cities for supplies along the way. More cars to check on the major road-ways, too," Cristian said, completely ignoring Don's complaints.

"Lead the way," I said, as I picked up one of the shopping bags.

Cristian swung the pack onto his back and started out. I followed without a word and I didn't look to see if Don was also behind us. My inner monologue was coming up with ways to make the man disappear. As if he could hear my concerns, Cristian slowed and dropped back so he was walking next to me. I looked up at him, but his gaze was fixed on the road ahead.

"Your mom. She's sick?"

His question surprised me, and I didn't respond for an uncomfortable moment. He looked down at me then, as if to make sure I heard him. I felt the familiar tears fill my eyes when I thought too much about my mom and her cancer. Now, it seemed even more unlikely that she would survive. Cristian looked away, my emotions seeming to make him uncomfortable.

"Cancer. It's the second time she's battled it. I talked to her yesterday--she called me at the courthouse—and she's getting weak. I think there may have been a reason she called even when I was in jury duty."

"What reason do you think she had?"

"I don't think the treatments are working this time. She sounded worse on the phone each time we spoke. But she wouldn't come out and say it."

"I'm sorry." His words were soft, and I could feel the sincerity in them.

"Thank you. I'm just terrified. Now, I don't know when or if I'll ever get there to find out."

Putting my fears into words was almost too much. I felt short of breath, as if we were running and not just walking along the sidewalk. A tear escaped my best intentions to not cry, and I swiped it away before Cristian could see. His hand on my shoulder told me he missed little.

"I lost both of my parents a few years ago. Ironically, it was a car accident. I know the pain," he said, his voice soft and just for my ears.

"I'm sorry, too."

"Thank you."

He removed his hand, and we continued down the road. I felt a different companionship with the man now. He was standoffish. He tended to growl and scowl. But there was something he was holding back. Maybe this was the end of the known world, but I was truly interested in finding out what that was.

CHAPTER
SIX
CRISTIAN

A few hours into the morning, we found ourselves passing a grocery store. There were looters running in and out, carts and bags full of goods. The lawlessness of everything went against my basic nature. But there was nothing I could do. I was one man without a weapon. And I had Marlowe to think of.

When had that happened? Within 24 hours of surviving with the small woman, I had started factoring her into my choices. While we hid behind an abandoned vehicle, watching the store, I weighed our options. We'd finished our remaining food for breakfast and only had two bottles of waters left and at least fifteen miles left to walk.

"So, Deputy, what's your plan here?" Don asked.

The man was getting on my last-nerve. I had imagined punching him in the face more than once. And when I saw the way his eyes stayed glued to Marlowe, I had a feeling I'd get the chance to do exactly that. I knew Marlowe was aware of his unwanted attention as well. She was staying as close to me as she could without it looking awkward.

"I'm not a deputy out here," I replied, a bite in my voice.

Don didn't take the hint, as he scoffed and rolled his eyes at me. I was moments away from throwing him out in the open just to see what the piranha in the parking lot would do.

"We need supplies. I'm just not sure this is the place to get them," I said.

Suddenly, shouts echoed from inside the store and shots rang out. A woman came staggering out of the broken doors of the store, gripping her stomach. Blood spilled from between her fingers. Another woman came came out of the store at a dead run. They had two full bags of items in one hand and the other hand was gripping a handgun.

"That's what you get! Don't try to steal from people!" the gun wielder screamed at the woman that was now on the ground, bleeding out.

"Does she not realize she's stealing?" Don said.

Neither Marlowe nor I responded to that. The woman with the gun disappeared around the side of the store, while another person checked on the woman she had shot. I fought against my instincts to help, but I was pretty sure a gunshot to the stomach would not be survivable without help from a doctor. Something we had no way of getting quickly.

"Oh, no," Marlowe almost whispered, her words barely audible above the breeze. I followed her gaze and saw a woman with a baby clutched to her chest approaching the grocery store.

That was the tipping point. I couldn't just stand by while a woman with a baby went into danger. I tightened the pack on my back. Marlowe and I shared a look, both on the same page. Standing together, we took off at a jog toward the woman. Hearing our footsteps, the woman froze and turned toward us with her features frozen in fear.

Marlowe spoke first, holding up her hands to show she had no weapons. "We aren't going to hurt you. But you can't go in there. It's not safe."

As Marlowe spoke, she pointed to the spot where the gunshot victim still lay, eyes open in death. The mother glanced over, and her face went pale. When she looked back at Marlowe, I could see her lip trembling.

"I need formula. I was supposed to go to the store yesterday, but I forgot and we ran out this morning." Her voice shook.

Stepping forward, Marlowe offered her hand to the woman. "I'm Marlowe. This is Cristian. We'll get the formula for you. You need to find a safe place to wait outside."

I could see it happening. The woman saw Marlowe, and she was unthreatening and calm on the outside. I doubted she felt like that inside, but she was doing a great job of projecting strength and trust to the woman. The mother was slow to shake her hand, but she eventually shifted her baby to one arm and her palm met Marlowe's.

The baby started to fuss, and the panic flared in the mother's eyes again.

"Just any formula will work?" Marlowe asked.

The mother looked toward the destroyed store. "I think whatever you find will do the job. He's not picky, and I doubt there's much to choose from."

Marlowe nodded. We waited for the woman to take shelter with the baby in a nearby parked car that had a door left open. Once they were out of sight, we turned toward the store. I realized Don wasn't with us and I glanced back to where we'd been hiding. His head peeked out from over the car hood and I wanted to scream at him to get into the store with us.

"Leave him. I feel better if it's just us," Marlowe said.

I nodded, knowing exactly what she meant. Together, we walked into the store. Just inside, we could hear, more than see, the chaos. People ran from aisle to aisle. Yelling at each other, or calling for their loved ones. I reached out and took Marlowe's hand in mine.

"We do not split up," I said.

"Ok." Her voice was barely audible, but she confirmed with a squeeze to my hand.

Leading the way, I pulled Marlowe behind me, keeping her

hand firmly locked in my grip. I ensured she remained mostly hidden behind me and my pack. When anyone came our way, I would dodge and push her against a wall or rack to hide her from prying eyes. It took a few aisles to find the baby supplies.

"She was right," Marlowe said, disappointment in her tone.

People ransacked the aisle. Broken containers of formula littered the ground, and it felt like such a waste. If people needed the supplies, why would they destroy something so precious? Marlowe stepped forward and with her free hand, she reached deep into a shelf and pulled out one can of lactose-free formula. She motioned for me to turn, and I did, letting her drop the can into the half full pack. Bending, she found two more with a smile and also packed those.

She moved to the diapers, and I followed closely on her heels. I kept looking up and down the aisle, making sure no one was sneaking up on us. If someone attacked us with a gun, I would have to surrender everything, or risk being shot. I wasn't interested in dying in a parking lot on what seemed like the second day of the apocalypse.

Marlowe inspected two packages of diapers and decided on one size. She then grabbed another pack of that to put into my pack. She held the other in her hand, because we were running out of space.

"We need to find supplies for us too, since we're already taking the risk," I whispered.

Holding out her hand with a nod, Marlowe agreed. I gripped her tightly again, and we started winding up and down the aisles. I wasn't confident we would find much, as there were still people running and leaving with full grocery bags of products.

A man sprinted past us with a case of wine. When he saw us, he hesitated for a fraction of a second, eyes darting to the items Marlowe was holding. His fingers twitched like he was weighing his chances, but then someone screamed from inside the store, and he bolted. I exhaled slowly. The hunger in his eyes hadn't been for the wine.

The beverage aisles were wet and sticky. But we were able to find bottles of carbonated flavored water. Regular water was probably best, but something was better than dying of dehydration. In the snack aisle, I found one pack of beef jerky sticks and a can of peanuts. We found a pack of rye bread, to which Marlowe scrunched her nose in distaste, but I packed it anyway. And in one check stand, we found an entire box of Almond Joy candy bars. This time, I made a face, and Marlowe smothered a giggle.

Without looking further, we raced for the front doors. Pounding footsteps came from behind us and I whirled, pulling Marlowe into me at the same time. She cried out in surprise as her slight frame collided with me. I wrapped both of my arms around her to keep her from going down and taking me with her.

Three men came running from the back of the store, holding beer and pet food. I pulled Marlowe with me into a shadowed area by the front door. The men didn't spare us a glance as they ran out. The two of us stood, breathing heavily, waiting for anything else to come out of the darkness.

When I felt like we were in the clear, I looked down at Marlowe. With her hands tangled in my dress shirt, she pressed her forehead against my chest. Her fear was palpable. Running my hands over her shoulders, I rubbed at her upper arms, trying to console her.

"We're fine. Everything is ok. I didn't mean to scare you," I said.

"Everything is scaring me. I'm sorry. I shouldn't be so freaked out." She pulled out of my arms and shook herself, as if she was loosening up all the muscles that had just tensed.

"I'd wonder what was wrong with you if you weren't a little freaked out."

"Well, then I've got good news for you. I'm more than a little freaked." She gave me one of her megawatt smiles, that I had only seen when she and Colleen were sharing a private joke. I didn't smile back, but I did the best I could not to frown.

We made it outside the store with no more interactions.

Marlowe didn't let go of my hand as we walked straight to the car that held the mother and baby. We could hear the baby wailing from across the parking lot. The sound was enough to even hurt my heart. When she saw us approaching, she popped open the door and climbed out, bouncing the baby in her arms.

Marlowe pulled out the formula and used a plastic bag she had grabbed to pack it up for the mother. She then handed her the packages of diapers, but realized it was too much for her to carry. Marlowe looked at me helplessly and I pulled one of the reusable bags I had stashed in my pack for the diapers.

"Thank you so much. I don't even know what to say." There were tears on the mother's cheeks.

Marlowe just smiled kindly at her. "Don't mention it. Take care of you and your baby. I'd get back home as soon as you can. You live nearby?"

"Just in the apartments, over there." The mother tilted her head toward a three-story apartment complex that was on the other side of the trees lining the grocery store parking lot.

"Good luck," I said.

The mother nodded and turned to flee toward her apartment. The entire grocery store task only took thirty minutes. But when we arrived back at where Don hid, he was pacing with a furious look on his face. He stared down at our hands, that were still linked, and his face darkened further.

"You just left me here!"

"You could have come with us," Marlowe replied.

"Instead of being a coward and hiding," I added.

Don's face darkened, his breath coming out heavier. His hands curled into fists, flexed, then curled again. It was like he was barely holding something in. And whatever it was, I didn't want it coming out. He glared at Marlowe, directing his anger at her. She didn't cower, just stared right back at him.

Knowing I needed to calm things down, if we were going to keep moving, I pulled off my pack. "Here. Have a candy bar. Maybe that'll make you feel better."

I handed him an Almond Joy. His face went blank at first, but he opened it and immediately started to shove it into his mouth. I handed a bar to Marlowe, and she gave me a small smile. I could see the tightness around her eyes. She knew she was at risk with Don around.

It was lunchtime, and we were all tired and hungry. I didn't feel safe staying so close to the store that was drawing a lot of attention. We continued walking, but suddenly Marlowe cried out and rushed toward one car that was parked in the grocery story lot. I moved after her, checking around to make sure she didn't run into a trap. She bent and when she turned back to me, she held a bunch of bananas. Her smile was wide and happy, so I gave her a small nod and motioned for her to come back to the road.

She gave Don a banana, which he walked away to eat alone. I watched him closely. He was going to be a problem, but I didn't know when.

"He was a pain the entire time during jury duty." Marlowe's voice was so quiet, I had to lean down to hear her.

"How so?"

"Always defiant. Refused to work together. Disrespectful. And he didn't want to convict the man, even though the evidence was cut and dried."

I nodded and stood straight. When Don looked back at us, I had stepped closer to Marlowe, and I didn't miss how his face changed when he noticed. Instead of playing into his attitude, I took Marlowe's elbow and encouraged her to move forward and start walking again. She shot me a small smile, and we both took a banana from the bunch and carefully packed the last two into my pack.

There was so much smoke rising into the air, the sun was soon hidden behind a gray haze. The air felt thick, and I couldn't contain the coughs that rose in my chest. We came upon a blocked intersection where a delivery van had flipped on its side. The back doors hung open. The accident had strewn mail and boxes all over the road. People had gathered to rip open the larger boxes, looking for anything valuable.

I led Marlowe away from the chaos, Don following close behind as we veered down another street. But as we rounded the corner, I saw we couldn't go that way either. In the distance, a fire devoured a small hotel building, its flames towering high. The blaze was intense enough that even walking on the opposite side of the street wouldn't be safe.

We turned into a narrow alley instead. We maneuvered around dumpsters and piles of rotting trash, passing tents that had been pitched long before the power had gone out. Eyes peeked at us through the tent screens. No one spoke or called out, though, and I was grateful for the quiet—our small group moved without interruption.

The silence gave my mind a lot of room to spiral. I didn't have family left to worry about, but that didn't mean I had no one on my mind. Sarah. Despite the fury I felt toward her—and toward myself, for how our marriage ended—she was still someone I had loved. She was in Seattle now, engaged to someone else. I found out through a congratulatory photo posted by a mutual friend on social media. Sarah didn't owe me anything, and I wasn't entitled to know what was happening in her life. But seeing that photo had been a gut punch, harder than I wanted to admit.

I shook my head to focus. Dwelling on Sarah wouldn't help now. The alley was narrow and damp, the walls closing in like the weight of the past I was trying to outrun.

Marlowe stumbled on a loose piece of debris, and I instinctively reached out to steady her. She murmured a quick "thanks," but her eyes stayed alert, scanning ahead. Don shuffled behind us, his breathing heavy and uneven.

"This better lead somewhere," he muttered, his voice grating against my nerves.

"Keep it down," I snapped, glancing over my shoulder. The last thing we needed was to draw attention.

We moved deeper into the alley, the faint glow of distant fires casting eerie shadows across the brick walls. The stench of rotting food and stagnant water grew stronger, mixing with the faint metallic tang of smoke in the air.

Then I heard it—a low, guttural growl, faint but unmistakable.

I froze, throwing out an arm to stop Marlowe. "Did you hear that?"

"Hear what?" Don asked, his tone dripping with annoyance.

Marlowe held her breath, her eyes darting to mine, then to the darkened corner ahead. The growl came again, louder this time, followed by the faint scrape of something moving against the pavement.

"Shit," I muttered under my breath.

"Is that... a dog?" Marlowe asked, her voice barely above a whisper.

"Maybe," I responded, unconvinced. Stray dogs weren't uncommon in the city, but this sound was different—more aggressive, more desperate.

I stepped forward slowly, motioning for them to stay back. The alley curved slightly ahead, its darkened recesses hiding whatever was making the noise. My hand brushed against my hip where my sidearm used to be. Now, it was nothing but muscle memory and wishful thinking. I cursed myself again for not finding a weapon sooner.

As I rounded the corner, the source of the sound came into view. A dog, or what used to be one. Its ribs jutted out under mangy fur, and its eyes glinted in the dim light. It bared its teeth, saliva dripping from its mouth as it growled low and deep, crouched like it was ready to pounce.

"Cristian?" Marlowe's voice was tight with unease.

"Stay where you are," I said, keeping my tone calm.

The dog stared at me, muscles tense, waiting for a sign of weakness. I didn't know if it was starving or rabid, but either way, it wasn't going to back down easily.

Behind me, I heard Don muttering curses, the shuffling of his feet making too much noise. "Why are we stopping? Just deal with it!"

"Shut up," I hissed through gritted teeth. The dog's ears twitched at the sound, and its growl deepened.

I glanced around quickly, my eyes landing on a broken wood handle leaning against a dumpster. It wasn't much, but it was better than nothing. Slowly, I reached for it, keeping my movements deliberate.

The dog lunged.

"Move!" I barked, swinging the broom handle in a wide arc. The makeshift weapon connected with the dog's side, sending it skidding across the pavement with a yelp. It scrambled to its feet, snarling, and came at me again.

Behind me, Marlowe pulled Don further back into the alley, her voice calm but firm. "Stay out of the way. Let him handle it."

I braced myself as the dog charged, this time aiming lower. I sidestepped and jabbed the handle forward, catching it in the ribs again. The animal faltered, wheezing, and then backed away, its teeth still bared but its movements less certain. Although it was attacking me, I felt sadness at having to harm the creature.

"Go!" I shouted over my shoulder. "Get to the other side!"

For a moment, it felt like a standoff. Neither of us was willing to back down. But then the dog let out a frustrated bark and darted away, disappearing into the shadows of the alley.

I exhaled sharply, my muscles trembling with adrenaline. Dropping the wood handle, I turned and jogged to catch up with Marlowe and Don, who were waiting at the mouth of the alley.

"You okay?" Marlowe asked, her voice steady but her eyes scanning me for injuries.

"Fine," I said shortly, wiping sweat from my forehead. I didn't miss the way her eyes continued to look over my shoulder.

"That thing was rabid," Don said, his tone accusatory. "It could have torn us apart."

"I would have torn you apart if you hadn't kept quiet," I

snapped back. His tone raised my blood pressure. He looked at me as if I asked the dog to find us in the alley.

Don muttered something under his breath, but didn't argue further.

Marlowe stepped closer, her hand brushing my arm briefly. "Thanks," she said quietly.

I nodded, my breath still unsteady. "Let's keep moving. The faster we're out of here, the better."

We moved on, the tension lingering like a shadow. The dog was gone, but the danger hadn't passed. It was just waiting for us further down the road. The threats in this darkened world were beyond any I could guess. As we walked, I kept Don in front of Marlowe and I. The threats weren't only those in the open. There was one with us already. And I wasn't sure how I was going to deal with that one.

Marlowe kept pace beside me, silent but steady. I tried not to look, but my eyes betrayed me. I could still see the freckles across her nose, even though dirt smudged the unbandaged cheek. A stupid detail to notice in a world collapsing around us. She'd genuinely looked worried about me and that made me feel something I knew wasn't appropriate for the time. I needed to focus. On survival. On the next step. Not on her.

What was appropriate? I was going to get her to my house, where we would hopefully be safe for some time. But what happened after that? I had told her I would help her get to her mother. How could I not offer to help with something so important? I promised that before I really had a plan for how it would work out. One foot in front of the other was all I could think of.

"At this rate, we're not going to be getting anywhere today," Don said over his shoulder.

"Do you have a better plan, Don?" I said through gritted teeth.

Marlowe laid her hand lightly on my arm. Her skin was soft and warm, and it was a distraction. Cooling down my anger over Don's insolence. Don suddenly stopped and spun. I reached out to grab Marlowe's arm, to keep a suitable distance between us. Again, I noticed the man's gaze go to my hand on Marlowe's arm. He had some sort of issue when it came to Marlowe. What I could imagine in my mind would be a nightmare for Marlowe.

"If you two would stop flirting, we could cover a whole lot more ground," he said.

Marlowe made an odd choking sound next to me, and she dropped her hand from my arm.

"Where are you from, Don? I realized you never said. But you agreed to come with us," I said.

Don avoided eye contact, and I waited patiently for his answer. Something wasn't right with the guy, and I needed to figure out what it was. Was it simple infatuation with a beautiful woman that wasn't giving him the time of day? Or was there something more sinister happening in his head?

Marlowe also waited for him to answer. She crossed her arms over her chest, as if to protect herself from his gawking. The t-shirt I'd gotten her wasn't tight, but you couldn't miss her trim form, or her her feminine figure that made her seem soft in all the right places. Don had missed none of those things. I knew, because I hadn't either.

"I live in Tualatin, too." His voice was a bit too high. If I had pulled him over and asked if he had been drinking and he'd answered in that tone, I would have tested him.

"So, you're going in the same direction, but to your own place?" Marlowe asked.

"Sure."

"That doesn't sound very convincing," I said.

Don scoffed and finally met my eye with a hard stare. "The world is falling apart around us. Sorry for not having a solid plan for what I'm doing to survive right this moment."

"Then maybe you can lay off us. We're also just trying to figure this out as we go," Marlowe said.

Don stared at her, and something unmistakable crossed his

face. Desperation. I knew then I wasn't just dealing with an irritating man. Don wasn't a nuisance. He was a predator waiting for the right moment. And I wasn't going to give him one.

I didn't miss the way Cristian casually put his body between Don and me. The man was sleazy, something I had realized while on the jury together. Somehow, he had passed all the lawyers' questions and played the right part to get into the room with us. But once he was there, it was clear he had his own agenda. And now, his agenda included me. Cristian knew it. So did I.

"We can get a few more miles today, but we probably have another full day before we get to Tualatin. Barring any other challenges," Cristian said.

He pulled the flavored water from his pack and handed each of us a bottle. I sipped the carbonated drink, wishing it was plain water. But I was glad we had something. Don guzzled his bottle and casually tossed it in the street. It joined piles of trash that other survivors had left or dropped.

Cristian's jaw tightened as the empty bottle clattered onto the pavement, but he said nothing. The tension was practically crackling in the air, though. I watched him inhale sharply, his hand flexing at his side like he was debating whether it was worth the effort to call Don out. I hadn't stopped wishing he would just punch the guy and be done with it.

"Thanks for that," I said, my voice dripping with sarcasm as I picked up the discarded bottle. It wasn't about the litter. It was about the principle. Don gave me a lazy shrug, looking entirely unbothered.

"What's the point?" Don said, gesturing to the trash-strewn street. "The world's already gone to hell."

"The point is not being a jackass," Cristian muttered, loud enough for only me to hear. I bit back a smile, grateful for his quiet solidarity. I didn't let Don see my reaction, not wanting to feed into his accusation of flirting.

"Let's keep moving," Cristian said more firmly, adjusting the strap of his pack. He led the way, his stride steady and purposeful, even though I could see the fatigue creeping into his shoulders. The man was like a human shield. Always in front, always braced for the next threat.

The streets grew quieter as we moved away from the city center. The occasional crack of distant gunfire or the low roar of fires reminded us that chaos wasn't far behind, but for now, it was just us and the desolate, trash-strewn roads. Everything felt too quiet. My ears were expecting to hear the growl of a vehicle, a plane, or helicopter in the air. Without power, I realized there was some sort of hum that we had gotten used to in our lives. Now it was gone, and the silence was deafening.

"We need food," I said after a while, my voice breaking the silence. My stomach had been grumbling for the past hour, but I hadn't wanted to complain. The little that we had grabbed from the grocery store in the morning had only lasted until lunch.

"Agreed," Cristian said without looking back. He pointed to a corner store up ahead, its windows dark and boarded up. "Let's try there."

As we approached, the building loomed like a hollowed-out husk of what it used to be. The front door hung crooked on its hinges, swaying slightly in the breeze. It had three gas pumps that no longer worked, but abandoned cars were sitting in front of them. Cristian motioned for us to stay back as he stepped inside first.

"Stay close," he said after a moment, waving us in.

The shelves were mostly empty, but a few items remained, scattered like forgotten treasures. Cans of soup, a couple of battered granola bars, and a half-crushed box of crackers. Cristian moved quickly, checking for anything else remotely edible or useful.

I grabbed the granola bars and crackers, stuffing them into a plastic bag. Don snatched up a can of soup, holding it up like it was some kind of trophy.

"Found dinner," he said with a smirk.

I ignored him, focusing instead on a cooler in the back corner. When I opened it, the smell clearly indicated that the products remaining were starting to spoil, but not quite rotten yet.

"Anything drinkable?" Cristian asked, his voice tight with focus.

"Not unless you want to die of food poisoning," I replied, stepping away from the cooler.

Cristian frowned but didn't comment. He moved toward a shelf lined with a few remaining bottles of soda. "It's not water, but it's something."

He grabbed the bottles, handing me one before tucking another into his pack. Don didn't bother waiting for an offer. He grabbed a bottle for himself and twisted it open on the spot, taking a long drink. I didn't think he understood the point of trying to survive or rationing. He was busy eating and drinking everything we found.

Once the pack Cristian wore was packed as full as possible, we left the store and continued on the road. The further we got from the most populated part of the city, we saw fewer indications that anything had gone wrong. More buildings had the chance to board up their windows before they were completely overrun. But in the distance, plumes of smoke were a constant reminder that nothing was normal.

As the sun dipped lower in the sky, the shadows grew longer, and with them came a creeping unease.

"We should find somewhere to sleep," I said, my voice quieter now. The streets felt emptier, like the world itself was holding in its pain.

Cristian nodded, scanning the area. "There's a church up ahead. If it's empty, it'll be safer than staying out in the open."

The church stood away from the road, its steeple silhouetted against the darkening sky. A beautifully manicured lawn surrounded the building. Beyond the grass, trees loomed. I was sure without the sun going down and smoke filling the sky, it was a beautiful scene. But as we walked down the long driveway, I couldn't help comparing it to the horror movies I had watched.

The front doors were locked. Cristian looked at the mechanism and shook his head, indicating he couldn't pick it to open it.

"Maybe there's an open backdoor." I hadn't meant to whisper, but the fear and darkness were closing in around me.

Cristian nodded and held out his hand to me. When I took it gratefully, Don made a disgusted noise that I ignored. I barely knew either man, but both had shown their characters since I had met them. And if I was going to trust someone to keep me safe, it was going to be Cristian.

Together, we walked around the church. Simple yet beautiful stained glass windows covered the walls. I definitely wanted to be inside and feel safe, but the idea of breaking a window to get into a church didn't sit right with me. Cristian must have felt the same, because he didn't look twice at any of the windows.

We found an addition added to the original church building when we circled around to the back. It had a door and regular windows. This door was also locked. But as he checked the windows, Cristian found one unlocked and forced it open. He turned to me in the dark and I thought I saw a small smile of victory on his face, but it was hard to tell.

He motioned for me to come closer. Crouching lower, he laced his fingers together and when I stepped into them, he boosted me through the open window. His pack followed, and then he pulled himself up. I could hear Don complaining outside, but I turned away and started to explore the room. Don grumbled but followed, pulling himself through with an exaggerated groan.

Inside, the air was warm but fresh. We left the window open to allow the cooler evening air to come in. We found ourselves in some sort of back office. There was a desk with a useless laptop open on its surface. Don walked right to the desk phone and picked it up, holding it to his ear. He hung up, finding exactly what we all expected. Nothing.

"This will do," Cristian said, taking off the pack and placing it against the wall.

I sat in the desk chair, exhaustion weighing me down. But when I looked at Cristian, I felt guilty for feeling tired at all. As far as I knew, the man hadn't slept in two days.

Cristian stood near the doorway, his silhouette framed by the faint light from the window. Even now, he couldn't relax.

"You should rest," I whispered.

He glanced at me, his expression unreadable. "I will. But not yet."

I nodded, understanding without him having to explain. Someone had to keep watch, and I knew he wouldn't trust Don with the responsibility.

"Do you think we could build a fire outside? Try to have a hot meal?" I thought about the cans of soup that we had packed in the pack.

Cristian looked outside and nodded. Opening the lock on the backdoor, he headed out into the dim dusk light. I followed, wanting to help since the idea was mine.

"Before you come out, grab some paper from that desk in there," Cristian called over his shoulder.

I didn't ask questions and went back in to sort through what was on and in the desk. I found Don, with a can of soup, the lid peeled back with its pull tab. He slurped it cold, without a thought. I sighed and ignored him.

"Just going to follow him like a little puppy, aren't you?" In the dim light, I could barely make out the sneer on his face.

"I'm going to help him, because he's helping me. Something tells me you've never played any team sports," I replied.

My first mistake was underestimating Don. My second was turning my back on him while I searched the desk. I barely had time to process the movement before my chest slammed against the desk, knocking the air from my lungs. The wood pressed into my cheek, grinding against the fresh wound Cristian had patched up. Don's breath was hot and uneven against my ear, his grip a steel vice on my wrist.

"What are you doing?" I cried out.

I could feel his body pressed against mine. It was grotesquely intimate, as he made sure every inch of his body touched mine. His hot breath fanned out over my face as he leaned over me.

"You uppity witch. Thought you were too good for me when we spent time together in the jury room. Thought you were so much smarter than me. Now what? What are you going to do now?"

Red hot fury rose in my body. Being a woman meant always being prepared for an attack. Being on edge every moment that you were in an unfamiliar place with unfamiliar people. It meant not being able to walk alone after dark, because some man would believe he had the right to my body.

Growing up, my mother put me in self-defense classes. "Marlowe, there's never the guarantee that someone will save you. You gotta save yourself," she'd say.

I started allowing my body to relax, as if I would not fight him.

He chuckled low in his throat, his body sinking into me even further. "Oh, I see. You want this, don't you?"

The answer to that was a resounding hell no. But I didn't want him to know that yet. He smelled of stale sweat and unbrushed teeth. I needed him to get comfortable. To believe he had the upper hand. I needed him to loosen his hold just a fraction so I could move. That moment didn't take long as his free hand started to slide down my arm, with a destination I wasn't interested in letting him get to.

Don didn't notice my movements until I had stomped hard on his toe and he moved his foot in response. He cried out in pain and some of his weight left the lower half of my body. Exactly what I needed. With more leverage, I slammed the bottom of my booted foot against his shin, hitting and pushing at the same time.

When his hand released my head, I used my arms and shoved back as hard as I could, throwing myself back. Don was off balance and he tripped backward, away from me. He regained his footing and didn't go down, but it wasn't enough to stop me. I took a running start and slammed my foot into his groin. He cried out and toppled like a fallen tree.

"You bastard! Never touch me again!" My voice echoed in the office and I knew Cristian would hear outside.

Moments later, I heard his pounding footsteps as he approached the open door. Without a decent source of light, I couldn't see his face, but he only paused for a moment in the door, before bending and heaving Don to his feet. The man sputtered and tried to protest.

Cristian's voice was deathly quiet, each word dripping with controlled fury. "I saw this coming. I saw it in your face, in the way you looked at her. And I should've ended this before you even had the chance. But honestly, I didn't think you were this dumb. You didn't even wait for me to be asleep or step away where I couldn't hear her." Cristian spoke while he dragged Don from the office.

My heart was hammering in my chest, and I had to bend over slightly to catch my breath. I had trained for this. Prepared for this. And yet, nothing could have prepared me for the feeling of his weight pressing me down, or the sick realization that some men don't see women as people, just opportunities. But I wasn't an opportunity. And I would not be a victim. It happened to other women. There were victims every day that couldn't get away. But that hadn't been me.

I jumped when hands fell on my shoulders. Scrambling back, I saw the outline of Cristian against the open door. He raised his hands before him to show me he meant no harm. I knew it was him, but my adrenaline spiked again, and my gaze bounced around.

"He's outside," Cristian said.

"What's stopping him from coming in?"

"I tied him to a tree."

I gaped at him. "You did what?"

"I had a paracord bracelet from REI. I unravelled it and used it to tie him up."

Suddenly, from outside, I heard bellowing. Not words. Just angry screaming. Cristian went to the door and shut it. I heard the lock click and then the desk chair rolling across the room. He then moved to each window, checking the locks and ensuring there was no way in.

"I don't think he can get himself untied, but just in case," he said.

My entire body was trembling, and I gripped my upper arms, trying to control it. The smell of something burning caught my attention and a small flame flared from a piece of paper Cristian held. He threw it into the metal trashcan that was next to the desk. Pulling it away from the desk, he fed more paper into it. He pulled books from the small bookcase that was against the wall, adding those to the growing fire.

As if he had a second thought, he went to the window we had come through and cracked it, allowing the smoke from the fire to be sucked out.

"I'll close it before we sleep, for safety. But for now, I think you need the fire. Come closer."

The office smelled like burnt paper and smoke, the makeshift fire in the metal trash can crackling weakly in the center of the room. The flickering light threw jagged shadows across the walls, but it didn't warm the chill I felt deep inside. I sat on the floor with my back against the desk, knees drawn up to my chest, my hands trembling despite my best efforts to steady them.

Cristian crouched in front of me, his expression unreadable except for the tightness in his jaw. He didn't say anything at first, just handed me a bottle of soda from his pack. I took it, twisting the cap open with shaky fingers, but I didn't drink.

"You okay?" His voice was soft, but there was an edge to it, like he was struggling to keep his anger in check.

I nodded quickly, too quickly, the motion almost making me dizzy. "Yeah. I'm fine."

He tilted his head, his dark eyes narrowing. "You don't look fine."

I let out a shaky breath, my shoulders slumping. "I'm not hurt. That's what matters."

Cristian exhaled, leaning back on his heels. His gaze flicked to the fire, then back to me. "What happened, Marlowe?"

I swallowed hard, staring down at the water bottle in my hands. The cap dug into my palm, where I gripped it too tightly. "He... he came out of nowhere. I didn't hear him. I was just trying to find the paper for the fire. He made some snide comment, and I shot back."

Cristian's jaw tightened, but he didn't interrupt. In stilted words, I explained how Don had attacked me. Thinking about it made my shaking worse. I screwed the cap back onto the soda, afraid I was going to spill it all over myself. I felt my chest tighten, the memory of Don's grip on my neck searing into my skin like a brand.

"How did you get away?" Cristian asked, his tone low and steady, like he was afraid pushing too hard would shatter me. He wasn't too far off.

I hesitated, forcing myself to meet his eyes. "I... I panicked. But then I remembered something, something my mom told me years ago. She had me take self-defense classes, and I remembered what

I learned. I stomped on his foot. I kicked him in the shin when he loosened his grip. Then in the balls."

"And then?"

I took a shaky breath. "He went down. Like a sack of potatoes. And then you ran in."

Cristian sat back on the floor, his shoulders tense. He ran a hand through his hair, his movements jerky. "You did what you had to do."

"I didn't even think. I just... reacted."

"And that's exactly what stopped him from doing even worse." His tone was firm now, leaving no room for doubt.

Tears welled up in my eyes, but I blinked them back, biting my lip hard enough to hurt. "I shouldn't have antagonized him. I should've known better."

"Don't do that," Cristian said sharply, leaning forward. "Don't blame yourself for his actions. You had every right to step away, and he had no right to put his hands on you. None of this is your fault, Marlowe."

His words settled over me like a blanket, soft and heavy. I hadn't realized how much I needed to hear them until now.

I nodded, my throat too tight to speak.

Cristian reached out, hesitating for a moment before placing a hand on my shoulder. His grip was firm, steady, and for the first time all day, I felt a flicker of safety.

"I'll keep him away from you," he said, his voice quiet but filled with conviction. "I promise."

I looked at him then, really looked at him, and saw the firelight reflecting in his dark eyes. There was anger there. At Don. At the world. But also something else. Something softer, more fragile.

"Thank you," I whispered.

Cristian nodded, his hand still resting on my shoulder. "We'll get through this, Marlowe. One way or another."

Not for the first time in since I met Cristian, I believed him. I had no doubts he would do what was necessary to keep me safe. Something in him made him be a protector. And I had a feeling it wasn't just the fact he was a Sheriff's Deputy. No, he did that job because he had the drive to do the right thing.

Cristian was determined to give me a hot meal, as per the original goal. He used metal pieces from the filing cabinet to create a place for a can to sit above the fire. I just sat and watched as his mind worked on the problem and found a way to fix it. His skills were impressive, and I found myself seeing him in a different light.

When he wrapped a hot can of soup in a piece of fabric, he checked the temperature himself before carefully handing it to me.

"Don't eat it too fast, blow on it. I think it's pretty hot."

I nodded and wrapped my hand around the fabric. The warmth from the can seeped through just enough to warm the ice from my skin. Cristian started the warming process again on a second can of soup, after he added two more books to the fire. He looked at me over the orange and red flames and when I wasn't eating, he motioned for me to start.

"I know you don't feel like eating, but you need something in your stomach. It's important for you to keep going."

Carefully, I put my lips to the can edge and sipped a bit of the soup. The temperature was perfect and I could feel my body warm from the inside out as I ate. Though I didn't feel hungry, I continued to sip, finishing the entire can under Cristian's gaze. He ate his in about three gulps.

He put the cans to the side, mentioning keeping them for cooking if we needed to on the road. I wasn't really keeping track of what he wanted to do. He pushed the trashcan with his foot until he could slide it out the door and leave it a few feet from the building. The fire inside it was already dying down, but that way we could close up the office and maybe get some rest.

"You need to sleep," Cristian said.

After disappearing into the main church building to check the door and any other access points, he returned with bench cushions. He created a bed in the office's corner with direct access to the church. Cristian seemed to think about all possibilities and prepare for the worse.

"So do you," I replied.

"I'll be ok."

I moved over to the cushions and carefully laid down. "I know you didn't sleep last night in the bookstore."

The dark circles under Cristian's eyes were deeper, and I hadn't missed him yawning when he thought I wasn't looking.

"We'll hear anyone trying to break in. You've checked all the locks at least twice. And I'd feel better if you lay with me." My voice trailed off at the end, wondering if I was asking too much.

Cristian hesitated just for a second before joining me on the cushions. With four of the cushions laid out, we could lay shoulder to shoulder comfortably. He covered me with his suit jacket again.

"Would you think it was weird if I asked you to hold my hand?" I asked.

I felt so alone, lying in the dark. The silence was thick and constant. It was easy to feel like we were alone in the world. With no technology, no noise that we were so used to, no social media to see smiling faces, it left us alone. And though Cristian was right next to me, we didn't truly know each other. I knew there was more to him than what I could see. But he didn't want to let anyone in to learn.

"Of course not," he replied.

Cristian didn't hesitate. His fingers laced through mine, rough and warm, anchoring me in the darkness. The grip was steady, a silent promise that I wasn't alone. His palm made mine feel tiny. But it was a comfort to feel connected to another human being that wasn't trying to hurt me. I turned on my side, so I was facing him and laid my head near his shoulder. Closing my eyes, I was positive I wouldn't fall asleep. The effects of my restless mind and anxious heart were too overpowering, preventing me from finding the calm and tranquility that sleep promised.

"Don't think about him, Marlowe. Don't think about what

happened. Have good dreams." His whispered words floated in the dark and circled around me.

I wasn't sure his words were going to change the outcome of my sleep. In my mind, I was reminding myself that it could have been worse. That I had fought off Don and made him pay for what he tried. I tried to fight off the sick feeling, as if his slime coated my skin. With my hand connected to Cristian, I imagined the slime disappearing, inch by inch. Because Cristian wasn't just a good man. He was the kind of man who stood between darkness and those who couldn't fight it alone. And tonight, I wasn't alone.

Marlowe's tiny hand in his was enough to keep him from falling right to sleep. As her breathing deepened, I was glad she could get rest after Don's attack. Thinking about the man, I wanted to rage and go back outside and make him pay for what he had done. Make him pay in pain.

As her tiny body shuddered next to me, I shifted, so I was a bit closer. The office was getting cooler, the later it got. And we didn't have blankets or anything for bedding. I felt bad for not providing something better for Marlowe. It wasn't necessarily my responsibility, but I wanted to take it on. I was going to protect her.

When I heard her scream while I was looking for firewood, I couldn't move fast enough. I suspected Don had some sort of plan of attack for Marlowe. But I thought he would come after me first, so I was constantly on guard. I hadn't expected him going for her directly. Guilt was heavy in my chest when I thought about how much worse it could have been if she hadn't screamed.

One thing she was right about, I couldn't keep running on no sleep. I was almost positive that we had safely locked ourselves inside the church building. Unless someone had keys or made a whole lot of noise to get in, we could sleep. The cushions on the ground weren't nearly the bed we both needed, but better than the bare ground.

I turned, so I was facing Marlowe. I studied her sleeping face in the dim moonlight that filtered through the dirty office window. Marlowe had handled Don on her own. She wasn't fragile. She wasn't helpless. And yet, when I looked at her, something clawed at my chest—a need to keep her safe, to shield her from everything out there. It wasn't rational. It wasn't logical. And I hated I couldn't push it away. I let my eyes drift shut, with Marlowe being the last image I saw.

When I woke, sunlight streamed through the office window, casting a soft glow across the room. The first thing I noticed was how close Marlowe was. There was no space between us. Her arm rested lightly around my waist, her fingers splayed against the small of my back. She rested her head on my shoulder, pillowed on one arm of mine while my other arm held her close, instinctively, even in sleep.

I stiffened, not sure how we got into the position and not sure how to get out of it without waking her. Staying still, I waited.

"I'm awake." Marlowe's voice made me jump. She snorted and pulled her arm away from my waist. "I didn't want to wake you. You needed the rest."

"I…I'm sorry. Must have moved in my sleep," I mumbled.

I quickly got to my feet and moved to the window in an attempt to act normally. I straightened my dress shirt, tucking it back into my pants and brushing invisible dirt from it. When I turned back, Marlowe was sitting up and running her hands through her hair. Once she seemed happy with the texture, she tied it up in a high ponytail. A few shorter pieces fell out and framed her face. Somehow, she looked even prettier than before.

Shaking my head, I pushed the thoughts away. We had too much on our plates for me to think about anything but survival.

"What I wouldn't do for a cup of coffee," Marlowe said.

"You aren't kidding," I agreed. I handed her the bottle of soda she'd left on the desk the night before. "Some caffeine at least."

She smiled softly and took the bottle. The quiet hiss of carbonation escaped as she opened it. After she sipped the soda, she stood and stretched her arms above her head. I checked the window again, not seeing anything to be concerned about. There had been no noises to wake us during the night and I was feeling energized after a full night's sleep.

Double checking the church, I found we were still completely alone. But Don was still outside. And I had to figure out what to do with him. As far as I was concerned, he was no longer welcome to come with us. Somehow, I needed to untie him. I wasn't willing to leave him to starve or die in some other horrific way. But we'd need to sneak away so he couldn't follow us on our trip.

Marlowe and I shared the box of crackers, eating the ones that weren't crushed and then taking turns pouring crumbs into our mouths. We ate one granola bar each, leaving us with four more in the pack. I knew it wasn't enough to get us far, but at least we both had something in our stomachs for the morning.

I went to the back door, glancing back at Marlowe before I opened it. "I'm going to check on Don. I'll need to untie him. Then we'll get away from here before he can follow."

She nodded, but I could see the tension around her eyes and the stern set of her mouth. Slowly, I unlocked the door and peered out, to make sure there wasn't someone lying in wait to attack. The back manicured yard led to a small fenced-in playground, with large trees beyond. Only the quiet breeze moved and made a sound.

I stepped out and closed the door immediately, continually checking corners and the darkness in the trees. The trashcan fire was right where I had left it, completely burned out. Ignoring it, I walked toward the tree where I had left Don, I waited to hear him screaming or any noise of him struggling. But he made no sounds. Something felt wrong.

When I got to the tree, I froze. The paracord was on the ground, cut clean. My stomach clenched. He hadn't struggled out of it. Someone had helped him. I grabbed the cord, thinking it would be useful later. Then I jogged back to the office. I burst through the door to find Marlowe looking through the books left on the book-case. She spun in panic, but calmed when she saw it was me.

"We need to go. Now."

A frown came to her face, and she moved toward me. "What's wrong?"

"Don got loose. I don't know how, but he's not where I left him. And I have no idea where he's gone. We should get out of here in case he comes back."

Fear crossed her face, but she seemed to swallow it down and nodded. She packed the few supplies we had back into the pack, and I yanked it onto my back. Instead of exiting through the back door, I led her through the church to a side door that we could unlock. I motioned to Marlowe to stay silent, and I carefully disengaged the deadbolt on the door.

The door lead to a small gravel path that ran the length of the church building. I stood silently, listening for the crunch of shoes on the gravel, or someone rustling through the bushes in front of the tree line. The screech of a bird seemed so loud. But there was no other sound that a human being could make.

I reached back, and Marlowe immediately gripped my hand. I tossed open the door and jogged toward the front of the church, staying close to the bushes. The line followed all the way around the lawn, leading up to the road. We could stay in the shadows until we got to there. Marlowe kept up, though I could hear her breathing heavier than me.

The cool air of the morning chilled my body as I began to sweat. My pack slapped against my back with each step, its weight a constant reminder of how little we had and how much we couldn't afford to lose. And losing anything to Don would be unacceptable. Marlowe clung to my hand as if letting go would somehow unravel everything holding her together.

"We can't keep this pace forever!" she called over my shoulder, her voice tight with fear.

"We won't have to," I said, though I wasn't sure who I was trying to convince—her or myself. "Just a little farther. After we get to the road, we'll find somewhere safe."

Safe. The word felt hollow, like a promise I wasn't sure I could keep.

Don's face flashed in my mind, twisted with fury as he fought against his bonds. I'd underestimated his desperation. Again. The moment I saw the shredded ropes, I knew we were out of time. Staying wasn't an option anymore. Not with a man like Don free to roam and pissed off enough to do something about it. I imagined he wouldn't hesitate to come after Marlowe again if he had the opportunity.

Suddenly, Marlowe's hand yanked out of mine and I spun to find her on the ground. She carefully lifted her hands from the gravel with a grimace and I crouched next to her to see what happened.

"I tripped."

"Crap, I'm sorry. I was going too fast."

I took her hands in mine and carefully brushed away the gravel bits and dirt. Nothing was bleeding, but there were some scratches. I helped her to her feet, and she bent her knee up a few times.

"Did you land on your knees?" I asked, bending to look.

"Yes. I'm fine. Let's just keep going," she said, pulling me to standing and starting back down the hedges toward the street.

I grabbed her hand again, clasping it in mine. "Let's be more careful."

She nodded, her expression tight. "I'm fine. Just… tell me you're sure he won't follow us."

I didn't answer right away, because the truth wasn't what she wanted to hear. If Don was anything, he was vindictive. He'd find a way.

"Don't worry about him," I said instead, though my voice lacked conviction. "Just focus on moving."

At the end of the hedge, we came to the main road. We would be in the open and easy targets if we stayed following the route Don knew we were taking. I hesitated, looking up and down the empty street. There weren't any houses to be seen, but stalled cars sat haphazardly along the asphalt. Everything looked the same as it did the evening before. Turning, I checked behind us, looking for any movement.

"Cristian." Marlowe's uncertain voice pulled my attention back to the street.

Down the street, a group of people were coming our way. There was shoving and jostling between them. Laughter rang out as if the chaos was their playground. I pulled Marlowe with me, into the shadows of the trees. I wasn't sure what the group was up to, but I didn't want to pull their attention to us.

We crouched behind the first row of trees, keeping ourselves hidden from the road. Swiveling my head, I continued to check that Don wasn't somewhere ready to sneak up on us. I wouldn't let him get his hands on Marlowe again, no matter what I had to do to prevent it. And he didn't want to find out what my limits were for that.

The group grew closer, and they seemed to be only teenagers, maybe a couple barely over eighteen. One of them picked up something from the ground and the next thing we heard was shattering glass from a nearby vehicle. The kids walked around the car and checked inside, pulling things out and scattering the owners belongings across the road.

"What are they doing?" Marlowe murmured.

"Looting, I guess. Creating general havoc."

"They're children."

"There are plenty of children that thrive on chaos. I saw it every day on the job." I couldn't keep the bitterness from my voice.

The number of times I had to cart kids to juvenile detention was more than I would have liked. Kids with a host of issues passed through my patrol car and it made it hard to not see the broken system the kids suffered in. The number of kids with mental health and addiction issues that just needed help broke my heart. They outnumbered the kids that liked to be harbingers of anarchy for the fun of it.

I wasn't sure where this group fell on that scale.

They passed on the other side of the road and we both watched them closely. All of them looked as if they had been on the road since everything turned off. A couple of them were wearing school backpacks. One boy was wearing a child's barbie backpack that looked brand new. They headed to the next cars that were left on the side of the road and broke out another window.

I shifted and sat down on the ground. Marlowe did the same, sitting close so our shoulders touched.

"Seems like they aren't in a hurry," I said.

Marlowe shook her head and sighed. Her gaze moved around and I knew she was thinking about Don.

"If he was close by, I don't think he would wait to make himself known," I said.

She didn't seem to acknowledge my statement, as she continued to check behind us in the dark forest. Nothing moved and I continued to watch the kids at the nearby car. If I had thought we would find anything useful in the vehicles, the kids were making sure to clean them out before we could. My mind whirled with plans on how I could guarantee food and water for us.

The kids disappeared around a far bend in the road twenty minutes later. In the distance, we could hear additional glass shattering and loud shouting. But we carefully left the trees and quickly headed in the opposite direction. As we walked, we could see the destruction the kids had dealt to vehicles and buildings along the stretch of road. Though businesses, houses, and other buildings were sparse, the kids wandered around and vandalized everything accessible to them.

We walked in silence for the first part of the morning. My stomach growled, and I knew Marlowe was also hungry. The soup the night before and crackers this morning were not enough to fuel our trip. We were careful to stay to the side of the road, where we could hide within the tree line should anyone appear, or we needed to run from Don.

The man didn't show himself. My not knowing his location felt worse than knowing he was following us. Every noise had me turning and looking over my shoulder. When a loud bird crowed on the power lines above us, Marlowe visibly jumped. She looked over at me sheepishly, but I pretended to have not noticed her panic. To be honest, the sound of the bird was the loudest thing we had heard in a long while. It was easy to be surprised by it.

The quiet between us was heavy, broken only by the sound of our footsteps on the cracked pavement. The streets were emptier here, the fires and distant gunshots muted by the quiet stretch of suburbia we'd slipped into. I'd steered us this way deliberately, away from the route Don knew, away from crowded streets, and away from more trouble. The man was a threat. She didn't argue when I'd suggested changing our direction.

Now, we just had to keep moving.

"We'll cut through the neighborhood," I said, pointing to a row of houses up ahead. They were the kind of places that had neatly trimmed lawns and kids' bikes on the front porches. Now the porches were empty, save for scattered debris and overturned chairs. The trimmed laws would only last so long as a reminder of a time that was gone.

"We'll find something?" Marlowe asked, her voice tinged with desperation but steady.

"We will," I said, more for her sake than mine. We didn't have the luxury of doubt.

The first two houses were stripped bare. Open cabinets, over-turned drawers, everything picked clean. Whoever had lived here had either fled or had never made it home before their house was stripped of valuables. The third house was clearly a short term rental. It was well furnished, but the pantry was almost bare. We found a box of dried pasta and a half-full bottle of water in a kitchen cupboard. Not much, but enough to keep us moving for a little while longer, if we could cook the noodles.

"We should try the next block," Marlowe said, straightening up from where she'd been crouching by a drawer. Her face was pale, but her jaw was set.

"Agreed," I said, slinging my pack over my shoulder.

We stepped out onto the front lawn as the sun moved past the zenith in the sky. When we crossed into the next yard, I heard it. A sharp creak, like something heavy shifting on wood.

"Marlowe, wait—"

I didn't get the rest of the words out before the porch she stepped onto gave way. The wood splintered and cracked, and Marlowe's scream tore through the air as she went down, crashing through the broken boards.

I was at the edge of the hole in an instant, peering down at her. She lay crumpled on her side in a shallow crawlspace, her face twisted in pain.

"Marlowe!"

"I'm—" She tried to push herself up, but her arm gave out, and she gasped, clutching her side.

"Don't move," I said, my voice sharper than I intended. "I'm coming down."

The drop wasn't far, but I found myself in a cramped space filled with the smell of damp earth and mildew. I crouched beside her, my eyes scanning for injuries. She had bent her legs up to her abdomen, and pressed her hand against her ribs, breathing shallowly.

"Broken?" I asked, gesturing to her side, thinking if she had broken ribs, we couldn't just call 911 and get help.

"I don't know," she whispered, her voice tight. "It hurts to breathe."

Her eyes locked onto mine, wide and scared, and for a moment, I felt that familiar surge of helplessness. But I shoved it down. I looked at things clinically. She didn't fall far, but she fell to the side, and she landed on a concrete block. A block that should have been holding a beam, but someone messed up and the beam was missing.

"Okay," I said, keeping my voice steady. "We're going to get you out of here."

It took everything I had to lift her without making it worse. She bit back a scream as I hoisted her out of the crawlspace and onto the grass, her face pale and slick with sweat.

"We can't keep moving like this," I said, crouching beside her as she tried to catch her breath.

Marlowe clenched her jaw, sweat beading along her temple. "We have to."

She tried to stand. The moment she put weight on her leg, she gasped, her face going ghost-pale. I caught her before she crumpled again.

"No, Marlowe. Not today. You're not walking when you can barely breathe."

I scanned the area, my mind racing. We couldn't go far, but we needed shelter. I tried the door of the house we were in front of. It was locked. But I didn't hesitate to make quick work of the deadbolt. The door swung open easily, and I listened for movement inside. When there was nothing, I helped Marlowe to her feet. I would have carried her into the house, but when I tried to lift her, the pain was too much for her to handle.

Once we were inside, I locked the door behind us. I helped Marlowe onto the couch before I went and checked the windows, pointing toward the street. There was no one outside that could follow us.

Satisfied that no one saw us come into the house, I returned to Marlowe. "Stay here. I'm going to check the rest of the house, make sure we're completely alone."

"I won't be running any marathons down the street anytime

soon." Her small laugh turned into a groan as she gripped her ribcage again.

"Maybe also let up on that stand-up comedy routine. We'll save all the laughs later."

She nodded, her face pinched with pain. "We can't wait too long, Cristian. We have to keep moving."

"We'll wait as long as we need to," I said firmly. "You're not going anywhere until you can walk without passing out."

Her eyes softened, but she didn't argue. She lay back, her breathing uneven, while I checked the rest of the house for its previous inhabitants. The photos on the wall confirmed that a small family lived in the house. Parents with two small children. The first door I opened in the hallway was a children's bedroom, the two kids clearly sharing. There were toys strewn all over. The mess was likely normal, and I could not piece together a story from it.

There was a bathroom that was also fairly normal. Though I noted things that were missing. A toothbrush holder with no toothbrushes. Towel rack with no towels. Yet the tub was full of bath toys small kids would enjoy. I checked under the sink and found a bin of first aid items. It was open, with some things scattered inside the cabinet. Someone had rushed through, grabbing things from the bin.

The real story unfolded in the main bedroom. Clothes were everywhere. A partially packed duffel was still sitting open on the bed. They had removed the bedding from the bed, leaving only a bottom sheet. The side tables had open drawers and random items were on the ground. It told me the tale of two parents in a panic, realizing they couldn't survive in the house alone. They'd packed up their most important items, clothing, and toiletries. Where they went from there, I couldn't tell.

I checked the father's clothes and was surprised to find we were close to the same size. He was slightly shorter than me and wider around the middle. But I changed into cargo pants, that were made of a lightweight material. With the boots I got from

REI, they didn't look too short. Getting out of the dress shirt I had been stuck in was freeing. I grabbed a t-shirt that was from some random truck stop in Idaho. Feeling much more comfortable, I finished my check of the master bedroom.

We were alone. Feeling confident in that, I went around the house and made sure all the doors that led to the outside were locked. A van remained parked in the garage. Just like all other newer vehicles, this one couldn't run. The family had left on foot. Windows in the roll up garage door let in enough limited light that I could search the shelves along the walls of garage.

They were an organized family. They neatly arranged and labeled heavy plastic totes that lined the shelves. I skipped ones that mentioned kids' clothes, toys, memories. I opened the tote labeled "camping". Inside I found a lantern, which wouldn't turn on and I didn't feel any surprise at that. I found two hiking sleeping bags that were rolled tightly in small bags. They were meant to be packed in a hiker's pack, so they were lightweight.

Setting aside the sleeping bags, I continued sorting through the items. There was a small first aid kit, something called a Life Straw, a foldable saw and much more. I continued to separate the items that were useful and those we didn't need to bother with. There was a backpack in the container, and I packed it full of the items I knew we needed to take with us.

Another container caught my attention, labeled "Scuba Gear". We would not be diving anytime soon, but I found myself curious what tools could be inside. Masks and fins were definitely unnecessary. The underwater flashlights didn't work. But at the bottom, I found something I definitely needed. It was stainless steel, with a line cutter at the end of the blade. I slid the blade back into the cover and put it into my pocket.

A case of water caught my attention. A few bottles were missing, but the parents probably realized there was no way for them to carry the case. I took the entire case into the house. Marlowe looked up as I entered, and her eyes zeroed in on the water. A soft smile, followed by a grimace played on her lips as she carefully sat up. I put the case on the ground and opened a bottle for her. She groaned softly as she sipped the water.

"Drink your fill, but slowly. Too much water might make you throw up. The pain from that would probably knock you flat," I said.

Marlowe nodded as she sipped again. I left two bottles by the couch and lifted the case to find the kitchen. It was just beyond the living room. As I expected, I found many cabinets open, and shelves emptied. However, the family could only carry a limited number of items. I didn't bother with the fridge. It was the third day since the power went out and I wasn't sure what the smell would be like.

I found two bags of chips, one opened and one still sealed. Before I finished checking the rest of the kitchen, I took the chips to Marlowe. She immediately popped one into her mouth. In her hand was a piece of paper. Holding it up, she raised her eyebrows at me.

Taking it from her, I scanned the handwriting. It explained that in case someone named Mike came to the house, they would meet him at someone's dad's house. Without electronic communications, the family knew they would have to go on foot to meet their relatives.

"Yeah, family. They're gone. Matches up with the note. They took whatever they could carry," I explained.

"I wonder if they made it." Her voice was soft, as if speaking too loud hurt. I watched her closely as she sipped the water between chips.

"Wherever it was, I hope so. There's a van in the garage that wouldn't start. I guess they could have had a second vehicle. If it was old, it might still have run. But I haven't heard an engine since everything stopped."

Marlowe didn't respond, just nodded thoughtfully.

I motioned toward the brick fireplace that occupied a corner of the living room. "It's definitely too warm for a fire, but maybe if I get one going, we could cook something for dinner. I think you need to eat something substantial to help your body with the healing process."

"Is there more food?" Her voice was hopeful, and I wasn't willing to disappoint her.

"I haven't checked everything. We have the pasta from the other house. They couldn't have taken everything with them when they left."

Turned out, I was right. There were several items that would hold us over for a few days. The first thing I went for was two cans of chili. They had beans and meat, both things that Marlowe needed. Not only for healing, but for energy—hers had dropped off drastically. Watching her waste away in front of me wasn't something I was willing to do.

The family had kept a small pile of wood on their back porch. I stepped out to bring wood in and stopped short when I saw the toddler sized play structure. My gut twisted thinking about little kids living through the same hellscape I was. It was hard enough wrapping my adult brain around the world coming to a standstill. From a child's perspective, it had to be a nightmare.

Inside, Marlowe was shifting around, unable to find a comfortable position. I dropped the wood and came to crouch in front of her. She smiled at me sadly.

"Did I seriously fall through the floor?"

"Well, the decking, yeah."

She groaned. "I've been known to be clumsy. But I won't take credit for this one. I'm sorry."

"What in the world are you sorry for?" I brushed the hair out of her face that had escaped her ponytail. When it fell back into her face, she blew up at it. It just fell into her eyes again.

"I'm sorry for slowing us down. You wanted to get home. Now you're here, waiting with me, cause I fell through a deck and hurt myself. And I look like a train wreck, but when I tried to lift my arms above my head to fix my hair, I thought I was going to pass out. So this is what you get."

I just blinked at her. At the moment, I was pretty sure telling her she was beautiful would be a bad move. She was injured and miserable. I tried to think of ways I could help make her more comfortable.

"I could help," I said before I could stop myself.

Marlowe blinked up at me, eyes wide with surprise. I wasn't sure why I'd offered, only that I didn't like seeing her struggling, looking so tired and defeated.

I cleared my throat. "Fix your hair, I mean."

Help with my hair? I felt like my ears heard one thing, but my brain wasn't processing it correctly. I tried to lift my arm to pat my head and only ended up squeezing my arm to my side, hissing in pain.

"Stop. Just let me." His tone was all business, so I just sat still while he went around the back of the couch.

I couldn't sit up or shift to make it easier for him. Having him help me with what felt like an intimate task had me just as tense as my injury. He moved carefully, as he pulled my hair tie from my ponytail. It caught slightly on a knot, and he blew out a breath.

"I'm sorry."

"That's the worst of my pains, Cristian." I smiled, though he couldn't see it. I also didn't bother trying to laugh, because it would have made me miserable.

My hair spilled around my shoulders before his hands gathered it back into a ponytail. He scraped his fingers along my scalp, smoothing the bumps and ensuring he captured all the loose pieces. I needed to swallow down the groan in my chest, as I felt the soothing pleasure of him running his fingertips along my scalp. Just like everything else he did, he was efficient in ponytail creation. Way too soon for me, he stepped away and took his hands from my hair.

"Better?" He asked.

I nodded. When he moved back to the fireplace, I tried to shift so I could watch, but it only hurt. I eventually found a propped up position that took some of the pressure from my ribs. The smell of burning paper was the first thing I noticed and then I heard Cristian adding logs to the grate in the fireplace.

He came back to stand in front of me. "I'm going to let the coals get going and find something to warm up the chili I found. I think a pot would be better than the cans, but I'll see what they have."

It was only a few minutes later that he came back in, looking celebratory.

"Luck is on our side. Well, now it is. They have all stainless-steel cookware. And it's the type with removable handles, so we don't have to worry about them melting."

"You learned this in the Boy Scouts, too?"

He gave me a small smirk before he set to opening the two cans of chili with a can opener. "You make fun, but those years taught me a lot. Not just survival, but leadership and courage. If I hadn't had the Scouts when… well, when things went bad, I probably wouldn't be sitting here with you right now."

He didn't meet my eye as he spoke. I was immediately curious about what bad things had happened and how they had shaped him as a man. But he didn't seem to want to talk about it and I wasn't going to push a man I had only met a few days before. We weren't in a normal scenario. We didn't meet on a social media site or run into each other in a coffee shop. No. We were surviving what seemed like the apocalypse. I felt closer to Cristian than I had to anyone in a long while.

Pouring the chili can contents into the pot, he looked at me with a cheerful smile. "We're eating well for lunch. And then I'll figure out dinner."

"Shelter, food. Shelter, food. Fight off attacker. Shelter, food." I counted off things on my fingers and it caused Cristian to actually laugh aloud. The sound seemed foreign, even to him, when he stopped abruptly and looked down at me.

He cleared his throat and lifted the pot. "Let's see if the coals are hot enough to do something with this."

Heating the food took longer than usual, with Cristian constantly stirring, to get an even heat. The smell of the chili caused my stomach to grumble loudly. When Cristian snickered, I knew he'd heard it as well. The waiting was pushing my hunger beyond the point of my controlling it. I had been doing well the last couple of days, keeping my needs to myself. We were all suffering. It wasn't just me.

Once the chili was sufficiently steaming, Cristian disappeared into the kitchen with the pot. Upon his return, he dished out the food into bowls, providing spoons. And I almost moaned aloud when he revealed a loaf of bread from behind his back. He laid down a paper towel on the cushion next to me and placed a stack of bread on it. The bowl was warm in my hands. Despite the warmth outside, there was something about hot food going into your mouth and spreading through your body.

We ate in silence for a few moments, but it was driving me nuts. "I'm trying really hard to not go face first into this bowl. I'm positive I've never been this hungry in my life."

Cristian looked up at me from his spot on the floor. "I doubt I have either."

"Even when I was just traveling up and down the West Coast, working minimum wage jobs, living in hourly hotels, eating out of vending machines. I was never this hungry."

"You did that?" He raised a surprised eyebrow.

I nodded as I swallowed another bite of chili-soaked bread. "My mom's first round of cancer sort of ate away at my teen years. It wasn't her fault, and I would have never left her alone while she was sick. But when I turned 18, and she was in remission, I wanted an adventure. I found it."

Cristian rubbed a hand through his hair. "I can't even imagine a life like that."

"You had a normal teen experience?"

"Define normal?"

I understood a redirection when I heard it. I hadn't really meant to lead back to his past, but it just worked out that way. Now, I wanted to know what was so difficult for him to talk about.

I shrugged in response to his question. "I guess normal is all relative. Maybe nursing your mother through cancer is considered normal for some people. I just know when I watched my friends going out as groups, to the movies or to the mall while I was driving my mom to and from chemo treatments, I thought what they had was normal."

"I remember people like that in high school. I wasn't one of those."

"I didn't picture that," I said with a small laugh. I grimaced at the pain that radiated from my ribs.

Cristian set his empty bowl on the ground and held up his finger, telling me to wait. I wasn't going anywhere, not while I still had chili and bread. I continued to wolf down the food, savoring the feeling of my stomach being full and not gnawing at itself. With Cristian out of the room, I actually debated licking the bowl clean. But as I threw the thoughts around in my head, he walked back in and I set the bowl down.

He shook a pill bottle and held it up. "Toradol. Not even generic. It'll help with pain and inflammation. There are twelve pills, but the label says to not take longer than five days. Not sure why, but one pill every four to six hours. That gives you a few days of help."

I held out my hand and he shook a pill into my palm. I didn't question his suggestion. I just trusted him. With the remnants of my bottled water, I swallowed the pill. Cristian then showed me a long piece of fabric that looked like a fancy scarf.

"We'll gently bind your ribs. It can help with support and lessen the stress on the rest of your body trying to keep still."

With his hands under my stiff elbows, he slowly helped me stand. The pain wasn't really any different if I was standing or sitting. It was just there, and it was severe enough to make me lose my breath. But Cristian was incredibly careful. I started when I felt my shirt inching up.

"Sorry. I really should look, just to make sure nothing is extremely discolored," he murmured.

I stared at the wall ahead of me, fighting the shiver that ran through my body when his fingers lightly ran over my ribs. I wasn't sure if it was because I was ticklish, or it was something about his skin being on mine. He was clinical with his check, and I felt silly for even thinking what I did.

"There is some bruising, but from what I can tell, nothing is dislocated and no bones protruding." He pulled down my shirt and slowly wrapped the scarf around my ribs.

When he tied off the material, my breath caught in my throat. The initial pressure felt painful, but after a moment, once I let my body relax, I could feel how the scarf was supporting my ribcage. Cristian watched me closely, and I nodded with a small smile. He seemed satisfied and helped me slowly sit down again.

"I'll handle the dishes," he said.

"This is where I say something about you cooking and I should clean. But I don't think I could even think to manage that right now."

He snorted as he picked up the empty bowls and disappeared into the kitchen. There was no running water, but I assumed he had a bottle to rinse the bowls. Or maybe he'd just leave them in the sink. We weren't going to live in the house. This was a temporary shelter before I could get back to walking and we could get to his place.

Sitting in the house and feeling somewhat safe felt foreign, though it had only been a few days. I hadn't felt settled since we left Hillsboro, but Don's attack had changed everything. It wasn't just unease anymore—it was the weight of knowing he had been waiting for the right moment. And I had been alone when it came.

"What are you frowning about?" Cristian asked as he came in.

I started to shrug, but when the movement pulled on my ribs I froze. "Just thinking about this house. I mean, I know we're not staying. But do you think we're safe here?"

"It's locked up tight. But I guess all that really means is someone would make a lot of noise trying to break in and loot the place."

"What about the food situation? Are we ok for a few days?"

Cristian looked toward the front door as he replied. "I'm actually going to check around the neighborhood. See if any of the other houses have anything left over."

"By yourself?" The nervousness in my voice was clear.

"I'll be ok. You'll need to stand up and lock the door behind me, though. And unlock it when I get back. Do you think you can manage?"

I'd figure it out.

Yet when Cristian walked out the door, I suddenly felt like I couldn't breathe. The silence of the house closed in on me. I limped around, looking at the photos on the walls. Studying the happy smiling faces of a mother, father and two little kids made me feel like I was an interloper. I was suddenly a part of the world they left behind and they had no idea.

Cristian had been through the house, and when he'd come back, he was wearing new clothes. He'd also had a second bag full of supplies. I doubted if I went through things, I would find things he missed. I couldn't know what would be needed after the world effectively ended. Even when I spent years on the road, I always had a roof over my head and could scratch a few bucks together for food. This was a different world.

Wandering back to the front of the house, I looked out to the street through the front windows. I searched for Cristian, but he was doing a good job of staying out of sight. Afraid of missing his return, I carefully pulled a piano stool over so I could sit by the window.

The street was eerie. Nothing moved. No people walking their pets or leaving to go to the store. No mail being delivered or Amazon trucks rushing up and down the road. All the things we expected to see each and every day were just gone. There was a deep sorrow and desperation sitting in my chest when I really thought about everything that was happening.

Movement across the street and three houses down caught my attention. I saw Cristian climb from a front window. He crouched, looking up and down the road, before walking across the lawn to the next house. He moved stealthily, and I was impressed. Even without being injured, I doubted I'd be able to mimic what he was doing. I watched him closely, studying how he checked the house, before trying the front door. Once the front door swung open, he stood off to the side, peering around the doorjamb.

I tried to imagine him in his uniform, entering a house in the same manner. It was easy to see. Despite the grime we had collected on our clothing and skin, he was still clean cut and professional. I looked like a bedraggled mess. At least he'd fixed my hair. One more thing to remind me that at the moment I didn't have anyone besides Cristian and my mother. And my mother was entirely too far away for me to get to.

Sadness hit as I thought about Mom. We didn't know for sure, but it seemed likely that whatever was happening in Hillsboro was at least statewide. Other states would respond to a state in distress. We hadn't seen or heard any sort of support. No engines. No planes flying over us in the sky. Mom was probably scared for me. And if I was right, she was suffering through the worst episode of cancer she'd ever had.

Movement out of the corner of my eye made me turn my head toward the end of the street we had come in. My breath caught in my throat. Someone was sneaking down the road. I stood shakily from my stool and moved so I could see more clearly in that direction, but also hide behind the wall. My heart hammered in my ears and I began to tremble.

There was no way for me to warn Cristian without giving away both our locations. The sun had started to dip and was casting long shadows across the road, making it hard to see the person clearly. At first, I thought my eyes were playing tricks on me. The shadow of the person seemed to multiply. But when the shadow got closer, I realized it wasn't just one person. There were three.

I looked over toward the last house I saw Cristian in. The front door stood open, making it an easy target for anyone looking to loot. I wanted to call out to Cristian, to warn him, but my throat felt like it had closed up. If they heard me, it would be over—for both of us. Instead, I pressed my palm against the glass, willing him to look out the door or window, to see me, to realize something was wrong.

He didn't.

The group of three appeared like ghosts from the shadows, slipping silently down the road. They moved with purpose, their steps deliberate, and their heads constantly swiveling like they were looking for something—or someone. My chest tightened as I watched: one tall, wiry man with a makeshift spear slung across his back a shorter woman with a knife in hand, her shoulders tense; and a younger boy, maybe late teens, clutching a crowbar so tightly his knuckles were white.

They weren't just wandering. Their steps were too deliberate, their heads constantly scanning like they were tracking something. The tall man whispered something, and the other two split off slightly, fanning out as if expecting trouble. Hunters, not scavengers.

My heart slammed against my chest, the sharp pain from my ribs making me wince. I had to do something, but what? Running outside was out of the question—I could barely walk without doubling over, let alone sneak up on three armed strangers. And shouting would only paint a target on me.

My hands shook as I scanned the room for anything useful. My eyes fell on a lacrosse stick that was propped against the wall near the front door. Likely the father's, along with the bag of equipment on the ground next to it. It felt laughably inadequate. My eyes darted back to the group, who had crept toward the house across the street, their weapons glinting faintly in the fading daylight.

I sucked in a breath, the sharp pain grounding me. I couldn't warn Cristian directly, but maybe I could create a distraction—something loud enough to pull their attention away from him. My gaze landed on a flowerpot, with fake plants, near the door, its ceramic edges chipped and jagged. It wasn't much, but it might work. I grabbed it, ignoring the stabbing pain in my side, and shuffled toward the back sliding glass door. My pulse thundered in my ears as I cracked it open, just enough to fit myself and the pot through.

I hesitated, my hands trembling. If this didn't work, I'd be leading them right to me.

Sucking in another shallow breath, I flung the pot over the back fence, aiming for the yard beyond. It hit the ground with a loud crash. The sound echoed down the empty street. I prayed that the crashing pot sounded like it was in the street over. As quickly as I could, I snuck back inside, being sure to lock the sliding door behind me.

I crouched back down near the front window, every nerve in my body on edge as I waited. The group had frozen, their heads snapping toward the noise. The younger boy whispered something to the others, his crowbar raised defensively. For a moment, they seemed torn—their attention split between the house where Cristian was and toward the direction of the noise.

"Go," I whispered under my breath, as if I could will them to turn away.

The woman gestured sharply, and they shifted direction, heading toward the street that would lead them behind the house. Relief surged through me, but it was fleeting. I had only bought

Cristian a little time, and if they came back empty-handed, they'd be more cautious—and angrier.

I watched as the three disappeared back into the shadows further down the street, my breath coming in short, painful bursts. Cristian's figure reappeared in the house across the street, oblivious to the danger he had narrowly avoided.

He needed to hurry. We needed to make a plan. And I needed to find a way to tell him what had just happened—before it was too late. He looked up, as if to check the house, and I gestured wildly. I couldn't see his face clearly, but he immediately jogged back to the house. I limped over to the front door, feeling even more sore, after hefting the flowerpot and throwing it.

Unlocking the door, I ushered him inside quickly, before flipping the locks again. I went back to the windows, carefully peering around the shade. There was nothing moving again, but I wasn't sure if it would stay that way.

"What's wrong?" Cristian asked. He dropped his bag, and it landed with a thunk, showing he'd been successful in his search.

"Three people were coming down the street toward you. They looked dangerous."

He joined me at the window, standing behind me and peering through the small opening I created with the shade. "I don't see anything."

"That's because I threw a flowerpot over the back fence to draw them away."

He pulled me away from the window to sit on the couch in the front room. The way he was looking at my face, I knew my pain level was written all over it.

"You shouldn't have done that. Are you in terrible pain?"

"It's not great. And what should I have done? Just let them ambush you? I'm not sure they actually saw you go into the house you were in, but you left the door open and I was afraid that would be an open invitation to search the same house. I had to do something." My words came out in a wheeze. I couldn't take a deep enough breath to spit out a full sentence without getting winded.

"It's too early to take another pill. Maybe you need to lie down and rest?"

I shook my head. "What about those people? Are we just going to stay here and risk them finding us?"

Cristian looked toward the front of the house, as if he could see everything and predict what was approaching. "We can't leave. Not unless we're forced to. I'll just make sure we have an escape plan if someone breaks in. I'm pretty sure the house directly across the street and the two next to it are still occupied. I saw movement in those. And maybe the one next door to us. We aren't alone in this neighborhood. Not completely."

I wasn't sure if that made me feel better or worse. We had broken into this house, this family's house. Granted, Cristian was a deputy, so I would follow his lead when it came to breaking the law. Were laws even still applicable if the police and other services weren't enforcing them? My mind whirled with our lack of options and the threat we could be under.

"I can see the wheels turning. We'll be ok," Cristian said quietly.

He motioned for me to climb to my feet again. He led me to the master bedroom. After he pushed the clothes to the floor, he disappeared for a moment, before returning with bedding. His efficiency also applied to making a bed. The corners all pulled tight, and he wiped a hand over the sheet to make sure it was smooth.

He helped me climb in. Untying my boots, he set them on the floor, but near to hand. Then he disappeared again, returning with another bottle of water, which he put on the side table.

"Covers?"

I nodded. Not because I was cold, but because I just wanted the comfort of a blanket. Cristian pulled a fleece throw over me. He gazed down at me for a long moment, and I could already feel my eyes drooping.

"Just rest, Marlowe. I'll watch out for you. Everything will be ok."

He double checked the windows, making sure they were locked. Then he pulled all the blinds tight, plunging the room into semi-darkness. I was the type that could sleep anywhere. But the darkness only made the room more cozy. My eyes were closed as I felt his fingers brush my hair back gently, barely skimming my skin. It was nothing—just a small gesture. But it sent warmth curling in my chest, something I wasn't prepared for.

I should have said something. Made a joke. Pulled away. But I didn't. I just sat there, too tired, too sore, too… something to stop him.

It wasn't like this meant anything. He was just being careful, just making sure I wasn't uncomfortable. That was all. But my body didn't seem to care about logic. Every nerve felt on edge, keyed into the way his fingers lingered for half a second too long before he pulled away.

I exhaled slowly, pressing deeper into the blankets. "Thanks."

Cristian hesitated, like he wanted to say something, then just nodded. "Get some rest."

I turned my head, staring into the dark. Rest. Right. I didn't think it would come easy tonight. I didn't think twice about trusting Cristian to keep me safe while I slept. The softness of the bed and the exhaustion of not only the crazy day, but the crazy apocalypse since that plane fell out of the sky and the power turned off, pulled me under into sleep.

While Marlowe slept, I searched the entire house for any weapons that could be used against the people she had seen. The best I could find were the kitchen knives, besides the dive knife I still had in my pocket. I didn't feel comfortable with that for defense, but it was better than nothing. The knives were sitting in random places around the house, where I could easily access them.

In law enforcement, you see the damage a kitchen knife can do. It was almost always domestic violence calls, where one spouse was abusing the other and it got to the point of attempted murder. There were the ones that succeeded as well. But I knew a lot had to go my way for it to actually work. The first goal was to just keep anyone from breaking into the house.

I pulled an armchair to the front window area and carefully propped the corner of the shade up, so I could see out. But I sat back enough so that I could hide in the shadows. When I was searching for supplies, it had been easy to recognize which houses had people in them, and which seemed empty. The unknown was if the people Marlowe saw were just looting, or if they had more nefarious plans.

The front room had a bookcase full of well-loved books. I

stood and browsed through. It had been a long time since I had held an actual book in my hands. E-books were my normal reading method, and I was a shameless fiction reader. Sometimes I would even read on my phone during breaks at work. Having easy access to books was going to be something I would miss.

Someone in the house was obsessed with old literary classics. Especially Charles Dickens. Multiple copies of A Tale of Two Cities, A Christmas Carol and Oliver Twist dominated two entire shelves. I picked one up and flipped through the pages. The old English style of writing just wasn't my thing. And I wasn't looking to be bored to tears. One copy looked fairly old. When I picked it up, I realized it was an actual first edition copy. Slipping it back onto the shelf, I thought about how it was nothing but a paperweight now.

I found a section of sci-fi and picked one with a cover that called to me. Sitting back in front of the window, I opened the book. I glanced up at the street often, making sure nothing moved that shouldn't. The houses were pitching deep shadows as the sun moved. I was happy that I wore a real watch, something that had no electronic parts. It read 8:15 PM. Our Oregon summer could be beautiful with long days. It made me wonder when we would again enjoy the warm days like we used to.

I was getting introduced to the main character of the book, who was a struggling engineer with a bigger purpose on a star-ship. As I turned the page, trying to focus, a flicker of movement outside pulled my gaze. I leaned forward, narrowing my eyes. What was that?

Nothing. Just shadows stretching across the pavement.

Still, the unease settled in my gut. Something felt...wrong. I slipped a scrap of paper into the book, because I refused to dogear a page even if the world was falling apart. I wasn't a heathen. Sliding to the side of the window, so I could more easily see without being seen, I noticed a couple coming out of the house across the street.

They were wearing backpacks and looked like they weren't

planning on coming back. The woman paused and looked back at their home. Grabbing her hand, the man I assumed was her husband gently tugged her down the driveway. Her face scrunched up and tears streamed down her cheeks when she looked at him. Her husband reached down and brushed his fingers across her face. I couldn't hear anything they were saying, but she looked up at him and nodded. He touched her chin and kissed her quickly before they walked down the driveway and headed down the street.

What was happening had caught people off guard. Looking for help was going to be the natural thing to do. But I already knew there was no one to help. We were all on our own. And we had to do what was necessary to survive. I wasn't sure where those people thought they were going to go.

I settled back in the armchair and picked up the book. Ten minutes later, a horrific scream broke the silence, and I was on my feet, dropping the book to the ground. Without thinking, I ran through the house to the bedroom where Marlowe slept. I busted into the room without slowing and she shot up in bed, crying out in pain as she moved too fast. I came to her side and sat on the edge of the bed.

"What happened?"

"What do you mean? You busted in here like hell was on your heels and I woke up. I forgot about my ribs and it hurt like hell." She was breathless, and I knew she wasn't telling me how bad it was.

"Didn't you scream?"

"Scream? No? I don't think I was having a nightmare," she replied.

Just then, another panicked scream echoed, and I realized my mistake. In my fear for Marlowe's safety, I hadn't understood that the scream wasn't from inside the house. It was outside.

"Stay here. Lock the bedroom door behind me and don't open it for anyone but me," I said, rising.

Marlowe's fingers dug into my forearm, slowing me. "Don't go out there."

"I can't just leave whoever it is. They sound like they need help. And those people you saw could be out there."

"You don't have any weapons. What can you do?"

"A lot more than you think. I'll be ok." I took the moment to brush a finger down her cheek, under the pretense of pushing hair behind her ear. "Just lock the door."

Her eyes were wide, but she nodded. "I will be really pissed at you if you die."

"Got it." I gave her a strained smile.

I waited until I heard the lock click on the door before I ran back through the house to the front window. I had the diving knife on me. And from the description Marlowe gave of the group, I had a feeling they didn't have guns. So it would be a hand to hand fight, with whatever rudimentary weapons they were carrying.

When I pulled the shade from the window, I found the woman who had left the house across the way, laying in the middle of the street. She was in a ball, with three people walking around her and taunting her. Looking around the rest of the neighborhood from my vantage point, I could see other people looking from their windows, but no one was going to help her.

The attackers laughed manically, a sound I could clearly hear inside the house. The front door of my house was too obvious, so I snuck into the garage. I remember there was a side door that led into a side yard. I ran to the garage, careful to not make a noise as I opened the door. Outside, I slowly approached the gate that opened to the driveway. I lifted the latch and it squeaked quietly, but I didn't think it was loud enough for them to hear over their own voices.

"C'mon, lady," a man sneered, his voice dripping with malice. "Don't make this harder than it has to be."

I crab walked to the side of the house where I could peer at the scene. I saw them. The three from before that Marlowe told me about. They'd surrounded the woman sprawled on the pavement, her clothes torn and her hands trembling as she tried to shield herself. The tall guy with the spear kicked her leg, just hard enough to make her flinch. The woman didn't cry out, but her body jerked, desperation written all over her face.

I looked around but didn't see her husband anywhere and my gut clenched. Her first screams had been terror and grief. The group must have taken care of him before attacking her.

"We can do this the easy way," the shorter woman in the group said, twirling a knife in her hand like it was an extension of her arm. "Give us what you've got, and maybe we let you go."

The woman on the ground didn't respond, just curled tighter into herself. All she had was her backpack, which was still strapped to her body. They had to know she had little to give them. People like them just wanted to terrorize others, getting off on hurting someone.

I clenched my jaw, forcing my breath to stay steady. The logical choice was to stay hidden. To wait.

But then she whimpered—small, broken, barely more than a sound. And that was it. I couldn't walk away, and even in a world gone to hell, I wouldn't allow three predators to tear someone apart.

I gritted my teeth and stepped out from behind the house, my fists clenched.

"Hey!" I barked, my voice cutting through the air like a whip.

The trio snapped their heads in my direction, their surprise replaced with annoyance. I walked down the driveway and planted my feet in the street, near the woman on the ground.

"Who the hell are you?" the spear guy asked, his tone flat but dangerous.

"The guy who's going to put you down if you don't walk away," I said, my voice steady despite the hammering in my chest.

The short woman laughed, her knife catching the dim light as she took a step toward me. "Big talk for one guy. You even armed?"

"Nope," I said, stepping closer. "But I don't need to be."

The spear guy sneered and moved first, thrusting his weapon forward. I sidestepped, grabbing the shaft and twisting hard. He yelped as I ripped it from his hands and rammed the blunt end into his gut. He doubled over.

Before I could follow up, the younger one—the kid with the crowbar—charged at me. I barely ducked in time, the metal swinging inches above my head. I surged forward, driving my shoulder into his chest, and slammed him into the side of a truck parked on the street. His weapon clattered to the ground, and I kicked it away, turning just in time to see the knife glinting toward me.

The woman was fast, her blade slicing toward my ribs. I twisted, but the edge grazed my arm, sending a flash of pain up my shoulder. I ignored it, grabbing her wrist and twisting it hard. She screamed and dropped the knife but before I could finish the job, the spear guy tackled me from behind, knocking us both to the ground.

I hit the pavement hard, the air rushing from my lungs. The bastard was on top of me, his fists raining down, but I managed to roll, using the momentum to throw him off. We scrambled to our feet at the same time, and I swung the spear like a bat, catching him across the jaw. He went down hard, and for a moment, the street was still.

Then I heard the gunshot.

It was deafening in the quiet neighborhood, the sharp crack echoing off the abandoned houses. My head snapped toward the sound, and I saw her. The woman who'd been on the ground, now standing, her hands trembling as she held a small handgun.

One attacker, the younger kid, staggered backward, his crowbar falling from his grip as he clutched his chest. He crumpled to the ground, unmoving.

I didn't have time to think. The other two froze, their eyes darting between the woman and me.

"Give me the gun," I said, keeping my voice calm as I approached her. She was shaking, her wide eyes fixed on the body in the middle of the street.

She didn't resist when I took the weapon from her hands. It was lighter than I was used to, but the weight of the moment bore down like a freight train.

I turned to the remaining two attackers, leveling the gun at them. "Leave. Now. Or you'll end up just like him."

The short woman hesitated, her gaze flickering between me and the gun. "You wouldn't—"

I cocked the hammer, my expression cold. "Try me."

That was enough. She grabbed the spear guy's arm, dragging him to his feet. They backed away slowly, their hands up, before disappearing into the shadows.

The silence was deafening. My chest heaved as I lowered the gun, my eyes settling on the woman who was still standing there, swaying slightly.

"You okay?" I asked, my voice softer, now.

She nodded, but her face told a different story.

"Come on," I said, de-cocking the gun and tucking it into my waistband. "We can't stay here."

She didn't argue, and as I led her away from the scene, I glanced back once, my grip tightening on the stolen handgun. The rules of the world had changed, but some things stayed the same. You don't leave someone to fend for themselves when you can do something about it.

Even if it costs you.

As we approached the side yard, the woman was murmuring to herself and I wondered if she hadn't fractured her psyche. I let her continue as I led her into the house. I locked all the doors behind us, making sure we were secure, on the off chance the two attackers tried to return and get their retribution.

When we entered the house, Marlowe was pacing near the

front door, her arms wrapped tightly around herself, her breath coming in quick bursts. The moment I stepped inside, her head snapped up. Her eyes locked on me, wide and frantic, scanning every inch of me for a wound.

"Cristian," she choked, her voice raw. Before I could say a word, she crashed into me, her fingers clutching at my shirt like she was afraid I'd disappear if she let go. "I heard a shot. I was so scared."

"It's ok. It wasn't my gun. And it wasn't me."

She stepped back, looking away and cheeks blooming with color. It was then she noticed I wasn't alone. Giving us room to come further into the house, Marlowe led the way to the front room. The woman stood, frozen and confused. I guided her to a chair, encouraged her to sit, which she did without a word or even meeting my eyes.

"You're bleeding!" Marlowe suddenly exclaimed, grabbing my arm and lifting it so she could examine the wound.

"Knife. It's not deep."

"I'll get the kit."

She limped off toward the bedroom where we had our bags and the supplies we were collecting for our trip. I had put together the first aid kid and now I figured it would come in handy. The adrenaline from the fight was waning, allowing the knife wound to make itself known.

The woman on the couch rocked back and forth, her constant mumbling continuing. I didn't want to scare her but needed to know if she had any injuries. Slowly, I crouched down in front of her, trying to get her to meet my gaze.

"What happened out there?" I asked.

"They…they…killed him."

"The man you were with?"

She slowly nodded and tears poured down her cheeks. She didn't bother brushing them away. "My husband."

"I'm sorry." I wasn't sure what else I could say.

She didn't acknowledge my words, just continued to rock. I

noticed a spray of blood across her chest. Pointing, I tried to get her attention. "Is that your blood?"

Her eyes widened, a horrified look coming to her face. She shot to her feet and erratically threw her backpack off her shoulders. Her body bucked as she tried to rip the t-shirt over her head. I climbed to my feet to try to help, not sure why she was stripping in the middle of the room, but clearly seeing she was in distress.

The shirt came off, and she looked down at her chest and she cried out again. She scrubbed at her skin, where the blood had soaked through and stained her skin. Her rubbing was violent, and all of her skin was turning red to match the blood spots. I grabbed her wrists, trying to calmly pull her hands away, but she yanked out of my hold.

"It's his. It's his. It's his." She repeated over and over as she stumbled and spun away from me.

Marlowe chose that moment to walk back into the room, the makeshift first aid kit in her hands. Her mouth dropped open, but she quickly grasped the situation. She dropped the first aid kit and approached the woman with her hands held out.

"Ok, ok. I can help you. We have water bottles, and I can get a washcloth. Do you want to clean off in the bathroom?" She said, her voice soft and soothing.

As if the woman just realized Marlowe even existed, she froze and slowly looked up. Marlowe motioned for her to follow, and they disappeared down the dark hallway. I saw a slight glow after a moment and figured Marlowe had lit a candle in the bathroom. A minute later, she appeared back in the room, pale and tears in her eyes.

"Her husband?"

I nodded. Marlowe's hand came up to cover her mouth. I wasn't sure what to say, so I just opened my arms and motioned for her to come to me. She didn't hesitate. Her face buried in my chest as she quietly cried. Her sweetness, innocence and kindness couldn't handle the evil that was appearing. I rubbed her back and let her get it all out.

Once her shoulders stopped shaking, she pulled back, a look of determination on her face. She swiped angrily at her face and took a deep breath. Bending, she picked up the first aid kit and motioned for me to follow her into the kitchen. At the sink, she poured water onto the gash on my arm. I hissed but let her clean the wound.

"Infection would be a real bad thing to get right now," she said.

"Agreed."

"Maybe we should check a pharmacy or something tomorrow. Just in case?"

I glanced at her profile. Her eyes narrowed as she inspected my arm. "You think we're leaving tomorrow?"

She looked at me, surprised. "We can't stay here. What if they come back?"

"I have a gun now. And they know it. The woman shot one of them. That's the shot you heard. The other two would need fire-power to come back. And in the dark, it would be pretty hard to attack without getting themselves killed."

"You're talking as if these people have common sense. It only took two days for them to turn into monsters. What makes you think there are limits on what they'll do?"

She used a paper towel from the holder to dry my arm and soak up the blood that still leaked out. After some consideration, she put two gauze pads together and wrapped two strips of tape around my arm to secure them. It felt wasteful using so many supplies for one cut, but Marlowe was determined to take care of it.

When we entered the front room again, the woman was standing in the center, looking lost. She started when we appeared but relaxed a fraction when it was clear we weren't the people that had attacked her. But she studied us closely.

"You aren't the Greens. Are you family?"

Marlowe and I shared a look before I replied. "The Greens are the family that lived here?"

The woman nodded.

"No. We aren't the Greens or family. And we didn't know them. We were just looking for somewhere safe to be," Marlowe replied.

"So you're no better than the people that killed my Bobby." She stepped back, wrapping her arms around herself.

I shook my head. "We wouldn't have come into the house if anyone was here. Marlowe got hurt, and I had to find somewhere she could rest before we kept heading toward my house."

She studied us quietly. Slowly, it seemed like her entire body deflated. Her face crumpled and tears appeared again. Marlowe rushed forward and wrapped her arms around the woman. I didn't miss the gasp that she tried to swallow as the woman's arms came into contact with her injured side.

While Marlowe comforted the woman, I thought about dinner. Searching the empty houses had yielded quite a few things and I figured we should fill our stomachs while we had the food. In the kitchen, I unpacked the backpack I had filled. In the cabinets, there were plenty of clean plates, but also a stack of paper plates. I pulled down a few.

One I filled with two different types of crackers. I poured beef jerky and mini smoked sausages on another. A third held dried apricots and freeze-dried strawberries. In the other room, I could hear murmured words. Marlowe had calmed the woman and was hopefully bringing her around to us staying in her neighbor's house. It was getting dark, and I wasn't interested in walking in the dark when anyone might follow us.

Setting the table for a touch of normalcy, I set the food in the center, as well as sodas and waters. I also added the remaining bread from lunch then I went to see if the women were ready to eat. They sat together on the couch, and Marlowe leaned back with her eyes closed. The neighbor woman looked up sharply, her eyes narrowing on me for a moment before she relaxed.

"I have food on the table. I'll grab some candles."

Marlowe opened her eyes, and she nodded. But I could see she was pale. I glanced at my watch. She had slept a good two hours before everything happened with the neighbor. She still had to wait another hour before taking another pill. I went to her, putting out my hands to help her slowly lean forward.

"What's wrong?" the neighbor asked.

"She may have cracked or broke her ribs. We aren't really sure. Didn't have a hospital we could head to," I said, giving her a small smile.

"How did that happen?"

I had Marlowe on her feet, her smile was forced when she met my eye. "Did you notice the hole in the end of the porch? We were coming from the side and she fell through."

She gasped. "Ray, the man in the photos, was trying to get homeowners' insurance to pay for the porch. Something about a rotten beam that was like that when they purchased the home. Insurance wasn't covering it, and he hadn't gotten around to fixing it himself."

"Well, I guess I'm superb at finding rotten wood." Marlowe's attempt at a joke fell flat.

We sat together at the dining table, and I lit two of the candles we had brought from the bookstore. It was enough light to eat by, if not see each other's faces all that well. Marlowe pushed the plates of food toward the woman first, but she took very little. Neither Marlowe nor I pushed her, understanding she was in a place we couldn't understand.

"I'm sorry. I realize I don't even know your name," I said.

"Oh, I should have introduced you! Cristian, this is Blair. Blair, Cristian." Marlowe motioned back and forth between us.

"Nice to meet you, Blair, despite the reason," I said.

"Thank you. I should have said that sooner." Blair's words were barely audible, which was something in an absolutely silent house.

"No thanks is necessary. I couldn't just stand by and do nothing."

We were quiet as we ate. I tried not to stare at Blair, but I noticed she barely put anything in her mouth. Marlowe carefully pushed the bottle of water toward her. Blair nodded and sipped from it before putting it down. She continued to stare off into the distance and there was no guessing what was happening in her mind.

So when she spoke, it was surprising. "Will you let me stay here with you? I can't go back to my house. Without…without Bobby there." Her head snapped toward the front door and she gasped. "I can't just leave his body in the street."

Marlowe laid a hand on her shoulder. "I'm not sure there's another option right now."

Blair looked at me. Even in the candlelight, I could see the pleading in her look. I swallowed the smoke sausage that had turned to sand in my mouth. Gulping down water to clear my throat, that seemed ready to close up, I met Marlowe's eyes across the table. She shrugged slightly, as if to tell me she didn't have an opinion.

"In the dark, there's not much I can do. But tomorrow, if you want, I can dig a grave at your house. In the backyard? It's the only thing I can offer. I don't know if there will be any services to help anytime soon. Without power, I'm not sure how we'll handle our…well, our dead." I tried to put the situation as delicate as possible, but I didn't miss the flinch on Blair's face when I finished.

She seemed to consider my offer before nodding without another word. Marlowe and I finished our food. Blair stood and wandered from the dining room into the interior of the darkened house.

"I'm going to make her a plate, to take to bed, in case she's hungry at some point," Marlowe said.

I nodded, thinking about how her compassion didn't seem to have a limit. Even when I knew she was in pain, waiting to take the next dose of meds, she was worried about a stranger. Although she and I were also strangers, tough moments had forged a connection. Emotions rose in me, but I shoved them down. There was no time for distraction.

I picked up a candle and followed Blair, finding her standing at the entrance of the hallway. Behind me, Marlowe followed with the plate and another candle.

"I'll sleep in the kids' room, if you don't mind," Blair said.

"Of course," Marlowe replied.

She walked by me, her hands full, and moved with Blair down the hallway. The door opened to the bedroom, and the light disappeared into the darkness. It was early for sleep, but with no sun and limited time with the candles, it made little sense to stay up for hours. And after everything I had been through during the day, I was exhausted. Sleep would come easy.

I went to the front room and pulled one shade back from the window. My eyes played tricks on me as I tried to concentrate and see if there was anyone sneaking up on us. A light in the sky caught my attention, and I craned my neck. The first thing I hoped for was a plane or helicopter, anything to show that the world hadn't completely stopped. I couldn't get a good enough look, so I rushed to the front door, just as Marlowe came out of the hallway.

"What is it?" she asked.

"Something in the sky."

"The auroras again?"

I nodded but added, "And something else. I need to get a better look."

"I'm coming with you."

Without me agreeing, she came to the door and opened it. I pushed my hand against it and looked down at her. I lifted the candle I was holding a little, so she could see my face.

"Maybe you should stay inside?"

Marlowe entered the circle of my candlelight. Her face was sad, and she wouldn't meet my eyes. "I'm not staying in here without you. It's dark. And you have no idea what you saw."

I didn't have the energy to argue with her. And leaving her in the house alone with a stranger, albeit a mourning one, wasn't something I wanted to do either. Together, we slowly stepped outside. I looked up and down the street, watching for any sort of movement that would indicate we had a threat nearby.

"Oh my god," Marlowe breathed next to me.

I glanced at her, thinking she'd seen something I didn't. But she wasn't looking at the street or nearby shadows. Her face was directed upward toward the sky. Following her example, I turned and looked up. The sky was lit with a similar aurora to what we had seen every night since everything started. A deep red with violet and pink dancing within it. At the edges, the colors faded out to blues and greens. It was still a shock to see something so vibrant in Oregon. But that wasn't the shocking thing.

"Are they falling stars?" Marlowe asked.

"I don't think so?" I had no idea what we were seeing.

They weren't small and didn't disappear like a shooting star. Instead, the objects would fall, then there would be a flash of fire before it continued into the atmosphere. I had never seen a meteor myself, but I didn't think this was what they looked like.

"Do you think something will fall on us?" Marlowe looked around anxiously.

I shook my head, watching the fire balls for a few more moments. Something suddenly occurred to me, and I tried to pull the knowledge together in my mind.

I swallowed hard, my throat suddenly dry. "If this was caused by a solar flare—an EMP-like event—then I think I know what those are."

She followed my gaze upward. "What?"

"Satellites." The word sat heavy in my chest. "They're falling to Earth."

Marlowe blinked, like she wasn't sure she'd heard me right. "Out of space? Seriously?"

She stared at me, waiting for me to tell her it wasn't as bad as it sounded. But I couldn't.

Her voice was quieter when she spoke. "That means..."

"That means we've lost everything." I forced the words out,

each one hitting harder than the last. "GPS. Internet. Cell service. Weather tracking. Defense systems. Even if the power comes back, none of that will."

I nodded, the realization pressing down on me like a weight I couldn't shake. "And if satellites are failing... that means this wasn't just Oregon. It wasn't just the U.S." I exhaled slowly. "This was global."

Marlowe let out a dry, disbelieving laugh, but there was no humor in it. "I feel like I'm living in the goddamn Twilight Zone. Next thing you're gonna tell me is that zombies are around the corner, ready to eat my brains."

I didn't laugh. Because as much as I wanted to say something reassuring, I couldn't. Instead, I turned and headed for the house, holding the door open for her. She followed, silent now. I locked the door behind us, my grip tightening on the handle. Losing everything we knew? That was bad enough. But not knowing what was still out there? That was worse.

I didn't mention any of these things to Marlowe. With her injury and the arrival of Blair, she had enough to worry about. We walked to the entrance of the hall, both looking at the closed door where Blair had gone to sleep.

"I guess that leaves us with the main bedroom," I said.

Marlowe nodded and turned toward the room. Inside, I knew there were two tapered candles on the dresser. They were likely meant to be ornamental, but they would be useful now. I used the candle in my hand to light the two tapers, taking one to each of the nightstands.

When I turned toward Marlowe, I saw she was in tears. Rushing forward, I took her hands from her face and tilted her chin up so I could see her eyes. "Is the pain bad? You can take a pill now. It won't hurt anything."

"It will probably help me sleep. I'm going to need something, because I feel like I'm just going to be left with nightmares all night. Today was horrible."

"I know. But we made it through another day. Even if there were moments where we didn't think we would, we did."

"To do what? Get up tomorrow and do it all over again? And know it's just going to get worse."

She pulled away from me and paced. I stayed where I was, letting her get out the emotions roiling inside her.

"Blair did nothing but leave her house and her husband was killed. She had a husband. They had wanted to start a family before all of this. And they never got the chance." She spun toward me, pointing to herself wildly. "I've done nothing with my life. Nothing! I'm a shift manager at a freaking Target. I've never had a relationship longer than a month since I settled in Oregon. And the only person who cares about me is hundreds of miles away and is likely not going to make it through this."

A sob tore through her, and I couldn't keep myself from reaching out to her. Carefully, I wrapped my arms around her shoulders, avoiding her injury and bringing her head to my chest. She cried. I could feel the warmth of her tears on my skin as they soaked through the fabric of my shirt. The disaster we were living amplified the sadness she was feeling. But I had a feeling these were emotions she had suffered through alone before everything fell to pieces.

ELEVEN

Thinking about my mother made my chest feel like it was going to crack in half. It was worse pain than my ribs. As I stood with my face pressed into Cristian's chest, all I could think of was what we were going to do next. Where was my mother? Who was holding her through the pain as the cancer continued to ravage her body?

Cristian said nothing as my sobbing finally slowed and I could take a deep breath. His arms were warm and comforting around my shoulders. Suddenly, I realized my own arms were around his waist, gripping his t-shirt. As I calmed down, I eased my hands open and released the material.

"Sorry."

"I figure we'll both have breakdowns eventually," Cristian said.

"You're just being kind. You don't seem to be fazed easily." I pulled back, but he didn't completely release me. His eyes bore into mine, a thoughtful look on his face.

"I'm realizing that you feel things much deeper than anyone I've ever met. And we're in the middle of what I would call a damn apocalypse. It makes sense you'd be a little upset."

I sniffled and looked away. It was embarrassing how he saw

me in a way no one else ever did. Probably because with everything happening, I didn't have the strength to hide the heart on my sleeve. I scrubbed at my face, forcing myself to push everything back into a neat little box I kept it all in. At the bed, I sat and started to bend for my shoes. Pain shot through my side, and I gasped. The sudden movement of straightening made the pain throb, and I was ready to cry all over again.

Cristian knelt and took one of my booted feet in his hands. Deftly, he untied it and slid it from my foot, then repeated the process on the other. His hand then appeared with a dose of meds, and an unopened bottle of water. I had no idea where he pulled them from, but it was like he always had what I needed. I swallowed the pills, and he helped me lie back on the same side of the bed I had napped on.

He blew out the candle on my side of the bed, before going to the other side and snuffing that one as well. I felt the bed shift as he climbed onto the mattress. An awkward silence seemed to stretch between us. Without the sounds of engines, lawnmowers or people, the world felt like it only existed in the room we were in.

I cleared my throat. "So, you don't have any family waiting for you? Anyone that would wonder if you're safe?"

Cristian was quiet for so long, I thought he might have fallen asleep. But he shifted and moved until his shoulder pressed against mine. "No. Like I mentioned, my parents are gone. I lost my only brother when I was a kid. My family was never really close to any extended family. And well, I doubt my ex-wife cares much."

"Ex-wife?" I couldn't mask the shock in my voice.

Cristian chuckled darkly. "I guess there was no chance to mention that. Yeah, we divorced a while ago. She lives in Washington, or did, with her boyfriend."

"I'm sorry." It was the only thing I could think to say.

"Don't be. It wasn't completely her fault. I was always too busy with work to really be a good husband. Granted, there should have been other ways to handle our problems, but divorce is what happened. It was the best thing for her."

"What about you?"

I felt his shoulder move, as if he had shrugged. "It wasn't about me."

"Marriage is about two people. And so is the divorce. Seems you should be allowed to have feelings about that."

"I had plenty of feelings about it for some time. But it was best to let that all go. I made a lot of mistakes and came to terms with that."

I struggled to imagine Cristian making mistakes bad enough to want him out of my life. I wondered if this could be a form of Stockholm Syndrome. As he talked about his ex-wife, I immediately felt on the defense for him. And I barely knew anything about him. But when he mentioned his mistakes, I could feel his regret in those words.

"People make mistakes all the time. If you really love someone, you work through those and try again. Or at least that's what I always thought." I wasn't speaking from any experience personally.

Even during my childhood, when my mother would date, she never brought men around me. I didn't learn anything about healthy relationships. My mom would lecture me when I dated boys as a teenager. Mutual respect was one of her highest requirements in a relationship. I had always wondered if men didn't agree with her, since she never got married or had a long-term relationship.

"My parents were like that. They never went to bed angry. Always talked through everything. I remember them laughing together all the time. Sarah and I had nothing like that."

"It must have been great to grow up in a family like that."

He shifted again. With the shades all closed, there wasn't even the ambient light of the moon to see his face. But I was sure he was lying on his side, facing me, even though there was no way he could see me either.

"You only have your mom?" He asked, though he knew the answer. It was him opening the door to the conversation, without blurting out that I was a loser for not having a family.

"Yeah. It was just the two of us. All my life."

"I think in some ways, that might have been a pretty good life, too."

I thought about the best way to put it. "It wasn't a bad life, by any means. My mom worked hard to give me everything she could. But when she got sick the first time, everything changed. I was a teenager in high school. I had to drive her to and from appointments. My school gave me a lot of leeway, allowing me to do things online and turn in work late."

"That sounds like a lot of pressure for a teenager."

I was the one to shrug this time. My mom's friends had often complimented me for the sacrifices I made to help my mom. To me, it wasn't sacrifice. "I didn't think of it that way." I finally said.

"How did you think of it?"

His question took me aback. No one had ever asked me how I felt about what was happening. They assumed everything, and I never contradicted. Looking like an ungrateful child after everything my mother had done for me was one of my biggest fears. My other, was losing my mother.

"I thought that if I didn't do it, who would? Without her treatments, I would have been completely alone in the world. And I wasn't ready to face that as a sixteen-year-old." His hand found mine in the dark. The reassuring squeeze helped me continue. "I felt so selfish for being angry that cancer stole my teenage years. I would be so mad at myself for my feelings when she would barely eat at dinner, because she would just throw it all up. As she wasted away to the skinniest, I had ever seen her, I thought the guilt would kill me."

"You were just a kid."

"Sure. It was a lot to carry. But my mom never made me feel like I had to do it. When she found out it came back last year, she never once asked me to come home. She never said she needed me. On the phone, she rarely wants to talk about how her treatments are going or what the doctors say. I think she feels bad about how things went when I was younger. And something about that makes me feel even worse." I snorted at that. "It's an all-around confusing, messed up story."

Cristian pulled the blanket over us as the evening cooled. But he didn't move away from me. My confessions came out easily, as we lay in the dark. Without the chance to see him judge me, I felt free with my feelings. It was a foreign feeling for me. I revealed myself to him, but he remained silent.

"Thank you," I whispered.

His deep intake of air made me feel a little nervous. But he just squeezed my hand and laid his head on his pillow. "Let's get some sleep. Being able to do things during the sunlight hours is going to change our sleep schedules."

I laughed lightly, trying not to move too much. "I worked evening shifts. And that made me a night owl. It's going to be a big adjustment for me."

"My shifts sometimes rotated, but I was mostly on a swing shift, which made me a night owl, too." He yawned before continuing. "But I think we keep using so much energy during the day, we'll easily fall into a pattern."

I felt a yawn trying to bubble up, but I tried to keep my lungs from fully inflating. Broken bones were something I had never experienced. Even as a kid, I was never into riding a bike or roller blading. I got the normal skinned knees, but had never broken anything. Cristian mentioned they could just be bruised, which would be a much better option. It would get us back on the road faster.

As Cristian had predicted, it didn't take too long to fall asleep. His breathing deepened before mine and it was almost the white noise that I needed to shut out the silence of everything else. Living in an apartment complex meant there were always voices, the sounds of footsteps, the slamming of doors. And that became what you knew and the melody by which you slept.

But staying asleep was a different situation. I rolled in my sleep, only to be woken by shooting pain in my side and gasping for air. Cristian woke up quickly and helped me shift me into a less painful position. The pain didn't just disappear, but throbbed like a wave through my middle. He helped re-wrap the bandage, taking some of the pressure off, but it didn't stop the pain completely.

Falling back to sleep was difficult. And I knew my issues were making it hard for Cristian. But he never complained. When slivers of light peeked around the shades, I was wide awake, staring at the ceiling. Earlier, I had tried to get up on my own. But after two unsuccessful attempts, I stopped trying. I wanted Cristian to sleep as long as possible.

"Good morning." His voice was gravel and handsome, which was ridiculous for me to think in the situation we were in. How could a voice be handsome?

"Morning." My voice was full of false cheer. When Cristian propped himself up on a hand, his eyes told me he knew I was faking it.

"Did you get much sleep?" he asked.

I was going to lie, but he watched me too closely. He saw too much. So I just looked at the ceiling and said nothing.

"Ok. Well, we aren't going anywhere today. You'll be able to nap."

I shook my head. "We could go. I can walk."

Cristian climbed from the bed and moved around it to come to my side. He put out his hands and easily pulled me to a sitting position. I held my breath the whole time, feeling the pain as it intensified. I repeated the phrase over and over in my head that I could handle it, I could handle all of it, if it got us on the road.

"There's no rush, Marlowe. You're in pain. Trying to hide it, but I can tell. Why are you trying to push?"

He bent and helped me slide my boots back onto my feet. He took the time to adjust all the laces until they were comfortably snug and tied. All I could do was stare down at his dark, wavy hair that didn't look like he had slept on it.

"I don't want to hold us up."

He stood and held out his hands again. Once I was on my feet, he held both of my hands in his and squeezed until I looked up at him.

"There's nowhere for us to be, except safe. And right now, we're ok. So let's stay that way and you can get a bit more rest. It's ok, Marlowe."

I was still unsure, but his eyes were so sincere. He looked at me again, like he was picking my brain apart. Reading me like a well-worn book he was learning page by page.

"Sometimes it's ok to think about yourself, put yourself first."

His intense gaze made me look away. There was a lot I never truly faced, never saw a therapist or talked about. And I had poured a lot of that out to Cristian in the dark while we lain together in bed. It made me feel awkward and wide open for him to see. He understood things about me no one other than my mom had seen. I wasn't sure how I felt about that.

We made our way to the front room. It was empty and quiet, and I glanced at the closed door where Blair had slept. Cristian made his way to the kitchen, and I followed. I wasn't sure I could just sit around and do nothing all day, no matter how much movement hurt. He had unpacked the food he found in the other houses, and I found him looking through cans. Turning toward me, he held up two.

"Chicken noodle or chicken noodle?"

I laughed. "Man, the options are just so hard to handle."

He grinned and started preparing breakfast. The stainless steel pot we'd used the day before now had a black bottom from being over the fire, the inside was clean and ready to warm our next meal. I took the pot from Cristian while he started a fire in the fireplace.

Setting the pot on the bricks in front of the fireplace, he straightened and found me watching him.

"I'm going to go outside. Check the perimeter of the house and see if anything has changed overnight. I doubt it, but just in case."

"I can come, too."

He tilted his head at me. "If I need to run, can you keep up?"

I grimaced and brought my arm up along my injured side. I opened my mouth, but snapped it shut when I realized I really had no defense.

His hand came up and rested lightly on my shoulder. "It's ok, Marlowe. I've got this. I'll be back in just a few minutes."

I walked with him toward the front door. He checked through the front windows first and he nodded to me as he opened the door and slowly walked out.

"Be careful," I called quietly.

"Yes, ma'm," he replied with a smirk.

I closed the door once he disappeared around the side of the house. Inside, it was uncomfortably quiet. I made my way to the front bay windows, where Cristian had pulled up an armchair. The corner of one shade was propped up and when I sat, I could see a portion of the street. My foot kicked something, and I looked down to find a book.

Holding my breath, I carefully reached for it. When I straightened, I was gasping, and the pain was red hot again. I cursed silently, angry at being injured. Though it had only been a day, I was tired of being in pain. It was just an added layer to all the worries I felt.

I read the back of the book, finding a sci-fi story I wouldn't typically read. There was a piece of paper marking a page early in the book. I opened up to that spot and started reading, not really caring about the story itself. After a little while, I heard movement in the house. Assuming it was Blair, I kept reading and didn't hassle the woman. I wasn't sure how to comfort a woman that had lost her husband in such a horrific manner. But I was pretty sure being on top of her all day wasn't the way to do it.

She didn't come looking for me, and the house was silent

again. I thought maybe I'd just imagined the sounds until the crack of a gunshot rang through the house like a whip.

The sound split the silence. My breath hitched. My knees locked. My brain screamed at me to move, but my body wouldn't obey. A strangled noise clawed its way out of my throat, somewhere between a gasp and a sob. My heart slammed so hard against my ribs, I could barely breathe through the pain.

I rushed out of the front room, still gripping the novel in my hands. It wasn't a weapon, but I held it close as if it would keep me safe. The first thing I noticed was the door to the children's room was now open. Glancing inside, I found it empty. The sheets on the twin sized bed had been thrown back and Blair's sneakers lay on the ground next to the bed. Her pack was at the foot of the bed, unzipped, but still packed.

Looking down the hall, I could see the door to the main bedroom open, and I tried to remember if we had closed it when we came out in the morning. Carefully, I walked toward it. As I was about to enter, I heard the front door burst open and slam shut. Pressing myself against the wall, I waited. Cristian came bounding down the hall, and I breathed a sigh of relief.

"Marlowe? What was that?"

I shook my head, looking back toward the bedroom door. "I don't know. I was looking for Blair."

"Did you see her? Talk to her?"

"No. I don't know where she is."

Cristian looked beyond me. Setting his hands on my shoulders, he squeezed and moved me to be behind him. "Go back to the front room, Marlowe."

"What? Why? I can help you look for her."

He looked back at me; his grim mouth was set, his face pale. "Please. Just go back to the front room. I don't want you to see this."

I started to push by him, not understanding why he was acting so strange. "See what? Don't be silly, Cristian."

He grabbed my arm as I tried to go by and pulled me to him. I looked up at him in alarm. During the few days we had been together, he had always been thoughtful in the ways he touched me or helped me. Now, his grip was steel, and he wasn't allowing me to budge. My confusion turned to fear as I waited for him to say something or release me.

"I know where Blair is. And you don't need to see what I'm going to see. There was only one bullet left in that gun. The gun I left inside the nightstand on my side of the bed."

His words sank in, and the implication was clear. I looked over my shoulder into the darkened bedroom. My stomach turned and everything seemed to slow. When I looked back up at Cristian, he nodded once, reading my thoughts as they crossed my face.

"She lost her husband," I whispered, the words sticking in my throat. My chest tightened, bile rising again. My own voice sounded distant, hollow. Clenching my hands into fists, my nails dug into my palms. "I should have checked on her. I should have done something."

Cristian's grip softened, and he again steered me toward the opposite end of the hall. I stopped again and looked at him. "You don't have to do this alone."

His face took on a knowing look, one that had seen many other things that were too much of some to handle. "This isn't new for me. I can handle it. I don't want you to have to. I'll be out in just a minute."

With that, he trusted me to not follow him. He disappeared into the darkness, and I watched, unable to force myself to follow. My stomach churned, and I rushed into the hall bathroom. Ignoring the pain in my side, I bent over the toilet and wretched. There wasn't much to come up, but my body expelled it all.

Gentle hands pulled my hair from my face. I couldn't seem to stop being ill and I started to drop to my knees. Cristian's arm came around my waist, careful not to crush my ribs, and slowly lowered us both to the ground. Once it was clear I wasn't throwing up any more, he lowered the toilet lid and flushed it. No water filled the tank, but the reminder of my vomit was washed away. He used the last toilet flush to hide my weakness.

A hand towel came into view. He thought of everything. Taking it from his hands, I wiped at my mouth before speaking. "Did she?"

"Yes."

"Oh god. I should have gone to talk to her when I thought I heard the bedroom door open." Tears slid down my cheeks as I imagined her last moments. Feeling alone and helpless.

"This isn't your fault. I don't think anything could have stopped her for long. If anything, it's my fault for not keeping the gun with me. I didn't imagine…" he trailed off.

I was sure he could imagine quite a lot. But the world wasn't what either of us knew. It wasn't the same one he served and protected, following a set of agreed upon laws. Now, anything could happen. Anything had happened. And though he used to be the one that prevented those things from happening, he had to endure them all now.

"Neither of us did. Her grief was more than she could handle." I leaned back into his embrace, realizing I hadn't felt alone since the power stopped. No, I'd had Cristian the entire time.

"I guess she didn't think surviving was worth it without her husband. She never mentioned if they had any other family nearby," he said.

I just shook my head in agreement. We hadn't really talked about anything beyond what had happened to her and her husband on the street.

"Did you see that a lot before?" I didn't want to say the word suicide. Saying the word out loud made it feel too real, too painful.

Tension caused the arm around my shoulders to go rigid. He cradled me carefully against his chest, where I could feel the beating of his heart. When he took a deep breath, it seemed to relax his limbs.

"It happened, yeah. It was never easy to see, or to talk to the families after. The worst ones were when we had to go to notify a family of a death in that manner. There are some I can never forget."

I put my hands on his forearm that lay across my chest. Squeezing, I tried to infuse him with my support. "That's horrible."

"Yes. It was. I have always told myself that it was better for the families to know than have questions about what happened. But that doesn't change the pain they feel. And there's always a lot of why's."

An image popped into my head of Cristian catching a woman wailing about losing her husband. It wasn't hard to picture. He had been nothing but supportive and reliable since we met. However, I was sure Cristian hid his emotions carefully. Because he didn't want to burden someone else, or didn't want to look weak. It didn't matter to me. He supported me and I needed to support him.

We sat on the floor in a comforting silence. I held on tightly to his forearm and his thumb rubbed up and down my arm. He didn't push for me to get moving, to get up, to get over it. No, he sat with me, held me, until I was ready to face what was happening around us.

"We can't stay here," I finally said. The idea of even sleeping under the roof with Blair's dead body in the bedroom was more than I could handle.

"Do you think you can walk? At least until we find a safe neighborhood?"

The fact that he agreed so easily told me he was just as bothered by the idea of staying in the house as I was.

"Yes. I might not be able to carry a pack, but I don't want to stay here."

He unfurled his body from behind me, climbing to his feet. I immediately felt cold, where his warmth disappeared from my back. He held out his hands and helped me to my feet. My side screamed in fury, and I didn't admit to Cristian that black spots dotted my vision for more than a second. When he looked down at me, I pasted on the best sad smile I could muster.

In the hallway, I found Cristian had already brought out the two packs we had been adding to. They had been inside the bedroom, Blair's ultimate resting place. I couldn't stop myself from looking at the door. He had closed it, though that didn't make it any easier. I could still picture the scene inside.

With one more glance at me, Cristian picked up the packs and went back to the front of the house. At the door, I hesitated. My gaze drifted toward Blair's room, where the silence was heavier than anywhere else in the house.

"I'm sorry," I whispered. Not that she could hear me. Not that it mattered. But I needed to say it, anyway.

Then I turned, following Cristian down the hall. Even as we stepped into the morning light, that shone through the living room windows, I knew the shadows of this house would follow me forever.

CHAPTER
TWELVE
CRISTIAN

I was quiet as I packed the food items I had left out in the kitchen. There was no knowing where we would end up or if we would find anything else. The fire I had started before checking the outside was burned down to the embers we would have needed to cook the soup. Instead, we stood together, slowly eating cold soup from the pot with spoons.

My stomach revolted against the food. Blair's body flashed across my mind's eye. The way she'd folded in on herself, the blood soaking through the sheets. I clenched my jaw and shoved the memory down. There was nothing I could've done. I knew that. But knowing didn't make it easier. I didn't stay to study the blood or position of her body. I'd only checked for a pulse, which put me closer to her than I would have really liked.

Marlowe's face scrunched as she put a small spoonful of soup in her mouth. I could imagine her stomach was feeling worse than mine. To encourage her, I continued to eat. Somehow, we got down to scraping the bottom of the pot. I offered her the last bite, but she shook her head and dropped her spoon in the sink.

I filled both packs with anything we could possibly need while on the road. At the door, I pulled the hiking pack from REI onto my back. I then put the smaller pack from the garage on my front

Marlowe looked at me with a pained expression. "I'm sorry."

"You were the one that broke the decking, huh? I knew it. You just wanted some sympathy."

She stared at me. I had been told that my humor was too dry and unusual for people to really get when I was joking. I didn't even look at her as I spoke, adjusting straps on the packs. She then let out a little giggle and my gaze found hers.

"So, you can be funny."

I shrugged, surprised that she even realized I was joking. "You don't need to be sorry. We'll manage."

It was midmorning when we stepped outside. Looking up, we could see nothing falling from the sky. What concerned me were the dark clouds rolling in. Marlowe's brows drew together as she looked up.

"I can't remember what the weather report was for the week," she muttered.

"Weather reports weren't accurate even before the world ended."

That garnered a snort from Marlowe.

We would need to walk in the opposite direction of the clouds, but they'd be on top of us before we knew it. Yet there was no way we were staying in the neighborhood. I started walking, but let Marlowe set the pace. It was clear she was determined to move fast, despite the pain she was likely in.

The wind picked up first, pulling at our clothes and causing Marlow's hair to come loose from her hair tie. It whipped across her face, and she kept trying to push it out of the way. We stopped once, so I could help her pull it back more securely. I looked up at the clouds that were now overhead. They darkened with the smoke that had swirled through the sky and met them high above our heads.

"Storm's here," I said, stating the obvious.

Oregon was normally dry during the month of July, but there were always occasional summer storms. The problem with those was they were sudden and could dump inches of rain in short periods of time. If the sun caused the solar flare which killed all the power, I wasn't sure the weather would even be predictable.

Twenty minutes later, the rain hit all at once. The skies opened and wept, dumping buckets of huge droplets down on us. The sound was deafening, rain hitting rooftops and abandoned vehicles. A river of water flowed down gutters, carrying debris that clogged the drains. Within moments, my clothes clung to my body, and the rain plastered Marlowe's hair to her face.

"We need to find cover," I called.

We had only walked a couple of miles since leaving the house. Between being buffeted by the wind and the torrential rain, the storm slowed us down. The rain chilled us, far colder than it had any right to be on a summer day.

I put my hand on Marlowe's arm, to make sure she didn't trip over any of the debris that was blocking the sidewalk. I felt her shiver and knew we needed to find shelter fast. Being cold and injured was going to make movement even more difficult.

My breath fogged the air as the rain pulled down the summer heat. I spotted a carport next to a warehouse and we rushed over to it. The rain falling on the metal roof was loud, even louder than normal after the silence of the three days.

Slinging off the backpacks, I dropped them to the ground before pulling Marlowe into my arms. Her entire body was shaking. I rubbed carefully up and down her back, using friction to warm her skin. Being careful of her injured side, I drew her into me and she wrapped her arms around my back.

"Yesterday, I would have loved to feel cold. Now I'm freezing and I hate it," she said.

I nodded, my cheek resting against her head. "We aren't used to dealing with temperature without power."

Lifting my head, I looked at the building next to us. Along the long expanse of concrete wall there were two doors and no windows. Marlowe's shivering worsened, and I needed to get her somewhere out of the rain, where she could take off the wet clothes and get warm.

"I need to check the other side of the building. Maybe there's a front door, something open. We need to get inside." As I spoke, a gust of wind blew the rain sideways, and we were drenched again.

Marlowe nodded, but seemed reluctant to let go. I was hesitant, too. Her needs came first, but I was cold, and it was better keeping her close. Instead of letting go completely, I reshouldered the packs and slung an arm around her shoulders. Keeping her tucked into my side, I guided us down the wall of the building. She turned her face and buried it in my chest, hiding from the slanting rain.

Around the front, as I had hoped, there was a wall of windows and a front door. But when I yanked on the door, it didn't open. I examined the lock, but didn't think I could get us in so we continued past the lobby.

I had my eye on the next building over. If we could get to the other side, we would be out of the direct path of the wind.

"Wait! Hello?!"

A voice from behind us, carried on the wind, caused me to spin. Again, I went for a gun I wasn't wearing on my belt. Marlowe gasped in pain as I pulled her with me. I steadied her with the arm around her shoulders, figuring I would apologize later.

At the door of the warehouse, an elderly man stood with the door propped open. He waved us over with one hand, while the other was shielding his face from the rain.

"What do you think?" Marlowe's teeth chattered as she spoke, telling me we had little choice.

I hesitated. The warehouse looked intact, but that didn't mean it was safe. I scanned the doorframe, the ground for fresh footprints, anything that screamed trap. Nothing.

Marlowe shivered violently against me.

"We need to get inside."

We moved toward the man and when we got to the doors, he moved inside and let us in. He shook his head, causing water droplets to fly from his gray hair. He turned his bright blue eyes on us and a friendly smile.

"You two look like wet rats," he said.

"We probably feel that way too," Marlowe replied with a small smile of her own.

I studied the hunched man. At a guess, he looked to be around seventy years old. His jeans were dirty, but he was dry and didn't look like he'd been suffering since the power went out. Short, with a slight hunch, he'd pulled his long, gray hair into a ponytail at the base of his head. The hunchback made him appear even shorter.

Marlowe and I dripped onto the dry entry rug. The lobby was dimly lit by the gray light that filtered through the front windows. But the back of the lobby was almost pitch black. There were two waiting areas with small coffee tables and chairs and couches surrounding. The tables were littered with empty bottles, paper bags, and food wrappers. The couches each had bedding on them.

"How many people are here?" I asked.

The man opened his mouth, but a voice from the back of the lobby interrupted him. A light came through the door, illuminating the face of an elderly woman.

"Harold! Don't leave those poor kids soaked and freezing. Bring them in the back!"

"Yes, dear." The man rolled his eyes with a smile.

The woman, no taller than the old man, came toward them and gave Harold a disapproving look. She was the epitome of a little old grandma. She wore a floral apron over her clothing, with a short cap of gray hair that seemed to naturally curl at the ends. She looked at Marlowe and me. "I apologize for my husband. I'm not sure what he's thinking. You two probably want to change out of those clothes. This is Harold." She gestured toward the man. "And I'm Carol."

"It's really nice to meet you. Thank you for opening the door," Marlowe replied.

"It was only luck that Harold here was doing his daily walk

around the warehouse and he saw you. We keep ourselves in the back, mostly." Carol motioned in the direction she came from.

"Are there more people back there?" I didn't get an answer to my question originally, and I wasn't looking to walk into a situation blind. Especially not with Marlowe freezing and injured.

"We have fifteen right now. Well, seventeen with you two added."

Marlowe patted my arm and gave Carol a knowing smile. "This is Cristian. He's a sheriff's deputy. He asks a lot of questions." I looked down at her with a frown, but she just flashed me a bright smile. "I'm Marlowe. We were headed toward Tualatin, but traveling in this rain doesn't seem like a good idea."

Carol came over and took one of Marlowe's hands in hers. "Oh, you poor dears. Of course, traveling by foot right now isn't possible. Come with me. I'll get you something dry. We have plenty of clothing in the back."

I stayed close behind Marlowe, as Carol pulled her through the lobby and into the warehouse. I'm not sure what I expected, but the open boxes lining the sides of the large room were not it. My eyes strained to see what was actually going on inside. Harold caught up with me and noticed my gaze.

"This was a shipping warehouse. Some sort of small shipping company. The boxes have had all sorts of products, from cookware, to clothing, to electronics that don't work. Carol and I have a place not far from here. We were on our way there when we saw people inside. We decided to stay. Better than being along, eh?"

As I had met none of the other people, I couldn't quite agree with his sentiment. I just grunted in response, hoping that would be enough. Ahead, I could see a general glow of light. Movement in and out of the light cast shadows around. The building had high skylights, but on the gloomy day, there was hardly any light coming through. Though, I wasn't sure even on the sunniest day, those windows would really do any good.

When we approached the group of people, all talking seemed to stop. Shadowed faces turned toward us and froze. Carol walked us directly to the center of the group, where several candles were lit. We were lit up for everyone to see. I pulled Marlowe to my side, keeping her close against the chance this was actually a dangerous situation. I didn't get a bad feeling from Harold or Carol, but there was no knowing.

Carol clapped her hands together to call attention. "Everyone! This is Cristian and Marlowe. The poor kids were trying to walk through the storm out there. And we just couldn't leave them. Katherine, do me a favor and warm up some water. I'm sure some hot tea would do them good. I'll take them to the clothing so they can change."

A tall, slender woman stepped closer to us. She was young, probably near Marlowe's age. She had red hair that was wrapped in some sort of bun on the top of her head. Shadows played across her face, but I could tell she was studying us. I tried to give her a small smile when Marlowe squeezed my hand, as if trying to give me some sort of direction. I wasn't sure what she was trying to tell me, but the woman named Katherine was entirely too interested in us.

Carol gestured for us to follow her, and she led the way with a single candle. The light didn't spread far. I held onto Marlowe to ensure she didn't trip and fall on something unseen. We turned a corner, and Carol took a moment to light a few candles that were on tables set in a square. In the center were boxes with clothing heaped on them.

"We haven't really sorted through anything, so the sizes and items are all mixed. But help yourself to anything you need. When you're ready, just use one of the candles to come back to us. I think someone is making a late lunch, if you're hungry?"

"Famished. Thank you," Marlowe said. I could hear her teeth chattering as she tried to put on a cheerful face.

Carol excused herself. Marlowe stood, shivering in the middle of the circle of tables, and looked around uncertainly. I went to the nearest box and pulled a few things out until I found a t-shirt that would fit me. I found another that was just a little bigger than

Marlowe. When I turned with them in my hands, she was still standing, her arms wrapped around her middle.

"I...can't...get my shirt off," she muttered.

Taking the hem of her shirt, I pulled it up just slightly. "See if you can pull your arms in, instead of raising them over your head."

Slowly, she pulled one arm through the hole and then the other. Once the shirt was around her neck, I looked at her for permission before continuing. She nodded, and I carefully pulled it over her head. I took a moment and laid the wet material out. Returning to Marlowe, I bent and untied her boots.

"My feet stayed dry, thanks to the great boots you got me," she said.

I glanced up, and she smiled down at me. As my eyes traveled down her bare skin, I caught sight of something that chilled me far more than the rain. Standing, I pulled Marlowe closer to the candles.

"Cristian, what—"

Marlowe sucked in a sharp breath as I lifted her arm away from her body. My stomach twisted.

Purple and black bruises stretched across her ribs, deeper than I expected. Guilt tightened around my chest like a vise.

"Jesus, Marlowe," I murmured, brushing my fingers carefully near the worst of it. "How long has it been like this?"

Marlowe looked down and tried to move in the light to see things more clearly. "I don't really know. I haven't looked since we wrapped it."

"I'm worried about internal bleeding. I need to feel around it and have you tell me where the worst pain is."

Marlowe nodded, and I pushed slightly on the bruising on her stomach. She didn't flinch. I moved more toward her side and her breathing increased just slightly. Carefully, I moved up her side, avoiding touching her ribs directly. When I finished, she sighed in relief.

"I think it's mostly just around the ribs. My stomach feels

bruised, but didn't hurt worse than that. It hurts the most near my ribs."

"We can't just get an ice pack. I'm worried about swelling. Maybe they have some ibuprofen or something that would help with that."

Marlowe grabbed the hand I was running over her bruise and pulled until my eyes moved to look into hers. "You worry a lot. I'm doing ok. I promise, I'll tell you if it gets too bad. Maybe we can find something to wrap around me again. That did help."

She smiled, and I tried to picture the freckles I knew sprinkled her face, but couldn't see in the limited candle light. I brought my free hand up and cupped her cheek. Guilt settled in my stomach. I never should have allowed her to get injured under my watch. Her smile had fallen away, and she watched me closely.

"This isn't your fault, Cristian."

I just stared at her, wondering for a moment if I had spoken out loud. But no, she had just been able to see on my face what I was thinking.

Shaking my head, I caressed her cheek with my thumb for a second before pulling away. "I should have protected you better. First Don, then the deck. I'm failing at this whole keeping you safe thing. Which is hard, because it was literally my job to keep people safe."

"That was with a gun, a car, power and an understanding of what was going on in the world. None of that applies anymore. And really, this isn't your job. This is survival. And we're both still breathing." She grimaced for a moment before continuing, "Even if it's a bit harder for one of us to do that."

When she smiled at her joke, I had to chuckle. "Let's get you in dry clothes. Last thing I need is you catching your death."

After helping her out of her shoes and wet jeans, I slid a clean t-shirt over her head, helping her feed her arms through the holes. The sweats I found were slightly big, but she tied the string and rolled them a few times. Once she had her shoes back on, she spun like a fashion model and posed, making me laugh again.

I changed quickly and found Marlowe trying not to watch me out of the corner of her eye. In my mind, I would admit I had gotten an eye full of her body. But I forced myself to be clinical and not listen to the male instincts that had suddenly come awake in my head. Instincts I had ignored since my divorce, as I threw myself into every other aspect of my life instead of women.

Marlowe was beautiful. I had known that the moment I met her in the courthouse. That hadn't been the reason I brought her with me. But it wasn't something I could completely ignore. Especially not as she clung to my arm as we carefully made our way back to the group. The little hands that wrapped around my bicep were warm and comforting on my chilled skin. I felt distracted by her nearness, now that we weren't running for our lives or braving a torrential downpour.

"Oh, you're back!"

The woman named Katherine came bounding toward us and I stopped short. Marlowe took one step forward to greet the woman, but Katherine bypassed her and came to stand uncomfortably close to me. I saw Marlowe's eyes widen as she looked at Katherine and then to me and back again. Her mind was working, and I could see she was weighing her options and also trying to figure out what I wanted her to do.

"We have hot water ready to make tea for you, Cristian."

Her attention was making me uncomfortable. And in that moment, I realized it was women like this, after Sarah left, that made me not want to try dating. Women that saw me and decided I was some sort of catch for them to reel in. I had no desire to deal with women who didn't care to get to know me. Katherine seemed to be one of those.

Deciding for us both, I moved around Katherine and took Marlowe's hand in my own. "Thank you. We'd both love a chance to warm up."

Marlowe sent me a soft smile and squeezed my hand. I pulled her close so I could whisper in her ear. "Thanks."

"She's on the hunt," she whispered back.

"Doesn't seem like the right time for that," I mumbled.

Marlowe looked over her shoulder at Katherine, following us. Her gaze was soft and kind. "She's scared. You look like a good option for safety." Her eyes found mine in the dim light. "That's why I'm keeping you around."

And then she actually winked at me. Winked.

Carol was standing near a camp stove that had a teakettle on the top. It was making a slight whistling sound. Turning toward us with mugs, she held out two tea bags.

"There's no sugar or anything, but luckily someone was getting tea from China," she said.

I took the mugs, and Marlowe opened each of the tea bags. Carol poured hot water, warming my hands immediately. I pointed toward two open chairs in the candlelight and Marlowe led the way. We sat away from everyone else while our tea steeped. No one tried to approach us, though Katherine stood watching us from the edge of the light. I could feel her eyes on me.

Looking around, I could see people doing numerous things. A man with a small child was sitting on the ground near a candle with toy cars in front of them. Harold stood with a circle of men, having a quiet conversation. I watched them for a moment, but nothing seemed tense or out of place. On the other side of the circle there were three women, who looked much older than Carol. They were knitting or crocheting, it seemed. A group of teenagers were in the shadows, giggling and whispering.

I accounted for the headcount Carol had given. There was no reason to distrust them, but I wasn't sure trusting anyone was a good idea, either. Marlowe moved closer, so our knees were touching. She blew on her mug and then took a sip. The little groan she made brought my attention to her face.

"This is what I needed," she said.

I nodded and sipped my tea, enjoying the warmth that spread down my chest and filled my belly. It was scalding, but I didn't even care. Even during the summer, it felt amazing after being caught in the chaotic storm. Color seemed to seep back into Marlowe's cheeks. She looked better, at least compared to the pale, shivering version of her that had stumbled in here less than an hour ago.

"So, Cristian." The voice cut through my thoughts like a knife. I looked up to see Katherine leaning against a stack of pallets. She had a smile that might've been charming in another life, but now, it felt like a calculated move. "What brings you two to this part of Oregon?"

Her eyes flicked to Marlowe briefly before settling back on me, the kind of look that didn't bother to hide its interest. I felt Marlowe shift beside me, her posture stiffening just enough that I noticed.

"Traveling south," I said simply, taking another sip of tea. There was no need for her to know we were headed to my home.

"South, huh?" Katherine pushed off the pallets and walked closer, her boots echoing on the concrete floor. "Long way to go in this weather. And with her condition." She nodded toward Marlowe, her tone just a little too pointed.

"We manage," I replied, keeping my voice steady. I didn't need to explain anything to her, but the way her eyes lingered on me made my skin crawl.

Katherine smiled, but there was something sharp beneath it. "Well, if you ever need someone to share the burden, you know where to find me."

Marlowe's posture stiffened beside me, her fingers tightening around her cup. When she spoke, her voice was smooth, but there was a sharp edge beneath it. "Thanks, but he's fine right where he is."

The words hung in the air, heavy and unmistakable. Katherine's smile flickered. She glanced between us, assessing, then shrugged. "Oh, I see how it is."

I felt Marlowe's hand brush against mine, her fingers curling lightly around mine. She didn't look at me. Her focus locked on Katherine, but the gesture was clear. I wasn't sure whether annoyance or a claim motivated her, but I wouldn't contradict her, regardless. I couldn't really take my eyes off Marlowe, as her spine straightened, and she stared at the bothersome woman.

"That's right," Marlowe said, her voice steady despite the faint color rising in her cheeks. "We take care of each other."

Katherine's eyes flicked between us, assessing, before she took a step back with a shrug. "Fair enough. Just thought I'd offer. Can't blame a girl for trying."

She walked away, leaving us in a silence that felt heavier than it should have. Beside me, Marlowe lifted her mug to her lips, but I caught the ghost of a smirk. I wasn't sure what was more surprising. The fact that she shut Katherine down so fast, or that I didn't mind it.

"You didn't have to do that," I whispered.

She shot me a look, her expression somewhere between irritated and embarrassed. "You didn't seem like you were going to say anything."

"Because it didn't matter."

"It mattered to me," she muttered, her gaze dropping to her tea.

For a moment, I didn't know what to say. This wasn't just about Katherine; it was about everything. Her injury, the storm, the strangers, had chipped away at her sense of safety. And I realized I wanted to be the one that was her sense of security.

"Thanks," I said finally, keeping my voice low.

She blinked, glancing at me like she hadn't expected that. "For what?"

"For watching my back."

She didn't respond, but her shoulders relaxed slightly, and the faintest hint of a smile tugged at the corners of her mouth.

We sat there for a while, sipping our tea as the storm raged outside, and for the first time since Blair's death, the silence between us didn't feel heavy at all.

The warehouse quieted as people readied for bed. Someone led us to the area of makeshift rooms, separated by pallets and boxes. It was a semblance of privacy that wasn't real. I didn't mind. The weight of the day, my injury and Blair were catching up to me and I wanted nothing but to shut my brain off for a while.

Cristian sat in the circle of candlelight, tinkering with a lantern someone had produced. Where they found an oil lantern, I couldn't be sure. Throughout the day, we had seen that the warehouse was full of lots of odds and ends. Most of the products were from overseas, but the survivors inside were finding uses for a lot of it.

Food was the one thing they seemed to have some concern about. Before the storm, they had done a run to a nearby dollar store. They had looted the entire canned food, beverage and candy sections. For seventeen people, if they were smart with their rationing, what was there could last them a week, at least. But I had heard Cristian having a hushed conversation with Harold about the plan for finding more.

We hadn't discussed it yet, but I got the feeling that Cristian had plans to stay in the warehouse for a little while. After he found the bruising on my torso, he had been extra vigilant in watching over me. Which led him to wanting to stay put so I could rest and heal.

I sat on the edge of the makeshift cot someone had offered, a double-sized camping mattress laid over a pallet. It wasn't much, but it was worlds better than the wet pavement we'd been walking on hours earlier. My ribs ached, the dull throb making it hard to sit still. The storm outside had finally settled into a steady patter, and the sound should've been comforting. Instead, it just made the silence louder.

Cristian stood and crossed the room, setting the lantern down on a crate near our corner. "That's as good as it's getting," he said, gesturing to the light. "It'll last the night, at least."

The original shippers couldn't send the lantern full of fuel, but a small testing container of fuel was inside the box. It would give us enough light to get ready for bed and maybe for a little while longer if I couldn't fall asleep.

Without me saying anything, Cristian kneeled at my feet to unlace my boots. Not being able to bend over and take care of my own shoes was an enormous source of frustration for me. But then the injury had brought me to depending on Cristian to undress me. I had felt embarrassed by needing the help, but I didn't miss the way he looked at my body as he checked the bruising. I could still feel his warm palm smoothing over my skin.

Mentally shaking myself, I pulled myself out of the gutter. I was just as ridiculous as the Katherine woman. Thinking of her had me glancing up. And unsurprisingly, I found her just a few "rooms" away, closely watching us.

To continue the ruse that we were some sort of couple, I lifted my hand and ran it through Cristian's wavy hair. His hands froze on my shoe, but he didn't look up.

"Act natural. Your favorite fan is watching." My lips barely moved as I muttered.

Cristian relaxed and went back to untying my shoe. My fingers toyed with his hair as he bent. Once the second shoe was off, Katherine had gone about her own business. I slid to the far side of the mattress, which put me next to the wall. I moved around until I found a position I could comfortably lie in. When I turned to look for Cristian, I found him sitting on the floor, back against the bed, watching the rest of the warehouse.

"You're not sleeping?" I asked.

"Not yet," he said, his voice low. "I'll keep watch for a while."

I frowned. "There's an entire group of people here, Cristian. We're not alone anymore."

His eyes flicked toward me, sharp and unreadable. "Doesn't mean we're safe."

I wanted to argue, to tell him to trust that not everyone was a threat. But the truth was, I didn't feel safe either, not entirely. The storm, the strangers, the way Katherine's eyes lingered on him, it all felt precarious, like the slightest wrong move could shatter the fragile peace they were building. I didn't want us to be the reason these people didn't survive whatever was happening to the world.

I shifted on the mattress, wincing as a sharp pain lanced through my side. Cristian noticed immediately, his brow furrowing.

"You need to rest," he said, his tone softening just enough to make me feel like I wasn't entirely an invalid.

"I'm fine," I lied, because saying otherwise wouldn't change anything.

He didn't push, but the look he gave me said he didn't believe me for a second. I shifted again until the pain dulled. Pulling the thin blanket up over the sweats I was wearing, I watched Cristian. His eyes moved as he scanned the shadows dancing around the warehouse. It was impossible to tell anything from the movement, only that something was moving.

"Thank you," I said instead, my voice quieter than I intended.

His gaze snapped to me, momentarily surprised. "For what?"

"For everything," I said, shrugging as much as my ribs allowed. "For... putting up with all of this. With me."

He shook his head, a small, almost imperceptible smile tugging at his lips. "I don't put up with you, Marlowe. You're tougher than you think."

The words sat between us, soft but unshakable, and I felt something inside me ease, just a little.

"Get some sleep," he said, his voice low but steady. "I've got this."

It felt good to know he was watching my back, just as I watched his. I hadn't realized I had fallen asleep when the mattress dipped. My heavy eyelids lifted, and I recognized the fuzzy outline of Cristian getting comfortable next to me. It was an automatic thing for me to reach out until I found his arm. He slid closer and slid an arm under my head.

Turning my face until my cheek pressed against his shoulder, I sighed in contentment. As I let myself slip back into sleep, my mind wandered to the luck I had when the world had stopped. The courthouse was just barely missed by the plane crash. Somehow, I found myself with Cristian. A man that was not only heroic, but not bad on the eyes either.

Throughout my life, relying on anyone other than myself had been close to impossible. Even my mother, with her illnesses, wasn't someone I could say would always be there for me. However, in the worst time that I could experience, a man found me that was willing to protect me, care for me and provide for me. He said he would help me go south to find my mother, and I tried not to doubt him. No one else had come through for me in that way.

However, the warmth of him lulled me into sleep. Even in a drafty warehouse, with the sounds of other people, I felt real comfort lying next to him. With him, everything felt like it would be ok. I wouldn't admit it to him, but the way Katherine looked at him drove me a little crazy. Staking my claim on him wasn't just for him. It was for me, too. I didn't want to lose my companion, my comfort.

The next morning, the rain was still sheeting from the sky.

Cristian and I stood at the front windows, and he sighed. I knew he had to be disappointed to not keep going, but he wouldn't say anything. Since my injury, he had done nothing but support and take care of me.

"You aren't thinking about going out there, are ya?" Harold's voice broke into our rain study as he joined us in the lobby.

Cristian shook his head and turned to him. "We'd appreciate being able to stay another day with you. I can't imagine this will continue through tomorrow."

Harold nodded with a kind smile. "You two stay as long as you need."

"We have some food in our packs that we could give the group, so we aren't cutting into your supplies," Cristian said.

"None of that. You'll need that when you get back on the road. We have all we need right now and more."

"Thank you, Harold," I said with a smile. I suppressed the grimace, as the pain in my side reminded me why we were delayed.

Harold tilted his head to the side and studied me. "Something wrong, young lady?"

I looked at Cristian. He smiled softly at me with a shrug, telling me I didn't hide the pain as well as I thought I had. Looking back at Harold, I waved it off. "Just a slight accident a couple of days ago. Still feeling a little pain."

"A little?" Cristian muttered.

"Why didn't you say something? We have a doctor here. Maybe he can take a look."

I was about to wave the idea off, but Cristian stepped forward, his hand on my lower back. "Thank you, Harold. I think that would be great. There was some bruising I saw yesterday that I'm concerned about."

"I'm—," I started to say, when Cristian cut me off.

"Downplaying things, because you're afraid of being a bother to people."

I looked down at my feet. My cheeks warmed, and I knew a blush was spreading across my face.

Harold led us back into the warehouse and to an area with supplies spread across a few tables that were pushed together. There was a man with wild blond hair wearing wireframe glasses bent over the table. In the light of a few tapered candles, I could see he was sorting through a first aid kit. He had piles of bandages, pill bottles, bottles of alcohol and saline solution, and other assorted medical supplies.

"Oh, hi Harold," he said, when he realized we had approached.

"Hi, Dave. Listen, this is Cristian and Marlowe. Not sure if you met them yesterday. Marlowe had an accident a few days ago and might be in need of your services."

Dave the doctor's face, got serious. He came around the edge of the table and motioned me to come forward. "What happened?"

"I stupidly fell through a front deck and landed on my side."

"She fell on a concrete block that I think hit her ribs," Cristian added.

Of course, he knew the details. I glanced at him from the corner of my eye and nodded to Dave. "I'm talented like that."

"I'll need to examine you."

Harold's feet shuffled. "That's my cue to leave!"

My hand snapped out, and I grabbed Cristian's sleeve before he could do the same. Our gazes met and he must have seen what I was asking without words, because he nodded to me. Dave watched us and nodded. Turning back to his table, a bright light flared to light.

"Where did you get that?" It had been days since we had seen anything with electricity and I was staring at the lantern.

Dave looked up from what he was sorting through. He glanced between us and the lantern. "What? Oh, the lantern. Weird thing. There was this caged area in the back of the warehouse. All sorts of random things were inside. I found this lantern inside a microwave. I'm not sure why it works. Harold thinks it's something to do with the microwave blocking electromagnetic waves or something. I only turn it on when I need proper light to do medical things. Trying to save whatever power it has, since I'm not sure running out for batteries is going to help right now."

The doctor led me to an area that was surrounded by hanging sheets. I motioned for Cristian to follow. I was more trusting than him and worried that might be to my detriment. If Dave tried anything, I'd rather have Cristian within arm's reach, instead of waiting for me to scream.

"Do you feel comfortable removing your shirt, Marlowe?" Dave asked.

I nodded and turned to Cristian, who expertly removed the garment causing no additional pain. The lantern light highlighted the deepening bruise on my side.

Dave inspected it at first, then put on his stethoscope. "Take a few deep breaths, if you can."

I tried my best, without moaning in pain. David moved the stethoscope around with each breath. I felt good about it, as the pain wasn't nearly as bad as it had been before. But I definitely wasn't able to pull in enough breath. Cristian watched my face closely.

After a few breaths, he pulled the stethoscope out of his ears. "That hurts, huh?"

I nodded slightly, grimacing.

"Well, sorry to say, this is going to get more painful. I need to palpate your abdomen. And it's going to hurt."

Panicked, I looked over at Cristian and he put an arm in front of me, barring Dave from touching me. "Why? If you know it's going to hurt, why do you need to do it?"

Dave didn't argue, just smiled in an understanding manner. "I understand you're worried about her pain. I have some meds to give her to help with that. The palpations are to check her organs for swelling or rigidity. I'm fairly certain the bruising is from a bruised kidney, but I need to make sure. As this happened a couple of days ago, I don't believe it's severe, or she would be doing much worse. I don't think she has any internal bleeding, as she doesn't seem to have symptoms of blood loss. I'll do the best I can to not hurt her more than necessary. Promise."

Cristian's entire body went rigid, his stance shifting slightly, blocking Dave from me without even thinking about it. His fingers flexed, like he was debating whether to push the guy away.

Cristian's jaw clenched. I squeezed his arm. "It's okay," I murmured.

Only then did he step back, his eyes never leaving Dave's hands.

I nodded. Determination flared. I wanted to be strong in front of him. And I didn't want him to think he needed to care for me as if I was an invalid. I was clumsy; I admitted. But I could carry my own weight in our survival.

Dave explained I needed to lie down, which was already the first painful step. Cristian turned and took my hands in his and slowly lowered me until I was on my back. I focused on my breathing, making sure I was getting oxygen through the entire process. Cristian held onto my hand, standing on the opposite side of the table from Dave. He looked up and nodded at the doctor, letting him know we were both ready.

Dave's hands were warm as he laid them on my bare stomach. He slowly pressed on the unbruised side and I didn't feel any actual pain. I could feel him pressing into my organs as he moved his fingers around and I watched his face, noting his focused expression.

"Ok, moving to the injured side now," he warned.

As soon as he pressed into the area around my bruised side, I gasped and squeezed my eyes shut. The pain was blinding and even with my eyes shut, I could see stars popping behind my eyelids.

Cristian's hand squeezed mine and his free hand brushed across my forehead to push back my hair. He leaned down so he could talk in my ear. "You're doing great. Only a few more minutes."

It felt like it was an eternity before Dave's hands left my stomach. When he stopped, I took the deepest breath I could without more pain. I opened my eyes and found Cristian right above me, his face a mask of worry. I tried a reassuring smile, though I was pretty sure it was more of a grimace. His hand was cupping my face, and his thumb swiped along my cheek.

"Well, good news," Dave said, pulling our attention to him. "Nothing seems swollen. You definitely have a bruised kidney on that side. But it doesn't feel extended or rigid. Have you noticed any blood in your urine?"

"I wasn't really checking," I said, glancing at Cristian, feeling exposed. But his focus was on Dave and his diagnosis.

"I need you to check for the next few days. We need to make sure you're drinking more water than normal as well. If urination becomes difficult or painful, I need to know immediately. I'll give you some pain meds. But you need to get comfortable. You need to stay in bed for a few days at least."

"A few days!" I exclaimed. I shut my eyes and brought my free hand to my face. Frustrated tears stung, and I didn't want anyone to see me being overemotional.

"The problem with this type of bruising, with no equipment to really see how bad it is, is that I can't tell you how long you need to stay still. I can't tell you how close you are to making it worse. I need to walk a line of caution here, so you don't end up with an injury I can't fix in this warehouse." Dave had taken on his doctor tone, and I knew he meant business.

When I opened my eyes, I just looked at him and nodded. He gave me a small smile in return. "I'm going to grab the meds. You can get dressed."

He left the small curtained-off area, and Cristian took my hands again. Pulling me into a sitting position on the table without a word, he worked my t-shirt back on.

"I'll make this up to you, I promise," I whispered.

Cristian looked at me, confused. "Make what up to me?"

"This," I said, gesturing to my side and around us. "This delay. I'll make sure I follow the doctor's directions and get on my feet as soon as possible. Then I'll walk as far as you say without complaint."

He sighed and leaned his hip against the table. Leaning down slightly, he brought our faces to the same height. "You didn't get hurt on purpose, Marlowe. There is no reason for us to rush anywhere. We've both been through a lot in a few days. Slowing down so you can recover is probably what we both need. You really don't like people taking care of you, do you?"

"I don't want to be an inconvenience."

"Have I made you feel like that's what you are?"

"Not at all. But I don't think you would tell me if you did feel that way," I replied.

Cristian smirked at me. "Oh, I'd tell you. You're not a burden, Marlowe. Everything will be ok."

Dave came back with a small plastic bag with medication and explained everything to Cristian and me. With orders to lie down and only move for the bathroom or emergencies. He was very serious about his instructions, repeating them to Cristian again, as if he figured I wouldn't listen. He wasn't far off with that assumption. I wasn't planning on laying in a bed for a week.

Cristian helped me off the table used for the exam. And he didn't let me deviate from going straight back to our assigned area. He rearranged the bedding to make an area where I could lie slightly inclined.

"I can do it. I'll be ok," I said.

Cristian ignored my comment and crouched to help take off my boots. Once those were off, he motioned for me to get into bed. Following his instructions, I carefully slid back until I was propped up. He pulled the blanket up, partially covering me.

"You're probably going to get bored lying around. I could look for a book or something for you to do?" Cristian said.

I nodded, though I was already feeling tired. I wasn't sure if it was because I didn't sleep well at night, or all the prodding by the doctor, but it had all sapped my energy. Cristian disappeared through the curtain surrounding of our room and I let my head fall back. He was trying so hard to take care of me. The best thing I could do for him was to get better as fast as I could.

Secretly, I was thankful I didn't have to step foot inside a hospital. It was impossible for me to not connect every hospital to my mother's cancer. I spent so much time with her, going through treatments, doctor's appointments and emergency room visits. Every moment I had to sit and suffer the antiseptic smell led to my anxieties around any sort of cleaning solution that smelled similar.

I had attended therapy several times after my mother survived her first round of cancer. The diagnosis was a form of PTSD from the emotional trauma I experienced. The fear I lived with, at such a young age, had weighed on me for a long time. My mother had needed me, and I never resented her for that. Getting cancer wasn't something she asked for either.

My entire life, I had only relied on my mom. Even before her cancer, it had always been just the two of us. Throughout my travels and my time settled in Oregon, I hadn't created any healthy relationships. Nothing that could help me understand that not everything ended up the way my mom and I had. I hadn't lost my mom that first time, but it was something I feared every day.

And now, I had the same fears, in addition to everything else happening. Not only did I worry about my mom and her cancer in California, I worried about being left behind. The thought came suddenly, unbidden, waking me up to an empty space beside me. Cristian was gone. The ache in my ribs twisted into something sharper, something worse. He wouldn't do that. I told myself that over and over. But the truth was, I wasn't sure.

Confused, I looked around, expecting to find Cristian in the room. But he wasn't there. My heart thudded in my chest. I had no idea how much time had passed. But as I shifted, a stack of magazines and one book slid toward me. The room was dim, so I wasn't able to actually see any of the pages.

Looking around, I found a candle on a small table near me. It hadn't been there before, and I realized Cristian had come back in and set things up to make it easier for me. Matches were next to the candle, and I struck one and lit the candle. I recognized it as one we had brought from the bookstore.

The light from the candle was just enough to help me see around our area. The moment I saw both of our packs sitting on the ground, I felt my heartbeat return to a normal rate. He hadn't left, or at least hadn't taken either of our packs. I relaxed back against the pillows, debating whether or not to get up and find him in the warehouse. Just as I was going to swing my legs from the bed, the sheet flipped open and Cristian walked in.

"Were you going somewhere? Need the bathroom?" he asked.

I shook my head. "I, uh, was feeling a bit confused. How long was I sleeping?"

"Just over an hour," he said, setting some more books down. "Extra sleep is probably good for healing."

I nodded, sinking back against the pillows. But as I did, I caught movement beyond the pallet walls. A shadow flickered in the dim candlelight, lingering for a second too long before disappearing.

Katherine.

I swallowed hard and forced my eyes shut, but sleep didn't come as easily this time.

Keeping Marlowe in bed for a week was torture. It was torture for me, and she was positive I was committing some sort of international crime against her. She didn't come straight out and tell me she was pissed, but she had a hard time fixing her face to hide her emotions. If she wasn't so cute when she was mad, I would probably be a whole lot more annoyed with how difficult she was being.

"It's been a week. Doctor Dave only said a few days," she argued.

"That was his minimum. And your bruising isn't clearing up as fast as he had hoped."

She crossed her arms and glared at me. The look almost made me laugh, but I kept that inside, just so I didn't goad her to climb out of bed no matter what I said.

"I'm tired of just lying around, Cristian. This is boring. And we need to get on the road. Staying here was never the plan."

"The plan formed when your bruised kidney became evident. We couldn't and still can't risk something becoming worse. How about I ask Carol to come in and play cards with you again, today?"

She narrowed her eyes at me. "Are you just trying to distract me from your plans?"

That was exactly what I had been trying to do. I didn't confirm or deny, knowing Marlowe would just call me out for lying. She had nothing to do but study me and she was getting good at reading my tells. I didn't like it, but I couldn't seem to hide things from her.

"Of course not. I wouldn't go scavenging without telling you I was leaving. I don't want you worrying."

Marlowe's voice was steady, but her fingers twisted the blanket in her lap, knuckles white. She was trying to keep herself composed, but I could see it—the tension in her shoulders, the way her jaw clenched like she was physically holding back from telling me not to go.

"I'll be fine," I said, adjusting the straps on my pack, pretending not to notice the way her breathing had tightened.

She let out a short, humorless laugh. "Right. Because everything's been going so fine lately."

I sighed, stepping closer, resisting the urge to kneel beside her like I had when helping her with her boots. "Marlowe…"

"Just…" She exhaled sharply, shaking her head. "I don't like this."

Neither did I. But someone had to go. "I just want to help. They took us in. I want to contribute. And this is a way I can."

"You know I don't disagree with that. But I can't help thinking of what will happen if you don't come back." Her voice had dropped to a whisper, and she wouldn't hold my gaze.

"I'm going to come back. You're safe here with the group. We're only checking a few stores about a mile away. I'll be back before you know it."

She didn't argue further, but she gripped her hands tightly in front of her. I double checked she had snacks, water and a new book. She was a fast reader, especially when the options were romance novels. The survival group found a few boxes of books and had them set out like a library. Every other day, Marlowe finished whatever I brought and I replaced it as soon as I could.

I pushed the book closer to her and a few magazines. Putting my pack on our pallet bed, I sorted through what was inside. Leaving the first aid kit and the reusable shopping bags inside, I pulled everything else out and left it with Marlowe's pack. I slung the pack on my back and turned to look at Marlowe again. She looked forlorn, and I felt a stab of indecision.

Leaning over her, I pressed a kiss to the top of her head. "I promise. I'll be back."

I didn't look back as I walked out of the room. Seeing her upset or worried would have pulled me right back. And I had already committed to join the group that was scavenging. In the lobby, I found Harold talking with three other adult men and two women. Bill, Roger and Kyle were the men. And the women included Katherine and a woman I had just met, named Molly.

Katherine turned to watch me as I approached, and her eyes wandered in a way I wasn't going to acknowledge. Since Marlowe had been bedridden, I had spent very little time outside of our room. During the short times I wasn't at Marlowe's side, Katherine had tried to talk to me. I responded in the simplest ways possible, making it clear I didn't have any interest in her. Admitting my interest in Marlowe was difficult, even to myself. I wasn't looking to complicate things with another woman.

"Cristian, hi! Thanks so much for volunteering to help today," Harold said, as I joined the circle of people.

I raised my hand in greeting and smiled. "No problem. I'm interested in seeing what's going on out there, too."

The group discussed the plan, with Roger taking the lead. We all had packs on our backs, ready to pack and bring back whatever we found. There was a list of things the group needed. One teenager had asthma, and their inhaler was almost empty. There was a need for blood pressure meds for two of the older women, as well as Harold. None of them lived close enough to make a run to their houses for their meds. So, a pharmacy was the only other option.

Harold unlocked the front door, and we slowly exited in a line. Roger led us along the border of the warehouse, sticking close to the building. At the far corner, I glanced back and saw that someone had pulled the front door closed. Roger scouted around and when he motioned for us to move forward, I took that as a sign we were in the clear.

Katherine slowed until she was walking next to me. I was too busy keeping my eyes on the road and checking behind us to even try to make polite conversation with her. As we exited the lot for the warehouse, we turned into a residential neighborhood. Many of the houses were trashed. Windows broken, doors left open, and even a few cars had crashed into garage doors.

Roger paused in front of a burned-out husk of a house, studying the scene. I moved forward through the group to stand next to him.

"This is what we have to look forward to, isn't it? Without power, a fire department or running water, there's nothing to stop fire," Roger said.

I was pretty sure he was talking to himself, but I replied. "Humans figured these things out before. I'm sure we'll get back on our feet."

Roger looked over at me with a frown. "You were in law enforcement, right? Why aren't you with your teams, or whatever, helping put this back together?"

"I wish I could tell you that law enforcement was ready for this. But we weren't. As soon as things went to chaos, there was no communication or way for anyone to coordinate. Most would have gone home to save their families. I had no way to even get to my station, let alone contact anyone. There's no plan for the world falling apart."

We continued until we turned a corner that led down a street holding a few larger stores. The shared parking lot was littered with trash, abandoned vehicles, and shopping carts. Roger moved forward, but I touched his shoulder and motioned toward a truck where we could hide.

"It's too quiet," I said.

"Quiet is good, isn't it?" Katherine asked. She had moved up to stand with Roger and me, half hidden by the truck.

"Yes. But we should just watch for a bit, to be sure," I replied, my eyes on the buildings in front of us.

"We don't really have all day," Bill piped up from behind us.

"We do if it prevents any of us from being hurt," I shot over my shoulder.

"Roger, you're the one leading this party. What do you say?" Bill asked.

Roger looked between Bill and me before assessing the box store that had a pharmacy sign and the grocery store. Shattered windows covered the entire front. I couldn't say what he saw, but what I saw was plenty of walls, dark corners and places to hole up. Being able to control a grocery store would be a prime location for survival. And to keep the store under your control, you'd need weapons. Something we didn't possess.

"I say we go in. Maybe we split up," Roger said.

I just shook my head and sighed. Not only was he not doing any reconnaissance but separating the group would make us even more vulnerable. Roger gave me one glance and I know he saw my disapproval on my face. But instead of heeding my warning, he started breaking us into groups. He put Katherine into a group separate from me, but she spoke up and demanded to be in the same group. I wasn't sure how to get the woman to understand. I wasn't interested.

Roger sent my group to the box store. The last store I wanted to step foot into without a weapon. Carts pushed through on either side, propped up the metal roll doors which had been partially raised from their normal closed position. It was the only positive sign I had seen. If someone was trying to keep the products of the store to themselves, they wouldn't leave the doors wide open.

The store had extremely high ceilings with rows of skylights. Luckily, with the sun high in the sky, there was enough light in the store without resorting to candles. The front of the store was completely trashed. Smashed products littered every surface; someone had pushed over the displays. I was careful in the way I picked my steps. Katherine followed closely, with Kyle behind her.

I saw the large pharmacy signage on the far wall, so I headed in that direction first. Just as I thought, the pharmacy was ransacked and in disarray. Since we were looking for meds that weren't narcotics or something that could be used as currency, the agreement was we would still search. We all had a written list of the medications we were looking for. I pulled my paper from my back pocket and moved around until I found light that would help me read it again.

Hopping the counter, I carefully set my booted feet on the shattered glass and medications that were spilled everywhere. Katherine climbed onto the counter and looked at me as if she needed help. Kyle hopped over and turned to help her down before I could move back. I didn't miss the flash of annoyance on her face.

Moving through the rows, I tried to see the labels on the items on the shelves. It was way too dark to make out anything clearly. Setting my pack out, I pulled out a taper candle and lighter. The wick flared with fire and the back of the pharmacy was suddenly full of shadows. Kyle joined me and we sorted through medications. He held up a box in victory, and it was the only inhaler on the shelf. Looking around, we didn't find any others in the vicinity or on the ground.

The medications for the older folks were a little more difficult, with longer, complicated names. I couldn't seem to memorize those. Kyle and I glanced at the lists and at the labels, back and forth. We only found two of the medications on the list. The time we spent in the pharmacy felt like half the day, but in actuality, it was only about thirty minutes.

Katherine stayed leaning against the front counter, watching Kyle and I search. I had a lot of strong thoughts about her lack of assistance, but my desire to ignore her won out. Jumping over the counter again, I started down a row. I could hear the woman huff behind me and let Kyle deal with her.

We wandered further into the store. Many of the shelves were empty, having been picked clean. I found a box of fish crackers and took the bags from the box, so they fit into my pack. The teens and the one child in the warehouse would enjoy the snack. Further down the aisle, there were loose cans on the ground, and I picked them up, putting them in Kyle's pack. It didn't matter what was in the cans. We could use any of it.

A loud noise from the front of the store caused me to freeze in place. Katherine started to walk by me, toward the noise, but I threw out my arm, blocking her way. Holding my finger to my lips, I moved her and Kyle toward the shelving. The shadows would hide us, unless someone came down the same aisle.

"What if they can help us?" Katherine's voice was louder than I would have appreciated.

"Better to act with caution than to just run up to any strangers in a store." My reply came out as a hissed whisper, hinting for her to bring it down a notch.

A few minutes later, we could hear conversation between people. And I immediately knew it wasn't anyone we knew. As the voices grew louder, a light seemed to approach. I heard them sorting through items they found on the ground. They were approaching our row and with the light they were carrying, they would expose our hiding spot.

Turning to look at Kyle, I motioned for him to run to the end of the aisle, hoping we could hide at the end before the group found us. He immediately turned and quietly jogged away. I physically turned Katherine, despite her still trying to see who was coming. With a hand on her back, I started pushing until she was speed-walking. At the end of the aisle, I moved her until she was next to Kyle. She shrugged me off and glared over at me.

"What is your problem?" Her voice was a whisper yell, but at least quieter than before.

"Needed to move quickly," I said, as I crouched to peer around the corner to watch the new group.

When they came into view, alarm bells went off in my head. Even without seeing details, I could recognize the police uniforms that two of the people were wearing. But there were things that didn't make sense. The uniforms weren't matching, and both were wearing jeans and sneakers. As I watched them, it wasn't just their clothing, but the way they moved and threw around anything that was in their way. They laughed loudly and shoved each other, as if everything was a big game.

"Those are cops," Kyle said, more loudly than I would have liked.

"I don't think they are," I whispered.

Kyle shot me an incredulous look as he stepped out into the aisle. I motioned for him to come back to us, but he just shook his head, annoyed, and started toward the men in the center of the store. Katherine started to move, but I put my hand on her shoulder and pushed her back down.

"Hey! Hi! Man, am I glad to see you!" Kyle exclaimed.

From our hiding spot, I could see when the lights the men were carrying swung toward Kyle. There was a beat before Kyle's voice came again.

"Wait, why are you pointing that at me?"

I peered around the edge of the aisle and could clearly see one man pointing their gun at Kyle's chest.

"Do you have supplies?" A man asked.

"Supplies? Just a few things from here. But there's more than enough back where I'm staying."

"Idiot," I muttered angrily.

"And where's that? Where are you staying?"

I couldn't hear Kyle's muttered reply, but he was slowly backing up. His hands were out in the open, as to show that he wasn't a threat. The gunshot cracked through the air, sharp and deafening. Kyle's breath hitched—his hands flew to his chest like he could hold the life inside. He staggered back a step. Then another. And then he crumpled.

It was only instinct that had me spinning for Katherine. Grabbing her, I clapped my hand over her mouth and sunk to the ground. She was in front of me and my free arm banded around her middle, keeping her from running. My hand muffled her scream, and the shot echo swallowed it.

She squirmed, and I locked my arm around her and pulled her back until I could speak into her ear.

"If you run now, they'll shoot you in the back. Or worse, if they realize you're a woman."

That caused her to freeze, and she stopped fighting me.

"They're going to go through his pack. We're going to go back around the aisle and as far down as possible before we run for the front door. Got it?"

She nodded her head. I slowly released her, and she melted back against me. The footsteps of the group grew closer as they moved toward Kyle's body. I peeked around once more and, as predicted, they were flipping Kyle and pulling his backpack from his body. I waited, trying to memorize any identifiable characteristics. The two in the uniform shirts came forward into the light as they sorted through Kyle's backpack.

"What did he say? You shot him too soon. He had more information," the shorter of the two said, shoving the man standing next to him. The other two of the group stood back, as if they were keeping an eye out. I ducked back behind the shelving, still listening but staying out of sight.

"He said warehouse. That could be anywhere," the taller man said.

"Right. We could have made him tell us where, you idiot. Instead, he's dead. And we have no idea where he's from."

"What does it matter?"

The sound of a smack sounded, and I assumed the short one smacked the tall one. "He's fed. He's clean. It's been what, almost two weeks since everything went to hell. This guy was staying somewhere good. And we could take it, if we knew where it was."

That was the last thing I needed to hear. Marlowe was at the warehouse. And they were unarmed. I had to get back to protect her. The warehouse wasn't an obvious destination near the stores. But if the group was any bigger than just the four men, they could easily split up and check any warehouses in a grid search.

I turned toward the next aisle, motioning to Katherine to stay low and stay quiet. She nodded, but her body trembled. Gripping her hand in mine, I started slowly walking from our hiding place, keeping my eyes down the aisles to make sure there weren't any others in the group wandering around. When we got to the further aisle from the one that held Kyle's body, I stayed crouched and ran toward the front doors.

Behind us, I could hear the fight heating between the two that seemed to be the leaders. I had no desire to stick around and find out who the winner of the argument would be. As we got closer to the door, which was the brightest part of the store, I paused. Katherine huddled close to my side and her trembling had become full body shakes now, making me worry she would go into some sort of shock before I could get her back to the warehouse.

Checking that we were for sure in the clear, I peered around the displays that circled the entrance. I didn't see any of the men and I grabbed Katherine, practically dragging her behind me. Once in the open, I picked up the pace and sprinted for the grocery store that the other group had gone into. Just as we got closer, Roger came out of the store, looking around with a worried look on his face.

When he saw us, his eye widened, and he dropped what he was carrying. "Where's Kyle?"

"Dead. We need to go, now," I replied.

"Katherine?" Roger asked, trying to get the woman's attention. But she stood, frozen in fear, gripping my hand and arm in a vise grip.

"I think she might be in shock. We need to get back to the warehouse. I have to tell everyone what happened," I said.

Bill and Molly came out of the store, both of their hands ladened with bags. I looked back toward the box store. The image of the group of us huddled in the parking lot with supplies would be too much for the men to resist. I didn't wait for them to agree. With Katherine attached to my arm, I started walking toward the nearest parking lot exit that would put buildings between us and the killers. The faster we were out of sight, the better.

Luckily, no one argued, and they all kept up. Even Bill and Molly with their loads. Once we were down the street and I felt like we could hide well enough, I paused behind a house in a small alleyway. Roger stood in front of me. His leadership was under threat, and he didn't like it. I could tell by the look on his face that he wanted me to explain.

So I did. I told them the entire story from start to finish. Katherine wept, and I let her bury her face in my chest. Putting my arm around her, I tried to console her best as possible.

Roger's face went pale as he took in what I was saying. "Kyle told them about the warehouse?"

"Not exactly. They didn't give him the chance. But from what I heard, they don't have a safe place to survive. They could tell by the way Kyle looked he'd had it good the last few weeks. That made the warehouse Kyle mentioned very appealing."

"There are warehouses all over the place. There's no way of knowing which one it was," Bill cut in. His normal negative demeanor was on full display. It made me want to punch him in the face.

"No one, or at least very few, people have working vehicles. That means everyone is coming and going from places that are within walking distance. It's not hard to figure out that Kyle wouldn't have walked days away from his home base," I said.

Roger looked between Bill and me. "You're saying that the warehouse might be at risk?"

"That's exactly what I'm saying. I need to get back to

Marlowe. And we need to tell everyone about the risk. Those men had weapons. There's no knowing how many more they have. Or if there are more people in their group. If the group is larger, the risk is greater. They could search the area more efficiently by splitting up."

Roger nodded then, finally tapping into my logic. We started off at a quick pace toward the warehouse. I took up the rear, with Katherine glued to me. Walking backward, with her holding on to my arm, wasn't easy. But I couldn't shake the feeling of being watched. There was no sound to indicate anyone following.

When we arrived at the warehouse, Roger pounded on the door loudly and I cursed under my breath. Looking around, I hoped we hadn't been followed, because Roger just turned on the vacancy sign for anyone in earshot.

Harold came to the door with a wide smile on his face. It faltered as soon as he saw us. He fumbled with the door longer than I liked. As soon as he swung it open, we rushed in and I turned and pushed it closed behind us. Flipping the lock, I stared out the glass and waited for anything to move. When the lot and street beyond were still, I ushered everyone into the back, where we wouldn't be seen.

Roger whispered to Harold and the older man looked at me, shocked. Then they called everyone together. Marlowe came from our room. Her eyes narrowed on Katherine, who was still clinging to me. I knew she'd understand once she heard what happened. Meeting her gaze, I tried to tell her that everything was ok with my eyes. She came to stand on my other side.

"What's going on?" She spoke for my ears only.

"We're going to need to go. I'm sorry. I know you needed a few more days of rest."

She looked up at me, not even a question in her eyes. "I'm ready to go when you are."

Harold stood in the center of the group, concern on his face. As soon as he delivered the news about Kyle, gasps and tears started around the room. He called me into the center to tell the story and I had to peel Katherine off me. Helping her sit, I stood next to Harold and told the story. Murmurs went up around the room and I knew that convincing these people to leave their safety was going to be close to impossible.

They hadn't seen the worst there was. Hadn't seen what was happening outside of their walls. They had a false sense of security. And that falsity would put Marlowe in danger.

"I understand this is a lot to take in. And I don't believe they were right behind us. But I don't think it will be hard for them to figure out where this warehouse is. I'm not here to tell you all what to do. But for myself and Marlowe, this doesn't feel safe."

After thanking me for the information and patting me on the shoulder, Harold dismissed me. I went to Marlowe, and she threaded her fingers through mine. We stood a little while longer, listening to the group discussion. The people of the warehouse were together by happenstance. They weren't family. Most of them didn't know each other before. Yet they weren't ready to let go of the stronghold they felt they had.

As the groups broke off to have individual discussions, I took Marlowe to our little area. There was no privacy, so I pulled her close to me so we could whisper directly to each other without any interference.

"Is it as bad as you said?" she asked.

"Yes. The scavengers will kill everyone in here if they find this warehouse."

Marlowe shuddered in my arms, and I hugged her closer.

"And Katherine saw it? Kyle's death?"

I shook my head slightly, my face sweeping through the hair that was loose from her ponytail. "She heard it. She broke down right after."

"Poor woman."

Marlowe's hands were on my back, and they gripped my shirt. I didn't speak. Just held her to me. Even with my job, it was still shocking to see someone shot in cold blood.

"I don't think we can stay. I want to help these people. But if they aren't willing to leave, I'm not sure there's anything I can do. We don't have any actual weapons. Those guys didn't seem worried about ammo."

The usual anger rose in me. Anger at myself for not being better prepared. For not having a weapon. For not being able to better protect Marlowe, and now, the people of the warehouse. With no semblance of normalcy coming back, I didn't believe the government was going to swoop in and save us.

"So when do you want to go?" Marlowe's breath tickled my neck as she spoke.

"First light. I don't think they can find the warehouse today. I'll ask Harold for a few supplies, to keep us going."

"Cristian?" Katherine's voice came from behind us, and she stepped through the curtains. When she saw us in an embrace, she paused, and indecision had her backing out.

"It's ok. What can we help you with, Katherine?" Marlowe said. She turned in my arms, so she was facing Katherine as well. But I didn't release her. I needed the feeling of her warm body, full of life, near me. It helped warm the cold that had infused me the moment I watched Kyle drop dead in the box store.

Katherine turned back to us, but her eyes were on the ground. The events of the store had changed the woman, subdued her. She finally looked up at us and her gaze was imploring.

"Can I go with you? I know you aren't staying. I live in Vancouver and have no way to get all the way back there and I don't want to be alone. But I don't want to stay here. I think you're right about them coming to find us."

Marlowe tilted her head back and up so she could look into my face. I felt bad for Katherine. I felt bad for anyone that was alone during this mess. Marlowe had been alone. I had been alone. Yet, we found each other. And had relied on each other through it all. I knew she didn't trust Katherine. But was that enough to turn her away?

It was as if we had the entire conversation with our eyes. Marlowe's soft and understanding. Her lips tilted into a small smile that I knew to be her kindness shining through. Before she spoke, I knew what she was going to say.

"Yes. You can come with us, Katherine."

Marlowe's words had barely left her lips when I heard it. Glass breaking from somewhere inside the warehouse. My muscles tensed. My hand moved instinctively toward my knife.

And then—

Gunshots. Exploding through the warehouse, rattling the walls, sending shouts and screams ricocheting through the space.

Cristian's hold on me tightened the moment the shots rang through the warehouse. I looked back at him; his jaw was tight, and his eyes wide.

"Cristian?" I whispered.

"I was wrong. They must have followed us somehow."

In a rush, Cristian moved to our bags. Lifting mine, he helped me swing it onto my back before he grabbed his own. He looked at Katherine, who was cowering near our bed platform.

"Do you have a bag packed?" He asked.

She didn't respond, and he just stared at her. I recognized her shock and fear. Stepping between them, I grabbed Katherine's face and forced her to look at me. I was shorter than her, but at that moment, I was commanding her attention. She blinked a few times when she realized we were almost nose to nose.

"You need to snap out of it. We need to go. Cristian is our best bet. Listen to him. Follow his directions." I patted her cheeks lightly with both of my hands. "Are you hearing me?"

She nodded and blinked again. Then she looked over toward Cristian.

"I still have my bag packed from the store."

"Where is it?" He asked.

"Near the cooking area."

Cristian nodded and moved toward the opening in the curtains. He peered out and looked back at us.

"Stay close to me. Do what I do. And if I tell you to do something, you do it immediately. Got it?"

I nodded. He grabbed my hand, and I reached back and grabbed Katherine. I would drag her with me if need be. She squeezed my hand, giving me hope she was with us and wouldn't get either of us killed.

Cristian bent low as he guided us through the curtains. The warehouse was in chaos, with everyone running around and trying to find places to hide. He paused, looking side to side. The coppery stench of blood filled the air before I even saw him. Harold lay face down, arms stretched toward Carol like he'd tried to reach her before the bullet took him down. His fingers twitched once. Then went still.

"Cristian...," I whispered.

"I see him. We need to go out the back. There's a door that only opens from inside. We'll grab Katherine's bag and then we're running."

His hand was steel around mine. If I wasn't so scared, I would have told him he was cutting off circulation. But I didn't want him to let go of me until we were far from the chaos. Voices echoed from the lobby, yelling and arguing. It sounded like someone demanding something and another voice was responding.

"Is that Carol?" I asked.

Cristian tilted his head, listening. He looked back at me, his face grim. Nodding, he confirmed my suspicions. The attackers had Carol in the lobby and they were demanding things from her.

"We can't leave her, Cristian. We have to help." My voice sounded more confident than I was feeling inside.

"What are you even saying? We can't help her! They have guns!" Katherine whisper yelled from behind me.

I didn't bother to look back at her. I waited for Cristian to decide what we could do. Katherine wasn't wrong. The men infiltrating the warehouse had guns. And we did not. But leaving the woman that had helped us handle the threat alone didn't feel right.

Cristian spun and pulled me closer to him, so we could talk quietly. "You two go get Katherine's bag. Go to the back door. In the parking lot, there's a delivery truck to the right. Hide behind it. I'll come for you."

The moment he started to speak, I shook my head. "You can't do it alone. I'm staying to help you. Katherine can go hide."

"Marlowe, I can't worry about you and concentrate on what I need to do."

"We worry about each other. That's the deal. I'm not going without you."

I couldn't put into words how I knew if I left without him, I'd never see him again. The pit in my stomach told me I couldn't leave him on his own. And that if I did, if I ran to protect myself, I would be leaving Cristian to die. And I wouldn't do that.

His eyes were so dark in the dim lighting in the warehouse. They stared into mine, and I knew he was debating the fastest way to get me out of the warehouse. I didn't want to fight with him and didn't want to delay helping Carol any longer. An idea popped into my head, and I grabbed both of his arms, just as yelling came from the lobby.

"I'm going to distract them. You sneak up and take them out."

"Take them out?" Cristian asked, his voice incredulous.

I lifted my hand to his face, and he leaned into my palm for just a second. "You can do anything you put your mind to. And I know you can do this. They won't hurt me. I'll make sure of that."

"How?"

"Other than supplies, what do you think men like that are after?"

Cristian opened his mouth to argue, but I clapped my palm over his lips.

"I can do this. It'll be ok. I'll have their attention on me. You handle everything else. And be fast with it. I don't want them to take me anywhere."

"Goddammit, Marlowe." Despite the fear, the growl in his throat and his hot breath against my hand sent a chill through me.

"You'll save me." I removed my hand and, without thinking, pressed a kiss to the corner of his mouth before turning and heading toward the lobby. Glancing back, I saw him watching me, but he snapped to attention. He quickly spoke to Katherine, and the woman disappeared toward the cooking area.

With a deep breath, I walked directly to the lobby. I unbuttoned the two top buttons on my shirt, letting my cleavage show a bit. With the sports bra and tank I was wearing under, my breasts were pushed up a bit more than usual. And if these men were anything like I was assuming, it would be an excellent distraction.

When I came into view of the men that had broken out the glass doors of the lobby, I knew they were exactly who Cristian had seen. Two men with guns were facing down Carol. Each of them was wearing a law enforcement shirt, but that was the only thing that looked official. Random tattoos, likely from prison or gang affiliations, covered them. One was tall and scrawny, while the other was short and stout. They were both filthy. A sign they hadn't been living well in the weeks since everything fell apart.

As soon as I appeared, both of the men swung their guns in my direction. I held up my hands, palms open, as I moved to Carol's side. Her face was ghost white. Her red-rimmed eyes stood out and tears were still spilling down her cheeks. I couldn't imagine the pain of watching her husband murdered in front of her. My mind flashed to Blair and her death. I had to breathe through my nerves and the nausea that flooded my stomach.

"Marlowe, you need to run," Carol said through her gritted teeth.

"I just came to see if I could help these gentlemen." I flashed the biggest smile I could pull off in the moment.

"Who are you?" The scrawny one said.

"Marlowe. Nice to meet you…," I paused, waiting for him to

fill in the space with his name, but he just glared at me. I put my hands on my hips and popped one out to the side as I raised an eyebrow. "Well, it's rude to not respond when someone introduces themself, isn't it?"

"Marlowe." Carol's warning was hard to ignore. I was trying to act tough, but my stomach was churning, and I felt like I was going to throw up on my shoes.

"It's okay, Carol. These guys and I are gonna be friends, aren't we boys?"

The men looked at each other, clearly confused by my friendly banter. I could see Carol staring at me as well, just as confused by what I was up to. There was no way to tell her to relax and not give me away. Not without risking Cristian, who I knew would sneak in at the right time. I had no doubt in him.

"What are you up to, girlie?" The short man asked. His gun was slowly lowering and not pointing directly at my face any longer.

With a smile, I tossed my hair. I literally tossed my hair. Aware that I was likely laying it on thick, I just kept my responses simple. "I just want to help. It's clear you boys needed some assistance, right?"

"We came for the supplies," the tall one said, his voice wary still.

"Sure. I understand. Are you all alone? That's too bad. No one should be alone right now. Especially not handsome men like you."

I almost threw up in my mouth, but I forced all my true emotions down and kept the look on my face light and friendly.

"There's more of us," the short one said.

Putting on a show, I looked behind them and then glanced behind me. I was really looking for Cristian, but he was nowhere to be seen. But neither was anyone else that could be with the two attackers.

"Not with us." The tall one rolled his eyes, as if I was an idiot.

"Oh. I thought maybe there were more of you good looking fellas."

I said fellas. I wondered if it sounded as stupid to them as it did to me. Out of the corner of my eye, I could see Carol's eyes bulging at me. I hoped she had spent enough time with me to know this wasn't real. But at the moment, her shock was genuine.

"So, can I help you find your supplies?"

The short guy stepped forward, walking by his tall friend. Carol's hand snapped out and grabbed my arm, trying to pull me backward. I turned and looked at Carol and winked for only her to see. Her brows pulled together, but as soon as I turned and put her behind me, it didn't matter. I could see Cristian sneaking behind the tall man.

"I'm sure you could be of some help, sweetheart. Name's Mike." The short man finally introduced himself, just as he was getting close enough for me to smell him.

I forced a smile but kept my breathing shallow, so I didn't gag on the stench radiating from Mike. Without taking my eyes off him, I kept Cristian in sight from the corner of my eye. Mike's hand came up, and he ran a finger from my collarbone down to the center of my cleavage. Revulsion rose in me, but I stayed as still as possible.

Mike's grin turned cruel and just as his hand opened and his palm brushed my breast through my shirt, a shout rang out behind him. Startled, he started to spin, but I didn't give him a chance. I knew what the shout meant. Moving quickly, I brought up my foot and slammed it into Mike's groin, which was closer to the ground than expected. He collapsed with a pained grunt, and I was able to see Cristian and the tall guy struggling over the gun in the attacker's hand.

Frozen, I watched the scene unfold and wondered if I should do something to help Cristian. The gun went off and the table to the left of me splintered when the bullet hit it. For a second, Cristian glanced my way, checking to see if I was hit.

"Run!" He bellowed.

Thinking about him not wanting to worry about me, I did as he asked without question. Grabbing Carol's arm, I pulled her from the lobby toward the back of the warehouse. A few people were still hiding behind pallets and boxes, maybe with nowhere to go or no idea of what to do. When Carol and I appeared, they rushed toward the older woman.

"Harold!"

"Oh my god, Carol, are you alright?"

"What's happening?"

Everyone spoke at once, but I didn't care about their questions. I turned to where I could see the entrance from the lobby and waited. And waited. Another gunshot rang out and everyone involuntarily ducked, as if the bullet was going to come through multiple walls and boxes. When two more gunshots sounded, I was running for the lobby, with Carol screaming after me.

I slowed and walked carefully around Harold's body, so I could come up on the side of the lobby that Cristian had. I hoped that if he was still fighting the men, or if they had somehow taken him down, I could sneak in. Peeking around the edge of the wall, I saw Cristian's back, heaving as if he had run a marathon. He held a handgun in one hand and pressed his other against his leg.

While I watched, he raised the gun and pointed it in front of him. I couldn't see around the front desk to see what he was looking at.

"Please, mister. Please. We're just trying to survive, just like you." The voice belonged to Mike and even in his short stature, he had to be on the ground in front of Cristian.

"You don't murder people so you can survive." Cristian's voice was low and threatening.

"I...I...I didn't wanna shoot the old man. That was Vic. And you already killed him. So like a life for a life, ok mister? We won't come back. I'll go and we won't come back."

Cristian didn't move an inch. I could see the tension in his back and the control he had over his arm with the gun. However, the hand that was pressed to his leg shook slightly and I could see that it was red with blood. I wanted to rush forward and help him, but I didn't know where the other gun was. My presence would distract Cristian, and I didn't want to do that.

"Leave the gun. And get out," Cristian said.

I heard the drop of the gun echo in the lobby and the scrambling of Mike to get off the ground. When he finally appeared around the desk, he was slightly bent, holding his groin. It gave me a slight thrill to know he would pay for his attack for a while. He crunched through the glass that was shattered on the ground.

Once he disappeared around the corner of the building, Cristian's entire body collapsed in on itself. Running forward, he turned just as I reached him.

"Are you alright?" he asked.

I stared at him in shock. "Am I alright? Are you kidding? Did you get shot?"

Cristian looked down, as if he wasn't exactly sure what had happened. "Just a graze, I think."

When he looked back up at me, I realized he also had a cut on his face. I reached up and tenderly touched around it and he winced. "One of them got you good, huh?"

"Marlowe, grab the gun the guy left. We can't stay here. They'll be back."

Grabbing the gun, I went back to him, and he started to limp toward the back of the warehouse. I pushed my shoulder under his arm and he reluctantly leaned on me as we walked.

"We need to get you to Dave. He needs to look at your leg," I said.

Cristian swayed slightly as I pressed closer to support him. His breath hitched, his jaw clenched tight. Sweat beaded along his hairline, soaking into his shirt.

"I'm fine," he muttered, even as his leg trembled under him.

Questions peppered us when we entered the back of the warehouse. Cristian was trying to focus and be nice, but I wasn't feeling any of that.

"Please, give us room! He's been shot. Where's the doctor?"

"I'm here, Marlowe. Bring him to the table!" Dave called from his makeshift clinic.

"Come on, honey. Lean on me. We'll get you fixed up," I whispered to Cristian, as he gave me a little more of his weight.

"Are you sure you're okay? I saw that guy try to touch you," he said through gritted teeth.

"You made sure he never got a chance. Nicely done. Let's worry about you for now, ok?"

Cristian didn't argue, which only proved my point. In the weeks I had known him, he had never once put himself first. He had to be in some actual pain if he did that now. I squeezed my arm around his waist and leaned my head on his chest as we walked. For the moment, I couldn't think about how close this all could have been. I needed to worry about one thing at a time.

In the clinic room, Dave instructed Cristian to remove his pants if he could, or he would cut them off. The limited supply of clothes had Cristian insisting on getting them off without cutting. I turned to leave, but he grabbed my hand.

"Will you stay?"

I thought about him staying with me throughout my examination. And how he had waited on me, taking care of everything from my medications, meals and even my boredom. For him, there wasn't much I'd say no to. I nodded and helped him ease his cargo pants over his wound. The sight of all the blood had me shaking, but I did my best to concentrate on the task at hand.

Once his pants were around his ankles and boots, Dave and I helped him climb onto the table. Dave immediately brought his lantern to Cristian's leg and probed around. When Cristian hissed in pain, I looked over at the doctor, ready to yell at him, but Cristian grabbed my hand.

"It's ok. He's gotta do it."

I squeezed his hand and leaned over his face. "Well, couldn't he give you something for the pain first?"

He squeezed his eyes shut and held his breath for a long moment before just shaking his head.

"Breathe. Holding your breath will make it worse," Dave said from his place by his leg.

"Doc, you have something I can clean his face with? Just a small cut. Doesn't need anything else," I asked.

Dave nodded toward a large first aid kit box. I sorted through the supplies until I found alcohol prep pads, a bottle of saline, and some gauze. When I leaned over Cristian again, I could see sweat dripping. Looking around, there was nothing to use, so I whipped off my top layer and blotted at his face. His eyes opened, and he looked up at me with an emotion I couldn't name. Whatever it was, it warmed my chest for the split second I saw it. But the next moment, he was grimacing again.

"Hey, I'm going to clean your cheek. Okay?"

He nodded slightly and closed his eyes. I decided talking would be a great distraction. And if there was one thing I could do, it was ramble about all the random things in my head.

"We almost have matching face wounds now. I bet our scars will be similar." This prompted a small smirk from him. Knowing he was listening, I continued. "When my mom was going through her cancer treatments the first time, she needed so much care. Her insurance didn't even cover all the treatments. One of her jobs ran a GoFundMe that paid for the rest of the chemo. But at home, I was her nurse. There was this one time, she had a fainting spell. God, that scared me. But she fell and hit her head. Because of all the medical bills, she refused to go to the hospital. So, there was I was. A teenager figuring out with the internet the best way to clean a head wound."

I took a moment to focus on the task at hand. I flushed the small wound out with the saline, making sure there wasn't anything in it. It was a small enough cut that it would scab up fairly fast. I then wiped around it and cleaned the blood with the alcohol prep pad.

"You know the worst part? Face and head wounds, they bleed so much. Even when they aren't that serious. I'm glad your face didn't get too bad. I'm not sure I could have taken care of it. Blood and I aren't the best of friends."

That prompted a slight chuckle from Cristian. "Learning new things about you all the time," he muttered.

The doctor broke in, moving up to join me over Cristian's face. "You need stitches. I don't have any sort of local anesthesia or pain med that's going to make this easier. I do have a bottle of whiskey. Would you like a few shots?"

Cristian shook his head. "We can't stay here. That guy will get the rest of his crew and come back. They won't stop. I have to get Marlowe away from here."

"Cristian, you can't just get stitches without something," I exclaimed.

"I can handle it. Just keep talking to me."

His eyes were serious and locked on mine. I found myself getting lost in their brown depths. The color seemed to swirl in the lantern light, even though I knew it was just an illusion. I nodded to him and looked over at the doctor.

"Do it."

He looked worried, but he nodded this agreement, before looking at me seriously. "I might need you to help hold him."

"If he wants to fight, there's nothing I can do to help you with that, Doc. So you better have a soft touch," I replied.

Dave blew out a breath, as he readied his tools. I continued to lean over Cristian's face and just stared into his eyes. I brushed my fingers through his hair and came up with another story to tell him about my life.

"I was a nomad for a few years. I think I told you that, right? It was like when I turned eighteen and my mother was healthy enough to be on her own, I lost my mind a little. Not in an illegal way. I was always a good girl." I had to chuckle at that. Though it was true, it was funny thinking about that now. Cristian started to smile, but then his eyes widened in panic and pain. Pressing a quick kiss to his cheek, I continued talking. "I went up and down the west coast, mostly California, to start. I would live in hotels for a few days or a week at a time. Usually holes in the wall. Looking back now, you would have never let me stay somewhere like that." I laughed again and even Cristian cracked a smile.

"Never," he whispered.

"So I would find some sort of waitress job or bagging at a grocery store. It would be just enough to pay for the hotel, a bit of food and then a bus ticket to move on to the next place. I met so many people. Some of the wildest free spirts out there. Back then, being a nomad wasn't popular and fun. It was usually for home-less people. But I wasn't homeless. I did it, because I wanted to. There were days I lived on nothing but vending machine food."

"Why?" Cristian's question was on a gush of air he expelled as his brow scrunched again.

"Hmmm, that's the question, right? I think I had this feeling of being suffocated. And then when I thought about that, the guilt would slam into me. So, I hid all of that behind the need to explore the world. Which is hilarious, because I've never left the West Coast, not really. I wasn't going to get to Rome or Paris on a bus. But that's what I told my mom, so that guilt didn't eat me alive. And it wasn't all bad. I mean, I learned a lot about myself out there. When I got up to the Canada border, I didn't even have a passport so I turned back south. I stopped in Portland, because it seemed like a good middle point before going home. But then I thought, why did I even have to go home? Why couldn't I live on my own? I had been doing it, even if not well, but I had taken care of myself. So I stayed here. That was a couple of years ago now."

"Still want to see Rome and Paris?"

I glanced down at what the doctor was doing as I answered. The man was bent over, his face a mask of concentration. "Sure. You want to take me someday?" I turned back and flashed Cris-tian a winning smile, and it prompted a slight smirk from him.

His grip on my hand tightened painfully, but I hid any reac-tion. He was literally having his skin sewn without pain medica-tion, with nothing but my random stories to distract him. I just hoped he didn't actually break any of the bones in my hand.

"Someday, yeah. We'll do that," he whispered.

I continued on, telling him funny stories of customers I dealt with while working at Target. Eventually, he closed his eyes and the only way I could tell how he was feeling was how his brows would pull together. I wasn't sure how long I was there, but my back began to ache. Despite the discomfort, I didn't even think about moving. I continued to whisper and run my fingers through his hair.

"All done. He really needs to be off this leg. He could easily rip these stitches," Dave said.

"We'll discuss it," I said, before Cristian could open his mouth.

Dave nodded. "You two take your time. I'm going to check in with everyone else to see if anyone needs anything."

With that, he was gone. Cristian squeezed my hand, pulling my attention back to him. His face was pale, and his hair was in disarray from my fingers and the sweat that had soaked him.

"How are you feeling? Do you want the alcohol now?" I asked.

Cristian shook his head. "Help me sit up, please."

He struggled, and I knew if I didn't help him, he would figure it out on his own. And he would likely hurt himself further. So, I leaned down and slid my arms under his back, encouraging him to wrap his arms around my shoulders. Once he was holding on, I leaned up, pulling his weight with me the best way I could. When he sat up, I could feel that he wasn't able to sit up on his own.

"Cristian, please. If we need to wait for you to heal, that's what we need to do."

Cristian was sitting on the table, looking down at me, his breathing steady but strained. His skin was pale, his face tight with pain, but there was something else there too. Something I couldn't quite place until — "You called me honey."

I froze, my hands gripping his arm and side as I held him up. The words hit me square in the chest, sending a wave of warmth straight to my face. I replayed the moment in my head. And there it was. Casual, instinctive, like it had slipped past my lips before I could stop it.

My throat went dry. "I…"

Cristian smirked. That infuriating, knowing smirk. Even stitched up and half-conscious from the pain, he still managed it. "Didn't realize I was your honey."

Oh, for the love of…

I let out a slow, measured breath and focused on my task, determined not to let him see my embarrassment. "Come on, Reyes. Let's get you up before you start getting ideas."

He chuckled, but I ignored it, slipping my arm under his and carefully pulling him upright. He tensed, his body rigid with pain, but I kept my grip firm, steadying him as he adjusted to the movement.

I risked a glance at his face. He was watching me, amused, despite the discomfort. I ignored the way my stomach flipped and focused on keeping him balanced.

"I'll pretend I didn't hear it if it makes you feel better," he murmured.

I huffed, shaking my head. "You definitely didn't hear it."

Cristian's low chuckle sent another rush of warmth through me, but I shoved it aside. He was barely standing on his own. I wasn't about to let my brain spiral over a stupid slip of the tongue.

Except, maybe it wasn't stupid at all. It just felt natural. In the few weeks we had spent together, I had started to care about Cristian. The realization of that struck me hard, and I felt foolish. I felt a bit confused about my feelings. Being in such close proximity alone with someone most of the time could be creating something unrealistic in my mind.

"I was just trying to be comforting. Did it work?" I shrugged as I helped him find his balance.

When I straightened and looked to check that he was still doing ok, I was surprised by the intensity in his gaze.

"Yes. Yes, it did."

My entire body felt sticky and slick at the same time. Sweat popped out of every pore it could. Sure, the warehouse wasn't the coolest place to be, but it wasn't nearly as hot as it was outside in the sun. The pain in my leg was enough to make me want to vomit, but I couldn't let Marlowe know that.

I knew that after I killed one attacker, his friends would come back with backup. The one named Mike played scared when he was alone. But it wouldn't stay that way. Killing either of them hadn't been my plan. But when the tall one spun with the gun after breaking out of my hold, I had to fight him for it. The firearm going off, and the shot slamming into his chest hadn't been the plan. Once it was done, it was done, and I had to think about the people I was protecting. Think about Marlowe.

As I snuck into the lobby, I almost gave us all away when I saw Mike touch Marlowe. It was a single finger, but I didn't miss the direction his hand was going. I saw red. Rage raced through me and instead of grabbing the tall one in a good grip, I attacked in anger. Inevitably, that was what gave the attacker an upper hand for just a moment.

Luckily for me, he was sloppy. I was stronger and likely better fed since the world fell apart. The two men were willing to do anything necessary to get the supplies they needed. Unfortunately for them, I was willing to go to any lengths to protect Marlowe.

I looked down at her now, as she was dragging my pants up my legs. Feeling like an invalid made me angry. But I couldn't be angry watching her gently caring for me. I could still feel her fingers in my hair. When I called her out for the pet name, she shut down on me. I mentally kicked myself for making things awkward. What did I really expect, anyhow? I wasn't interested in some random relationship caused by the apocalypse. I hadn't been interested in one before the world fell into shambles. Now was definitely not the time to find myself emotionally attached to a woman.

Reining in my random feelings, I shifted, testing my stitched leg. The pain increased immediately, but I could bend my knee and move slowly. The bullet had struck my left thigh, ripping through my pants. I figured I was lucky it was a through and through. Having the doctor dig around for a slug would have likely pushed my pain threshold beyond its limits.

Marlowe pushed her shoulder under my arm again and gripped me around the waist. She scrutinized every move I made. She clocked every grimace, likely filing it away to lecture me about later.

"Cristian? Marlowe?" Katherine's voice caught us as we were leaving the clinic.

"Here," Marlowe called back.

When the woman appeared, she looked scared. Her red hair was wild around her face, escaping the bun she normally wore.

"What in the hell happened?" Katherine asked.

"Long story. We need to go," I said, before Marlowe could change our plans.

She made an annoyed sound in her throat, but she didn't argue.

"Can you grab our bags? We dropped them by our room and didn't get them again," Marlowe said.

Katherine nodded and ran off. Carol came to meet us as we hobbled toward the back of the warehouse.

"What are you doing?"

"We need to go. Now." My gaze swept the warehouse one last time. Too many blind spots. Too many people remained frozen in shock. They compromised the front entrance, but what about the loading dock? If those men circled back, they'd come from behind next. No way to cover all the exits. No way to guarantee anyone here would survive.

"And you all should, too." I said.

"I'm not sure where I'd go," Carol said.

Marlowe and I exchanged a look. It was easy to read her thoughts. It was one reason things were so easy between us. I pushed that idea away and nodded to her, letting her know I agreed.

"Come with us, Carol. We're going to Cristian's home," Marlowe said.

Carol looked at us uncertainly.

"It's in Tualatin. If not for the storm, we would have gone straight there. You opened the doors and welcomed us in. Come with us. You have a place there. A safe place. And you won't be alone," I said.

Her eyes were brimming with tears. She wasn't looking at us, but at Harold's body.

"He was all I had here. Our children, they wanted to be world travelers. Our daughter is living in Paris. An artist. Our son, working with Doctors Without Borders in Africa. I feel like I'll never see them again now. He was it." Her voice was soft and heavy with grief.

Marlowe laid a hand on her arm. "I'm so sorry, Carol. But Harold wanted to protect you. That's what he would still want. Let us help you. You don't have to stay with us if you don't want. But we need to get away from here, in case the attackers come back. This warehouse is full of things they will want."

"And if they have more guns, the two I took from them won't be enough," I added.

Carol sniffed and pulled herself up straight. "We need to warn everyone that they definitely need to leave now. The teenagers left as soon as the shooting started. And I'm pretty sure a few others fled out back. Dave isn't sure what he's doing."

"A doctor would be a useful addition, since the two of us seem to keep getting hurt," Marlowe said sarcastically.

Just then, Katherine arrived with our packs. Before Marlowe released me, she made certain I could balance, then swung the heavier pack onto her back. I didn't miss the quiet rush of breath that came from her. Even though she had rested, I was certain her ribs weren't fully healed. She handed the lighter pack to me, and I raised an eyebrow.

"Put it on, or I'm taking both," she said.

I grudgingly did as she instructed, knowing I wouldn't admit that the additional weight didn't feel terrific.

"Let's tell everyone what's happening. I'll pack my bag and then we'll go," Carol said.

We met with the last few survivors that were still in the warehouse. Dave and Katherine were there as well. Carol quickly let everyone know she was leaving with our group. Folks exchanged glances and many appeared unsure of what to do. I understood. Everyone had believed, as things fell apart, that someone would come to the rescue. Police. Fire fighters. Military. But there was no one. We were on our own.

"Anyone that wants to accompany us to my home in Tualatin is welcome. No one has to be alone, unless that's what they chose."

Marlowe's hand tightened on my side where she held me. No matter what, I would protect her. She would come first in whatever group we collected. I wouldn't tell her that, but I made the promise to myself. I wouldn't fail Marlowe.

In the end, Katherine, Carol, Dave and, surprisingly, Roger joined us. Roger remained quiet as we made our way to the back of the warehouse. Between him and Dave, they carried all the important medical supplies the doctor had found and collected. Carol and Katherine's packs were heavy with food and we all grabbed extra clothes as well.

At the backdoor, I pulled the gun I had at the small of my back. I held it in front of me and pointed at the door. Gesturing, I told Roger to open it and stand back. Everyone moved to the side except Marlowe, who wouldn't allow me to walk on my own. Though she was likely correct that I would fall on my face after a few steps, I didn't like the idea of her being unprotected.

Luckily, there was no one lying in wait for us. The back parking area of the warehouse was silent. Cars that would likely never start again still sat in their parking spots. Judging their ages, I saw nothing I thought would still work. As we made our way along the back fence, my frustration grew. I was slowing everyone else down.

At the end, we turned down a residential street that seemed to run parallel to the larger main road. I wanted to avoid all main roads for as long as possible. We had no idea of the location of the attackers' group, so no matter what we did, it was a risk. I wished I had even one advantage I'd had as a cop. When doing door to doors, or even just writing a ticket, I'd had the ability to look up information at the touch of a button. Or call backup to locate a suspect. Now, every move we made was completely blind.

Marlowe didn't complain as she continued to support my injured side. We walked in sync as best as we could. I was taking smaller steps to mitigate some of the pain, which also matched Marlowe's stride. I kept scanning the area, looking for threats. Carol, Roger and Dave walked ahead of us, while Katherine brought up the rear. It wasn't where I wanted her, but I had enough to worry about.

I tucked the gun containing most of the remaining rounds at the small of my back for easy access. The other gun was in the bottom of my pack. I knew the caliber of each gun and planned on keeping them in my possession. Finding additional ammo was on the list of priorities now. I wouldn't allow my group to be unprepared again. Two handguns weren't an arsenal, but it was better than kitchen knives and my fists.

Coming out the other side of the small neighborhood, we skirted close to the fence along the road. Across the street was a field and green space. We were making our way out of Hillsboro into the farming area between cities. The flat land didn't leave many places to hide if we were to get caught in the middle, and no way could I run.

I tried to keep my focus sharp, but my body was betraying me. Each step sent a fresh wave of fire through my leg. My vision blurred at the edges. I forced myself to blink it away. If I let myself stumble, Marlowe would try to hold more of my weight, and she was already carrying too much.

"We need to stay on the side with the trees," I said, my voice rougher than I intended. "If we're in the middle of that open field, we'll be sitting ducks."

Dave glanced over his shoulder at me and then did a double take. I had a feeling I looked a lot worse than I knew. He slowed down and stopped, forcing Marlowe and me to stop in front of him. He pulled a handkerchief from his pocket and mopped at my forehead. Then he looked into my eyes, studying me.

"You need a break."

"It's only been like twenty minutes." My tone was terser than I'd meant, but I didn't want everyone worrying about me.

"It's been like an hour, Cristian," Marlowe said from my side.

I was moving slower than I had realized. If I estimated, we were only a mile and a half from the warehouse.

"He can't keep going like this. I know he thinks he can. But my medical opinion is we need to find somewhere to stop and rest. He needs weight off that leg and I'd like to check the stitches," Dave said, holding up his hands as I tried to walk by him.

Marlowe's grip tightened, holding me in place. I looked down, and she lifted her face toward me. Her cheeks were red, and I noticed her hair was wet with sweat. She was pushing too hard helping me and I hadn't even noticed. I maneuvered, so that I could pull my pack off. I had a bottle of water in the side pocket and I put it into Marlowe's hand. She sipped and tried to hand it back. I pushed it back toward her mouth and she drank more.

As we looked around, we faced limited options. Going back toward town could put us into the path of the attackers we faced at the warehouse. We were in no shape to fight. In the distance was a large, expensive looking farmhouse. If it was empty, it would be comfortable. It would also be an easy target.

Beyond the trees that bordered the fancy house, I could just barely see another roof. I pointed, and the group turned to look.

"If that house is empty, maybe we can regroup there."

"Why not that one?" Katherine asked, pointing toward the house I had dismissed.

Marlowe answered before I could. "Too obvious. It would be a target for looters."

She looked up at me with a confident smile and I smiled in return. Looking over at Katherine, I nodded my agreement with Marlowe. Without further discussion, we made our way toward the hidden farmhouse. I was hoping it was empty, because if not, I wasn't sure how much further we would have to go.

Dave hadn't been wrong. I'd reached the end of my endurance. My limp grew worse, and I leaned on Marlowe more than I wanted. The pain in my leg was intensifying. Stars sparked my vision and I focused on my breathing to ensure I didn't pass out. I pictured taking Marlowe down with me and accidentally crushing her small body under my much larger one.

We came to the end of a long gravel driveway. I couldn't contain the groan when I thought about limping down the uneven surface.

Marlowe's arm squeezed me. "I got you. We can make it."

"I'm going to go check and see if it's empty first. No reason for Cristian to limp all the way down there if we're going to find out we can't get in," Roger said.

I could have kissed the man for thinking of it. Katherine

volunteered to go with him and the rest of us headed for the shade of the trees that stood on one side of the drive. With Dave and Marlowe's help, I slowly sat on the ground, my back against a tree. The doctor crouched and looked in my face again. He held the back of his hand against my forehead.

"How bad is the pain?" he asked.

"On what, a scale from zero to one hundred and fifty?"

He smiled. Not in a way that seemed like he enjoyed my joke, but more as a doctor that had heard all them all. "Whatever scale you'd like."

"It's worse than when we left. If that helps."

"It does."

Dave doused his handkerchief with water and held it to my forehead. The material shouldn't have felt so cool, as none of us had enjoyed cold water for weeks. But when he pressed it to my skin, the coolness surprised me and made my eyes flutter closed.

"Hold this for a moment," he said.

Once I had the compress handled, he stepped away, pulling Marlowe with him. They shared a whispered conversation, and I watched, but couldn't pick up anything. She looked over at me a few times, concern in her eyes. She nodded to whatever Dave said before responding. The man's eyes widened, and he shook his head. But Marlowe wasn't up for an argument. She sliced her hand in the air, ending their dispute.

She spun on her heel, and Dave looked bothered, but he didn't stop her. She kneeled next to me, taking the wet cloth from me and mopping my neck and cheeks. I tried to get her to look at me, but she pretended to be focused on cooling me down.

"Hot day," I mumbled.

She nodded, but didn't meet my eyes. Something felt off, but exhaustion was pulling at my mind, making it hard to focus on what was happening around me. I let my head lean against the tree and closed my eyes for a moment. I figured it couldn't hurt to get a little rest while waiting for Roger to come back.

The shaking of my shoulder snapped me awake. Marlowe

stood over me, her eyes round with worry, but when I blinked, she smiled quickly and held out her hands.

"Roger says the house is actually empty, like someone was in the middle of moving. So, it's safe for a bit."

She grunted under the weight of helping me up, and Dave grabbed me under one arm as I worked to find my balance. He watched me warily, and I nodded, shaking out my arms and waking up my body. Marlowe was right there, pushing under my arm so she could help me to the house. I squeezed her shoulder, letting her know I appreciated her help.

The gravel was hard to limp along and more than once I was afraid I'd go down. Apparently, realizing Marlowe couldn't handle my weight on her own, Katherine appeared on my other side and slung my arm around her shoulders. I was worried about her getting the wrong idea, but when she looked over at Marlowe, I saw them exchange a worried look.

"What is it?" I asked.

Marlowe's smile was bright. And probably the most fake smile I had ever seen on her face. "Nothing. Just want to get you to the house without us all going down."

I frowned at her. But she wasn't wrong. I wasn't stable, and the gravel moved under foot, especially on the side where I couldn't put my full weight down. I had no desire to fall, either. Instead of trying to figure out what Marlowe was lying about, I focused on the placement of my feet.

Before I knew it, we were at the front steps of the farmhouse. Roger had the front door open. From the broken front window, I assumed he didn't know how to pick a lock. The house was definitely old, but someone had clearly cherished it. The floors inside were well polished, even with the marks of wear and tear in the expected places. There was a large dining room table, wrapped in moving blankets, with matching chairs covered in plastic wrap.

The kitchen was empty, all the appliances moved to wherever the owners went. Roger unwrapped a chair and Marlowe helped me sit.

"What's the rest of the house look like?" I asked. My mind went into defense mode, thinking about the different entrances and how many we would need to watch for intruders.

"Just one other door, at the back. It's locked with a deadbolt. I didn't bother trying to open it. There's three rooms, other than the dining room, living room and kitchen. There's a dresser in one, similarly wrapped and some cardboard boxes in another. Doesn't look like anyone has been here since everything went down," Roger explained.

"What's behind the house? Any roads? Fields?" I asked.

Roger shook his head. "I glanced out to just double check. There's a backyard, surrounded by chain link. Outside the fence, there are large trees that had probably been planted for privacy. I couldn't really see anything beyond that. It would be hard for someone to sneak up on that side, because they would have to be out in the open once they climbed the chain link."

"We need to have a watch at all times. If we stay here through the night, they need to wake up everyone if someone shows up," I said.

"We can take care of it, Cristian. Maybe we should get you comfortable," Marlowe said.

I looked at her, confused. "I'm fine."

"Doctor's orders," Dave cut in. "You need off that leg. And it needs to be elevated. We don't have ice to help with swelling, but we need you to rest it."

"Well, Doc, I'm not sure how I'm going to do all that. If you haven't noticed, we're sort of hiding from a possible gang," I replied.

Marlowe's hand was on my shoulder, massaging softly, as if she was trying to calm me. She leaned so her face was in front of mine, so close that she blocked the view of anyone else in the room. It was easy to focus on her. She was beautiful. My confusion seemed to open the door for thoughts about her appearance. She was petite, but I had a feeling she could be scrappy. Her warm brown eyes searched mine, as if she had asked me a question and I hadn't answered.

"Huh?" I asked, not sure if I had missed something.

She shook her head and smiled. Leaning forward, she pressed her lips to my forehead. But where I thought she was giving me a sweet kiss, she stayed for a few seconds before pulling back. Looking over at Dave, she grimaced and nodded. I didn't like the way they were communicating without speaking.

"What's going on?" I asked.

Marlowe and Dave continued to look at each other, and I just stared at her, waiting to see if she would answer me. It was Dave that spoke instead.

"I'm a bit concerned about your injury. It's been a few hours since the shooting, and I'm concerned about the possibility of an early infection."

My eyebrows shot up. Taking a moment, I evaluated the feelings within my body. Beyond the pain, I wasn't noticing anything that seemed significant. I was tired. But I figured that was to be expected. Even if it was just a flesh wound, someone shot me.

Dave pointed at the table. "Can someone take the blankets off the table and make a bed, best as possible? I think we need to have him lie down and then we'll elevate his leg."

"I'm fine. I don't need any of that," I argued.

Marlowe crouched next to me, taking my hand in hers. "Just listen to the doctor. Please."

The concern in her voice and eyes made me want to do anything she asked. I looked around at the faces of our small group. Letting them join us felt like the right thing to do, and I didn't want to be a liability to any of them. Looking back at Marlowe, I nodded my agreement, and she smiled a genuine smile for just me.

Roger and Carol worked together to unwrap the dining table. In one bedroom, they folded the blankets on the ground, trying to make a makeshift bed. Dave and Marlowe helped me into the room as Katherine unpacked all our bags on the large dining table. As I limped into the bedroom, I tried to remember how many supplies we'd brought with us.

"I'm not sure how long we can stay here. We might not have enough food," I muttered.

"Let us worry about that. You're going to rest and heal. And once you're ready, we'll be back on the road," Marlowe said.

Between the two of them, they lay me on the folded blankets. It was better than the bare floor, but it wasn't comfortable by any means. I didn't complain. Dave left the room to find something that would work to elevate my leg. Marlowe sat on the floor with me. She brushed the hair that stuck to my sweat-slick forehead.

"Damnit, I'm sorry Marlowe."

She smiled down at me. "Who needs to stop apologizing now?"

Dave returned with one of the smaller cardboard boxes. Carefully, he lifted my injured leg and put the box under my thigh as best he could. I felt like a hinderance, but my exhaustion was too much to keep fighting.

Marlowe didn't leave my side. Instead, she sat next to my head, brushing my hair with her fingers. I tried to say something. To thank her, maybe, or tell her to wake me if anything happened. But my tongue felt too heavy.

The soft hum of her voice reached me through the haze, but I couldn't hold on to it. The world tilted sideways. And then there was nothing.

Worry and panic created a sick mixture in my gut. As Cristian fell asleep, I studied his pale face. He claimed to feel fine, but it was obvious he had a slight fever. And from Dave's reaction, that was just the beginning of something. With everything we had been through, I hadn't once imagined I would have to manage things without him. Cristian was stronger than the apocalypse. It was what I knew about him. His strength. His determination.

Dave came into the room and motioned for me to follow him out.. After I laid an extra sweatshirt over his chest in lieu of a blanket, I slipped away from Cristian, who's eyes moved in sleep.

In the hall, Dave's face was grave, making me more fearful.

"How bad is it?" I asked.

Dave scratched his forehead. "It's hard to tell. I don't have enough equipment. I have a few things, but no antibiotics or antibiotic ointment. If I had, I would have used it right away. I cleaned the wound as best I could but I think we're seeing the start of infection."

"Ok. Infection. Cristian's strong. He can fight anything."

"He seems healthy. But this could be more than he can handle."

I rubbed my chest, the ache in it growing. "What can happen?"

"My concern is that the infection will grow worse and he'll develop sepsis. Without antibiotics, that's life threatening."

"He could die from this."

Dave nodded and patted my arm. I closed my eyes for a second and took a couple of deep breaths, trying to calm my heart. In my mind, I pictured Cristian, healthy and vibrant, staying up all night to protect our group. I thought about him protecting me from Don and then leading us away from where he could find us. How he looked after me when I was injured. I pulled from all the strength he had given me since everything had collapsed.

"What does he need?"

"Antibiotics. Pills and topical would be best, since I doubt we could find intravenous. He's going to need to stay hydrated and fed. And to keep him comfortable, some sort of pain medication. But that's not the priority."

I nodded. "So I could find most, if not all, of it, at a pharmacy, right?"

"For the antibiotics, yeah, we need a pharmacy. Or a hospital or clinic."

"Can you write down the meds to look for?"

Before I even stopped speaking, Dave was already shaking his head. "You can't go. It's not safe."

I grabbed his hand between mine, making sure he was paying close attention. "You're a doctor. You cannot leave him. His survival relies on you and your knowledge. This is the best way I can help him."

He still looked unsure, glancing toward the room where Cristian slept. "He won't like it."

"If he wakes up and I'm gone, he's going to lose his mind," I murmured, gripping the back of the chair for balance.

Dave nodded. "Probably."

"But if I don't go, he might not wake up at all."

That thought settled like a stone in my gut. I exhaled slowly. I would wait until morning. Let him rest. But if his fever spiked any higher, I was going, whether he liked it or not.

In the dining room, Katherine and Carol had sorted through the sparse supplies. There was enough food and water for a few days, if we rationed. But Cristian couldn't heal if he was only getting a small ration. I drank from a bottle of water that Carol handed me, but with each sip, I thought about how Cristian needed it more than me. It made me stop drinking. Katherine came to me with a small bag of trail mix in her hand.

"You can't help him or yourself, if you're too weak," she said.

I looked at the woman, who just a week ago was hitting on Cristian. She had backed off, mostly. Though it was clear she wanted his attention more often than not. I couldn't blame her. He was a good-looking man. And he exuded confidence and safety. And in a situation where you're completely alone, someone that could take care of you felt important. But she looked at me now, with sympathy and understanding. I took the trail mix from her and opened the bag.

After chewing a few nuts and raisins, I looked over to where Carol was sitting against a far wall. "How is she doing?"

Katherine followed my gaze and her eyes were sad as she studied Carol. "She's not talking a whole lot. I'm not sure she's really facing the reality of what's happened. She and Harold had been married since they were eighteen. High school sweethearts. They told us the stories when we all first met in the warehouse. I'm not sure I would know how to go on."

"I've never had anything that important in my life except my mother. So, I can't imagine how she feels."

"Well, you have Cristian now," Katherine said, reminding me of the part I needed to play.

"Yes. I do. And he's the only thing getting me through all of this." I realized I wasn't faking a relationship. It was the absolute truth.

Katherine looked toward the hallway, and I didn't miss the wistful look on her face. But when she looked back at me, she wiped it all away and showed me genuine concern. I didn't know what the woman's deal was, but as long as she kept her hands off of Cristian, she could stay with us.

With everyone fed as best as we could, we came together, without Carol or Cristian, to discuss the needs of the group. Dave, Katherine, Roger and I huddled in the kitchen, hoping to keep our voices from disturbing either of the others.

"We're going to have to stay here, at least for a few days," Dave said.

"We don't have enough food and water for that," Roger replied.

"We also have no beds, blankets, or anything to be comfortable for a few days," Katherine added.

Both had decent points. I moved to the window above the sink. It pointed toward the front of the house and from there; it looked as if the farmhouse was the only thing in the world. Though I knew just on the other side of the trees, there was the fancy house. The one we had avoided, out of fear someone looting it while we were inside.

"The other house. We should go there," I said.

"You and Cristian said—" Roger started, but I cut him off.

"I know what we said. And I'm not suggesting we stay there. But we could bring supplies from there. If it's empty. We should go check now, before dark."

I looked at each of them and could see the uncertainty in their faces. They looked back and forth, as if what I was saying made no sense. I could feel the heat rise in my cheeks. I wasn't used to being the one making plans for others. Traveling and living on my own was only about me. There was no reason for anyone to follow my ideas.

"I'll go with you." Katherine volunteering surprised me.

Roger sighed. "Well, can't let you two go alone, can I?"

"Dave, stay here to keep an eye on Cristian, ok? I'd feel better knowing he's not alone," I said.

The doctor nodded, and I didn't doubt it was relief I saw on his face.

The three of us emptied our backpacks completely. In Cristian's bag, I found one gun he had taken from the attackers in the warehouse. It was heavier than I expected for such a small gun. I'd never even held a gun, let alone shot one. But I understood the need for it, especially now. I tucked it into the side pocket of my bag and sent a prayer to the universe that I didn't somehow shoot myself in the butt.

The sun burned high overhead, blasting us as we stepped outside. I shaded my face, looking around the yard. It was a simple setup. If the owners had any lawn furniture, they'd taken it with them. There wasn't one random chair or piece of landscaping tool. Just overgrown grass surrounded on two sides with large trees.

I walked toward the trees that separated the land between the two farmhouses. There was no fence on the side of the gravel drive, so we could walk through the copse and find ourselves on the outskirts of the neighboring field. Walking into the field made me feel incredibly exposed.

The house ahead of us was too far away to see movement inside. Without discussing it, I was sure going toward the back would be a better idea, so I walked in that direction. I imagined if someone was watching, they would do it through the large panoramic windows that lined the wall of the house. Roger and Katherine followed silently.

The thought of Cristian's possible infection preoccupied me. I had a feeling when he found out I went out scavenging, he wouldn't be thrilled. It was time for me to make some decisions about our survival. He had done too much already. If he wasn't used to someone caring for him, he would need to learn. I wasn't going to let him die.

At the back of the farmhouse, we paused and watched the windows. The shades remained open. But it was dark inside, making it hard to determine if there was someone just waiting for us to break in. Glancing at Roger, he shrugged in response to my unspoken question.

Slowly, I ascended the stairs. They creaked underfoot, and I hissed out a frustrated breath. At the top, I slid to the side of the windowed backdoor. I peered into the corner of the glass and stood frozen, waiting. Nothing seemed to move. Running my finger along the window, I found a layer of dust on the outside. I couldn't be sure what that meant, but maybe nobody had used the door recently.

The handle turned easily, and the door swung in silently. I stayed just outside, listening for anything that would indicate we weren't alone. But everything was completely still inside the big house. I motioned to Roger and Katherine, and they both came up the stairs to join me.

"Seems empty," I whispered.

Inside, the house seemed undisturbed. The feeling of abandonment hit me hard, and I wondered what happened to the people that lived in the beautiful home. There were shoes of various sizes near the backdoor. I tried not to think about any children that might have lived here. How did families deal with their children being at school, possibly miles away when everything crashed?

The kitchen was the first room we came to, and Roger went directly to a door that opened onto a pantry. "Bingo."

He stuffed boxes of sugary cereal, jars of peanut butter, almond butter, Nutella and honey into his backpack. Katherine opened another cabinet but found only glasses and plates. She moved to another and found spices. Under the sink, she pulled out a small case that said first aid on it. Taking that from her, I popped it open, only to be disappointed by the various sized bandaids and half tube of antibiotic ointment.

Nevertheless, I put the kit in my bag and moved from the kitchen, leaving Roger and Katherine to worry about food. There was a half bath on the bottom floor, with a medicine cabinet behind the mirror. Over the counter medications lined the shelves. I didn't bother to read the labels. Everything went into my bag. I also shoved in the two rolls of toilet paper from the rack on the back of the toilet. If there were comfort items, I was taking them.

Katherine was folding a blanket from the couch when I walked into the living room. There was a basket next to a lounge chair that had a few more blankets and throw pillows. She moved that to the backdoor, so we could just take the whole basket. I climbed the stairs, and realized something didn't feel right as I reached the top. An unfamiliar smell hit my nose, and my arm hairs prickled.

"Guys! Can you come up here?" I called down.

It didn't take long for Roger and Katherine to both rush up to meet me. Immediately, Roger grabbed his nose and Katherine seemed to blanch.

"Is that smell what I think it is?" I asked.

Neither of them answered. But together, we moved down the hallway. The first door was open, and led into a neat office. The next room was a dimly lit bathroom, with sunlight streaming in from a small high window. The last door was closed. We didn't need to open it, though. There was a note taped to the wood. Roger pulled it down and read it quickly, before handing it to me.

"In the end of times, with the star named Wormwood above our heads, we want to go together to heaven's gates. May our children and grandchildren repent, and our Father allows them to meet us in his divine heaven when their time comes." I whispered the words, my heart heavy.

"Are you kidding me? Religious idiots!" Katherine stormed away, going back down the stairs.

I stared after her for a long moment. Her reaction was emotional, and it made me wonder what really upset her. I taped the note back to the door. The couple wanted to be together, in the end. Maybe I couldn't agree with the fact that they gave up so soon. But they made their choice. And I wanted to leave their resting place alone.

Downstairs, I found Katherine rummaging through a hall closet. As Roger walked by us, back into the kitchen, he raised his eyebrows at me. I shrugged and waited while he moved out of earshot.

I looked at Katherine's back, since she wasn't acknowledging me. "Are you ok?"

Her head dropped, but she didn't turn. Instead, she sorted through the jackets that were hanging in front of her, pulling ones off hangers. I wasn't sure what she thought we were going to do with them in the middle of summer, but I wasn't going to ask.

"You seemed angry up there. If you don't want to talk about it, that's fine," I said.

When she didn't speak, I started to turn away. But her sigh stopped me before I left the hallway.

"My parents are, or maybe were, devout Catholics. They live in Indiana. I imagine this is all happening there, too."

"You think that's why..." I pointed upstairs, not wanting to mention what we had found.

"Makes sense. The Wormwood reference? That's from Revelations." Katherine spun to face me, and her eyes were red and her cheeks were wet. I suddenly realized this was hitting very close to home. "The ironic part? If this was the rapture or whatever, they wouldn't have had to commit suicide. They would have been taken by God. And by committing suicide, they just committed one of the biggest sins and won't make it to their heaven."

I just stared at her. Religion wasn't something my mom ever introduced into our home. But I knew that suicide was a big no go for anyone that went to church. Katherine spun back to the closet, moving things around on the floor, until she pulled out a duffel bag. She moved to the laundry room off the kitchen. I followed quietly.

"I'm sorry. You must be really worried about your parents," I said.

Katherine checked the dryer and pulled out clean towels. Joining her, I started folding so they could fit into the duffel bag. There was a shelving unit on one side that had additional towels and sheets. I pulled those down as well. Without mattresses and no way to really move them to the older house, we needed as much as possible to make beds.

"We weren't that close. But something like this…well…it makes you really reevaluate the choices you made. They aren't bad people, not really. They just didn't agree with me leaving the church. When I moved out here, they assumed I had become some hippy that was living in a commune." That made Katherine snort, and I couldn't help my own smile.

"Well, I guess we're sort of creating a commune now, aren't we?"

Katherine smiled. "I mean, so far we're not doing too bad. Though we have lost people." Her smile fell, and I knew we were both thinking of Harold.

It made me realize I didn't really know anything else about Katherine. Her opening up about her parents was a lot of information in a short time. I had been busy judging the woman for her obvious interest in Cristian, that I wasn't treating her the way I should have. Though I still didn't want her trying her hand with Cristian, I wasn't capable of being an unfriendly person for a long period of time.

"You didn't know anyone in the warehouse before you got there?" I asked.

Roger walked into the laundry room then. "None of us did, really. I mean, obviously Carol and Harold were together. And the teens were friends who were trying to get home from school. But other than that, we were all strangers."

"I worked in an office building less than a mile from the warehouse. But I live in Vancouver," Katherine said.

The idea of being that many miles from home with no means of transportation had to be awful. Not to mention having to cross the bridge to get into Washington. The bridges were always packed with travelers. If all of those vehicles just stopped at once, I couldn't imagine the chaos. Not to mention if any of the drawbridges were open, they would be stuck that way.

Katherine continued, breaking into my end-of-the-world

thoughts. "Most of my co-workers had families or someone to get home to. I have my cat. Who is an outdoor cat and will probably survive this better than me. So, when I walked by the warehouse, still not super sure where I was going to go, I saw Harold. He was walking around the perimeter of the warehouse. We struck up a conversation. And well, you know how he was. He invited me in. And that's where I stayed."

"I think Harold invited most of the people in that were in the warehouse when you arrived," Roger said, a fond smile on his face.

"He definitely saved Cristian and I from drowning," I said.

"I just didn't have plans, beyond staying alive day to day," Katherine said.

I nodded. "That's likely the theme of life now."

We finished packing as many of the linens and towels that would fit in the duffel bag and the basket. At the backdoor, we stood looking back into the house.

"We can always come back for more of the food," Roger said.

With the three of us, we could only load down each of our backpacks. There wasn't enough water, which would be the biggest challenge. Something we would have to figure out at the house. But we did have enough to last our small group a week. It wasn't going to be the most nutritious time.

Katherine and I held the basket between us and Roger carried the duffel as we hurried away from the house. We were about halfway through the field when the sound of breaking glass echoed from the house. Frozen I spot, I slowly turned to look at Katherine. Roger was ahead of us, and he slowly spun to look at the house.

"Run," I whispered urgently.

The basket jerked between us, nearly spilling the blankets as we ran for the trees. My pulse was a hammer in my throat. Behind us, another crash of glass echoed, closer this time. I risked a glance over my shoulder. A figure stepped onto the back deck.

I sucked in a breath. He was too far to see clearly, but he wasn't just looking at the house. He was looking for something.

Someone.

"Go," I whispered, shoving Katherine forward. I wasn't waiting to find out if he'd seen us.

Just as we reached the trees, I heard more breaking glass behind us. My hold on the basket failed, and I spun to hide behind a tree trunk. Scrambling, I dropped my pack and dug to find the gun that I had. The weight in my hand didn't feel comforting, but I would defend myself if it came to that.

Roger pulled out a pair of binoculars next to me and hid, while trying to see the house we had just come from.

"Where in the world did you find those?" I asked.

"The upstairs office."

We whispered, though I doubted our voices could carry all the way to the house. We were too far away for me to make anything out, but Roger studied them and then held the binoculars out to me. I peered through and didn't recognize the man. He didn't seem to be looking for anything in particular, just searching around the house he had broken into. He could have been any survivor we had seen in the days since everything collapsed. Dirty, mismatched clothing, a hat on backwards, likely holding back greasy, unwashed hair.

"Let's go," I said, slowly backing into the shadows. I wasn't trusting anymore strangers.

When we arrived back at our farmhouse, we were greeted by shouting. I immediately recognized Cristian's deep timber. Running into the house, I found Cristian on his feet, trying to push past Dave. If he had been at full strength, there was no way the smaller man could have stopped him. But now, it was clear Cristian was sick, and he was barely putting weight on his leg. Dave had his hands out in a calming gesture and his voice was soft as he encouraged Cristian to lay backdown. Carol stood off to the side, her eyes watching the scene in front of her, but her expression blank.

"Where is she?" Cristian yelled. "You just let her go out there? Without me? Who's going to protect her?"

I dropped my bag by the dining table and rushed to Cristian. He gripped my arm, his fingers burning against my skin. His forehead was damp. His breathing was uneven, too shallow. When his eyes locked onto me, they were glassy, unfocused, like he was seeing something else entirely.

"Where were you?" His voice was rough, confused.

"Hey, honey. I'm right here." I put my hands on his chest to try to calm him.

He blinked a few times, the confusion clearing, and he calmed instantly when he saw I was there and safe. His hands came up and cupped my cheeks. He brought his forehead to mine, pressing briefly as he exhaled shakily. For a second the gesture took me aback, but then I realized how hot his palms were. The fever was rising. I covered his hands with my own, leaning one of my cheeks deeper into his hand.

"I'm ok. Everything is ok. You should be laying down." My voice was low and calm, trying to bring him down a few levels.

"You can't do that. You can't just leave me."

Confused, I shook my head. "I didn't leave you. I wouldn't."

"But you were gone." His confusion deepened, while his temper cooled immediately as he looked around the small group of us in the farmhouse. "I'm sorry. I thought…"

"You thought your girl here was in danger. That's ok. But it would be best if you laid back down," Dave said. He smiled his doctor smile, clearly not put off by Cristian's outburst.

Cristian nodded, but when he took his hands from my face, he grabbed my fingers and wouldn't let me move away. "You'll come with me?"

"Of course. Just let me get some stuff to make you more comfortable, ok?"

He took a long time to nod and release my hand. He let Dave prop him up and limped back into the bedroom. Once they disappeared, I released a deep breath.

"He's not doing good," Katherine said.

"No. He's burning up. Maybe some meds I found can help," I replied.

"Is he hallucinating or something?" Roger asked.

I shook my head. "I don't think so. I think he just panicked. Cristian is a protector. He thinks my safety is one hundred percent his responsibility."

"He cares about you. Of course he wants you safe," Katherine said.

I dug the bottles of pills from my bag and lined them up on the dining table. I grabbed the ibuprofen, knowing it would help with his fever. Taking that, a bottle of water and one of the thick blankets, I turned toward the hallway.

Before I walked down the hall, I paused and looked back at Katherine. "It's my turn to keep him safe."

Nothing made sense. The walls seemed too far away, then too close. Voices swam through my head, warped, like they were coming from underwater. My own name sounded foreign when Dave said it. Marlowe's name, though, that was the one thing that cut through the fog.

When I woke up, I had looked for her immediately. I felt like I'd been asleep for days, when in reality it had been an hour. Dave informed me that Marlowe had gone to scavenge. I heard what he said, but all I heard was she'd left. She'd left me.

Panic rose, and I had no control over it. I lurched to my feet, causing agony so great I thought I'd fall back on my ass. But I couldn't get the idea of Marlowe being attacked, hurt or, worse, killed. My foggy brain wasn't capable of suppressing the feelings that she evoked in me, and I found myself caring more than I wanted to.

When I saw her face, I had to grab it. I traced her freckles with my thumbs, reassuring myself that she was alive, whole, and standing in front of me. I could pull her into my arms if I wanted. Could kiss her if I wanted. No, that wasn't what I wanted to do, was it? The confusion was genuine, and Marlowe looked up at me with such concern that I knew something wasn't right.

Dave helped me down on the packing blankets, and I collapsed back and closed my eyes.

"She doesn't leave again, got it, Doc?" I meant to sound forceful, but the words came out in a whisper.

"I'm sure she's not going to leave you, Cristian."

His words meant very little. Marlowe was headstrong. If she wanted to do something, she was going to do it. But my energy waned again and I drifted off.

Whispers just outside my door woke me. I peered through my lashes to see Marlowe, her arms full of blankets and pillows, talking to Dave. He was looking at a bottle and nodding.

Marlowe tiptoed in and created a small nest of blankets next to me, then tucked one around me. Opening my eyes, I watched her. She didn't look hurt or scared. I felt reassured that nothing had happened to her when she left the farmhouse.

She caught me staring and got to her knees next to me. "Hi."

"Hi."

"I have some pills for you to take." She held up a white bottle and a half full water bottle.

"What are they for?"

She looked at me before brushing my hair back and pressing her hand to my head. "You have a fever. We need to bring it down before it gets too bad."

"Fever?" The confusion was back and I realized it was the fever messing with my mind. So when Marlowe went to put three small pills into my mouth, I lifted my head to swallow some of the water.

She carefully cradled my head and slid a pillow under.

"Where did you get the pillows?" I asked.

She tucked me in, avoiding my gaze. "The house next door."

"The one we avoided?" I didn't have the strength to accuse her of anything. But I wasn't thrilled with her going to the house we specifically said wasn't safe.

"We were careful getting it. And well, it was empty. The people that lived there…they were gone."

Her voice was sad, and she still wouldn't look at me. I turned her face with my palm until she looked down and met my gaze. "What is it?"

"They were dead. They committed suicide."

She then told me about the note and the little that she learned about Katherine. That was more information than I needed at the moment, and I let my eyes close while she talked.

"Sorry. Let me get you something to eat. And then we'll rest. It's been a long day," Marlowe said.

She started to get up, but I snapped out my hand and grabbed her. "You're not leaving again, right?"

Marlowe's fingers curled tighter around mine. "I won't go anywhere without telling you."

It wasn't a no. I tried to hold on to that thought, tried to keep my grip on her, but my fingers felt distant, uncooperative. My eyelids drooped against my will. I fought them open again, just long enough to see Marlowe still there, watching me.

"I mean it," she whispered.

I floated between sleep and wakefulness. I could hear murmured voices in the front room, though I couldn't make out any words. I was worried about Carol. When I went looking for Marlowe, the older woman didn't say a word. But I was so focused, I hadn't taken the time to see how she was doing. She'd lost her husband in a pretty horrible way. But she didn't seem ready to give up the way Blair did. I hadn't known Blair. We had spent time with Carol, and she had showered us with kindness. I couldn't imagine the same thing happening to her.

Lying there, I waited for Marlowe. My body felt worn to the bone and I couldn't stay awake. The next time I woke, Marlowe was pulling the blinds closed. She'd lit a small candle lit, but shadows cloaked most of the room, and no light came from the window.

"How long was I asleep?"

"Not too long." She kneeled next to my head, the candlelight barely bright enough for me to see her features.

She produced an open can with a spoon in it. Holding it up, she flashed me a bright smile. "It's not hot. We haven't figured out a way to cook without giving away our location. But it'll be good on your stomach."

She helped me sit up and lean against the wall. After moving the candle closer, she carefully held a spoon of soup up to my lips. I allowed her to feed me, though I figured I could have done it myself. The soup was some sort of vegetable and didn't taste half bad, even cold out of the can.

"How much food is there?" I asked.

"Enough for a week or so. We thought we could go back, but..." Marlowe hesitated, stirring the soup.

I narrowed my eyes. "But what?"

She sighed. "Someone else was there."

My exhaustion lessened instantly. "Did they see you?"

Marlowe shook her head and held the spoon near my mouth. "No. But we saw him. He wasn't looting, he was looking. Searching."

With a grunt, I opened my mouth for the bite. After swallowing, I continued my questioning. "You sure he wasn't from the group that attacked us?"

"I wouldn't know. I only saw the one guy that you let leave, Mike. How can you tell just by looking at someone that they're dangerous if they aren't attacking you?" She shrugged, continuing to feed me.

She scraped the bottom of the can and put it aside once I finished, then brought a cup of juice for me to sip. I was surprised and took my time enjoying it. Marlowe sipped from her own cup. Sitting in silence was comfortable with her. She leaned against the wall with me, our shoulders touching.

Though the silence was okay, I wanted to hear her voice. "Where did you get the juice?"

Marlowe laughed quietly for a moment. "It was an unopened bottle in the pantry. We figure we all need to finish it, since we don't have a fridge. Enjoy it while we can!"

She held her mug toward me, and I clinked mine against it. "Cheers"

"Cheers," she said, smiling at me over her mug. After another sip, she turned to look at me. "How are you feeling? And tell the truth."

I smirked. She had figured me out so quickly. "The pain is there. It feels worse than when we left the warehouse."

She nodded. She leaned toward me, and I held my breath. But instead of anything I pictured happening, she pressed her lips to my forehead.

"Your fever is still there, but I think the meds helped. It'll be time for another dose in the middle of the night. I'll try to wake up."

"Why do you do that?"

She sat back down and leaned back, squinting at my face in the limited light. "Do what?"

"Kiss my forehead like that."

Her face looked surprised for a moment, and then she dropped her eyes. "Sorry. I didn't realize. I just…well that's how my mom used to check my temperature when I was sick. She always said it was more accurate than hands. And since we don't have a thermometer, I thought it was the best way. I'm sorry."

I took her hand in mine and laced our fingers together. "Don't be sorry. I appreciate you taking care of me. I wish I didn't need it."

She squeezed my hand and slowly leaned against my shoulder until her head was lying on me. I leaned my head on hers.

"We take care of each other, right?"

"Right."

We both finished our juice, and Marlowe went to the kitchen to refill the mugs. When she came back, she had fruit snacks to share as well.

"Were there kids living over there, or something?" I popped a gummy fruit piece into my mouth.

Marlowe's face fell, and she looked at the wall across from us. "They were grandparents."

Her words felt heavy on me. We had been moving so much, surviving since everything happened. I had little to think about outside of myself and figure a way to survive. Marlowe had her mom. But other than that, we didn't have people to worry about. So many others did. It was a lot to wrap my mind around.

"It's so hard to imagine what life will be like if things don't go back to normal," I said.

"Do you really think it could go back? Will everything come back?" she asked.

Her voice sounded hopeful, and I wished I had a good answer for her. But I didn't live in a world of hope. Not before the world fell apart, and definitely not now.

"I don't know, Marlowe. I really don't." I said the words quietly, hoping that would lessen the sting.

We sat in silence, with the candle flickering, throwing shadows around the room. I watched them move along the walls and thought about the grandparents who'd decided death was better than living through this. I thought about Marlowe's mom and if she was healthy. I thought about Marlowe, as her warm body pressed against my side, and wondered what the future held for the two of us.

I even thought about Sarah. The same bitter anger didn't strike me when I thought about her now. Instead, it was just a form of grief. At the loss of someone I once loved. Someone I hadn't treated the way I should have and to whom I'd now never get the chance to say that I was sorry. We didn't have to end our relationship hatefully, even though it wasn't meant to last.

The drowsiness almost beat out the sadness, but not quite. Marlowe helped me lie back in my makeshift bed. She stretched out next to me, pulling a fluffy blanket over us both. I put my arm out, inviting her to lie closer. She didn't hesitate. Laying her head on my shoulder, she put her arm across my chest.

That was the last thing I remembered before passing out. After that, my memory was full of images and broken sounds. Much of it was Marlowe. Hands on my chest. Cool. Soft. Marlowe? I tried to say her name, but my lips wouldn't form the words.

"He's burning up." Marlowe's voice, thick with worry. Dave's voice followed, lower, more measured, but I couldn't pick out the words.

Marlowe's fingers brushed over my forehead again, soothing. Familiar. I needed to tell her something, though I didn't know what. Needed to keep her safe. But my body didn't listen. The words wouldn't come. The world tilted sideways, and I let it take me.

CHAPTER
NINETEEN

Cristian stirred in his sleep, waking me. The room was almost pitch black, and I had to feel around until I found the lighter and candle I'd brought into the room. The light flared. I tried to evaluate him. His skin was flushed, and he was clearly uncomfortable. I looked at the watch Dave had given me to track Cristian's medication. It was an hour after his next does was due.

Armed with three pills and a water bottle containing enough for a sip, I kneeled next to Cristian's head. "Hey, Cristian. Can you wake up for me, honey?"

His eyelids fluttered, but he didn't wake. I ran my fingers over his cheek and was alarmed by its warmth. I repeated his name again and shook his shoulder softly. His face turned toward me, and his eyes opened just slightly.

"You need your meds. Can you take them if I help you?"

All I got in response was a grunt, so I took that as a yes. Scooting behind his head, I propped it on my lap and carefully placed the pills in his mouth when he opened. Then I poured just a little water between his lips, and he swallowed. He coughed, and I panicked for a moment, until he settled and swallowed again.

I was about to move away from him, but he mumbled something and turned in my lap. Cristian sighed, his grip around my waist tightening as if his fevered mind wouldn't let me go. I froze, my heart slamming against my ribs.

"Marlowe…" The way he said my name sent a ripple down my spine. Like a thought slipping free before he could catch it. He turned his face against my thigh, his breath burning through my pants. "Don't… go." His fingers curled, holding onto me, but he wasn't awake.

I swallowed hard. It was just the fever talking. He didn't know what he was saying. Right? I ran my fingers through his damp hair, trying to soothe him, trying to tell myself it meant nothing. That I wasn't reading into it.

But I didn't move him. Because if it gave him even the slightest comfort, I wasn't going to take that away from him.

Carefully, I straightened my legs, but let his head continue to rest against my thighs. I knew he didn't feel well. His fever seeped through my pants, proving just how bad things were getting. It happened so fast, but Dave had explained to me how dirty bullet wounds could be. And he didn't have what he needed to clean it sufficiently in the warehouse. He'd done the best he could and now we faced a situation that wouldn't solve itself.

Cristian's dark hair was damp, sticking up in places, and his face, despite the fevered flush, looked peaceful for the first time in hours.

"He's just sick," I muttered under my breath, as much to convince myself as anything else. "He doesn't mean anything by it."

Still, I couldn't bring myself to move him. He needed rest. I adjusted myself against the wall, leaning back so I could balance his weight more easily.

Cristian sighed in his sleep, the sound low and soft, and something in my chest tightened. I hesitated for a moment, then reached out, brushing my fingers lightly through his hair. It was something I used to do with my mom when she couldn't sleep. Simple. Soothing.

Except this didn't feel simple. Why didn't this feel simple?

The steady rhythm of his breathing slowed, his body relaxed further and his head grew heavier, as he drifted deeper into sleep. I stayed there, running my fingers absently through his hair, trying to ignore the strange warmth spreading through me, something that had nothing to do with his fever.

He wouldn't remember this in the morning, I told myself. And that was for the best.

The exhaustion from the past few days pulled at me again, and I let my head rest against the wall. Cristian's presence was a heavy, grounding warmth against my leg, and despite everything, the chaos, the fear, the uncertainty, I found myself relaxing.

Before long, my eyes closed, and I slipped into a dreamless sleep, my fingers still tangled gently in Cristian's hair. That was how Dave found us in the morning. He was quiet as he came in, but his presence in the room startled me awake. His eyes were soft and kind as he smiled at me.

"How's your neck feeling?" he asked.

I rolled my head around, feeling a ping of pain from sleeping in such a weird position. But it didn't matter. Cristian slept solidly through the rest of the night. Dave was touching his face and was checking his eyes. It was then I realized Cristian was starting to shiver.

"What's happening to him?" There was no way I could hide the fear in my voice.

"The infection is getting worse. I don't think his body will be able to fight this off on its own."

It felt like a punch to my gut. I looked down at him. Even with his hair sticking up in random directions from sweat and me playing with it, he was beautiful. I wasn't sure if I had thought about that before. But he was. Beautiful. And damaged. I couldn't blame him for that. Losses in life made us into who we were. His created a man that couldn't stop protecting everyone else.

What if I lost him? The thought hit me so hard I felt like I'd been punched in the gut. I exhaled slowly, grounding myself. This wasn't about what I could or couldn't do. It wasn't about fear. It was about the fact that Cristian didn't get to die on my watch and it was time for me to protect him .

"I'll go," I said.

Slowly, I untangled myself from Cristian's embrace. I was immediately chilled, losing the heat of his body against mine. I climbed to my feet and Dave pulled me to the side of the room.

"This is really dangerous, Marlowe. Cristian was out of his mind when he realized you left before. And that was just to go next door. You're going to have to go back into town to find even a fraction of what we need. I'm not even sure how long it would take."

"Well, it can't take too long, or he won't make it, right?"

Dave looked over at Cristian, who had crossed his arms over himself, as if he was trying to keep himself warm. But the doctor didn't speak.

"He could die, right, Dave?"

He nodded and looked me in the eye. "Yes. If this goes too far, he could die."

"I won't allow that to happen. Not if I can do something to help."

I could see Dave's indecision, but nothing could deter me. The determination must have showed on my face, because the man nodded and sighed.

"Before you go, we should undress him. Give him a cool sponge bath. Try to bring his fever down a bit that way."

Between Dave and me, we were able to get Cristian's shirt and jeans off. We left his briefs. No one really knew that Cristian and I weren't actually a couple. But the idea of him being completely nude did something to my stomach that was inappropriate while he was so sick.

He didn't even wake completely as we moved him around. At one point, he moaned my name, and I tried to let him know I was with him. But he didn't open his eyes. Once he was bare, we took some of the last water we had and wet down a washcloth, sponging him down.

"What about water for everyone here?" I asked.

"There's a well out back. I'm going to see if I can figure it out. There's got to be a manual way to get water from it," Dave replied.

Dave moved to his leg, examining the wound, which even I could see was red. He rinsed it with a small amount of water and patted it with a cloth. Grimacing, he shook his head.

"There's puss. Definitely infected. I need to remove the stitches to clean it out, but I don't want to do that until I have better supplies."

I nodded. "I'll leave today. I'll get my bag ready."

Dave covered Cristian with a blanket, but didn't dress him. With one look at me, he walked out of the room. Grabbing my bag from the corner of the room, I checked what I still had packed. I made sure I had the small first aid kit and an extra set of clothing. There was also a lighter, a pack of matches, and two candles. A reusable water bottle hung from a carabiner. It was empty, so finding water would also be something I'd have to focus on.

At the last moment, I took the gun from Cristian's bag again. I could pull the trigger if needed. Clumsily, I checked the ammo the way I'd seen Cristian do it. I could tell the gun had only a few bullets. It was better than nothing, and I tucked it into my backpack. After packing, I sat down next to Cristian.

"You're going to be so mad at me," I whispered with a sigh. I laid my hand on his bare shoulder. It was so much warmer than it should be. Just further evidence I was doing the right thing. Leaning over, I pressed my lips to his forehead. This time it had nothing to do with checking his fever. I paused, pressing my forehead against his. "Do not die. I'll never forgive you."

I strapped on my bag and looked at him once more. Fever flushed his olive skin. Part of me wished he would wake up and tell me I couldn't go without him. Just so I could believe he wasn't as sick as Dave said he was. But he didn't stir. There was no doubt that I had to go back into town and find whatever I could to help him.

In the dining room, Katherine had a pack on. She looked at me expectantly, and I paused in confusion.

Dave came to me with a box of meat sticks, two cans of soup, and two boxes of juice. "She wants to go with you. I agreed, because I don't think you should be alone."

"Cristian wouldn't want anyone else in danger on his account," I said.

"Cristian will murder us all in our sleep if you somehow don't return," Katherine replied.

"I'm coming back." Looking at Dave, I made sure he heard me. "If he wakes up, you make sure he knows I didn't leave him. I'm not leaving him. I will be back."

Dave nodded and moved around me to put the food in my pack. "I wish we could spare more. But with the guy in the neighboring house now, there's no way to know where else we can scavenge."

"I'm going to look around. I think it would be better for me to try to scavenge houses while you scavenge for Cristian." Roger shrugged and gestured to the table that was less than half covered in the food items we found. None of which was water. They had one more bottle of unopened juice to enjoy before they had to figure out the well.

"Be careful when you go out. We can't afford to lose anyone else," I said.

Roger snorted and then nodded to me. "Me be careful? Think about yourself, sister."

"She won't be alone," Katherine said.

Dave was packing food into her pack as well. I could admit that I felt better about not being alone. Not that I was sure Katherine would be the best backup, but at least she was another set of eyes to watch out for me.

The doctor came back to stand in front of me. He handed me a piece of paper with a list on it. "The first choice should be a hospital or clinic. The items marked with stars at the top are the most important."

Looking at the list, I saw that "injectable or oral" was written next to the antibiotics at the top. Next on the list were topical antibiotics. He also had listed several antiseptics, but he also had raw honey listed and I pointed to it, looking at Dave.

"Raw honey has some natural antiseptic properties. It's far, very far, from my first choice. And it has to be raw. That is only if you can't find any of the others listed," he said.

"What kind of doctor are you?" I asked.

Dave barked out a laugh, and I couldn't help but smile a little. "I had a private practice. But when I was young and had a lot of time on my hands, I read a lot about the history of medicine. Much of that applies to a world without active healthcare options."

I patted his shoulder. "You, Dr. Dave, are an excellent person to have around. Take care of my guy, ok?"

"I've got him. Get back as soon as you can."

I nodded goodbye to Roger and realized Carol was nowhere to be seen. "Be sure to keep an eye on Carol, too. She's probably having a really hard time."

"Everything will be ok here, Marlowe. Don't worry," Dave said.

There was no way I wouldn't not worry, but I was determined to help Cristian. I walked through the front door. Once outside, I checked the surrounding yard to make sure there wasn't anyone around that we didn't know about. Katherine silently stood behind me.

"You don't have to come with me. You could stay. It would probably be safer," I said.

"Safer, while I just hide away, and Cristian gets sicker? Or we all starve because we can't find enough food? No. I'll do my part. You need someone to watch out for you, too."

"And maybe you could win points with Cristian?" I asked.

I wasn't sure Katherine had fully let go of whatever she

thought she had for Cristian. We'd been playing the part of a couple since the moment we arrived at the warehouse, a convenient illusion that offered safety and kept prying eyes at bay. But if Katherine's sudden helpfulness had more to do with him than me, I wasn't going to stand by and pretend not to notice.

"Hey." Katherine's voice, low and casual, pulled me from my thoughts. Her hand brushed my arm, light enough to seem friendly but deliberate enough to demand my attention. I turned to meet her gaze, and she offered a small, knowing smile. "Look, I may have been...interested at first. I mean, can you blame me? Have you seen him?"

She jerked her chin back toward the house, and for a moment, I could picture him exactly as he'd been, restless on his makeshift bed, his dark hair damp with fever sweat but still impossibly striking. She wasn't wrong. Cristian had that kind of quiet intensity that turned heads, even in a world that had fallen apart.

"But I get it now," she continued, her tone lighter but her words cutting sharper. "You two made it pretty clear. And honestly, I can see it. The way he looks at you? That man's already spoken for."

Her words hit me harder than I expected, and I forced my expression to stay neutral. The way he looks at me? It was all part of the act, wasn't it? Cristian played his role well, too well, but I couldn't shake the uneasy flicker of doubt creeping in. Was Katherine seeing something real between us, or was she just buying into our carefully constructed lie?

I swallowed, giving her a tight nod. "Good. I'm glad we're on the same page."

The edge in my voice betrayed the storm of questions brewing beneath the surface. Did Cristian even realize the signals he was sending, or the ones I might have been giving off without meaning to? And why, despite everything, did I suddenly care so much about the answer?

Pushing my intrusive thoughts back, I started down the gravel drive with Katherine falling into step next to me. We were silent as we arrived at the main road. I knew we'd have to pass the driveway of the neighboring house, and I didn't want to risk being seen by the man we saw break in.

"Let's cross here and walk in the trees on that side of the road until we get away from the farmhouses," I suggested.

Katherine didn't need to be told twice, as she knew the same thing I did. We moved quickly and once we were in the shade of the trees, we headed back toward town. My mind raced with the knowledge I had of the area. Had I ever seen a clinic, immediate care or hospital?

"Do you know where we could find a hospital or something like that?" I asked Katherine.

She thought about it for a moment before speaking. "I think there's one of those Zoom clinic like places on this side of town. I feel like I drove by it before. Is that what we need?"

"Do you think they have medications on hand?"

She shrugged. "I wouldn't know, if I'm being honest."

The not knowing where we could find the supplies to save Cristian made me sick to my stomach. I wondered how long he would last without the assistance of medication. The idea of him being even more ill or even dying without me made my eyes burn with tears.

"Hey, don't cry. We'll get this done and be back before you know it." Katherine's hand touched my arm in a sympathetic gesture.

I wanted to believe what she said. To have confidence in myself. To know that I could step up and provide for Cristian when he needed me, but in the back of my mind there were doubts, sitting and threatening my resolve. I felt like I was a teenager again, watching my mother waste away during cancer treatments. But this time, the treatments depended solely on me.

We walked for a while in silence, and I knew both of us were getting hungry and thirsty. I hadn't even thought to eat breakfast before leaving. My need to help Cristian had overridden common sense. Once we were far enough from the farmhouses, I suggested having a seat and eating something small. We sat near the large trees to keep ourselves hidden, and each had a snack from our packs.

"We are going to need to find water soon if we're going to keep up this walking," I said.

Katherine nodded as she sipped from her juice box. We both only had one box each for hydration. That would not be enough for the trip we were facing.

"We passed that old corner store when we were leaving town. I know Cristian didn't want to enter it because it looked trashed, but maybe now would be a good time to take that chance."

I remembered the building Katherine was referring to. It was unlikely there were any supplies left, but for just the two of us, if we could just find a couple bottles of water, it would help. I thought about Roger checking around to find more food for the farmhouse, and I hoped he was successful. If they could get water from the well, things would look much better by the time we got back.

"Is it weird that I'm still in shock?" Katherine asked suddenly.

"In shock about what?"

She gestured around us. "All of this. The world. Everything just coming to a stop. If I let myself really think about it, I still feel really shocked."

"I'm not sure when that shock will wear off. But I think we're stuck in this situation for the time being. Finding ways to not only survive but thrive should be our ultimate goal. Maybe someday the government will show up again and help us. But right now, we have to help ourselves."

Katherine snorted. "The government. They couldn't even help on day one. It's like they disappeared from everywhere. I never even saw a police officer or a fireman after everything happened. Let alone anyone within the military or any other government agency."

"I did. And they were no better prepared than anyone else.

Almost immediately, it felt like we were on our own. Nobody is coming to help us anytime soon."

With that last dark thought, we packed up our trash and got back to walking. If I remembered correctly, we would reach the corner store within the hour. If it had not been further ransacked, we could get lucky. Luck was the only thing I could hope for at this point.

I felt bad that I didn't have more things to talk to Katherine about. But I was too worried about the fake relationship between myself and Cristian to really talk about anything in our past. Because the woman might wonder why I wasn't including Cristian in the stories.

If I was honest, a large part of me didn't want to admit what was between Cristian and I wasn't real.

So far, from what I could tell, Katherine and I had little in common. However, the woman had come to help me, for whatever reason, and I felt better not being alone. I glanced at her out of the corner of my eye and wondered, and not for the first time, if her red hair was real. I chastised myself for being unkind and tried to think of something we could talk about.

Katherine took that problem out of my hand as she sighed and spoke. "If we ever get to Cristian's house, you aren't planning on staying there, are you?"

"The only person I have in the world, besides Cristian, is my mother. She was sick. And she's in Northern California."

I could see Katherine looking at me out of the corner of her eye, but I just kept looking around. I was avoiding her gaze, but I knew it was important to keep an eye out around us.

"Cristian will go with you?"

It always came back to him and my trust for the woman went out the window. "I assume so. We discussed the prospect of looking for her."

"Cancer, right? My grandmother died of cancer. Was your mom getting treatment?"

I nodded, but didn't speak. I was already aware how unlikely it was that my mother would survive this apocalypse.

"I'm sorry. I shouldn't have brought it up. I was just trying to make conversation."

"It's fine. It's reality, right? Reality is, she was getting treatment. This was the second time around. I think…I'm pretty sure the last time we talked, just before all of this, she wasn't doing well. She wouldn't admit it, but it was clear in her voice it was bad. I can't be sure she's even still alive."

A sob choked my words, and I clapped a hand over my mouth. I froze, not caring if anyone saw me on the side of the road. The grief tried to claw its way up my throat, and I fought to push it back down. I had been thinking the same thing for days, but with all the surrounding craziness, I had kept that in a box and away from my consciousness. Katherine stood watching me silently. When she acted like she was going to lift her arms toward me, I held up my hand and shook my head.

"No. I'm okay. I just…I can't talk about it."

Katherine nodded and stepped back. "That's fine. We don't have to."

As I got myself under control, I heard something. I looked at Katherine and realized it wasn't just in my head. We both swung toward the sound, which was coming from around a bend in the road.

"Is that an engine?" Katherine exclaimed.

I nodded, but started to back off of the road, grabbing Katherine's sleeve to follow. She looked at me incredulously. "What? We should flag them down! We haven't seen a working vehicle since the beginning."

"There's no knowing who they are," I said urgently. "Cristian thought that older vehicles may still run. We just hadn't found one. That sound is going to draw every person out. And I'm not willing to take that risk."

We'd left the safety of the trees behind and had little protection. We reached a cluster of bushes just as the engine grew deafening. I pulled Katherine down behind them, crouching low, my body pressed against the dirt and brambles. The bushes were sparse, offering little more than shadows and hope. My breath came in shallow bursts as I strained to listen.

The vehicle came into view—a truck, battered and streaked with mud, its engine roaring like a predator on the hunt. Two men sat in the cab, the driver's arm hanging out the open window. I couldn't see their faces, but their movements were casual, too casual, like they had no reason to fear anyone.

The truck slowed as it approached the curve we'd just walked, the tires crunching on the gravel shoulder. My stomach twisted.

The driver leaned out, scanning the area. His voice carried faintly on the wind, though I couldn't make out the words. The passenger laughed. A low, cruel sound that set my teeth on edge.

"We can't let them see us," I whispered, gripping Katherine's arm tighter.

Her face was pale, her eyes darting between me and the truck. "What if they do? What if they—"

"They won't." I had to believe that. If we panicked, we'd only make things worse.

The truck rolled to a stop, the engine idling loudly. One man climbed out, stretching his arms over his head like he didn't have a care in the world. He said something to the driver, who laughed again before cutting the engine.

My heart sank. They weren't leaving.

Katherine's breathing quickened, and I pressed my hand against her arm to steady her. "Stay quiet," I whispered. "Don't move."

The passenger door opened, and the second man climbed out, pulling a rifle from the truck bed. He slung it over his shoulder casually, like it was an extension of himself.

Panic clawed at my chest, but I pushed it down. Think, Marlowe. Think. Two women alone out here would be easy pickings for these men. And though I couldn't know their intentions for sure, I wasn't willing to risk it.

"Get ready to run," I whispered to Katherine, my voice barely more than a breath.

Her eyes widened in alarm, but she nodded. I didn't know where we'd go, but staying here wasn't an option if they spotted us.

The second man started toward the shoulder where his friend stood, his rifle swaying with each step. My fingers dug into the dirt as I watched, helpless.

Then, as suddenly as it had begun, the first man stopped, unzipped his pants and started to urinate. The driver joined him. They both paused, exchanging words I couldn't hear, and after what felt like an eternity, they turned back toward the truck.

I didn't breathe. Neither did Katherine. The driver rolled his shoulders, stretching, his gaze flicking toward the trees. Toward us. I swallowed hard, willing myself into the dirt. He took a step forward, squinting, his boot crushing the exact spot where our footprints led into the brush. A slow, crawling sensation crept up my spine. He knew something was off.

He turned toward the passenger, muttering something. Katherine's fingers dug into my wrist, and I clamped my hand over hers, warning her not to move.

The driver exhaled, shaking his head. "Ain't nobody out here. Let's go."

The passenger laughed, zipping up his pants. "Yeah, well. For now."

Relief flooded through me, but I didn't move. Not yet. The engine roared back to life, and the truck continued down the road, kicking up gravel and dust.

I waited until the sound faded completely before exhaling.

"Are they gone?" Katherine whispered, her voice trembling.

"For now," I said, my voice harder than I intended. "But we need to move. Quickly."

She nodded, and we slipped out of the bushes, sticking to the shadows as we continued down the road. The danger hadn't passed. It never really did. But for now, we had to keep moving.

For Cristian.

Time didn't exist. Not in any way that made sense.

I felt as if someone had submerged my body in wet cement, every muscle slow, heavy, and reluctant. My head pulsed with heat, and my skin burned where the blanket touched it. I tried to move, to wipe the sandpaper grit from my eyes, but my arm barely responded. The second attempt was sluggish, my fingers uncoordinated, like I wasn't fully inside my own body.

A voice cut through the haze. Not hers.

"Cristian?"

My stomach twisted. Marlowe. Where was she? I forced my eyes open, blinking against the harsh slant of light filtering through the window. My pulse spiked as I turned my head too fast, searching for her, for the warmth I remembered falling asleep next to. But I was alone. I blinked at the bright light that filtered into the room from the small opening in the window covering. Looking around, I found Dave sitting next to me.

"Hey. Let's get some water in you and another dose of ibuprofen," he said.

He brought a cup to me and carefully helped me lift my upper body. Once I swallowed the pills, I looked down and realized I wasn't wearing a shirt. Lifting the blanket on my legs, I found no pants either. I looked over at Dave, confused. He set the cup down and uncovered my wound, and I tried to see it. I could see the skin around the stitches was red and angry. White fluid oozed out of the wound. Dave took a cloth and blotted at the nastiness.

"It's infected," he said.

Dave didn't need to explain to me the risks of a bullet wound. In law enforcement, we were well aware of everything that could go wrong. However, since it was a through and through, not hitting anything vital, I had hoped it would be an easy healing process. Instead, even I could see the wound wasn't happy.

"Okay. So, what do you need to do?" I asked.

Dave shook his head. "I can't do anything right now. I don't have the supplies."

"What do you need?"

He pulled the blanket back up and patted my shoulder. "We've got it handled. You just need to rest."

His words echoed in my ears. I looked around the room, as if I thought Marlowe would suddenly materialize. She didn't. My gaze fell instead on my bag against the far wall. And I remembered how hers was leaning against mine when we went to bed. My eyes snapped over to Dave and he could see the thoughts on my face. He diverted his gaze.

"Where. Is. She?" My voice came out rough, hoarse from sleep and the fever burning through me. The words scraped against my throat.

Dave hesitated. That was enough to send my pulse into a frantic, pounding rhythm. I shoved against the mattress, trying to sit up. The world swam violently, tilting sideways. My stomach clenched, bile rising. I braced my hand against my knee, forcing my body to obey me, but every muscle felt like dead weight.

"Cristian, stop!" Dave cursed, his hands pushing against my shoulders. "You're going to pass out."

"Not until you answer me." My breath heaved, my vision dark at the edges. There were two Daves, blurry and wavering in the heat rolling off my skin.

"The first thing she told me to tell you was she's coming back. She's not leaving you."

At the moment, that didn't comfort me. But she seemed to have known what my first thought would be. I continued to stare at Dave as best I could, while my vision blurred and cleared.

"She wouldn't sit by and watch you get sicker. And I know what my limitations are. I can't treat an infection without antibiotics and other medical equipment. But she wanted me to stay with you, in case anything happened."

"So you just let her go."

Dave grunted. "Have you tried to stop Marlowe from doing anything?"

I hadn't. We had been on the same page basically since the power went out. I never had to really tell Marlowe to do anything.

"I couldn't stop her. We needed Roger to look for food here. So Katherine went with her," Dave said.

"Katherine?" I couldn't hide my shock.

"She wanted to help."

Katherine helping seemed like a long shot. She'd been questionable from the moment we stepped into the warehouse. But Marlowe couldn't turn her back on her completely. Her heart was too kind and she could see the woman was alone and felt unsafe. I couldn't be sure why Katherine would leave the relative safety of the farmhouse to help Marlowe. The idea that Katherine was there to watch Marlowe's back should have made me feel better. It didn't. Because I should be the one out there. Not her.

Not my girl.

I stiffened. Where the hell did that come from? I scrubbed a hand over my face, like I could wipe the thought away. Like it hadn't snuck in before I could stop it. But it was there, stubborn and unrelenting.

My girl.

I clenched my jaw, forcing my focus back to the real problem. The fact that she was out there, that I wasn't, that I had let this happen. It wasn't just the fever talking. I knew that. It was the way she'd stayed up with me last night, her fingers brushing through my hair. Her voice soft and steady as she kept me tethered to reality, though she thought I was asleep. It was the fire in her eyes when she argued, the determination in her steps, the way she'd taken on every challenge with a resilience that made me want to protect her even more.

It had been there all along, creeping in quietly like a thief in the night. I'd ignored it, buried it under excuses. This isn't the time, this isn't the place, but now, with her gone, the truth slammed into me. A truth I wasn't sure I was capable of facing.

"Cristian," Dave said, pulling me out of my spiraling thoughts. "She can handle herself. She's strong."

I laughed bitterly, the sound hollow. "I know she's strong. That's not the problem." The problem was that she was risking everything for me, and I hated the thought of her facing whatever dangers were waiting out there without more backup. Katherine was something, but neither of them were ready for what they could face.

"You care a great deal about her." Dave's words weren't a question, just a quiet observation.

I stared at him, my jaw tight, the fever making it harder to keep my emotions in check. "Of course I care," I retorted, though I didn't direct my sharpness at him. "She's... she's been the only constant I've had in this craziness. And now she's out there, risking her life, because I couldn't—"

I broke off, my hands clenching into fists. The room was stifling, the weight of it pressing down on me, but it wasn't the fever or the pain in my leg that made it hard to breathe. It was the thought of Marlowe not coming back.

"Cristian," Dave said, his tone firm but gentle. "You're not the only one who feels responsible for someone. She knows what she's doing. Trust her."

Trust her. I did, more than I trusted myself. That wasn't the issue. The issue was that I wanted to be the one protecting her, not the other way around. I wanted to keep her safe, hold her steady when the world was falling apart. I wanted…

I stopped the thought before it could form completely, clenching my jaw against the surge of emotions I didn't know how to process.

She wasn't mine. Not really. We were just two people trying to survive in a world that had gone to hell. That's all this was.

Except it wasn't. Not anymore.

I leaned back against the wall, my body trembling with the effort of staying upright. "She'd better come back," I muttered, more to myself than to Dave.

Dave nodded, his expression thoughtful. "She will. For you."

His words hung in the air, and I couldn't bring myself to respond. I didn't know what scared me more. That she might not come back, or that she would, and I'd have to face what I was starting to feel.

Suddenly, Roger burst into the room. He was out of breath and red-faced. My head snapped up at his appearance, and Dave turned to look at him.

"There's a vehicle!"

In the ensuing silence, I heard the low growl of an engine.

"Where?" I asked.

"Down the road. I was out, looking down the road to see if there were any other houses we hadn't seen to scavenge. And I saw something moving in the distance and then heard the sound. I came running back," Roger said.

"How?" Dave said.

"Older vehicles probably work right now. I've been looking for one but hadn't found anything."

As we talked, the engine sound grew louder. I tried to climb to my feet. Dave tried to force me back.

"They might come here. We need to be ready. My bag. Has a gun." My voice was broken as I gasped through the pain and dizziness that assailed me.

"You're going to fall," Dave exclaimed.

"Get my bag."

Roger ripped open the bag. Pulling out the gun, he checked the safety and looked over at me. "I know how to use this. You can stay in bed."

"Like hell," I muttered.

I was finally on my feet and didn't even care I was only wearing my boxer briefs. Lurching toward the door, I caught myself on the doorjamb and followed Roger down the hallway. The farmhouse was quiet as they all listened to the engine, once so familiar, but now loud and foreign. I made it to the front windows and, leaning heavily against the wall, pulled the shade to the side.

"Were they headed toward us?" I asked

Roger stood next to me with the gun in his hand. "Not down the driveway, but on the main road, yeah."

I looked back at Dave. "Which way did Marlowe and Katherine go?"

Dave's face went pale, and I had my answer. I cursed under my breath and looked back out the window. A part of me wanted the vehicle to drive down the gravel drive. Let them come toward us, instead of in the direction the women had gone. My head swam and I could feel sweat beating along my skin. My leg throbbed, but my fear for Marlowe outweighed the pain and the fever.

We stood there and watched as pick-up passed the driveway. It moved slowly, as if the occupants were checking out the area. But they didn't turn toward our house. I didn't move from the window even when the engine's growl faded into the background.

"We need a car like that," Roger said.

I nodded. It had been one of my goals. But we hadn't gotten lucky yet. When she got back, after I chastised her for taking the damn risk in the first place, we'd need a plan.

I turned from the window and nearly fell into Roger. To his credit, he didn't drop the gun as he caught me and held me on my feet.

"Doc? Granted, my man here has an impressive body and all that, but I'd rather not sit and hold him like this."

I tried to pull away and stand on my own, but my legs didn't get the memo. Dave rushed to my side and threw one of my arms over his shoulder.

"He needs to be back in bed. Help me."

"I can do it." My words came out, though I didn't believe them myself. I didn't want to accept that I was so weak.

"Sure, sure, buddy. You're a regular Fred Astaire, ready to dance across the house," Roger said.

I turned my face to look down at Roger. Even sick, and barely able to move, I was almost a head taller than him. I wanted to glare, but it didn't come across, because Roger just rolled his eyes at me. I wanted to punch him in the face. My emotions ranged all over the place. Worry about Marlowe, interest in the new feelings I'd discovered, and anger at myself for not being healthy.

Between the two of them, they muscled me down the hallway back to the bedroom. Dave warned Roger to go slow as they lowered me to the ground. It didn't matter how fast or slow they went. The bedroom spun like a top, and I squeezed my eyes shut. My stomach pitched and rolled, pushing a queasy feeling up my throat. I took shallow breaths through my nose, hoping everything would settle once I was lying down.

"What is it?" Dave asked.

"Feel sick," I muttered.

A wet rag pressed against my forehead. Though the water was probably room temperature, it felt cool against my fevered skin. Dave flipped the rag every few moments, letting the cool side touch my skin. After a few minutes, the sick stomach feeling settled. But I was so exhausted, I wasn't sure how to open my eyes or communicate.

Falling into a fevered darkness, all I could think about was Marlowe, and if I would ever see her again.

CHAPTER
TWENTY-ONE
MARLOWE

The small corner store looked just as bad as it had when we first went by. Someone had shattered front windows and the door hung on one hinge. As we approached the front, I noticed what looked like a spray of bullet holes decorating the outside walls.

"Why do people always turn on each other when things go bad?" Katherine muttered, kicking at a spent bullet casing near her boot.

I scanned the empty street, my stomach tight. "Because fear makes people desperate. And desperate people do whatever they have to."

Approaching the open door, I coughed and covered my mouth. Katherine joined me then stepped back when she caught a whiff.

"What is that?" she asked.

I knew what it was. We'd recently smelled something similar. "Pretty sure someone died here."

I entered, watching the ground. Glass crunched under my boots and shell casings mingled with the shiny shards. A dark brown circle stained the cheap linoleum in front of the register counter. From the smears of blood, I figured the injured person lived long enough to move to safety.

To ease my mind and to ensure no one was hiding in wait for us, I followed the marks. They circled the long counter that blocked the now empty cigarette displays and scratch-off lotto tickets. Though I knew what I was looking for, the decomposing body that was on the ground behind the cash register still took aback me. It looked like it had been an older man. He was wearing a shirt with the store logo just barely legible through the bloodstains. In his limp hand was a gun. I didn't know what type, all I knew was it could be holes in people. Like the one in Cristian

Katherine came up behind me and gasped when she saw the corpse.

"He tried to fight them off," I murmured, my voice barely above a whisper. "Didn't stand a chance."

I imagined the man either owned the store or maybe his family did. Like many, he probably thought things would go back to normal. And if he allowed all of his product to be taken without payment, they would have lost everything and had a hard time recovering. But in the end, people weren't going to wait to see what happened. The fear was too heavy.

Turning away from the body, I took in the store's destruction. People had not only torn through it for supplies, but had shot up the place during the looting. Katherine and I made our way toward the back, which held the refrigerated items. Refrigerated case doors had been shattered or propped open. Shelves and racks were empty. I pulled an energy drink can from one fridge and an ice tea from another. Everything else was empty.

"Great," Katherine groaned.

"Better than nothing." I motioned for her to turn around and I slipped the two drinks into her backpack.

We sorted through the remains of the store, finding a box of individual bags of peanuts, and one bag of goldfish crackers that were likely crushed to a powder. I found a lighter that still worked and figured even though I had a lighter already, we could never have too many. The rest of the store felt like a complete loss. We started to make our way back toward the entrance when the noise of an engine roared outside.

I grabbed Katherine by the sleeve and pulled her back into the shadows of the store. Peering around the broken shelves in front of us, I could see the truck from earlier idling in the parking lot. I couldn't make out the men inside, but I had a sick feeling that they knew we were in the store.

"What the hell?" Katherine asked.

I shook my head, not having an answer to what was happening. It just felt bad. Staying low, I spun to look at the back of the store and spotted a door. I crab walked to the door and though the knob turned, it seemed to be stuck.

"They're getting out," Katherine hissed, her fingers gripping my arm. "Marlowe, they know we're here."

"I can't get this open!" I whispered back, yanking back on the door as hard as possible.

Suddenly, the door flew in, throwing me back and causing me to land in a sprawled mess. I started to reach for the gun from my bag, but I froze, looking at who stood in the doorway. Where I had expected to see a large man, a small teenage boy stood. Or at least that's what I thought I was looking at. The figure wore a ball cap, hiding their hair completely. A bandana covered their face. The clothing was nondescript and filthy. One hand held a hammer, and the other was still on the door.

"Hey, come on!" The voice was sharp, insistent, and definitely teenage.

"What?" I asked, completely confused.

"Those guys are bad news. They wrecked the store when this all started."

Katherine had turned and was surprised to find the newcomer. "Who in the hell…"

"Later!" he hissed, his tone urgent. "You ladies need to trust me on this. If they catch you…" He didn't finish the sentence, but his panicked look said enough.

I scrambled to my feet and Katherine was on my heels as we ran out the back of the store. The teen closed the door quietly and motioned with a finger to their covered mouth. Katherine and I exchanged a look and nodded at the kid. They turned and ran directly into the trees behind the store. Inside, we could hear the men's voices now and I heard one of them mention women. With no desire to stick around and see what the men wanted with us, I took off after the teen who might have just saved our lives.

We dodged trees and logs that littered the ground. I climbed over a downed tree that the teenager jumped off in some sort of artistic way. Yeah, no, I wasn't trying to do any of that. The kid looked back at us at one point and I swore I saw them sigh in frustration. We weren't quite fast enough for them.

When they slid to a stop, I barely noticed a small building hidden behind some camouflage someone had put up. The teen disappeared behind a sort of screen and when we didn't follow, reappeared and motioned for us to get moving.

"You good with this?" Katherine asked.

"Going into the murder house with the unknown person who pulled us from the murder store? This is either the safest place or the stupidest decision I've ever made," I muttered. "Guess we'll find out soon."

Katherine's mouth was open as she stared at me. I just shrugged and bent to go under the material that was hanging in front of the structure. She didn't hesitate, following on my heels. Beyond the camouflage, a small structure, little more than a shed, met our gaze. But the teen was in the open door, motioning them forward.

Steeling myself for the real possibility I was going to be murdered, I entered the building. The inside wasn't any larger than it looked from the outside. Katherine stayed so close that I could feel her breath on my neck. I reached back and found her hand, squeezing it to try to comfort her.

The inside of the shed was dim, and my eyes didn't adjust quickly. A light suddenly flared to life in the corner, and we turned to find the teen lighting a large pillar candle with their back to us. The candle looked like one of the huge ones you would find in a Catholic Church. It had been burned about halfway down, clearly used often.

With their back to us, they discarded their hat and untied the bandana from their face. Turning, I was surprised to find that the teen looked even younger than I had originally expected. Definitely male, and really just a child, he stared at us.

"What are you, ten?" Katherine blurted before she could stop herself.

"I'm thirteen," the kid shot back, straightening like that extra three years made all the difference.

"And by yourself?" I asked.

He nodded, the dirty blonde hair, released from his hat, flopping into his eyes. "The dead man in the store? That was my grandpa. I lived with him."

"I'm sorry," I said.

"Those men, they killed him. The store belonged to our family. Papa didn't want to open when the power went out, he was worried about looting," the boy explained.

I wasn't sure what to say. The boy moved around the small room, pulling things off of stacks he had. I watched him, realizing the entire place was full of food and other supplies.

"I'm Marlowe. This is Katherine. What's your name?"

"Toby."

"Nice to meet you, Toby. From the look of the store and your Papa, you've been alone from almost the beginning?"

He nodded, not looking back at me. "It was the second day that they showed up with the guns. Papa pushed me out the back when the men threatened him."

I winced. The boy had almost been a victim like his grandfather.

"I ran." Pain laced the boy's voice. He turned to look at us. When he met my eyes, the sadness was clear. "I was a coward. I ran."

"No. You were not a coward." I stepped forward. My chest ached with what the boy had been living with, all alone. With no one else to support or comfort him. "Your grandfather wanted to protect you. And he did. He knew something bad was going to happen. And he knew his job was to keep you safe."

"I could have helped him!" Toby exclaimed.

"With the hammer? Sorry, kid. Judging by the number of bullet holes, the men were heavily armed," Katherine said.

Toby just shook his head. He didn't speak, just turned away from us and opened something with a can opener.

"So, you live in here?" The question was pretty much rhetorical. I could see where he had set up his bed roll against one wall. There were paper products stacked around the bed area. All sorts of different food and beverage items lined the three remaining walls. It seemed like Toby had visited a few stores since his grandfather died.

"After I found Papa… you know, gone… and the store was empty, I had to figure something out. The houses felt too obvious, like everyone would check those. But I remembered this shed. I used to play here when I was little, back when Papa made me stay at the store after school. He didn't like it. Said it wasn't safe. Guess it's a good thing I didn't listen, huh?"

I nodded. "And all the food? And toilet paper?"

"You ever tried to use something other than toilet paper?" He shuddered and I couldn't suppress the laugh that bubbled up.

"Yeah, no one wants that. But where did you get it all?" I asked.

"Some of it is from the store. Papa stored products in the backroom. They weren't able to take it all at once. So, after they left, I went back and took everything I could. Took me a couple of days."

"Smart kid," Katherine said.

"Well, thanks for helping us. I'm not sure how those guys knew where we were," I said.

"Probably followed you. They've done it to others. I've seen them take…women."

A chill went up my spine at what that probably meant for those women. I was even more thankful now that Toby took the chance to come rescue us before the men found us hiding in the store.

"How have they not found you?" I asked.

"I'm small. I stay hidden anytime anyone is around. Hung the net outside and made sure you couldn't see the shed from far away. They don't expect a kid. It's easy to stay invisible when no one expects you." Toby flashed us a sideways smile, and I could see a small gap between his front teeth.

He was just a child, even if he was surviving on his own. Eventually, something would come along that would be bigger than he could handle. I admired him for holding out for so long, making smart decisions and then saving Katherine and me from an uncertain fate. But there was no way I could just leave him living in a shed, where it was more likely he would start a fire and burn to death than grow old and survive safely.

"We have others in our group. But one of them is sick. Do you know of any hospitals or clinics that are still intact near here?" I asked. I knew it was a long shot, but the kid seemed to know his way around.

Toby thought for a moment and then shook his head. "I haven't traveled far into town. Only once." He looked down at his feet for a moment, a look of sadness passing across his face. "After they killed Papa. Some of their group came back on foot, and not in the truck. I think that truck is the only vehicle they have that runs. Anyway, they came back to get stuff. I could hear them laughing over Papa's dead body. I was so mad. So, I followed them, but I lost them in a neighborhood. I couldn't follow too closely, or they would have seen me."

"They probably went into a house or somewhere they were staying," Katherine said.

Toby shrugged. He held out a can to each of us. Minestrone

soup. We thanked him and started to eat the soup with the plastic spoons he provided. Toby sat on a small wooden chair he had in the corner of the shed and ate a can of something as well. He watched us openly, and I had to wonder if he were thinking what I was. That we needed to take him with us.

"Where's the rest of your group?" he asked, breaking the silence first.

"About an hour from here, at an empty farmhouse," Katherine said.

"How many of you are there?"

"Six. No one as young as you," I said.

Toby nodded thoughtfully.

"I could help you find the place you need. Get what you need for your sick friend. Then maybe…"

"Well, we could definitely use some help!" I said with fake enthusiasm, but the way Toby's face brightened, he didn't realize it. "And I think we could use someone with your skills. We were in a warehouse for a while. But like your family store, people eventually showed up to try to take it from us. So, we're back on the road."

I saw the way Toby's shoulders seemed to straighten, and he sat up in his chair. Standing, the boy was probably almost six inches taller than me. And even had a few inches on Katherine, who was also taller than me. When I was honest, I would admit that pretty much everyone I knew was taller than me. And now the thirteen-year-old that saved my butt was also taller than me.

"So what do you say, Toby? Want to join us?" I asked.

I watched his face and for a moment, his true age showed. His expression held hope. At thirteen, he still had the pudgy cheeks of a child and he chewed the inside of one as he debated my offer. His eyes glanced around the shack, and I imagined he was weighing his chances.

When he returned his gaze to me, he looked determined. "I'll help you find the supplies for your sick friend. Then I'll go back with you."

Relief washed over me. If he had refused, I wasn't sure I would have felt comfortable just leaving him behind. I would have had to, for Cristian's sake, but it would have weighed on my heart and mind. If Cristian had been with me, he never would have left the boy, no matter what the boy wanted. I could almost hear Cristian convincing Toby to come with us, while making sure the boy thought it was all his idea.

I finished my can of soup, happy to have a full stomach. Toby also had bottled water and both Katherine and I gulped ours dry. Taking pity on us, he refilled them, and after we finished eating, the three of us sat in silence for a long, uncomfortable minute.

"I'm sorry, I don't want to rush you, Toby. But our friend is really ill. We need to get going to find the supplies we need. Are you ready to leave?"

Toby nodded and pulled out a large backpack that was leaning against the wall by his bed. He shoved a few pieces of clothing in it then rolled a blanket and pushed it to the bottom.

When Katherine and I didn't move, he turned with raised eyebrows at us. "Pack any of the food and water you want. I doubt we'll be back for it. Might as well take what we need now."

It was hard to choose as we sorted through the cans. I opted for the ones that would be more filling. Chili, ravioli and chicken soup. Katherine and I split the granola bars between our bags. In a box, Toby had bags of trail mix with dried fruit. I filled the side pockets of my backpack with as many of those as I could fit. Then I added as many water bottles as I could.

Feeling better about our supplies, I pulled my backpack on and winced at the additional weight. Though my ribs didn't hurt nearly as bad as they had a week ago, they were still tender. The weight of the backpack would likely aggravate the injury, but I wasn't going to say anything about it. I couldn't get the image of Cristian, lying there unresponsive, out of my head. I'd handle the pain that came with my healing ribs to get back to him.

Looking in another box, I saw cans with the labels torn off that had wood shavings and some sort of solid white substance inside.

I held one up to Toby. "What's this?"

Moving to my side, he picked up two of the small cans and stuffed them in his bag. "My Papa taught me to make them. You can use them for cooking or fire starters. You should each take a couple."

I handed two cans to Katherine, who inspected them. Not questioning it, I packed two in my bag as well. I had lighters, but if I needed light, or to cook something, they'd come in handy. Toby packed food into his pack and we all double-checked our bags. He pulled his hair back and trapped it under his hat again. He tied the bandana around his lower face and faced us.

"Why hide your face?" Katherine asked.

"I didn't want people to know I was young. Makes me a target."

The teen impressed me. He thought of things that wouldn't have occurred to me.

"Do you know the best way to get back to town?" I asked.

Toby nodded. "Yeah. And we should go away from the store and not back to the main road for a while. I've wandered that way a few times."

"Lead the way," I said, gesturing toward the door.

Toby took one long look around the shack. It was hard to tell what he was thinking with only his eyes visible, but he was making a big decision for himself. With resolution, he turned and slowly opened the door. He peered out and then stepped to the camouflage curtain and moved beyond it. Katherine looked at me and I nodded for her to follow.

Outside, the sun felt too bright after being in the shack's darkness. I had little time to acclimate, though, as Toby was already forging a path through the forest. He led us away from the store and to a trail not visible to the unfamiliar. I tried to think like Cristian, but no matter how I looked at the young boy, I could find nothing to be suspicious of.

We hiked through the green space, with little talking. Toby seemed to like being quiet. After all of his sneaking around and hiding, that made sense. And it was likely the safest option for us until we were further away from where the killers seemed to hang out. Every so often, I could see a glimpse of a road, but Toby continued to lead us parallel to it.

As we hiked, I evaluated my body and breathing. My ribs hurt, but not any worse than before. The backpack was heavy, and I propped my hands under the straps to keep the pressure off my torso. I watched where I put my feet. We couldn't afford one of us getting injured, and I refused to be the one to get hurt yet again.

We stopped and Toby lifted his bandana to sip water. Katherine and I did the same. It was hard not to overheat, even in the shade of the trees. The sun was high in the sky, lunchtime having passed. I pulled a pack of trail mix from the side of my bag and after pouring part of the bag into Katherine's hand, I went to share with Toby, but he shook his head and held up a bag of Cheetos.

For a moment I thought about telling him it wasn't the most healthy option, but I kept my mouth shut. He'd been living on his own and doing his own thing. He didn't need a stranger coming in and telling him how to eat. I wasn't sure I'd had Cheetos since I was eighteen and living on my own. At one time, I'd resented my mom for not letting me eat the same foods all the other kids ate. It only took a few years for me to realize I preferred the real foods she always provided.

Now looking at Toby, someone who had kept himself alive for weeks, I realized so many things that seemed important before, just weren't. Calories were calories. Of course, there were better foods for the body. But right now, we could never be sure where our next meal would come from. If the boy wanted to eat Cheetos, he could eat them.

We began walking again. Toby was a decent guide. Though he could have moved faster without us, he looked back often to make sure we weren't being left behind. We could have found the road easily, since we were walking parallel to it, but it was nice to have someone that knew where they were going. I had been in the area for years and still used GPS to get from one place to another. Those times were over, it seemed, for now.

As the trees thinned, Toby slowed. Standing behind a large tree, he waited for Katherine and me to move up next to him. In the distance, we could hear the sounds of people, and Toby's gaze scanned ahead nervously.

"What is it?" I asked.

"I've avoided people this whole time. I'm just not sure when it's the right time to come out of hiding, ya know?"

I touched Toby's arm and when his eye met mine. I gave him a warm smile. "You're not alone right now."

Not that I was any better than he was at defending myself. But what I hadn't shown him was the gun tucked at the small of my back, moved there when I was packing the food into my pack. Could I actually shoot someone? I wasn't sure. I wouldn't know until the moment came. And I hoped it never would.

"There's a walk-in clinic a few miles that way," Katherine said, pointing past the rooftops. "Might not have much, but it's a start."

Toby nodded, and we moved down the trees, keeping the street in sight, but not leaving the shadows. The closer we got to the town, the more noises came to us as people moved around. It shouldn't have surprised me to see people in the distance. Everyone was doing the same thing we were. Just trying to survive.

We came to the end of the trees and stepped out onto the street, moving between abandoned cars. A squeak from behind me had me spinning to check on Katherine. She stared intently at a car I had just passed without inspecting. She was pale and had frozen next to the sedan.

Rushing back to her, I grabbed her arm. "What is it?"

Katherine's voice trembled, barely a whisper. "Marlowe... we're not making it back, are we?"

CHAPTER
TWENTY-TWO
CRISTIAN

When I woke again, Dave was sitting beside me, his face lined with exhaustion and something else. Concern. His voice was calm but firm as he went through the usual questions, checking my symptoms like he was ticking boxes off a mental list. I tried to focus, but my thoughts were sluggish, my body heavy with fatigue.

I couldn't stop shivering. Every inch of me felt ice cold despite the suffocating summer heat pressing in from the outside. Dave wiped a sheen of sweat from his forehead, his shirt sticking to his back, but I barely noticed the warmth.

"It's the fever," he said, his voice softer now. "You're burning up, but your body thinks it's freezing."

"Marlowe?" The word rasped from my throat before I could stop it. My tongue felt thick.

Dave's forehead scrunched, and he shook his head. "You've only been asleep for a few hours. No, she's not back yet."

A few hours? It felt like days had passed in the darkness of my fevered sleep. Time slipped through my fingers, lost somewhere between dreams and reality, and the only thing I was certain of was the gnawing anxiety in my gut. Marlowe. The second I was awake, she was the first thing on my mind, but I couldn't hold on to the thought long enough to ease the worry tightening in my chest.

I tried shifting, testing the weight of my body, and pain shot through my leg like a blade carving through flesh. I gritted my teeth, the ache worse than before, spreading outward with every slight movement.

The doctor noticed. He always did. Reaching out of my view, he produced a few pills in his palm. He motioned for me to let him help me sit up. It took more effort than it should have, but I let him guide me, my muscles trembling with the strain. I took the pills without asking, swallowing them down with a sip of luke-warm water.

"Still just ibuprofen?"

"Sorry, it's all we have."

Marlowe had gone to the neighboring house, even at her own risk, to try to find things to help me. I wasn't going to complain about what she could find. And she had been so close to being caught by whoever broke into the house after them. The farm-house we were in was much more nondescript, and unlikely to catch the attention of someone looking to loot. But I was in no position to protect anyone.

"There's two guns in my bag," I said, my voice rough. "You or Roger should have them. Just in case."

Dave's expression flickered, and I realized the truth before he said, "Marlowe took one."

I groaned, dragging a shaky hand down my face. "Of course she did."

"She didn't hide it," Dave added quickly. "I saw her take it, and… I didn't stop her. Figured it was better she had something to protect herself with."

I clenched my jaw, but deep down, I couldn't argue. I hated the idea of her out there, alone, armed with nothing but good intentions and sheer determination. But I also knew Marlowe. She wasn't reckless. She was just… desperate. And the truth was, if I were in her position, I would have done the same damn thing.

The fever clawed at my mind again, pulling me back under its weight, but the last thought I had before slipping into restless sleep was of her. Marlowe, out there, in the unknown. And all I could do was wait.

I hated waiting.

TWENTY-THREE

Dusk crept in, swallowing what little light remained, and we still hadn't found the clinic Katherine swore was nearby. She'd started off confident, but after too many detours, too many wrong turns to avoid potential threats, her certainty unraveled. Finally, with tears brimming in her eyes, she admitted in a whisper, "I think I'm lost."

The fact that she was talking now was an enormous relief. After she saw the dead family in the sedan, I wasn't sure she would be able to keep going. It wasn't until she told me we were all going to die that I noticed the decomposing bodies in the car. I'd slapped my hand over my mouth to keep the scream bubbling up from escaping.

There was a man at the steering wheel, slumped over. I guessed a gunshot wound to the head. A woman sat in the passenger seat. Her head rested against the window, dried blood streaking the glass. She'd also taken a bullet to the head. The backseat was the worst part, and I refused to study the scene further. Maybe it was a blessing that the two children died with their parents. But that would be something I'd contemplate later. Getting away from the car was my priority.

I dragged Katherine away, but she craned her neck, her gaze

locked on the car. When we were finally out of view, she turned and trudged next to me, but only because I was holding onto her arm. I eventually twined our fingers together, to make sure she didn't break off from me when I wasn't paying attention. Her silence was suffocating. I didn't blame her. It was hard to imagine we could survive any of this.

Toby seemed unfazed by the whole thing, even though he had walked around the car, peering into the windows. Alarm bells went off in my head, wondering how much the boy had seen to desensitize him so fully. Another problem for later. I wondered if Dave had any mental health training, because we were going to need it. All of us.

"We can't keep wandering. We need shelter," I murmured, scanning the street for anything that didn't scream 'death trap.'

Most of the stores in the shopping district we were in had been vandalized. Windows were smashed, doors hung open. Even the sidewalk was starting to show signs of society crumbling. Unkept grass was growing unfettered, while weeds pushed up in the crack of of the concrete where they could. The rainy days must have helped them expand and grow when humans couldn't stop them. It wasn't much, not yet. My mind added more, and I knew if things didn't come back, we wouldn't recognize anything in a few months.

Toby stopped in front of a building that looked like it was two stories. He looked up and stared. I followed his gaze and wasn't sure what he was thinking. The bottom floor looked like it was a high-end toy store. Interesting place for people to loot, but I guessed if people were taking care of kids, toys that didn't need electricity might be in high demand.

"I think it's an apartment upstairs," Toby said.

I glanced up and saw what Toby was studying. The shades were open and there looked like there was a potted plant sitting on the windowsill.

"What if someone's still inside?" Katherine whispered, her voice uncertain.

I tilted my head, still staring up at the windows. "If someone's up there, they'd have the blinds shut tight, staying hidden. My guess? Whoever lived there never made it back."

"We need a place to stay overnight," Toby whispered. "I don't think wandering then would be a good idea. I've seen what can happen after dark."

He didn't need to elaborate. The worst of humanity was rising to replace the order we had before. And until someone or something strong came in to control the chaos, we were all at risk. We stepped into the wreckage of the toy store, the floor littered with shattered plastic and discarded boxes. I crouched, tugging on a pink string poking out from the debris. A doll's head tumbled free, her stitched smile eerily intact. Her body was nowhere in sight. Had two people fought over her, yanking until she came apart? Until she wasn't useful anymore?

Sighing, I tossed the doll head onto the trash-strewn ground. The store, a shell of its former self, had long been looted for anything worth taking. I didn't know what it would be like to shop in such a fancy toy store, but I guessed there was clientele for it. A single mom, with multiple jobs, just to make ends meet, didn't buy expensive hand sewn dolls for her daughter. I grew up just fine without all of that.

At the back of the store, a door led to a narrow staircase. I motioned for Toby to get behind me and I climbed the stairs. There was only one high window at the top of the stairs that let in the smallest bit of light from the waning day. Carefully, I climbed each stair, ensuring I didn't trip and tumble down, taking Toby and Katherine with me.

When we reached the top, there was a small landing. The door to the apartment was there, and it was closed. Suddenly, it occurred to me we didn't have keys, and I had no idea how to pick a lock. Toby walked straight to a small potted plant that sat at the far corner of the landing and picked it up, revealing a rock underneath. After showing us the rock was fake, he slipped the bottom open.

"Hide-a-key. Figured there was no other reason to have a fake plant, where there's no sun, sitting on the landing." He just shrugged when we stared at him. "My Papa had one too. Because I was always forgetting my house key."

I took the key from his hand, thinking I should be the first one through the door. Slipping my hand behind me, between my back and my pack, I wrapped my fingers around the gun. This wasn't an old western movie, and I wasn't some quick draw. But I didn't want to burst into the apartment with a gun in my hand.

Katherine reached out and grabbed my arm. "What if…what if we find the same thing we found at the farmhouse?"

Toby's eyebrows quirked up, as he had no idea what we were talking about. And with everything he had experienced since the end, I wasn't looking to tell that story. The telltale smell that we had recognized in the farmhouse, wasn't filling the hallway. This wasn't a perfect science.

I shook my head at Katherine. "It'll be fine."

I didn't actually know that. But I wasn't sure what else to say in response. What would we do if I opened the door only to find dead bodies? The darkness in the hallway was already deepening, and we didn't have long to find a different place to stay for the night. The landing was out of the way, but there was no way to secure the location, since the door from the toy store couldn't be locked. This possible apartment was our best option. And if we were faced with the worst case scenario, I would handle it to keep us safe for the night.

The deadbolt clicked open quietly. I didn't realize I was holding my breath as I slowly opened the door. The silence of the world made hearing people much easier. But if they were ready for us, we could be walking into an ambush. Lifting my hand over my shoulder, I motioned for Toby and Katherine to wait at the door.

I entered a small living room. The windows we'd seen from the street let in the remaining glow of twilight light. A couch, small flatscreen TV and lounge chair filled the room, almost more than it could contain. None of the pieces matched, but there was an eclectic, artistic feel to it. Just beyond the living room lay a small galley kitchen. A bistro table, only big enough for two, took up most of the extra space near the kitchen. On the counter sat a coffee pot with the dried remains of the last brew.

A small hallway led to a bathroom with a toilet, shower, and a small pedestal sink. I cringed when I caught my reflection for just a moment. My greasy ponytail was in total disarray and there was a smudge of dirt on my cheek. I didn't bother to clean up. It was pointless. Leaning in, I ran my finger over the scar tissue on my cheek. After a few weeks, the skin was pink and healing, but I was sure I would be left with a lasting memory of the plane crash.

There were two closed doors in the hallway and Katherine's worry came back to mind. Preparing myself for the worst, I opened the first door. I released a held breath when I realized it was just a linen closet. The shelves were full of sheets, blankets, and towels. I suddenly felt exhausted and thought about how taking one of those soft-looking blankets to wrap up in would be nice.

Standing outside the last door, I hesitated. A sound reached my ears, and I froze with my hand above the doorknob. Leaning toward the door, I put my ear close to the wood, waiting. Suddenly, a mourning meow came, and I realized the sound I had heard was scratching. Slowly, I opened the door and peered in.

The bed was made and empty bed. I pushed the door open and a gray ball of fur streaked toward me, forcing me to jump out of the way. The cat ran into the front room and I heard the voices of Toby and Katherine as they saw the fluff ball.

"Come on in," I called to them. "It's empty."

I heard the front door shut and Toby's quiet words as he tried to sweet talk the cat. Katherine found me in the master bedroom. The room stank, as the litter box was overflowing, and the cat had possibly soiled the bed and carpet in the room. I held my hand over my nose and mouth, trying to not breathe in the toxic fumes. Rushing to the window, I opened it and let the air flow in.

The only reason the animal was alive was the large bag of cat food that was in the closet. The door was open only a fraction, but it was enough for the cat to squeeze through and rip the bag open. There was a large water bowl on the ground that was bone dry. But also a glass on either side of the bed that may have had water at some point.

"Toby, the cat probably needs water," I called to the front room.

"On it," he called back.

I could hear the cat meow, and it was pitiful. Armed with a box of litter, I searched until I found a laundry basket in the closet. I put fresh litter in the basket's bottom and brought the whole thing out of the bedroom. Putting it on the ground near the window, I hoped the cat could figure out that it was its bathroom now. After bringing some food out as well, I closed the bedroom door and sealed the smell away.

"He's been alone this whole time?" Toby asked.

I nodded. "Don't know if it was from the beginning. But the state of that room tells me he had been locked in there for a long time. We don't want to go back in there."

Katherine pulled the shades on all the windows, making sure they were secure before pulling out one of the homemade fire starters from Toby's shed. She set it on a small side table that was next to the couch and lit it with her lighter. The wax concoction lit right up. It gave off just a small amount of light, but it was enough to move around the small room.

I went to the kitchen area and started opening cabinets. I found a six-pack of soda bottles and pulled them out to go with whatever we ate for dinner. There was little else to eat in the kitchen. Either the people living there kept little food on hand, or they were home when everything happened and packed to leave. They did have an extensive collection of herbs and spices. Something I planned on going through before we left to see if there was anything we could take with us.

After I handed out sodas, I sat in the living room. The feeling of exhaustion struck again, and I wasn't even sure I would have the energy to eat before falling asleep. Back at the linen closet, I pulled all of the blankets from the shelves and brought them into the living room, handing them out to Katherine and Toby.

Slipping off my boots, I massaged my feet for a moment before curling up in the lounge chair. I watched Toby pet the cat. The animal had quickly warmed up to him, once he provided the much needed hydration for him. Katherine was sorting through her pack. She produced a can and popped it open by its pull tab. Not bothering with a spoon, she poured the contents into her mouth, her eyes focused in the distance. We all were settled in our own worlds.

Gun shots rang out, and I jumped from the chair. Grabbing my pack, I pulled the gun out. The shots didn't sound like they were in our building, but they were close enough to make me nervous. Toby and Katherine were both on their feet. Katherine glanced at the gun, but if she was surprised to see it, she said nothing.

At the window, I slipped the corner of the shade back to check the street in front of the building. Everything was pitch black. It was a darkness that felt thick and unavoidable. Even when I had camped out, because it was cheaper than paying for hotels sometimes, there was always distant light. Even in the most remote woods I had been in, I could still find a light on the outside of an outhouse. Now, there was nothing.

I let my eyes adjust a bit, hiding them from the small flame we had in the apartment. The moon wasn't full, but eventually I was able to see movement in the shadows. There were two people running from building to building, hiding behind corners and in alleys. I couldn't tell who they were running from and I strained to look further down the street. Another gunshot sounded, and it was definitely closer this time. The two figures took off in a dead sprint, passing below our window and continuing down the street.

Another shot and one runner tumbled to the ground. In the darkness, the fall looked dramatic, but I couldn't be sure what actually happened. I heard a yell. It was a man's voice, and I was pretty sure it was a man's silhouette, bending over the fallen person. A deep wail rose, but it was quickly cut off as the man stood up straight. His head swung from side to side as he looked for a place to hide.

"Do we help them?" Toby asked.

"Like you helped us?" I asked. I could see Toby nod at the other window, where he was also watching. Shaking my head, I said, "No. Someone is shooting at them. I don't think we need to bring that down on us."

Katherine stood behind us and when I glanced back, I found her with her arms wrapped around her middle. I could understand her fear. The same emotion was trying to take over my brain. But when it rose, I pulled Cristian's image from my memory and built a new wall of resolve. No matter what was happening on the street or anywhere else in town, I couldn't give up. There was no one else to push forward for him. It was going to be me.

Toby and I watched while the man seemed to try to pick the fallen individual off the ground. I couldn't tell if the person was alive, unconscious, or dead. But they weren't helping the man. Out of the corner of my eye, I saw more movement on the other end of the street. Someone walked toward the pair that were struggling to get out of the open. The approaching person raised their arm and though I couldn't clearly see, I imagined there was a handgun pointed at the figures in the street.

I could see what was coming. And I didn't want to see it. Realizing I wasn't the most impressionable in the room, I stepped to Toby's side of the window.

"I don't think you should see this, Toby."

The boy looked at me, his eyes full of knowing. "I've seen worse."

"I know, sweetie. But when you don't need to see it, you shouldn't. This is all making you grow up really fast. And you've done a great job. This isn't something we can stop or fix. Move away from the window, okay?"

I took the curtain from his hand and let it fall back into place. He didn't fight against me as I moved him back to the couch, covering him up with his blanket again. Just as he looked up at me, multiple gunshots echoed down the street. He winced and closed his eyes. I wanted to hug him. But I knew that wasn't appropriate. Instead, I laid a hand on his shoulder for a moment, while we both accepted what was happening around us.

The night went quiet, as if the gunshots caused everyone else to be silent and small. I doubted anyone would venture out if they had heard the killings. We were in a place where the strong weren't always the good guys. They weren't all Cristian. Someone who cared for others without question. Some, like the person who had the gun in the street, used their power to take from others.

Letting those thoughts settle into my mind, I curled back into the lounge chair with my fluffy blanket. The sinister side of society was always there. I wasn't completely blind to that. But without the normal controls in place, like police, laws and government, that foulness rose to the top. We couldn't always fight against it. There was nothing the three of us could have done for the victims in the street. But maybe, someday, there would be people that would rise and fight.

I wasn't sure where I fit into society now. What would have happened to me if Cristian hadn't taken me from the courthouse? A question that had replayed in my mind over and over. Why was I spared when that plane fell from the sky? It had to mean something. I wasn't religious, wasn't sure if I believed in a higher power. But I had to believe that my life meant something, and that was why I was still here.

My mind was still whirling as I fell asleep, sitting up in the chair.

I felt pressure on my leg. A dull, throbbing sensation that sharpened as awareness returned. My eyelids refused to cooperate and for a brief, fevered moment, I half-believed Dave had taped them shut. A stupid thought, but my brain wasn't exactly firing on all cylinders. Finally, I could crack one eye open and was surprised to find bright light streaming into the room.

Coughing, I tried to speak, but my tongue was thick and my throat felt like sandpaper. A figure leaned over me and it took a long, confused moment for me to realize it was Dave. It wasn't Marlowe, the person I was hoping to see. At first, I forgot. She had left to get me help. And if the doctor was with me, I had to assume she hadn't returned.

Reading my thoughts, Dave smiled kindly. "Not yet, man."

"What time is it?" My voice was barely a whisper.

"Mid-morning. Around nine, I think."

Where had she slept? I hoped she knew not to stay out at night. To find somewhere safe to rest and only travel during the day. I tried to remember if she and I had ever talked about that. I didn't think so.

The doctor went through the same process of getting meds

into me then applied a cool compress on my forehead. It felt like heaven.

Moving down to my leg, Dave sighed. "This is probably going to hurt. But I really want to clean as much of this as I can. Roger was able to get water from the well. Don't ask me how he figured it out, but he found some sort of hand pump mechanism. I boiled this water this morning for over thirty minutes. It's cooler now. It's the closest thing I have to sterile."

"Do what you gotta do, Doc." I meant to sound strong and tough. Instead, the words came out broken and whispered.

I tensed involuntarily, anticipating the pain I was about to feel. And it didn't disappoint. Dave carefully poured the water onto the wound. At first the coolness against my heated skin felt like relief, but just as I thought I was in the clear, white-hot, searing pain, like fire licking at raw nerves, exploded in my leg. The throbbing pulsed harder, sharper, until I could feel it in my teeth.

"Sorry," Dave muttered.

I was about to say it wasn't so bad, but then he patted the wound with whatever cloth he had. The pain was almost unbearable. I gasped and slammed my teeth together before I cried out. Dave was quick with the cleaning, but then probed the area with his fingers and my body bowed, trying to get away from the inspection. I released a string of curses, no longer able to keep it all inside.

"Did you know there are studies that have proven that cursing can help with physical pain?" Dave asked.

The information made little sense until I realized he was referring to my outburst.

"Not sure that's helping me right now." My teeth were clenched so hard, my jaw was starting to ache and tremble.

The process felt like it took forever. By the time Dave finally wrapped a clean piece of cloth around my leg, I was on the verge of blacking out. The pain lasted even after he sat back, looking down into my face.

"The wound is swollen and hot to the touch. Not that I doubted the infection before, but it's really clear now."

The pain was unbearable, raw, and unrelenting. I felt the sting behind my eyes before the tears spilled, trailing hot down my temples. I didn't bother wiping them away. Dave's eyes held sympathy, and I looked away. I felt weak and vulnerable. I barely knew the doctor and badly wanted to be alone. But really, I wanted to be with Marlowe.

Not that I had known her much longer than anyone else in the house. The connection I was acknowledging more and more made me comfortable with her. Would I have felt like I could break down in front of her? She would have said she wasn't judging me. I knew she would comfort me and try to take care of me. In my condition, I wouldn't have been able to stop her. Just like I couldn't stop her from going out to save my life with only Katherine at her back.

Complications with Sarah made it hard to allow someone close to me. When I thought about Marlowe, I couldn't help but think about my family. The one I had lost piece by piece throughout the years. First, my brother. Gone in a drive-by shooting, wrong place, wrong time. Another statistic, just like that.

I was too young to really understand the impact that loss had on my life. But now, I recognized, I became the sheriff deputy I was, because I was always trying to save other little boys like him. My parents couldn't understand why I had to distance myself from them, to become the man I wanted to be. My brother's death wasn't their fault. They died, in a car accident, believing I thought it was all their fault. That was one of my biggest regrets.

Slowly, I fell into a painful sleep, even though I had just woken. The cleaning of my wound had taken all the energy I had. The last face I saw before oblivion was my mother's. I hoped it wasn't because I was getting ready to meet her in the afterlife. She smiled at me, and I swore I could feel her kiss my forehead.

CHAPTER
TWENTY-FIVE
MARLOWE

Waking up had become an exercise in readjustment. I no longer opened my eyes expecting the familiarity of my bedroom ceiling, the hum of the fridge or the streetlight glow through my curtains. I couldn't even be sure I would see my apartment again. Really, that wasn't an enormous loss. I hadn't amassed a lot of important possessions. Even so, I felt sadness over losing that sense of normalcy, of being in a place I had become comfortable in.

My neck was stiff from sleeping in a weird angle, and I sighed when I looked around the living room. Toby lay curled on the couch, his light snore indicating he still slept deeply. The cat was sleeping between his legs. Turning my head and then stopping because it hurt my neck, I found Katherine sitting at the dining table. She had a book open in front of her. I wanted to make a joke about her reading ability, but I decided against it. She had dark circles under her eyes. With the way Toby was spread out on the couch, I wasn't sure where or if she slept.

Standing, I stretched my back and rolled my neck. That was going to be annoying for the day. Katherine looked over at me and there was so much on her face, but exhaustion definitely outweighed everything.

"You didn't sleep, did you?"

"I couldn't."

I sat across from her at the table. "You could have woken me."

She snorted. "If either of us needed sleep, it was you. You went from trying to heal from messed up ribs, to being on the run, to worrying about Cristian. I wonder when you last had a full night's sleep."

I wasn't going to admit that I didn't think I had slept a full night since my bed, the night before the world fell apart. That was until I fell asleep in the lounge chair. A stampeding herd of elephants probably couldn't have roused me.

"I guess I was tired," I said.

Katherine nodded and held up the book she was reading. It was a cocktail book, but the drinks were all built around foraging.

"This is probably the most crunchy book I've randomly found."

I couldn't stop the laugh that bubbled up. And then felt bad, as Toby shot up on the couch. His hair was sticking up at all angles and he blinked like an owl around the room.

"Sorry, kid," I said, with a wince.

He shook his head and ran his hand over the cat that was now pressing against him for attention. I wasn't sure what we were going to do with that animal. I couldn't in good conscience just leave it in the apartment. It would die. Glancing around, I imagined there was a cat carrier or something we could use to take him with us.

"We should get going," I said, gently prodding them. I didn't enjoy being a leader, but I felt like I had wasted too much time already.

After a search of the closets and risking the smell of the bedroom, I was absolutely astonished to find a cat backpack. A real, honest-to-god, ridiculous-looking astronaut-style cat carrier. I turned it over in my hands, brushing off dust, staring at the little bubble window. The absurdity of it almost made me laugh. The cat seemed to know the situation. Toby opened it and the furry creature jumped right in and sat looking at us. As Toby zipped him in, he settled comfortably.

"Do you know what his name is?" I asked.

Toby nodded. "Yeah. He has a name tag. Apparently his name is Apollo."

"A Greek god, huh? Well, I guess he should behave with dignity. Hopefully, that means he'll be good on this trip," I said with a smile.

I found a drawer with zipper storage bags and picked the largest for cat food. Packing it full, I was sure it was enough food for this trip and days after. Though I didn't want to leave the poor thing behind, I knew I was also saddling us with another dependent. I found myself wondering if Cristian was a cat or dog person. Or neither? We hadn't taken the time for basic pleasantries so far.

We also added a small duffel bag to our supplies. Optimism had me believing we would fill another entire bag with the supplies Cristian needed right now and anything we could use in the near future. With a doctor on our team, there were probably numerous items that he could use to treat wounds or illnesses. I slung the duffel across my chest, making sure it rested on the opposite side of my injured ribs.

We were careful as we left the apartment. Nothing on the landing or the stairs indicated that someone had wandered through during the night. The toy store was as much of a disaster as before. There would be no way to tell one pile of destruction from another, so I could only assume it was all the same.

The street stretched out in eerie silence, bathed in the illusion of safety that only daylight could offer. But I knew better. I knew that feeling was false. As most survivors probably knew as well. We had to pass the spot where we saw the murder during the night. Oddly, there were no bodies. The puddle of drying blood was the only storyteller. All other evidence was gone. I looked up and down the street and in the nearby alley between buildings but there was nothing.

"Where did they go?" Toby asked, clearly having the same thoughts as I was.

I shook my head. "I have no idea."

"That's weird, right? That feels really weird." He'd pulled his bandana across his face again but his eyes were wide as he looked around for the dead bodies he expected.

"Maybe they had family or friends that didn't want to leave them on the street," Katherine suggested.

It was a probable explanation. Though I had to agree with Toby. I didn't say it out loud, because I didn't want him to worry. But it did feel weird. It was likely family members wanted to bury their lost people. The work that would take would be immense, without any sort of power or large equipment. It was impossible for me not to put myself in their shoes. If I ever could find my mom in all of this, she might already be dead. Could I just leave her? Or would I feel the need to put her to rest?

We walked along in silence. When we passed a pharmacy, we saw that someone had ransacked it. Katherine and I agreed we would come back to it if we weren't able to find the supplies we needed in the clinic. She was positive it wasn't much further now.

After a few wrong turns and a growing sense of frustration, we finally reached the clinic—a squat, beige building with a sign that promised Same Day Care! Unsurprisingly, it looked as if it had been looted. I had lied to myself, wanting to believe this would be easy. The pop of the hope bubble in my chest felt like my lungs deflating all at once.

"Well. Maybe there's some stuff left behind," I said, infusing my words with the determination I wanted to feel.

The inside of the clinic was a lot of open space. Sitting near the center of the office was a round desk that must have been for people to check in. There were papers scattered across the surface and all over the floor.

Katherine bent and picked one up and tossed it after reading a few words. "Patient records. A lot of good those will do now."

Private exam rooms lined the area. They were small, made of walls of frosted glass. A few of the front panes were cracked, where looters had tried to break out the glass. But they withstood whatever assault was brought down on them. Along the row, someone had used black spray paint to write random phrases.

Toby pointed to one that said End of Times. "These people serious?"

"It's easy to understand how people are connecting this with things that happened in the Bible." Katherine said the words as she walked into an exam room. She didn't make eye contact with either of us and I knew from what she had told me about her religious upbringing, she wouldn't expand on it further.

I entered another exam room, where someone had crushed the blood pressure machine on the ground. The destruction had no purpose other than to break things that no longer worked. If we ever got power back, even a semblance of the previous world, so much would have to start over. The paper normally covering the exam table lay completely unrolled. Did a cat cause this chaos? I snorted at my own inner monologue.

Someone had overturned a cart in the corner, but all the drawers remained intact. I picked it up and got it back on its wheels. Immediately, I found the cart locked. Something secured against theft was a good sign. However, I had no idea how to get it open. Before figuring that out, I searched the rest of the room. I found a box of gloves and put those into the duffel bag.

In the main room, I went to the center desk. There was no way it would be so easy as finding keys in a drawer, but it was the first thing I thought of. I pulled open each drawer, pushed around office supplies, grabbing whatever could be useful. I packed away two pairs of scissors. They weren't medical grade, but they were sharp.

I heard a jingling sound of keys and looked over to find

Katherine picking up a keyring. Joining her, I found a small pile of individually packaged gauze and bandaids on the counter.

"All I found in here so far," Katherine said, and I swept them into the duffel bag.

"What are the keys?"

"Don't know yet. They were shoved under the exam table." Katherine was studying the ring, sorting through each key.

"There's a locked case in the room I was in. I was hoping to find keys, but it can't be that easy," I said with a hopeful grin.

Katherine shrugged and tossed the keys to me. I rushed to the room I was in and started trying the keys that looked small enough for the drawers. When one slid in and it clicked open, I was stunned. The top drawer revealed a thermometer, tweezers, syringes, medical scissors, the same stitching kits that Dave had at the warehouse and more. I cheered out loud as I started packing all the items into my duffel.

"Marlowe?" Katherine's voice made me freeze.

I immediately heard the fear that laced her voice. Kicking myself mentally, I realized we lacked someone watching the clinic's front to prevent an ambush. I knew when I turned, I would see someone with Katherine that we didn't know. Slowly, I slid my hand to the small of my back at the same time as I turned toward the door of the exam room.

As expected, there was a large man behind her. One of his large paws was clamped down on Katherine's upper arm. I didn't dare take my eyes off of him, but I couldn't see Toby anywhere nearby. Relief blossomed. He had to be hiding. I hoped he stayed out of sight.

"Something we can help you with?" I asked.

I pulled my shoulders back, trying to look strong and hide the full body tremble that was happening.

The man sneered at me and yanked Katherine backward. "Was just coming back for that case. Thanks for opening it for me."

It was a split second decision and I couldn't be sure it was the right one. His grip on Katherine, with no gun pointed at me, convinced me he was unarmed. He was using his size and surprise as his weapon. If I was wrong, I could get us all killed. Including Cristian, who would never know what happened to me when I didn't return to help him.

Pulling my arm from behind me, I pointed the gun directly at his head. I watched his eyes widen in surprise. And immediately, I knew I was going to win my gamble. He didn't move, didn't counter my threat. Just stared at me. I stared back, as I lifted my free hand, and wrapped it around the one that held the gun. In my mind, I thought I looked experienced, but in truth, I had no idea if I was even holding the gun correctly.

"I opened it for us. You can leave. Once we're done, you can have whatever is left." I kept my voice even and neutral.

He hesitated, calculating, but I could see the doubt creeping in. He wasn't sure if I'd pull the trigger. I wasn't sure either. But I didn't let that show. I lifted the gun just a little higher.

When he didn't move fast enough, I motioned with the gun. "Let her go. Now."

"You aren't going to shoot me, little girl," he said.

"Do you want to risk that? Over some gauze? I don't think so. Let her go. I won't ask again."

Katherine's face was pale, and her mouth dropped open as I spoke. I avoided looking at her or I'd lose the confident facade I hid behind.

The grizzly man shoved Katherine forward. But because I predicted he would try to use her to knock me down, I moved to the side. She stumbled and caught herself on the exam table. I kept the gun trained on the man, who was still not moving toward the exit.

Without Katherine in front of him, I could get a better look at him. His hair was long and unkempt. Clearly, he hadn't been working very hard to keep himself clean, maybe since even before everything fell apart. His clothing was in tatters in some places and his eyes were red rimmed and bloodshot. He was twitchy, which told me there was something in this clinic he probably felt he needed, very badly. If he hadn't grabbed Katherine, I imagined I would have felt bad for him.

Realizing he had lost his leverage, he suddenly looked defeated. His gaze slid to his hands and then at his surroundings. I didn't take my eyes off of him, waiting for any sudden movements. When I pulled the gun out, I had taken off the safety, like I'd seen Cristian do. If the man rushed me, I would have to pull the trigger. It was the last thing I wanted to do.

"I'm sorry," he whispered, before he turned and fled.

I went to the door of the room and leaned out just far enough, with the gun still pointing in his direction, to watch as he ran from the clinic. He disappeared around some stalled cars that blocked my view. I waited another long moment before releasing a breath.

"Holy crap, Marlowe! Would you have shot him?"

I didn't turn to look at her. I didn't have an answer. Instead, I stepped further out of the exam room and called for Toby quietly. The teenager popped up from behind the front desk, Apollo still in his backpack, clutched in his arms. The boy looked frightened, and I rushed over to the desk.

"Are you ok?"

He nodded. "He didn't even know I was over here."

I reached out and patted his shoulder before finally looking at Katherine. "And you?"

"I'm fine. I still want to know what you would have done with that gun."

I clicked the safety on and slipped it back into the back of my pants, making sure my shirt hid it. "I would have done what I had to."

"Which could have been shoot the guy?"

I stared at her, incredulous. I had saved her life, and she was questioning me? "I don't think we have time for this discussion. We need to get everything we can out of here and get moving. More people will come."

I thought she was going to argue at first, but she just sighed and nodded. "You're right."

Without another word, she turned away from Toby and me and went to a different exam room we hadn't checked yet. Toby followed behind me and we went through the remaining drawers of the cart. There were boxes of individual dose packets of over-the-counter meds. They weren't strong enough for Cristian, but I packed them anyway.

I reached the bottom drawer, and it was full of labeled amber-colored bottles. Excited, I started picking them up and frowned at the words that looked like a different language to me. I compared the list from Dave to the labels until I cried out when I matched one. Then I found a few blister packs that also had a name he had written as a second choice. Then I grabbed anything else that ended in "in", as Dave noted as the last option.

There were two boxes of single use topical antibiotics, but no full bottles. Those would have to do. Other medications that I recognized for allergies or stomach issues also went into the duffel. I paused. Why would I leave anything behind? Without reading any additional labels, I threw every package of medication into the duffel.

Toby was rummaging around in the top of the cart and he held up two boxes to show me. "This stuff is great. I cut open my eyebrow once. They used this stuff like glue to close it up without stitches."

I smiled and opened the duffel so he could drop them in. "Everything is good to go."

Coming out of the exam room, we found Katherine, shoving mini bottled waters into her backpack.

"They had a small snack stash in the last exam room. I guess they didn't use that often for actual patients." She handed Toby a box of organic fruit leather and me a few bags of mini cookies.

"Either for the employees, or people with low blood sugar or something?" I mused.

"Their foresight is our boon. Now let's get the hell out of here. I'm not interested in being held captive again."

I couldn't agree with that more. We gave Apollo a moment to

stretch his legs. Surprisingly, he didn't venture far from Toby. The cat had bonded with the boy quickly, likely a trauma response to being left alone the way he was. Toby found a container to pour a little water in and let the cat drink. He also wanted to give Apollo the chance to eat a little food, since we weren't sure when we would stop again.

I didn't want to be caught unaware again, so I found a place in the shadows where I could easily see the door, but anyone approaching wouldn't see me. Every once in a while, I would glance back at Toby and Katherine. I couldn't fight the smile that came to my face when I saw her rubbing her hand along the cat's back. Her face held a delight I had never seen. Maybe bringing Apollo along would do a lot more good than just saving an abandoned family pet.

The cat went back into his carrier without fuss. It was almost a little eerie the way he looked out the window and watched everything around us. His eyes were green and though they weren't human looking, when I stared into them, I swore there were emotions behind them. If I had to guess, he probably felt a lot of sadness, realizing his family wasn't coming back.

It was midday when we left the clinic. I guided Katherine and Toby around the corner of the building, so it wasn't obvious that we were coming straight from there. What we had in our bags would be highly valuable to the right survivor. It was everything to me. I wouldn't let anyone take it from us.

We walked quietly, keeping conversation to a minimum. At times, I heard Toby murmuring. I thought he was talking to himself, but then I realized he was actually talking to Apollo. Thinking about it, I realized Toby had been on his own for a couple of weeks. That's a long time for a teenager to have no one to even talk to, let alone have anyone to care for him. I was looking forward to getting him back to our people.

I knew we wouldn't make it back to the farmhouse before dark. The thought of breaking the rules and traveling at night tempted me. But after what happened the night before, I didn't want to risk us being hunted down on the street like animals. We couldn't stay in the same place as we had the night before, or it would take us more than a full day to get back to the farmhouse. Too much time.

Judging by the sun, we didn't have enough time to make it to Toby's shed, either. I needed to find a space somewhere in between. Picturing the walk through the trees, I wasn't sure what we would find.

As we walked, Toby moved forward to walk next to me. "I know somewhere we can stay. It's not exactly comfortable, though."

I smiled over at him. "How did you know that was on my mind?"

"Figured it had to be that or your friend. And since I figure you don't want to take an extra day, we need to find a place for the night. But, like, not too soon. Right?"

"Smart kid. What are you thinking?"

Two hours later, and just before the sun fell below the horizon, we arrived at a small post office.

Toby stood in front of it, motioning with his arm. "I haven't seen anyone really go in and out of here when I've been around."

"Definitely not comfortable," Katherine added.

"But hopefully at least with one office that we could secure from the inside," I said.

The front door was unlocked, allowing PO box owners access to their mail. Boxes had been pried open and mail scattered. Coupons, newspapers, magazines, and envelopes covered the tile floor.

Katherine stooped and picked up a magazine that had a celebrity on the front. "I didn't get to read this issue."

She hadn't struck me as a celebrity gossip rag reader, but I was learning many things about the woman. At the counter, someone had forced the gated barrier halfway open. It was dark in the back, with no windows allowing even a sliver of light in. But it didn't seem like there was anything for anyone to come back for.

I took off my bags and put them on the counter. Boosting myself up, I carefully dropped behind the register. Toby handed over Apollo's bag and joined me. Katherine handed me the fire starter we had used in the apartment. We had doused it and didn't want to leave even a little behind. It was too useful.

With the can lit, we slowly moved further into the back. As I had hoped, there was one office, with a name tag on the door. The name didn't matter, but the title looked like it was someone in charge. I checked the doorknob and found that it could be locked from the inside. The three of us entered, and I secured the door behind us.

Even with the light, it was entirely too dark in the room. I rummaged in my bag and pulled one of the jar candles I had. Lighting that threw our shadows against the walls, but gave us enough light to figure out the situation. Toby let Apollo out of the pack and the cat immediately checked the room by sniffing and running from corner to corner.

"He's going to need a bathroom break," Toby said.

"Let's take him outside," Katherine suggested.

I nodded. "Stay together. I'll figure out what we have for dinner."

Being left alone gave me time to settle my thoughts. When Katherine and I had left to find the medical supplies for Cristian, I knew it would be hard. Hell, I even knew we could face the chance we wouldn't return. That thought had to be pushed way back, or I wouldn't have had the guts to keep going after the first small challenge.

Now there was a teenager with us. And a cat. I poured some water into a small bowl Toby had packed into Apollo's bag. And then made a pile of his food next to it. He didn't seem to mind eating off the ground. Which was helpful since we couldn't exactly cart around enough supplies to make everything perfect for him.

Putting out a can of chili for each of us, along with bottles of water, dried fruit and a candy bar, I felt decent about our dinner.

Not for the first time, I wondered what food would be like moving forward. I had been trusting Cristian to figure this out for me. But what if something worse happened, and we became separated? I needed to learn how to provide for myself. Plants and I weren't friends, though my houseplants seemed to stay alive. I had grown nothing edible.

Leaning against the wall, exhaustion pressing down on me, I thought of Cristian. Had he woken yet? Had he realized I was gone? Would he be angry? Or worse, would he think I had abandoned him? The idea twisted something deep in my gut. No. He had to know. He had to know I was coming back. I wanted to believe that this warmth that spread through my body when I pictured him wasn't a one-sided thing. But what did I really know about how the grumpy sheriff's deputy felt about anything?

The heat was oppressive, like a suffocating blanket. I wasn't sure where I was, but the light was all wrong. Too dim and hazy, like a sun struggling to break through thick smoke. It reminded me of the smoke that had filled the sky during the first days of everything falling apart. I stumbled forward, my legs sluggish and unsteady, each step dragging me deeper into a place I didn't want to be.

Then I saw them.

"Cristian, mijo," my mother called softly, her voice like a melody I hadn't heard in years. She stood a few feet ahead, her hair falling in soft waves around her face. The way I remembered it before life took its toll. Before losing my brother. She was wearing the simple yellow dress she always loved, the one she used to wear on Sundays, the one that matched the sunflowers she kept on the kitchen table.

My father was beside her, tall and broad-shouldered, his arms crossed the way he always stood when he was thinking. He had a disappointed look on his face. Or maybe it was sorrow. It was hard to tell anymore.

"Cristian, come here," my mother said again, her tone gentle but tinged with sadness. Her smile didn't quite reach her eyes.

I wanted to move toward them, but my feet felt like they were sinking into the ground. "Mama… Papa…" The words stuck in my throat, heavy and foreign.

"You never came back to us," my father said, his voice low and measured, like it always was when he wanted to make a point. "You left us, Cristian."

"No, I didn't…" My voice faltered, my chest tightening.

"You never even tried," my mother added, her eyes glistening with unshed tears. "After we lost Julian, you just…drifted away."

Julian. The name hit me like a punch to the gut, and suddenly, the air felt thinner, harder to breathe. My older brother, gone in an instant, a bullet meant for nothing and everything. The image of his small body crumpled on the pavement flashed in my mind, unbidden and brutal. It was a memory no young child should have seared into their brain. Even now, I can remember the color of his blood as it puddled under his small body.

"I didn't drift away," I whispered, my throat tightening. "I just…I didn't know how to stay."

"You blamed us," my father said, his voice harder now, sharper. "You thought it was our fault."

"No!" The denial ripped from my chest, desperate and raw. "I never blamed you. I blamed…" Myself. The word stuck, lodged somewhere deep inside, where I couldn't reach it.

It had always been in the back of my mind. Growing up, believing the wrong one of us had died. Julian was bright and kind. His future would never be fulfilled, and it felt wrong and like I was being robbed every day that I still breathed. And though I was only a small child myself, I always thought it could be my fault. He was outside that day to play with me because I had cried when our father wouldn't take me out. It was my fault.

"You left us alone with our grief, Cristian," my mother said, her voice trembling now. "We needed you, but you were too busy running away."

"I wasn't running," my voice choked on the words I didn't

even believe. "I just...I wasn't enough. I couldn't be enough. Julian was everything, and I—"

"You were our son, too," my father interrupted, his voice breaking for the first time. "But you never believed that, did you? You were too busy trying to be what you thought we wanted."

The ground beneath me felt unsteady, like it might give way at any moment. I took a step forward, reaching for them, but they stepped back, the distance between us growing even though I hadn't moved.

"I'm sorry," I whispered, the words barely audible. "I didn't know how to fix it. I didn't know how to be what you needed."

"You were always enough, mijo," my mother said softly, her eyes brimming with tears now. "We just wanted you to come home more. Spend time with us. To let us love you."

But they were fading now, their figures dissolving into the hazy light. I reached out again, desperation clawing at my chest. "Wait, please, don't go. I didn't mean…"

"Cristian."

My father's voice was distant, echoing in a way that made it hard to hold on to.

"We're proud of you, mijo. We always were. But you have to forgive yourself. You have to allow happiness into your world."

The light grew brighter, blinding, and I staggered back, the weight of their absence pressing down on me all over again.

"Mama! Papa!" I shouted, but there was no response. Only silence.

When I woke, the fever still clung to me, and the ache in my chest was worse than the pain in my leg. The dream left me hollow and raw, my parents' faces etched into my mind as if I'd just seen them yesterday. The guilt lingered, sharp and unrelenting, but somewhere beneath it was the faintest trace of their words.

"You have to forgive yourself."

When the farmhouse came into view, I picked up my pace. It didn't matter that I was exhausted. My legs ached, my ribs throbbed with every breath, but none of it mattered. The night had been long and restless, my thoughts looping endlessly, replaying every risk, every near-miss. Cristian was my entire purpose for this trip. And I couldn't stop wondering what that meant in the larger scheme of things.

The door swung open before we reached the porch. Anxiety drew Roger's face tight.

"What is it? What happened?" I demanded.

He shook his head, ushering us inside the house. Everything looked basically the same. There were three sleep areas that resembled nests set up around the living room and dining room. Numerous food items covered the table. Proof that Roger had scavenged while we were gone.

Dave stepped into the room from the hall, and he looked relieved to see us. I yanked the strap of the duffel up and over my head, holding it out to him.

"There's everything we found in here. I mean, I think we all have some in our packs too. But this is most of it. What happened? Is he ok?" I started to walk by the doctor, but he reached out and stopped me.

"He hasn't been conscious in about sixteen hours."

My chest felt like it was seizing, air not flowing in or out of my body. The floor felt like it was tilting under me. I slowly turned to look at him and saw the sympathy on his face. Sixteen hours wasn't just a long time. It was too long.

"What does that mean?" My voice cracked, and I felt my hand being taken. Looking over, I found Katherine, her hands holding one of mine. She looked at Dave, waiting for him to explain to me.

"I can't be sure. But if you have antibiotics in here, we need to get them into his body immediately. Then I need to clean his wound out properly."

"There're kits for stitches," I explained, going to yank the duffel back from him.

Dave didn't let me grab the bag. He slowly set it at his feet and laid his hands on my shoulders. "I'm sure you have everything I'm going to need. Why don't you, Katherine, and your new friend take a minute to clean up? Then you can come sit with him."

I had forgotten about Toby. Turning, I found Toby standing right at the front door. He looked ready to throw the door open to bolt from the house. It made me mad at myself for not making sure he was comfortable when we came in. I was so panicked about Cristian, I struggled to think about anything else.

Moving to him, I smiled and tried to convey that he was safe with us. I introduced Roger and Dave, since they were both standing there.

"Toby here saved our lives," Katherine said.

"He did?" Roger asked. "Well, I need to hear that story. Why don't we get you some water, Toby? So you can clean up. And then you can tell me what trouble you had to get these girls out of."

Toby looked at me, and I nodded with an encouraging smile. As he was about to walk down the hall, Carol walked out of a bedroom. She startled to a stop when she saw the boy. He was taller than her, but it was clear he was young enough to be her grandson. Her eyes took in his appearance, and she asked, wiping her hands on her jeans.

"Well, we have a newcomer. Hello, there. I'm Carol."

And in that moment, I knew the woman would attract Toby, just as she had attracted me. I was grateful to see her up on her feet and not sitting in the corner, completely checked out from the world.

Katherine moved to my side, whispering quietly. "This might be really good for Carol. A kid to take care of."

I couldn't agree more. Carol had lost her husband. That loss wasn't something that would just easily go away or fade. But if she had somewhere to put her energy, someone to take her mind off of that constant pain, maybe she could keep going day to day. She put her arm lightly around Toby's back, likely because it would have been awkward for her to lift her arm to his shoulders and they disappeared into the bathroom at the end of the hall.

"How are supplies?" I asked. I pulled the clean clothes from my pack, prepared to clean off with a paper towel and change myself into partially clean materials.

"Got the well working. It's a hand pump, so it's work, but it's water. We're still boiling, since we can't be sure. Roger has been boiling and filling the tub, so we have it on hand. He also found food at another house. So, I think we're doing ok, for now."

Katherine unloaded the items we still had in our packs, adding the food to the table. The surface was almost full, and that gave me a small sense of comfort. But I didn't have an appetite to even speak of. I could see buckets sitting in the kitchen and I pointed. Dave nodded, and I stripped out of my shirt right there.

Using my hands, I scrubbed at the dirt on my face, arms, and hands. I did the best to get clean. Without waiting for my skin to dry, I pulled my new t-shirt over my head. Turning, I found Dave had disappeared down the hall, but Katherine stood there with a bemused look on her face.

"He's a doctor, right? Isn't seeing people strip something pretty normal for him?"

When I just raised my eyebrows in confusion, she laughed. "When you pulled your shirt off, he spun and hauled it down the hall."

I laughed, too. "He's actually seen almost all of my upper half anyway, when he inspected my ribs. Maybe when it's medical, he doesn't mind." I sobered and pulled my dirty cargo pants off. Pulling my clean leggings on, I looked at Katherine again. "I just can't stand out here and wait. I need to see Cristian. And I don't want to bring any more germs near him."

"Go be with your guy," Katherine said, gesturing down the hall. "I'll figure out how to get our clothes cleaned."

Overwhelmed by so many emotions, I walked up to Katherine and wrapped my arms around her. She hugged me back.

"Thank you. Really. Thank you for going with me. Thank you."

"That was a lot of thank yous," Katherine mumbled, her hand patting my back as if she didn't know what to do.

Pulling back, I knew tears filled my eyes, and my emotions overflowed. "I know. It just needed to be said. I would have been so scared by myself."

"You would have gotten it done."

I shrugged. "Maybe. But being alone out there would have been terrifying. Thank you."

"You said that already."

I snorted and patted her shoulder as I walked by. "I'll probably say it again."

When I entered the bedroom, Dave was pulling medications from the duffel, mumbling to himself. But I barely noticed. My gaze flew to the bed, needing to see him.

Cristian lay on the floor, on the makeshift bed they'd pieced together for him, motionless except for the faint rise and fall of his chest. His skin was pale, too pale, and his dark hair clung to his forehead, damp with sweat. His body seemed smaller somehow, like the fever had burned away the strength that had always radiated from him. I didn't understand how he had changed so much in the time I was gone.

Dave went to the window and pulled open the shade. The bright summer sun streaked across the room. It only highlighted how bad Cristian looked. I crossed the room without thinking, dropping onto my knees beside him.

"Cristian," I whispered, my voice breaking on his name. I reached out, my hand trembling when I brushed the damp hair back from his face. His skin was a furnace beneath my fingertips.

"Like I mentioned, he's been unconscious for almost sixteen hours." Dave's voice was measured, but I heard the worry he masked. "The fever's still holding steady, but he's weak. If the antibiotics don't work…"

His words trailed off, but I didn't need him to finish. The tightness in my chest told me enough. If the antibiotics didn't work, Cristian wouldn't survive this. Tears blurred my vision, and I bit my lip hard, refusing to let them fall.

I leaned closer to Cristian, my hand still resting on his forehead. "Hey," I murmured, keeping my voice soft. "I'm back. I told you I'd come back, didn't I?"

He didn't stir.

A crack split my resolve, and I sank lower, my head bowing until my forehead almost touched his. "You can't leave, you hear me? You don't get to leave me here." My voice was barely above a whisper now, shaking with the fear I couldn't hide. "You're too damn grumpy and hardheaded to give up now. So, don't. Don't you dare."

His breathing hitched, just slightly, and I froze, my heart lurching in my chest. I waited, holding my breath, but he didn't move again.

The silence stretched, the only sound the soft rhythm of his breaths and the pounding of my own heart. I didn't realize I was crying until a tear slipped down my cheek and fell onto his arm.

"You have to wake up," I whispered, my voice breaking completely. "I need you to wake up."

I didn't care how much he bossed me around, or how he made me question everything I thought I wanted. It didn't matter that I wasn't sure how to handle the growing feelings. None of it mattered now. All that mattered was keeping him here, alive, with me.

I took his hand and laced my fingers through his, holding on like it would keep him tethered to the world. His hand was heavy and limp in mine, but it was warm. That was something.

"I brought back everything we need," I whispered, my thumb brushing over his knuckles. "You just have to hold on a little longer, okay? I've got you. I've got you."

Dave knelt beside Cristian's leg, peeling back the makeshift bandage to assess the wound. The moment he did, I turned my face away, swallowing the bile rising in my throat. The skin around the bullet wound was angry and swollen, a deep, inflamed red, with streaks of infection creeping outward like poison seeping through his flesh.

"This is bad," Dave muttered, reaching for the supplies we'd managed to scavenge. "If we'd waited another day, maybe even a few more hours, I don't think he'd have made it."

The words slammed into me like a punch to the gut. I'd barely made it back in time. My throat tightened, but I forced myself to focus. Cristian was alive. And that meant we still had a chance.

"What do we do first?" My voice was hoarse, my exhaustion clawing at me.

Dave didn't answer right away. He was too busy working, laying out supplies. A bottle of sterile saline, a packet of gauze, forceps, a small knife, and, most importantly, a bottle of antibiotics.

"The first thing we do is get this wound cleaned up," he said, glancing at me. "You're gonna want to look away."

I didn't.

I stayed, watching as Dave used the forceps and scissors to

pull and remove the original stitches. The second the saline hit the infected tissue, Cristian jerked, a low, pained moan escaping from his cracked lips. My heart clenched, but I forced myself to stay still, gripping his hand tighter.

"He can feel that?" I asked in a small voice.

"Yeah, even unconscious," Dave said grimly. "Even if he's not fully aware, his body still reacts."

I nodded, though the ache in my chest was unbearable as I watched him work.

With careful, precise movements, Dave used the saline to flush out the wound, wiping away pus and dead tissue with a piece of gauze. Cristian twitched, his brows drawing together, but he didn't wake.

When the wound was as clean as it could be, Dave reached for the antibiotics.

"He's in no shape to swallow," I said, my stomach twisting. "How do we…"

"Crush it," Dave said, already working. He pulled out a small, flat metal surface and used the back of his knife handle to grind one of the antibiotic tablets into fine powder. "We'll mix it in water and get it into his system another way."

I swallowed hard. "How?"

Dave's eyes moved between me and Cristian. He pulled a syringe from the kit, one of the oral dosing syringes we'd found in the clinic. "We dissolve the powder in water and give it to him slowly. Either by letting it drip down his throat or between his cheek and gums."

As he started the process of dissolving the pill, I looked at Cristian uncertainly. "And this will work?"

"It's the best option we have. He'll choke if we try to put a pill down his throat. Injectable would have worked faster, but I knew finding that was a long shot. The antibiotics will absorb through the soft tissues in his mouth or drip down his throat."

I nodded, pressing my lips together as I watched him tilt Cristian's head slightly to the side, parting his lips just enough to slide the tip of the syringe into the space between his cheek and gums.

"Slow and steady," Dave muttered to himself, pushing the plunger ever so slightly. The liquid seeped into Cristian's mouth, and I watched as his throat fluttered—an automatic reflex, forcing him to swallow.

My breath caught. "Is it working?"

"It's getting in there," Dave confirmed, giving another small push of the syringe. "We'll keep going, little by little. If we do too much at once, he could choke."

I nodded, my fingers still laced through Cristian's, my thumb brushing over his fevered skin. I hoped if he could feel the pain, he could feel the comfort of his hand in mine.

After what felt like forever, the first dose of antibiotics was in his system. It wasn't much, but it was enough to start fighting the infection.

Now all we could do was wait.

I exhaled shakily, leaning forward until my forehead brushed against Cristian's damp skin. "You're not getting out of this that easy," I murmured, my voice barely audible. "You don't get to leave me behind."

He didn't respond. But for the first time, I let myself believe— just a little—that maybe he'd fight his way back to me.

CHAPTER
TWENTY-EIGHT
CRISTIAN

The world was thick with heat and darkness, pressing down on me like a weight I couldn't shake. My limbs felt like they didn't belong to me, heavy and useless, my body a shell that burned and ached in ways I couldn't understand.

I wasn't sure if I was awake or still drowning in fever dreams, but something was different. The surrounding air wasn't as suffocating, and the fire that had been consuming me for…God, how long? It felt distant now, like embers instead of an inferno.

And then something solid.

Soft, warm, grounding.

A body against mine.

My eyes cracked open, not feeling as heavy as before, though it felt as if someone had poured sand directly on my eyelids. I blinked against the discomfort. The darkness was total. As I lay still, but awake, I counted the breaths of the body next to me. For a moment, I wondered if I was still dreaming or even hallucinating.

I tried to move, but my body only responded with a small twitch. But it was enough for the deep breathing to stutter. Then a touch, soft against my forehead, running down my cheek. I shivered at the sensation, not from the cold, but because it felt real.

Not like the warped, twisted memories that had tormented me in sleep.

A voice followed, quiet, shaking. "Cristian?"

Marlowe.

I swallowed, my throat dry and raw, my lips cracked. It took effort just to open my mouth, and when I did, my voice barely made it out. "What...?"

"Oh my god," she whispered.

Then her body and her warmth disappeared from my side. I wanted to cry out, to reach out, to stop her. To grasp the hallucination, dream, whatever she was, and hold her close. I wanted to believe it wasn't all in my fevered mind.

A light flared to life in the room, and I had to squint against the small candle flame. I finally stopped fighting it and let my eyes fall closed again.

"Marlowe," I rasped, my voice scraping out of me like gravel.

She made a sound, something small and pained and I felt her hand wrap around mine, her fingers threading through mine like she had no intention of letting go.

I focused on that. On her hand in mine, on the heat of her skin, the steady strength in her grip.

"Where...?" I forced the word out, but everything still felt distant, disjointed. My head pounded, my body felt weak, but my instincts told me to understand, to get my bearings.

She must have known what I was asking because her voice came again, soft and steady.

"We're still in the farmhouse. Dave's here. You're safe."

Safe. I needed to tell her it wasn't my safety I was worried about. It was her. I wanted to tell her I had been so afraid that I would never see her again. That she took too big of a chance for me. But even as those thoughts mixed in my mind, I couldn't force the words out of my mouth.

I tried to move my hand, to tighten my fingers around hers, but it was pathetic. The best I could manage was a twitch. But she didn't let go.

Time stretched, the silence between us thick with something unspoken. I wasn't sure if I was awake or still drifting, but I clung to the sound of her breath, the way she was still here.

I swallowed hard, forcing a few words out, hoarse and weak. "You came back."

She sucked in a sharp breath, and I felt the way her fingers trembled slightly against mine.

"Of course I did," she whispered, fierce and unshaken, as if the idea of being anywhere else was unfathomable. Her grip on my hand tightened, and for the first time in days, I realized—she had been just as afraid as I was. "Where else would I be?"

I wanted to say something—thank you, I'm sorry, never do something like that again—but my body was failing me again. The exhaustion was dragging me back down, pulling me under before I could fight it. But this time, it didn't feel like I was drowning in a pit of despair and fever. I felt like I could finally rest. I relaxed, my grip on her hand loosening, though she didn't release me. She wasn't letting go. And for the first time in what felt like forever, I wasn't fighting to hold on. I wasn't alone.

"He barely opened his eyes. Is that good or bad?" I asked, keeping my voice in a whisper.

Though I wanted Cristian to wake up, be vibrant and alive, it was clear he was exhausted. So was Dave, who I woke up out of a dead sleep as soon as Cristian drifted back off. I was afraid to release his hand, leading him to believe I was leaving him again. I wasn't doing that. Not again. Not unless it was to save his life. I planned on telling him that once he was better.

"He spoke. He knew you were here. And his fever is coming down. Those are all good signs," Dave said.

It was too dark for the doctor to check Cristian's leg. It wouldn't have been necessary, anyway. He had checked it every few hours since I got back with the supplies. Roger had a constant stream of sterilized water ready to rinse the puss from the wound as it leaked out. Dave seemed happy with the progress, explaining to me every time I panicked about the wound that it wasn't getting worse. And that was just as good of a sign as Cristian waking up even for a moment.

"What do I do?" I chewed my lip, looking down at Cristian's face, shadowed in the limited candlelight.

"Go back to sleep. You've barely slept a solid eight hours since you got back. And Katherine said you only slept a few hours while you were on the road. You want to take care of him? Take care of yourself. Doctor's orders."

I snorted at his doctor joke. He was right. I knew that. I only fell asleep when the exhaustion was too much to fight. But other times, I lay in the dark, counting Cristian's breaths. It was ridiculous, but I was so panicked that he would just stop breathing. That he would die and leave me alone.

Not that I was truly alone. Katherine sat in the room with me for hours when she wasn't busy doing something. Toby came in and visited with me as well, with Carol on his heels, fussing over him. When the older woman came into the room, she would take the time to tuck Cristian's blankets around him snuggly, making sure he was as comfortable as possible. Even Apollo had curled up in my lap once, as if he just knew I needed a cuddle.

Lying down, I pulled my makeshift pillow close to Cristian's shoulder again. Even in the short-lived relationships I had in my life, I was never a cuddler or even someone that enjoyed having someone stay the night. But something about the world coming to a screeching halt changed my opinion on that. The need for human connection was something new for me. I had no desire to fight that new feeling.

With my forehead pressed to Cristian's shoulder, his skin finally not feeling like flames could erupt at any moment, I fell asleep.

Fingers in my hair woke me.

Soft, slow movements, brushing through the strands, tracing the waves.

I stirred, blinking against the brightness that filled the room. The last thing I remembered was the heavy pull of exhaustion dragging me under, the warmth of Cristian beside me, the rhythmic rise and fall of his chest telling me he was still breathing. Now, daylight poured through the window, cutting across the floor in golden streaks. I had slept through the rest of the night, maybe longer.

But that wasn't what had startled me awake.

Fingers. In my hair.

I stiffened, expecting to see Katherine or Carol trying to gently wake me, maybe checking on Cristian. Panic flared at first, thinking someone was going to tell me something had happened in the night. But the touch was too tentative, too deliberate.

I sucked in a sharp breath and sat up so fast it made me dizzy. My heart slammed against my ribs as I turned, my pulse roaring in my ears. The hand in my hair belonged to Cristian. He was awake. Not just fever-stirring, not just twitching in restless sleep. Awake.

His eyes were open, framed by dark lashes, though the deep lines of exhaustion and sickness still etched his face. His skin was pale, his body thinner than it had been days ago, but his lips—his lips curved slightly at the corners, the barest hint of a smile playing there.

Relief hit me so hard I nearly collapsed back onto him.

A strangled cry left my throat, my hands flying to his chest, needing to feel him, to be sure I wasn't imagining this. "Oh my god," I whispered.

Cristian's gaze held mine, unwavering despite the exhaustion darkening his features. Then, voice rough like gravel and barely above a breath, he murmured, "Never again."

I froze, tilting my head, trying to make sense of the words. Never again?

Still trying to steady my racing heart, I leaned down, pressing my lips lightly to his forehead. He was warm but not burning. The fever had broken. He wasn't sweating, wasn't shivering. He was here.

Cristian's arm moved, slow, weak, but deliberate, and he wrapped it across his body, pulling me closer. I sucked in a breath. The gesture was careful, cautious, as if he wasn't sure how much strength he had or if I would let him. It was as if he was asking me a question without words and, at the moment, I didn't know what the answer was.

His face turned slightly, and I felt his breath against my neck, warm and uneven.

"…Marlowe."

My name. Just that. But something about the way he said it, soft, weighted, real, shattered something inside me. For a moment, I couldn't move, couldn't breathe. Was he still fever-drunk? Was this him or the remnants of an illness clinging to him like shadows? Slowly, carefully, I pulled back, just enough to meet his gaze.

"I'm here," I whispered, searching his face for signs of delirium, for anything that might tell me this wasn't real.

His dark eyes locked onto mine, the fevered haze replaced with something else. Something solid, something unshakable. Then, more certain than I expected, he rasped, "Never again."

He paused.

"You don't…" His breath caught, his grip tightening slightly around my wrist. "You don't ever do that again."

My throat tightened. My lips parted, but no words came out.

"…Do what, Cristian?" I asked, barely above a whisper.

His jaw clenched. "Go out alone."

His voice was hoarse but firm, threaded with something raw, something undeniable. It wasn't a question. It wasn't a request. It was a demand, a vow, a crack in the armor he had spent so long building. I didn't know everything that had happened in his life to create the wall he had erected. But I knew I wanted to know. And I wanted to be the one that took down that wall.

I could have argued. Told him I had no choice, that I'd done what I had to do. That I couldn't sit by while he slowly faded away and maybe even died. But looking at him now, pale, weak, clinging to the edge of consciousness, I couldn't.

Because the fear in his voice was real. Because, for the first time, Cristian wasn't just fighting to survive. It felt like he was fighting for me.

I swallowed hard, my hand still resting against his chest,

feeling the weak but steady beat of his heart beneath my palm. I nodded once.

"I won't," I whispered. What I wouldn't say, at least not now, was if his life was on the line again, I would do whatever was necessary.

He shifted and grimaced. "How long have I been asleep?"

"Before I got back, almost sixteen hours. Since then? Maybe another twelve?" I couldn't really pinpoint what time it was, nor did I know what time he had partially woken in the middle of the night.

"I've been having crazy dreams."

"Want to talk about them?" I didn't really expect him to take me up on the offer. But I found myself really wanting to pick his brain. To know what was going on during what I was sure were fever induced dreams.

He shook his head, and I couldn't help but feel slightly disappointed until he spoke. "Another time. I'm really thirsty."

"Oh god, of course you are! I'm sorry. What was I thinking? Did you know Roger figured out how to use the hand pump on the well?" As I spoke, I poured a little water from my bottle into a cup. "They're still boiling it, just to be sure. I mean, well water is probably usually clean. But who knows what went out with the power?"

I was rambling and Cristian knew it. He didn't reply, just slowly raised an eyebrow. Slipping a hand under his head, I helped angle him so he could sip the water. Once he finished the little that I had poured, I helped him lay back down.

"I'm still so exhausted."

"It's the infection. I think it's taking everything out of your body, trying to fight it off. But Dave has gotten two antibiotic doses into you. Actually, I think the third could be due any minute," I said, moving to get up.

Cristian's hand came out and landed on my thigh. "Where are you going?"

"To get Dave. You need your meds."

"No need, I'm right here." Dave entered the room just at that moment and Cristian completely relaxed once he knew I wasn't leaving his side.

"Hey. How are things looking?" Cristian asked.

Dave went to his leg and pulled out the supplies he had been using to clean his wound. "Better since we were able to start cleaning it out. Still pretty angry, though."

I looked away again, not loving the queasy feeling that rose whenever I watched Dave clear out the puss. I'd never had a huge issue with blood or injuries. When Cristian first got hurt, I didn't feel sick about it. But the infection was more than I could handle.

Instead of looking down at his leg, I took his hand in mine and squeezed.

I smiled sadly down at him. "Pretty sure this is going to be painful. Maybe we can give you pain meds now that you're awake."

"Here we go," Dave warned.

I knew when he poured the water onto the wound. Cristian's eyes widened for a moment before he squeezed them shut tightly. His breathing got shallow, and his grip on my hand was almost painful. I didn't have the words to console him. Brushing his hair back from his forehead, I tried to soothe him.

"Talk to me. Tell me what happened." Cristian's mouth barely moved as he spoke, his jaw was too tightly clenched.

I remembered how he wanted me to tell him stories when he got stitched up. Distraction was his pain killer when there was nothing else.

"There's not too much to tell," I said.

Dave snorted, and I shot him a glare. I wasn't ready to tell Cristian everything that happened while Katherine and I were out looking for supplies. I had no doubt that hearing about our two near-death escapes would not thrill him.

Cristian's eyes flew open, and he focused on me. His brow furrowed as he tried to decipher the look on my face and the sound that the doctor had made.

"Well, we ran into a few issues, but really, they weren't serious. And we both made it back in one piece. Not a scratch on either of us. I can't say the same for everyone out there, though. Nothing is coming back on. There's no government presence. No police. No military. Just people running wild. The first night, we found an abandoned apartment. There were people being hunted on the street outside the apartment, right there in town."

"Damn it, Marlowe. You shouldn't have been in danger like that," Cristian said on a groan that sounded half exasperated and half painful.

"Cristian, every day is danger. The world is gone as we knew it. And, honestly, I don't think it's coming back anytime soon. We need to make plans and keep each other safe and healthy."

Cristian nodded seriously, his eyes locked on mine. He grimaced again, and I tried to pick my words carefully. "Katherine was a great partner, too. She watched my back. And I haven't even told you the craziest part."

"It gets crazy?" he asked.

Truth was, I wasn't telling him the biggest stuff. Just things to keep his mind off the pain.

"Well, not that crazy. But Katherine and I didn't come back alone. We brought a teenage boy and a cat. Toby and Apollo."

"Is Apollo the boy or the cat?"

I laughed lightly. "The cat. He's one of the most well-behaved animals I've ever seen. He is totally content just being carried around in this little backpack that has a circular window for him to look out of. I realized we were definitely taking on yet another thing to care for. But I think he's a great comfort to everyone."

"Animals have a way of bringing comfort and happiness to humans. There are studies about the increase of dopamine and serotonin in the human body during happy interactions with pets." Dave carefully covered Cristian's leg and moved up closer to his head. "How do you feel?"

"The pain is still bad. When you cleaned it, it started to radiate throughout my entire leg. But I can handle it," Cristian said.

"Marlowe and Katherine brought back several medications. A few for pain. No reason to suffer. Think you can swallow a couple of pills?"

Cristian nodded, and Dave disappeared for a moment. When he came back, he had a fresh bottle of water and two pills. Katherine followed with Toby on her heels. Apollo was in the boy's arms, his little gray head pressed into Toby's neck. It was like the cat thought he was a baby. But Toby looked lighter already, and he'd only been with us for a little over three days.

Carol and Roger hovered at the door, and I turned to smile down at Cristian.

"The whole gang is here."

He started to struggle, and I understood he wanted to sit up. He wasn't far from the wall, so after some arranging and lifting on my part, he could lean propped up against his pillow. I tucked the blanket around his waist, working hard to ignore his bare torso. When my skin brushed his, I could tell his fever was coming down. He reached out and pulled me to sit next to him.

Dave held out the two pills for Cristian to take, along with the water. As Cristian swallowed the meds, his eyes were on Toby. I could see his calculations as he studied the boy. It wasn't unkind. But I was sure his instincts from being in law enforcement kicked in.

"Good to see you awake," Katherine said. Her voice was slightly shy, but I wasn't worried about whatever attraction she had to Cristian anymore.

"Thank you." His voice was still gravelly. He shifted his gaze from Toby to Katherine. "Thank you for being there for Marlowe."

She patted Toby's shoulder and before I could warn her not to tell Cristian the details, she laughed and said, "Well, really, it was Toby that saved us."

"Oh?" He raised an eyebrow in my direction.

I glared at Katherine and her eyes widened as she realized what was happening.

"Umm, yeah. So, I mean, I'm sure Marlowe will tell you the story when you're rested," she stammered.

I knew without even looking at Cristian that he would not wait to hear the story. I sighed and smiled up at Toby. He did deserve the credit for taking the risk and saving us. And I knew it would gain him Cristian's admiration.

"Toby got us out of a store, where we were about to be found by some not great people. He hid us in his shelter, fed us, and we decided he didn't need to be alone anymore, so he came with us." Turning to look Cristian in the eye, I continued seriously. "He was extremely brave. And we were very lucky he found us when he did."

It was obvious Cristian was struggling with his frustration. I knew we would have a conversation later, hopefully in private. But after giving me a long look that said plenty, he looked up at the teenager. I turned as well and found Toby blushing.

"It's really great to meet you, Toby," Cristian said. "Thank you for helping my friends. And I guess you helped to find the medicine I needed, so thank you for that too."

"Marlowe's the awesome one. She—"

"Did absolutely nothing beyond what was necessary." I cut off Toby and his brow creased in confusion. But Katherine caught my intention and her hand squeezed his shoulder.

I knew the boy was about to tell Cristian about the man inside the clinic. But I wasn't ready to have him upset with me about another thing. I wanted to enjoy the fact that he was awake and seemed to be getting better. A part of my brain wanted to tell him how I had been feeling. But it felt too big, too soon.

Carol came in closer to Cristian, kneeling next to us and looking into his face. She patted his cheek, just as grandmother or mother would. He reached up and held her hand to his face for a moment longer, and she smiled at him.

"How are you?" he asked.

Her smile dimmed, but she shrugged and said, "As good as anyone could expect me to."

He nodded and then tried to stifle a yawn. Carol stood and walked out of the room with Roger.

"I think it's time for the patient to get some more rest," Dave said.

"I've been sleeping long enough," Cristian tried to protest.

"Though your fever seems to have broken, your body is still fighting this infection. You're doing better. But let's not tempt fate," Dave replied.

Cristian sighed, but he didn't argue further. It would have been useless. Exhaustion lined his face. He was present, aware, no longer lost in the haze of sickness. His color was returning, his voice stronger, and the relief that had settled over me was so heavy it felt like I might sink into it. But I didn't disagree with the doctor. I refused to let Cristian be a stubborn patient and make himself sick all over again.

Everyone said their goodbyes and Carol returned for a moment with two mugs of warmed soup. I smiled appreciatively. My stomach rumbled at the smell, and Carol chuckled as she left the room again.

Turning toward Cristian, I held up a spoon to his mouth, but he shook his head.

"You first," he said.

Exasperated, I took a bite of my soup before holding the spoon to his mouth again. On it went, taking turns with the mugs, until we'd both finished our meal. It wasn't the most filling, but for Cristian, it was just about getting something in him that was more than water.

We had talked little beyond necessities—his pain, his fever, the sips of water I forced him to take, and now the food I convinced him to eat. But there was something between us, a weight neither of us was ready to touch yet.

I sat cross-legged on the floor beside him, folding and unfolding the edge of the blanket over my lap, my fingers restless. Cristian was repositioned to lie on the makeshift bed, one arm draped lazily over his stomach, his other hand resting just close enough to mine that if I moved even an inch, we'd be touching.

But I didn't move. And neither did he.

Then, his voice, low and rough, broke the quiet. "I meant what I said."

I blinked, dragging my gaze to his. His dark eyes were already on me, steady but unreadable.

"About what?" I asked, though I already knew.

His fingers twitched against the blanket, like he was working up to something.

"About you going out alone." His voice was hoarse but firm. "Never again, Marlowe."

I let out a soft exhale, shaking my head. "Cristian—"

"No." His tone was sharper this time, surprising me. "I need you to hear me on this."

I pressed my lips together, studying him. There was something behind his words, something deeper than just the need to keep me safe.

"I thought—" He broke off, jaw clenching, his fingers curling into the fabric of the blanket. When he spoke again, his voice was lower, tighter. More vulnerable than I'd ever heard it. "I thought you weren't coming back."

The admission sent a sharp pang through my chest. I shifted slightly, facing him fully, but he wasn't looking at me anymore. He focused his eyes on something beyond me, his brows furrowed as if battling himself. I could have reassured him. Told him I had survived, that I was fine, that it hadn't been as bad as he thought.

But that would have been a lie. So I stayed quiet, waiting.

Cristian exhaled sharply through his nose, rubbing a hand down his face. "You don't understand. Lying here, knowing I couldn't do anything—" His voice caught, and he shook his head, like he was trying to rid himself of the thoughts. "I don't...I don't let people take risks for me, Marlowe. Not like that."

My throat tightened. Not since his marriage. Not since his life had unraveled into something he didn't know how to fix. I swallowed hard, the weight of what he wasn't saying pressing down on me.

"You would have done the same for me," I said softly.

He scoffed, finally looking at me again. "Yeah. And that would have made sense."

I frowned, confused. "What's that supposed to mean?"

Cristian hesitated, like he hadn't meant to say that out loud. Then, instead of answering, he shifted, adjusting slightly like he was testing the limits of his body's strength. He grimaced, but his eyes never left mine.

Finally, after a long beat, he exhaled and muttered, "You shouldn't have had to risk yourself for me."

I narrowed my eyes. "Why? Because you don't think you're worth saving?"

Something flickered across his face. Something raw and unguarded. But he shuttered it just as quickly. He glanced away, his fingers tightening around the blanket before releasing it again.

"It's not that simple," he said, voice quieter now.

I let out a slow breath, studying him. His walls were still there, still strong, but they were cracking, just enough for me to see through them.

"You think I don't know what it feels like?" I asked, keeping my voice soft. "To believe you don't deserve what people are willing to do for you?"

His throat moved, but he didn't answer.

"I made my choice, Cristian," I continued. "I went out there because I couldn't..." My voice wavered, and I shook my head, gathering myself. "I couldn't just sit here and lose you. I wouldn't."

Something shifted in his expression. The air between us felt different, heavier, like the next words spoken could tip something over the edge. His fingers twitched against mine, but he didn't speak. Didn't have to. I finally understood. He wasn't just afraid of what could have happened. He was afraid of losing me. So I let him off the hook.

"For what it's worth," I murmured, offering him the smallest smile, "I don't take orders well."

A rough exhale left him, almost like a laugh, but it was tired and tinged with something else. He didn't argue, didn't push the point. Instead, he let his fingers brush against mine just slightly longer than before, before closing his eyes, the weight of exhaustion pulling him back under. Without thinking about the meaning of it, I slid my hand into his.

I stayed. Because even if he couldn't say it yet, I knew. He had needed me to come back. And despite whatever guilt or hesitation still lingered in his heart, he didn't want me to go anywhere. And God help me…I wanted to stay. Now. And forever.

One week. That was my limit.

I had tried to stay still, tried to follow orders, but patience had never been my strength. The farmhouse walls felt smaller by the day, the air thicker, the quiet heavier. I could no longer stay still, stay off my leg or take it easy. The pain was much better, though not completely gone. My walk did not thrill Dave. But I was only walking around the farmhouse. The warm fresh air and sun on my skin felt like heaven.

Well, it was the next best thing to having Marlowe nursing me back to health. She had been at my side almost every minute for a week. I wasn't sure if it was because I had shown my vulnerability and worry about her disappearing, or if she was still playing interference between Katherine and me. My insecurities believed it was the second thing.

The object of my thoughts appeared as if they made her materialize. She stopped at the corner of the house, her hands on her hips, looking annoyed with me. Dave had likely sent her to babysit me. I was finished with being coddled. We needed to get on the road.

Roger had done a good job keeping food on the table. But even he said he was having to go further and further out to find things.

None of us wanted him staying out overnight alone. I wouldn't let Marlowe go again. And in turn, she refused to let anyone else go, either. So, we were getting low on canned and dried foods.

The last house, though, had been a fantastic find. An overgrown garden in the back produced zucchini, cherry tomatoes, basil, lettuce and carrots. Once it was cleaned, we ate everything raw, seeing no need to go to the trouble of cooking it. The basil was especially delicious with the tomatoes. When Roger brought the produce home, we'd feasted and had full stomachs for two days.

Now we needed to move on to a place where we wouldn't starve. As I approached Marlowe, I studied her. It wasn't just the belt that I was sure had been tightened a few additional notches. It was the way her collarbone was a little sharper, the way her shirts hung looser. She never said anything, never took more than her share, but I saw it. I saw how often she pushed half her portion toward Toby when she thought no one was looking.

I didn't say a word about the food. Truthfully, I blamed myself for her not having enough. It was my job to protect her and care for her. Instead, she was busy taking care of me and making sure a child was eating. It was who Marlowe was. I knew that, even only knowing her for a month. When you spent almost every waking moment with someone, it wasn't hard to figure them out.

"I'm sorry, warden," I said when I approached the corner of the house where Marlowe stood.

She shifted, switching which hip she had popped out. Her cherub face, darkening freckles, and sparkling eyes turned up toward me. I could see her lips fighting a smile at my words.

"You aren't a prisoner, Cristian. Just don't always make the best choices for yourself, now do you?"

I stretched my arms above my head, reaching for the sky. "Exercise is good for the body."

"Technically against doctor's orders, today, though, isn't it?"

She was full of sass and I couldn't help the step I took that brought me just a little closer to her. I was rewarded with her eyes widening slightly and her head tipping back further to look me in the face.

"I don't take orders well, either."

Her face brightened as she laughed and then she clapped a hand over her mouth, but her eyes still danced with humor.

"You're a problem, Mr. Reyes."

Problems were exactly what I was thinking about while I walked, but it wasn't me I was worried about. I looked around us, at the vast farmland that we had no capabilities of farming. Roger had looked through some vehicles that the farm still had, but he only found machinery that needed parts or was long rusted. Whoever had moved from the farmhouse definitely had no desire to come back. Leaving us with little choice but to leave as well.

Marlowe's hand reached out and brushed my arm. "What are you thinking?"

"We need to get ready to go." I looked over at her and saw that her brow had furrowed in thought.

"But to where?" she asked.

"The original plan." I met her gaze, making sure she knew I wasn't wavering. "My place first. We get settled, we figure out our next steps. Then, if it's still what you want, we go find your mom."

Her breath caught, just slightly. "You're still willing to come with me?"

I frowned. "Marlowe, you think I'd let you do that alone?"

"I thought...well, it's not your commitment. It's my mom. That's asking a lot from you."

How did I tell her that for the first time in a long time, I knew exactly what I needed to do. I knew we were in an extreme circumstance, but somehow fate had put me with someone I would do anything for. And though it seemed crazy, I felt like my eyes were more wide open now than they had ever been with Sarah. But I couldn't say any of that to Marlowe.

"It's important to you and I want to," I finally said.

Marlowe hesitated for half a second. Just long enough for me to see the moment she made the choice. Then she stepped forward, sliding her arms around my waist like she needed the contact as much as I did.

I froze for a split second before wrapping my arms around her and holding her to me. I had touched Marlowe in many different ways over the time we'd been together. But each time felt like it had been for the purpose of caring for her or helping her. This was different. It was an embrace for no other reason than we wanted it. And I didn't want to let her go.

"Thank you," she mumbled against my chest.

"For what?"

"Not leaving me behind in that courthouse."

I pictured her that day. Wearing a too business-like for jury duty sheath dress, her hair in a disarray around her head, a cut on her cheek from where she had barely missed having an actual plane crash into her. She was beautiful then. But I hadn't understood what that meant until long after getting away from the chaos of the courthouse. Leaving her behind had never even entered my thoughts.

"Thanks for trusting me," I quietly said.

Her arms tightened before she slowly released me. Reluctantly, I let my arms fall back to my sides, and she stepped back. Her cheeks were a beautiful pink, and she didn't meet my eye. She looked around, as if she thought we might have an audience. But if anyone inside saw us, they didn't interrupt.

"When do we leave?" she asked.

"Tomorrow."

That night, we all sat together, packing the supplies that would fit into each of our packs. We would take turns carrying the duffel that was full of medical supplies. Once I was well enough to see what Marlowe had brought back, I was even more concerned about what had happened while she was out. She had been carrying around items that would be worth a great deal to anyone that caught her.

With all the bags packed with food and clothing, we each tied a blanket and towel in a roll somewhere on our packs. We didn't know how long the trip would take, but we wanted to be able to bunk wherever we stopped. My guess was at least three days, depending on what trouble we ran into. No one wanted to stay behind, and no one had better ideas about where to go. So, my house was the goal.

After we packed what we could carry, we worked together to cook everything that was left. Sitting in the warm glow of candlelight we ate canned peaches, fruit cocktail out of plastic containers, soup, and canned peas. I counted each bite Marlowe put into her mouth. If she knew I was watching, she didn't let on. It would have made me seem like a stalker. But I was worried about her getting enough calories for what lay ahead.

Though we weren't really together, the group had generally understood that Marlowe and I shared a sleeping area. The ruse to originally protect me from Katherine's attentions had carried on, though I hadn't planned on it. Yet having Marlowe by my side at night helped me sleep better.

After locking up the house and pulling the shades tight, Marlowe and I made our way into the room we were using. She closed the door behind us, while I carried the small canned light Toby had given us. I had the teen explain to me how his grandfather had made the fire starters. They gave us more light for a longer period of time than any of the candles we had. I was impressed and planned on finding more supplies to make more of them when we could.

We settled on the floor, pulling our blankets over us. Tonight, Marlowe shifted restlessly. I wasn't sure what she was looking for, but I finally reached out for her. She sighed and moved closer to rest her head on my chest.

"Sorry. I don't know why I feel so nervous about tomorrow," she said.

I pulled her in until her body was flush with mine and breathed her in for a long minute.

Then, remembering something Toby had said during dinner, I asked, "Why does Toby think you're such a badass?"

Marlowe's entire body froze, and I knew there was something she wasn't telling me. Her fingers started moving in an erratic pattern on my chest, tracing invisible lines on my t-shirt.

When she didn't speak, I prodded. "Marlowe. What happened out there that you didn't tell me?"

She launched into a whispered story, speaking so fast that I was sure I missed a good portion of what she said. But when I understood she'd held a gun on a man who was holding Katherine and threatening to take the medical supplies they needed for me, I went tense.

"But everything ended up fine. We're fine. I'm fine. You're better. It's fine," she muttered, clearly recognizing my stress.

"Let me get this straight," I said slowly, my grip tightening slightly. "You went out for me. You found what we needed. Then a man tried to take it from you. Likely would have hurt you. And instead of backing down, you held a gun in his face."

Marlowe shrugged, like it was nothing. But it wasn't nothing. I had faced men like that my entire career. I had faced worse. But Marlowe?

"More or less, yeah."

I let out a ragged breath and squeezed my eyes shut. It didn't matter. I could still see it all in my mind. And my brain took that moment to suggest all the things that could have gone wrong in that scenario. Sure, they hadn't. And Marlowe, Katherine, with the addition of Toby, had made it back to the farmhouse safely. But for some reason, knowing she was in such danger, my heart couldn't seem to find its regular beat.

"I guess I should teach you how to shoot," I said.

I let out a slow, steady breath, trying to push down the frustration bubbling under my skin. It wasn't anger at her. It was fear. Fear that I had been useless when she needed me, that I hadn't been there when she was forced to stand her ground with a gun she barely knew how to use.

That realization sank deep, heavy and unshakable. I tightened my arm around her.

Marlowe sighed, like she could feel the shift in me, the way my pulse hadn't quite evened out yet. She always noticed. Even when I tried to keep things buried, she had a way of peeling back the layers, seeing what was underneath.

"I really thought you'd be furious," she murmured, breaking the silence.

"I am," I admitted. "Just not at you."

She shifted, her chin grazing my chest as she tilted her head to look at me. I could only make out the vague outline of her face in the room's darkness. "Then who?"

I let out a quiet, humorless laugh. "Myself. Fate. The entire goddamn world."

Marlowe said nothing for a long moment. I felt her fingertips still against my shirt, then start moving again, slower this time.

"You know," she said, voice soft, thoughtful, "I don't really believe in fate. Not the way some people do. Not in the 'everything happens for a reason' kind of way." She made the motion of quotation marks against my sternum.

I tilted my head slightly, looking down at her. "No?"

She shook her head, her cheek brushing against my shirt. "No. I think things just happen. Random, unfair, impossible things. And the only thing that matters is what we do after."

My chest tightened. Because she was right. The world had shattered, and instead of looking for reasons, all we could do was keep moving forward.

"You made a choice," I said, exhaling slowly. "To protect Katherine. To stand your ground. And I hate you had to, but..." I hesitated, the words sticking in my throat before I finally forced them out. "But I'm proud of you."

Marlowe stilled completely. Her breath hitched, just slightly, and she pressed her forehead against my chest like she wasn't sure what to do with my words.

Something shifted inside of me, something I wasn't ready to

name. I closed my eyes, my grip tightening on her, pulling her closer like I could hold on to whatever this was between us before it slipped through my fingers.

I wasn't sure what else to say, so I said nothing. Instead, I reached up and tangled my fingers in her hair, smoothing it back like she was something fragile and breakable, even though I knew she was anything but. Marlowe exhaled slowly, her body relaxing against mine as if this were her rightful place.

For a long time, neither of us spoke. Tomorrow, everything would change. We would leave this place, head toward my home, toward something permanent. Something we both knew we needed but were too afraid to say out loud.

She was thinking about it. I could tell by the way her fingers started tracing patterns on my chest again, the way her breath had slowed but wasn't quite steady.

"Do you think it's possible?" she asked quietly.

I frowned. "What?"

She hesitated, then murmured, "A future. A real one. Not just surviving."

I felt my chest tighten again.

Because I wanted to tell her yes. I wanted to promise her we would build something, that my house could be more than just a place to sleep—that it could be a home. But I had made promises before. And I had broken them.

Still, when I spoke, my voice was steady. "If it's possible," I said, pressing my lips to the top of her head, "we'll find it."

Marlowe exhaled slowly, and I felt a little of the tension leave her. As we both relaxed, I didn't miss the way she fit perfectly inside my arm. Her head on my shoulder, her arm across my stomach in a soft embrace. I waited for a feeling of panic or claustrophobia. Neither came. Instead, I felt calm and, as Marlowe's breathing slowed and became deeper, mine followed suit. Falling asleep, my mind was still reeling with the work and possibilities ahead of us. But doing them together made everything feel worthwhile.

In the morning, I woke before Marlowe. I could hear movement in the front room, quiet voices whispering back and forth. We hadn't made a plan for how early to leave. But I didn't want to wait until mid-day. Somehow, we had shifted in our sleep, and I now spooned Marlowe, with my arm around her waist, anchoring her to me. Her head rested on my arm and her fingers were intertwined with mine.

Slowly, I shifted away from her, stretching and testing the movement of my healing leg. There was an ache, but it was so much better than it had been just days before. Marlowe rolled toward me and her eyes slowly opened and focused on me.

"Ready for today?" I asked.

She looked uncertain for a moment but nodded before climbing from our makeshift bed. In comfortable silence, we both changed into our travel clothes. Dave came in to check my leg, making sure nothing had reopened and for his own peace of mind, he wrapped the healing wound in gauze and an ace bandage for additional protection.

Everyone gathered in the farmhouse's front room when Marlowe and I arrived. Though we'd left a few things behind, the house was almost back to its original empty state. I wondered if someone else would come and take refuge. Maybe they could build a life for themselves on the farmland. Those just weren't our plans.

Everyone picked up their packs and got things strapped onto their bodies. I made sure to tuck one handgun at my back, just in case. After the stories about Marlowe and Katherine's trip, I had little confidence getting to my house unscathed. I laughed along with the group as Apollo got comfortable in his pack, which was strapped to the front of Toby's chest.

Looking at each face in the group, I was surprised at what I was part of. Despite my injuries and inability to lead, those faces now looked to me for guidance. I nodded and went to the door.

Cautiously, I opened the door and stepped onto the porch. The morning was cool, but with the sun bright, I knew the Oregon

August heat would hit us before midday. I stepped down the porch steps, listening for any human movement nearby. Hearing nothing, I turned back toward the open door.

Marlowe was waiting, always waiting for me to make the first move. But when I held out my hand, she didn't hesitate. She came to me instantly, sliding her fingers into mine. Like she already knew this was where she was meant to be.

I held on as she stepped down to stand beside me. We both took in our surroundings while the rest of our group joined us, but all I could feel was the weight of her hand in mine, like an anchor and a promise all at once.

She turned and squeezed my hand, looking up at me. Her face was full of trust. And something else. Something dangerous. Something I wasn't sure I could walk away from.

"Ready?" I asked, my voice quieter than before.

"Yes." She squeezed my hand again, her voice steady. "I go wherever you go."

ALSO BY COURTNEY KONSTANTIN

The Sundown Series

Prepared

Alone

Survive

Alive

Torment

Vengeance

Ruination

The Babysitter of the Apocalypse

Babysitter of the Apocalypse: Prequel (Freebie!)

Babysitter of the Apocalypse, Book 1

Babysitter of the Apocalypse, Book 2: We Don't Talk to Strangers

Echoes of the Flare

Whispers in the Dark